A CORNISH ORPHAN

A CORNISH ORPHAN

by

Sheila Jeffries

Magna Large Print Books
Gargrave, North Yorkshire,
BD23 3SE, England.

British Library Cataloguing in Publication Data.

A catalogue record of this book is
available from the British Library

ISBN   978-0-7505-4723-9

First published in Great Britain by Simon & Schuster UK Ltd., 2018

Published in Large Print 2019 by arrangement with
Simon & Schuster UK Ltd.

Magna Large Print is an imprint of Library Magna Books Ltd.

Printed and bound in Great Britain by
T.J. (International) Ltd., Cornwall, PL28 8RW

To my lovely sister, June.

Chapter 1

Porthmeor Beach,
St Ives, 1929

'There's something red out there in the sea. It could be a child.'

'Where?'

'There ... look ... between the waves. See it?'

'Briefly. It's too small to be a person. I reckon it's a red cloth, or a coat.'

'But it moved ... I saw it!'

'Wishful thinking, lad.' Vic scrutinised his son's expression. An eager, over-zealous face, reckless and compassionate. 'Don't you go out there, Arnie. We've done enough. We got 'em all – tragic it is – a tragic day for St Ives.' Both men glanced towards the top of the beach where the bodies of drowned sailors were laid out in an orderly line, their staring eyes covered in an assortment of fabric: sailcloth, old curtains, even coats. It had been hard to find enough to cover them all, to give them dignity after they'd been dragged, heavy and limp from the sea, or disentangled from the foam-spattered wreckage and seaweed piled on the shore.

'There wouldn't have been a child on a cargo ship,' Vic said. 'Forget it, Arnie.'

But Arnie Lanroska wasn't one to give up. He was a strong, young Cornishman, a proud

11

member of the lifeboat crew, a baritone in the male voice choir, a husband, a dad. His keen eyes searched the swell of silver waves, still massive from the storm that had raged through the night, driving a ship onto the rocks. Splintered and smashed, she had capsized with terrifying speed, in the dark, the crew flung into the sea, without lifejackets, before the lifeboat could even be launched.

Arnie felt he was the last man standing, watching the tide, believing someone was out there, clinging to a piece of timber. Alive. Abandoned. He sensed it. As if in response, the sea tossed it up again. Momentarily he saw a tumble of blonde curls, a tiny, lost, expectant face, appearing and disappearing in the troughs between waves.

'It's a child. A little girl.' He stripped off his sweater and trousers. Arnie was exhausted, but the glimpse of that small face touched a raw memory in his heart and gave him energy.

'I'm sure it's a child. I have to go in, Dad.'

'I hope you're not right.' Vic squared his aching shoulders and stood guard as his son stripped down to his swimming shorts. In the lion-coloured light of an October afternoon, Arnie dashed through the clods of seafoam the wind was tearing from the fringes of the Atlantic.

He dived into the green curl of a towering wave, cutting under the surf, his strong, lithe body swimming expertly above the undertow of an ebbing tide. The longing in his soul drove him forward. A little girl. He'd always dreamed of a little girl who would look at him with shining eyes and call him Daddy. He and his wife, Jenny, had two boys, Matt, nine, and Tom, five, but their first child had been stillborn. Perfect, but dead. A girl. Heartbroken, Arnie had cradled her in his rough, cupped hands, her skin cold, her sleeping face uncannily like his mother, the delicate features distinctly a Lanroska. 'You'll live in my heart, for ever,' he'd whispered, and he could see her now, as he thrashed his way through the hungry sea. It reopened the disappointment etched so deeply into his heart when he'd stared bleakly at her closed blue eyelids and realised he would never see his daughter's eyes. A door had slammed over their dreams, the lock tightening with every moment of holding their dead baby girl, the helpless heat of Jenny's tears as she'd pressed her shocked face close to his. The cruellest blow had come from his own grandmother, known as Nan, who had turned on the grieving couple with tight-lipped, imperious spite. 'It's your fault that baby was stillborn. I warned you – but, no, you didn't listen, did you?' It hurt bitterly, especially as Nan seemed triumphant, showing no compassion when her chilling prediction came true. It had caused a rift in the family. Jenny and Nan hated each other and the boys were kept away from Nan despite her grand house and magical garden where they might have enjoyed playing.

Arnie had grown up in St Ives, close to the sea, listening to its voice, its secret inner world, its rages and its peace. It was how he knew the child was out there; he felt her pulse beating across the water, sensed her life in the same way as he could sense a dolphin before it appeared.

13

A cone of sunlight sprinkled stars upon the water as he surfaced. Momentary light. He swam through timber and flotsam. And then, in a ribbon of clear water, he saw her: a little girl, her cheeks flushed, her fists clinging to the broken half a door. She wasn't crying. She was silent, her eyes assessing him through tendrils of honey-coloured hair.

Any possibility of bonding with her quickly vanished with the storm-surge heaving and plunging around them. He'd have to grab her and go, swimming on his back, hands clasped around her chin. She wasn't going to like it. She would be terrified, and too small to understand he was rescuing her, not trying to kill her.

'Don't worry, little one, I'm Arnie. I've come to get you.' That didn't sound right, shouted into the wind. The child looked at him silently. Did she speak English? There was no time to find out. 'Let go of the wood. I'll hold you safe.' Arnie touched her small arm and felt the tension in her as she tightened her grip. She wasn't going to let go. All he could do was keep her afloat and stay with her. Until what? The ebbing tide wouldn't carry them ashore.

Arnie waved and shouted towards the beach with all the power he could muster in his voice. 'I need some help. A child. Alive.' From the crest of the next enormous wave he saw Vic's solid navy-blue figure on the sand. 'Need help!' he yelled again, and moments later Vic had torn off his clothes and dived into the sea.

'Who's this? A princess?' Vic surfaced beside them, his hair slicked back by the water, showing

14

his bald patch. But his eyes had a sparkle and the child responded with a slight quiver of her lip, then a shift of the terror in her eyes, a silent, steely message. She wasn't going to let go of the door, even for Vic.

'You hold tight then, Princess,' Vic said. 'We'll have you snuggled up by the fire in no time.' Together, father and son steered the broken door through the waves with the child on it. Still she didn't cry. Splinters drove into Arnie's hands as he clenched the rough timber, fighting to keep it steady. His muscles burned with the effort of swimming only with his legs, his arms pushing the door through the turbulent water. The relief of feeling the sand brush his feet was huge. Emotional. After twelve harrowing hours of rescues, using his last reserves of strength to haul bodies from the sea. Trying not to care too much. Trying not to shout at God about why not a single one of them was alive, despite their efforts, despite the prayers going on in the village church. And now – to find a little girl, alive and not crying. A miracle that echoed down the corridors of Arnie's mind, right back to the stillborn baby. This little girl was safely ashore. Alive. Her eyes open. A pulse beating in her neck. Arnie wanted to collapse on the sand and weep instead of striding manfully out of the sea with Vic. Carefully they put the door down on soft white sand.

'There you are – you're safe now, Princess.' Vic squatted down and got eye contact with the shocked little girl. Arnie gulped. It was always the same. His dad, one step ahead of him, knowing exactly what to do, how to talk, how to warm the coldest heart with the light of his smile. An inappropriate thought at a time like this. He watched the child slowly unfasten her small hands from the wooden door. She examined them, a frown drawing her downy eyebrows together. Then her eyes widened, searching the beach. Who was she looking for? Arnie sat himself between her and the line of dead bodies, not wanting her to see them.

'What's your name?' he asked, but she didn't answer, her big eyes glancing over him as if the question was quite irrelevant.

Vic shook his head. 'She doesn't want to talk,' he advised. 'Best let her be. Maybe she don't speak English.'

'ARNIE!' He turned to see Jenny bustling along the sand, a blessed figure in her fruit-stained apron and shabby blue dress, her plume of dark hair blowing sideways. A group of village women were with her, their faces unusually serious after the storm had brought unasked for tragedy to their beach.

'Your hands!' Jenny immediately noticed his bleeding fingers. 'They're full of splinters.' Her eyes glowed with concern. 'I'm so proud of you – a proper hero, aren't you? Now, enough is enough, Arnie – and you, Vic. Time to come home.' Then she gasped, noticing the child still sitting on the door. 'Is that ... a child ... from the wreck? Surely not.' She knelt down on the sand and looked at her. 'Darling. You poor little mite.'

The villagers gathered round, curious, wanting to help, wanting to share the ambience of hope her rescue had generated.

'Where'd you come from, dearie?'

16

'Where's yer mum and dad?'

'Was you on that ship?'

The bewildered child looked from one to the other, and for the first time a single teardrop escaped down her rounded cheek.

'She don't look Cornish, do she?' said Maudie Tripconey, always one to spread controversy. 'Don't belong 'ere, that's for sure.'

Jenny reached out and touched the little girl's face. 'She's freezing. She's dangerously cold. I'm taking her home.' She scooped the wet child into her arms, and the little girl didn't resist but leaned her face against Jenny's comforting shoulder.

'Look at her red velvet dress,' Maudie Tripconey said. 'She came from a rich family. Look at the lace petticoats underneath. That's quality lace, that is. You be careful, Jenny, what you're taking on.'

'She's a child in need.' Jenny flung a contemptuous stare at Maudie. 'Now no more of your doom and gloom. We need to get her in the warm. It's getting dark now. And you two men, stood there shivering – where's yer sweaters? Come on – hot soup waiting on the stove. Some for you too, little one.' She pulled at her shawl, and wrapped it round the silent child who was studying Maudie Tripconey with just a hint of hostility in her eyes.

'If she's an orphan, she should go straight to the orphanage,' Maudie Tripconey called as Jenny swept by with the child in her arms. 'You wait 'til your nan hears about this. She's up there watching by her garden gate.'

'I don't care what she thinks.' Jenny walked on, refusing to look up at Nan's gabled house, its windows like watching eyes high on the cliff above the little harbour town.

But Maudie wouldn't or couldn't stop berating the family. 'You can't feed your own two boys, Jenny Lanroska, leave alone feed another one.'

'Hold your tongue, woman.' Vic's direct, honest eyes challenged Maudie who shut her mouth and folded her arms in defiance.

Arnie and Vic gathered their boots and sodden clothes in two disorganised bundles and followed Jenny's determined back, the child's face with its tumble of bright hair bobbing over her shoulder. Being careful to avoid the line of dead bodies, she walked up through the rocky end of the beach, past the lobster pots and fishermen's sheds, and into the cobbled street. Their home was in the Downlong area of St Ives, a huddle of granite cottages on the saddle of land between the harbour and Porthmeor Beach.

Still the child was silent, but her eyes were closing, the lids heavy. She was falling asleep, listening to Jenny singing. A Cornish sea shanty, sung by generations of home-going fishermen and tin miners; whether they were wet, cold, tired or destitute, there was always the singing. Spreading hope, spreading peace. Soon the deep voices of Arnie and Vic were joining in, even as they stood back to let the undertaker's cart roll by on its way to the beach. Two shaggy black horses, a black, covered wagon, a grim-faced top-hatted driver. Followed by a second cart. And a third.

But the Lanroska family went on singing. Singing a lost child to sleep. A child saved from the tragic wreck. An orphan. Who was she? It didn't

18

matter. The Lanroskas had taken her to their hearts.

Jenny carefully unbuttoned the red velvet dress from the sleeping child, the fabric dark with seawater. Mindful of the need to get her warm, she had laid her on the rug in front of the Cornish range, its door flung open to the purr of flames and the soothing heat of burning driftwood. The ornamental brass on the huge black stove had a reassuring gleam, and the flames tinged the steam from the big kettle and made flickering reflections in all the cooking pots, the brass bellows and fire tongs. Jenny hung the sodden dress over a drying rack where it steamed with an unfamiliar perfume, exotic and spicy, as if it had been kept in a drawer infused with an evocative eastern fragrance. The dress had a pocket with something hard and knobbly inside. Jenny didn't investigate; her priority was to remove the child's wet clothes, and wrap her in something warm. She opened the lid of the tall oak settle and pulled out a cream hand-knitted shawl that had belonged to her mother.

Under the dress were the layers of lace petticoats which she deftly peeled off, and under it was a liberty bodice, a pair of frilly bloomers and a vest. All soaking wet and awkward to remove from the sleeping child whose cherubic face didn't change even when Jenny rolled her to and fro and sat her up to get the clothes off. It was when she peeled off the last garment, a vest, that Jenny made a shocking discovery. The child had smooth, creamy skin, but her little back was

19

covered in ugly red weals, criss-crossed over her tender shoulder blades and down over her buttocks and the backs of her legs.

'Arnie!'

'What is it, love?' Arnie left his bowl of soup and came to her, appalled to see Jenny's eyes brimming with horrified tears.

'Look. Look at her. The poor little mite. She's been beaten.'

Arnie knelt on the rug, his face glowing in the firelight, and together they stared at the little girl's back while she slept.

'Those marks ... they look inflamed ... some are weeping. What could she have done to deserve it? How could anyone hurt a child so badly?'

'Looks like she was whipped with the buckle end of a belt,' Arnie said grimly. 'It must be hurting – but she wasn't even crying. She's a brave little girl.'

'I was praying her parents were alive,' Jenny said. 'But now...'

'Whoever did that should be hung, drawn and quartered. Doing that to a child.' Arnie reached across the sleeping child and drew his wife close to him, their heads pressed together in wordless emotion. It felt the same as the moment when they had gazed down at their dead baby. But now it had moved on into a new life, a new chance, a chance to heal and nurture this strange, ship-wrecked, silent child. 'We have to keep her,' Arnie whispered, and the words hung in the air like a pair of ornate entrance gates, metal, and shining, and strong.

Jenny nodded, overwhelmed by the unbreakable bond she had with Arnie, thinking it was a precious gift of love and protection for this little girl. Jenny's pragmatic, maternal mindset told her she couldn't linger and indulge the intense feeling. She must tend to the child's needs.

'Fetch me the iodine and the roll of cotton wool,' she said. 'And I can't wrap her in a scratchy shawl. Silk. She needs some silk. Mother's blouse.'

While Arnie rummaged in the dresser drawer for the iodine, Jenny opened the lid of the settle again and fished out the blue silk blouse her mother had loved so much. It would make a cool, kind layer against the child's injured back.

'How old would she be?' Arnie asked as Jenny dabbed the dark gold iodine tincture gently over the wounds, blowing on them to dry it.

'Six – maybe seven – we won't know until she talks. We don't even know her name.' Jenny rolled up the sleeves of the silk blouse and threaded the child's arms into it. 'A good job Mother was petite. Even so, it's miles too big. She's very deeply asleep, Arnie, and I must watch her all night – she could be ill from getting so cold – I mean, really, dangerously ill. Hypothermia, they call it ... and I know we can't afford the doctor. I'll nurse her as best I can.'

Arnie made the fire up, piling chunks of driftwood and nuggets of coal scavenged from the harbour beach. He spread a tartan rug over the wicker chair. 'You sit here with her, Jen. And when you think she's properly warm, bring her into our bed. Let her sleep in between us.' He lit a new candle from the fire and replaced the stump of wax in the brass candlestick. 'I'm bone weary. It's been a hard day – worst day of my life, Jen. I need to sleep it off. Can't ever forget those bodies laid out on our beach. I'll never go down there again without remembering. It's brought sorrow to our happy town.'

Jenny nodded, torn between comforting her shattered husband and nursing the child. She let Arnie settle her in the chair, wrapped in the blanket, with the child's still damp mane of hair draped over the arm of the chair, the curls rippling as they dried in the firelight. 'Kiss the boys goodnight for me,' she said, glad that she'd asked Millie from next door to put Matt and Tom to bed. She listened to the thump of his footsteps climbing the narrow stairs, heard him go into the boys' bedroom, the comforting twang of bedsprings as he tucked them in. Then the sound of him slumping into the sagging mattress they shared in the front bedroom. Normally they slept with the curtains drawn back, with the moonlight and starlight and the eternal pounding of the waves. But tonight, Arnie had closed the shutters as if to shut out the world.

A blend of love and anxiety simmered in Jenny's heart as she sensed the child relaxing, growing warmer, recovering in the blessing of sleep and firelight. Outside, the granite walls of the cottages echoed with the roar of surf breaking on Porthmeor and Porthgwidden. The narrow streets of St Ives were full of sand and broken roof slates which the storm had sent crashing down onto the cobbles.

The thought of those nameless bodies being

loaded into three undertaker's carts haunted Jenny. In a clear sky, the light from the sea extended the October twilight into a mystic hour, a coming home hour when cottage windows flickered with firelight and the Sloop Inn rang with laughter. Tonight there was no laughter. Only the crunch-crunch of men's boots heading purposefully down the cobbled streets towards Porthmeor.

Gently rocking the sleeping child, Jenny listened, aware of sorrow drifting through the streets like windblown sand. She sensed the compassion, the powerlessness carried in every heart. She wanted to be out there, sharing the burden with the community she loved. A community that did what it had to do, made unanimous decisions in total silence, as it was doing now, doing the last act of love for the dead sailors of a wrecked ship. Jenny listened, knowing exactly what was going to happen.

She hadn't cried for years but now the tears flowed, the breath burned in her throat, and she heard what she'd been waiting for. The men of St Ives, some of them so old they could hardly walk, had gathered to sing the dead sailors home. In perfect harmony, their voices rang out, warm and strong as they had always been:

Eternal father strong to save
Whose arm doth bind the restless wave...

The hymn was followed by another, and another until the slow clop of horses and the rumble of carts filled the street, and Jenny felt the shutters tremble as the solemn procession thundered past her door. A slit of light from a lantern shone between cracks in the shutters, the gleam of a horse's eye, then the long shadow of the death wagon. The sound faded, leaving only the hushed waves of low tide, and the piping cries of turnstones who gathered in twittering flocks at night to feed along the rocky shoreline.

The child's brow was warm. Jenny carried her upstairs and laid her down on the mattress. Without bothering to undress, she climbed in beside her, reaching across the bed for Arnie's hand. She lay awake, worrying. How would the little girl feel when she woke up, in a strange bed, between two strangers? Would she be terrified? How hard would it be, to cope with her and with the two lively boys? Could they find enough food and clothes for her? Jenny felt sure of only one thing. Love. There would be enough love to go round, always. Comforted by that certainty, she finally fell asleep.

At dawn, Jenny awoke to the sound of brushing from the street outside as energetic women with brooms swept up the sand and gathered the clinking roof slates into stacks against the walls. She turned over in bed and found herself looking into a pair of bright, strong, fathomless eyes. 'You're awake,' she breathed. 'Don't be frightened. You're safe now, and we're looking after you. I'm Jenny.'

The child gave her a quizzical glance, then looked down at the blue silk blouse she found herself wrapped in. Her small hands emerged from the creases of fabric. They were dimpled and very mobile, touching the silk, the coarse blanket, and twiddling locks of her hair which was now dry.

'Your dress is downstairs, drying by the fire,' Jenny said.

The child didn't seem interested. She twisted round, and her mouth fell open as she saw Arnie's stubbly face asleep on the pillow. She looked back at Jenny and put her finger to her lips. 'Shh. He's asleep,' she whispered.

'That's Arnie,' Jenny said. 'He rescued you from the sea.'

'Shh.' This time it was louder, and fierce. *A bossy little madam,* Jenny thought. *Like me. We should get along fine.*

'Will you tell me your name?' she asked, but the child shook her head.

'Then what shall I call you? Princess? Goldilocks?'

No response.

'How about Cinderella?'

Silence. And a rising tension. Jenny had a startling thought. *What if this beautiful little girl had lost her memory? What if she didn't know who she was?*

'Shall we get some breakfast?' she suggested, getting out of bed. She pulled out the towel she'd put there in case the traumatised child wet the bed. It was dry. 'I've got some elderberry cordial ... with honey ... would you like some?' Jenny headed for the stairs without further persuasion and was pleased to hear the little girl's feet running after her.

Together they looked at the velvet dress, a lighter shade of red now that it was drying. 'You can't wear it yet. It's still damp,' Jenny said, but

25

the child didn't seem to care. She was preoccupied with extracting something from the pocket, a black velvet pouch, its knobbly contents evidently precious to her. She wound the drawstring firmly around her wrist, and threw Jenny a look that clearly said, *'Hands off. This is MINE.'* She sat at the table, clutching the velvet pouch while Jenny warmed the elderberry cordial and honey on the stove. She gave her a thick slice of home-baked bread with butter and damson jam, surprised when the child took a knife and skilfully cut it into dainty squares, which she ate without getting in a mess.

'You're a proper little lady,' Jenny said.

The beams in the ceiling creaked alarmingly, and from upstairs came the sound of running feet, bedsprings, and squeals of laughter, followed by Arnie's groans of protest, then a roar as he pretended to be a lion. 'Don't worry, little one.' Jenny saw the child freeze with anxiety. 'It's only my two boys getting up. They're waking Daddy. Little monkeys.'

The big eyes rounded again as the child watched the stairs, her body poised for flight, like a bird on the edge of a roof. A beam of morning sunlight picked out a single curling strand of her hair, and Jenny noticed her eyes were dark blue like the deeps of the ocean. *Behind the round cheeks and the stubborn silence was an old soul,* Jenny thought, *a tender flower cruelly uprooted, torn away from everything she knew.*

'Who's SHE?' Matt pointed at her from the stairs, with Tom following him. 'She's sitting in MY chair.'

'Don't you be so rude,' snapped Jenny. 'This little girl came from the wrecked ship.'

The boys looked at each other, and Tom gave Matt a shove. 'We gotta say hello nicely, Daddy said.' He barged past his brother and ran downstairs, crossed the kitchen and stood in front of the little girl, his eyes treacle brown and solemn. 'Hello. My name's Tom Lanroska. What's yours?'

'Lottie.'

It felt like a breakthrough. The first time Lottie had spoken. 'Bless you, Tom.' Jenny ruffled his mop of dark hair, glad of her five-year-old son's disarming friendliness. She smiled at Lottie who sat uncannily still, as if she'd broken a spell and stopped breathing.

They all listened to footsteps tip-tapping on the cobbles. Footsteps that sounded oddly menacing. The front door had an iron knocker like the head of a lion. It was rapped, three times in an unfriendly manner.

Jenny smoothed her skirt, and went to the door, aware that she had slept in her clothes and hadn't yet washed or done her hair.

Two women in uniform stood at the door, their faces grave and unsmiling.

'Mrs Lanroska?'

'Yes – that's me.'

'We understand you have a child here from the wrecked ship. We've come to collect her.'

Chapter 2

'S'Nives'

Lottie got down from the table where she'd been eating her breakfast. She tried to push the chair in neatly, but Matt was waiting to reclaim it, his eyes smouldering with resentment. He snatched the chair from her fingers, and Lottie felt a huff of unfriendly breath on her cheek. 'That's MY chair, not yours.' Matt's voice had rough edges, like stones. 'And why are you wearing my granny's clothes?'

Lottie snuggled into the cosy shawl Jenny had given her to cover the silk blouse. She looked steadily at Matt, and the scars on her back started to burn and prickle as if his unfriendly attitude had somehow reawakened the pain. She didn't like his narrow nose, his scabby, bony knees and his dirty bare feet. Choosing to ignore him, she studied the younger boy, Tom, who was still baby-ish and plump, his sturdy legs anchored firmly in front of her, his eyes shining brown and knowing, as if a wise wizard lived inside his chubby face. She smiled at him and his eyes glowed with joy.

'Is that her?' The tallest of the two uniformed women at the door peered in, and the west wind from the sea gusted in, lifting the heavy damask door curtain. 'Can we come in?'

Jenny stood in the doorway, her back straight.

28

'Wait there.' She turned to shout up the stairs. 'Arnie! Come down here – right now, please.'

They all looked at the stairs, and Arnie's hairy legs appeared, bounding down the bare wooden steps. He was clad in a thick red and grey tartan dressing gown. He grinned at Lottie but she didn't smile back.

'Is this your dress, Lottie?' Tom asked, and he walked over to the drying rack by the fire, touching the red velvet in awe, and fingering the cream lace petticoats. 'It's pretty.'

'Keep away from the fire, Tom,' Jenny hissed. 'I've told you and told you.'

'Ah – you'll be Mr Lanroska.' The tall woman held out a leathery hand. 'I'm Miss Trevail from the orphanage in Truro. We've come to collect the child. I believe you rescued her from the shipwreck.'

Arnie frowned. 'What authority do you have to take her?'

'She's an orphan. Isn't that a good enough reason?' Miss Trevail lifted her sagging chin in a confrontational manner. Her ice-green lizard eyes glinted at him. The other woman nodded like an obedient accomplice.

'No, it isn't a good enough reason,' Arnie said. 'Me and Jen want her to stay here with us. Don't we, Jen?'

'That's right. We do,' Jen said staunchly. 'Poor little mite. She's only just arrived, and look what she's been through. It's not fair to move her again the very next morning.'

'But it's the right thing to do,' insisted Miss Trevail. 'We can care for her and discipline her

29

properly, keep her clean and train her to work hard.'

'She doesn't need an institution. She needs a home.' Jen stepped forward and propped her arm against the doorframe, barring the two women from coming in.

'But you can't look after her here.' Miss Trevail wrinkled her nose disapprovingly. 'This is a hovel. And look at the state of those two boys. I've never seen such dirty feet. Filthy.' She peered inside. 'And this is a two-up, two-down cottage in what is, frankly, a very rough area. Our orphanage in Truro is one of the best in the country.'

Jenny flew at her. 'How DARE you criticise my children and my home. My children are loved, not regimented. You've got a cheek, coming here telling us Downlong folk what to do.'

'But ... Mrs Lanroska ... I mean ... look at the sand on the stairs!'

'Don't you Mrs Lanroska me. If you lived in a cottage with a west-facing door and a storm blowing, you'd have sand on your stairs. We were all too busy caring about the shipwrecked sailors yesterday to go sweeping up sand. A bit of sand never hurt anyone. You go on back to Truro and sit in your fancy orphanage. Us Downlong folks don't need the likes of you in St Ives, telling us what to do.'

'I'm not telling you what to do, dear. We've come to collect the child – what's her name?'

'Lottie,' shouted Matt from the table.

'Right. Then Lottie is an orphan, and she must come with us to live in the orphanage.' Miss Trevail spoke slowly and loudly, hanging on to her consonants, as if Jenny was stupid.

The words broke into Lottie's consciousness. She'd been listening to Tom who was showing her a broad bean he was growing in a jar of wet newspaper. When she heard the word 'orphanage', Lottie's eyes went black with terror, the way they had been when Arnie first saw her in the sea.

'You've got to go to the orphanage,' Matt said, gloating.

'Eat your breakfast and be quiet, you tactless little spriggan,' barked Arnie, and Matt glowered.

A disapproving huff of wind made the fire flare in the stove.

'I really think we should come in.' Miss Trevail took a step forward. She brandished a brown leather suitcase with hard corners and brass buckles. 'We've brought a case for your clothes, Lottie – and what's that you've got in your hand? Where's your clothes?'

Lottie was clutching the black velvet pouch. Her lips quivered, and Tom put his arm round her. 'Don't cry, Lottie.'

'You are not coming in.' Jen braced her arm against the doorframe. 'That's right, Tom, you look after Lottie.'

But Lottie wasn't crying. She had steel in her eyes, and her mouth pursed tightly. In silence she gathered her clothes from the drying rack, folded them neatly over one arm, and walked towards Miss Trevail. Arnie and Jenny looked at each other. Surely Lottie wasn't going to choose the orphanage over their cosy home?

'There you are!' Miss Trevail looked triumphant. 'She's going to be sensible.'

Lottie walked right up to her in a moment of silence where everyone seemed to be holding their breath.

'Open the suitcase please,' Lottie said clearly. She looked up at Miss Trevail, who failed to notice the glint of artful intelligence in the little girl's frightened eyes.

Miss Trevail fumbled with the stiff leather buckles on the suitcase and when her hands were busy, Lottie saw her chance and took it. With one wild glance at Jenny, she slipped deftly between the two portly women and fled down the street, her bare feet flying over the cobbles, her bundle of clothes clutched tightly against her, her blonde curls waving like a flag.

'Now look what you've done,' Jenny glared accusingly at Miss Trevail. 'Made her run away. How's she going to find her way back? She don't know where she is.'

'St Ives is a good place to hide.' Arnie looked at Miss Trevail's shocked face, his eyes twinkling with amusement. He pointed a finger at her. 'You go back to Truro, and don't come here again. We'll take good care of Lottie. There's a train due in half an hour. Go on. Go.' He took Miss Trevail's hefty arm and turned her around.

'Don't you manhandle me.'

'Calm down. We don't want a rumpus.' Jen imagined how Miss Trevail's furious face would look to a small child. More than intimidating. Those cold lizard eyes were terrifying, and anger radiated from her pockmarked skin like invisible bristles. 'Arnie's right. Go – and take your posh suitcase with you.' Their faces were close now,

Jenny and Arnie and the two starchy women, a clash of wills.

But before anything else could happen, the streets of Downlong echoed with shouts and the rumble of handcarts. Two women scurried by, breathing hard, a bundle of empty baskets over their arms. Then an old man hobbling as fast as he could with a rickety handcart.

'Arnie!' Vic turned up next, his eyes alight with excitement, pushing a cart he had made from driftwood and towing a box on wheels. 'Cargo!' he yelled. 'Get yourself down 'Gwidden. And Porthmeor.'

Jenny's eyes rounded. 'What is it?'

'We don't know. It's in wooden crates, coming ashore off the wreck. There's plenty – but we gotta be quick – afore the police get there.'

Arnie pulled some clothes on and grabbed two fish baskets from the stack outside the door. He gave Jenny a quick peck on the cheek and a wink. 'Gotta go. Get what we can.'

'What about Lottie?' Jenny called after him.

'I'll look out for her.'

'She could get hurt.'

'She'll come back.'

Jenny gave Miss Trevail and her crony a little push. 'GO. Before you get mown down by this lot.' She waved her arm at the advancing horde of people now thundering down the street with baskets and carts, their faces alight with the prospect of plundering cargo from the wreck. They didn't see it as stealing. It was their right, and their reward for the hard work of living in St Ives, the pilchard packing, the rescues. A storm-wrecked

33

ship brought sadness, and treasure too. Sometimes it was crates of whisky and brandy, sometimes household stuff like cutlery and china, sometimes precious tins of food, food they'd never tasted, like salmon and pineapple.

Jenny watched the two women sidling along, close to the granite walls, hanging on to each other as the entire population of St Ives poured down the narrow streets towards the sea. She smirked when Miss Trevail's hat was knocked off by a flying fish basket. Seagulls wheeled and screamed overhead as if caught up in the excitement.

All she could think about was Lottie, out there clutching her only possessions, the black velvet pouch and her dress. Jenny thought of those tender little feet running over the cobbles. More pain. Undeserved pain. Seeing the cruel wounds on her back had upset Jenny and rekindled maternal love and a sheltering instinct. She wanted to protect this beautiful child who had suffered so much. Already she felt the ache of losing her.

Normally Jenny would have joined in the scrum to salvage booty from the wreck, but today she felt committed to finding Lottie. *I have to stay here, in case she comes back,* she thought, *and please God, she will come back.*

Lottie crouched behind a stack of lobster pots, her heart beating wildly as she watched the two women walk past in their prim navy-blue hats and squeaking shoes. Never again would she go to an orphanage. She needed to know where those women were going and if they would be coming back for her. If they were, then she'd stay in hiding

– for ever.

Dodging in and out of doorways and bobbing behind walls, Lottie shadowed them along the harbour, past the lifeboat house, to a high wire fence with notices in scarlet letters: DANGER, KEEP OUT and MINE CLOSED. She stared through the wire at the high granite chimney, the silent, rusting machinery and small trucks with iron wheels. What a place to hide.

Lottie almost forgot about the two women as she surveyed the overgrown site. She had no idea it was a tin mine with deep shafts and tunnels under the sea. Grass and thrift, bindweed and bramble colonised the piles of stone and heaps of iron. Seagulls sat motionless on every available perch, their blue-grey wings neatly tucked, their yellow eyes noting her without interest. A flock of turnstones ran to and fro, pecking the ground, their matchstick legs going so fast that they seemed invisible. Entranced by the cute little birds, Lottie lingered, tempted by sprays of black-berries glistening on the brambles. Then two rabbits appeared, hopping and nibbling grass, pausing to listen, their ears rim-lit by the emerg-ing sun. Lottie held her breath. She had never seen a wild rabbit, except in story books. But when she moved, both rabbits scuttled into holes and disappeared. Lottie made up her mind that one day she'd come back, find a way in under the fence and play there, in peace, away from dictatorial adults. It would be the kind of healing freedom she'd never had.

She pressed herself against the fence as a don-key trotted past pulling a cart laden with empty boxes, driven by a man with a hooky nose and greedy eyes. He didn't look at her but seemed to be hurrying towards the sea, like everyone else she had seen. Over here on the other side of the rocky headland of Pedn Olva, there was a glimmer of sunshine on the sea, a sanctuary from the great rolling storm waves, a glassy stillness about the wooded cliffs above a deserted beach. It wasn't the beach where the ship had been wrecked. Lottie frowned, anxious now as she followed the fence around the abandoned mine.

The whistle of a train broke into the lagoon-like silence of Porthminster Beach and the vast curve of Hayle Towans beyond. Godrevy Lighthouse shone white like a tooth at the far end of the bay, and Lottie could see surf breaking over its rocky island. She saw the plume of white steam from the train puffing through the hills, and ahead of her was a high granite wall. The two women were struggling up a flight of steep stone steps.

Hidden behind a clump of palm trees, Lottie watched their reddening faces, hearing their wheezing breath as they reached the top of the wall and disappeared. She ran up the steps, her heart thumping, ready to run for her life if they turned back and discovered her there. The granite twinkled with flecks of black and clear crystal, cold under her touch. At the top she crouched, peering over a low wall, amazed to see a railway station, and a steam train chuffing slowly into the long platform as if it had emerged from a page in a story book.

Her heart lifted when she saw the two women go into the station. She ran to the railings, awed by the towering black engine hissing against the barriers. Through the clouds of steam she observed the bulky shapes of the two women climbing into a carriage. Where could they be going? The orphanage in Truro? Well, she wasn't going with them. Ever. Lottie gave a little skip of joy. Truro must be far away, over those distant hills. She didn't know what Truro was, but she imagined a grim, grey orphanage with frowning windows. The scars on her back burned, and a question bobbed into her mind. She looked around for someone who might know the answer. There was a porter collecting the green cardboard tickets from people getting off the train. He looked friendly.

Lottie was still afraid someone might grab her, throw her onto the train, and call her an orphan when she wasn't an orphan. She waited until the train steamed off into the wooded hills, and then she approached the ticket collector. 'Excuse me. May I ask you a question?' she said in a clear voice.

'Yes, Miss.' He looked at her attentively. 'What do you want to know?'

Lottie took a deep breath. 'Is this America?'

'America!' A broad grin spread over his tanned face. 'Nah, course it's not. Get on with 'e. This is S'nives.'

Lottie felt hope and energy draining out of her.

The ticket man noticed her sudden aura of defeat. 'Was you joking?' He squatted down to bring his face level with hers.

Lottie shook her head wordlessly. S'nives. She was in S'nives. A place she'd never heard of. All that desperate terror she'd been through as a stowaway on the creaking, rolling, salt-drenched ship, then the shock of being thrown into the cold sea. Had it been for nothing? She swallowed, caught in the disappointment just as she'd been caught in the wreckage and the storm. She felt cold and sick.

'Where's yer mum and dad then?' the ticket man asked. His eyes glowed with concern for this strange little waif who stood before him in a blue silk blouse, miles too big, a cream shawl with its fringe trailing in the puddles, and a bundle of red velvet and lace clutched tightly against her body. 'You lost, are you?'

Lottie backed away, her eyes fixed on him in case he grabbed her. Questions about her mum and dad inevitably preceded her being seized by clamp-like hands, bruising her arm, marching her off to be taken prisoner by merciless adults. Before he could catch her, she twirled around and ran, feeling sick and shaken. She hurried down the stone steps too fast, lost her balance and tumbled to the bottom, banging her elbows on the granite, and leaving the red velvet dress and petticoats strewn over the sooty wet steps.

Expecting the ticket man to come pounding after her, Lottie picked herself up, fighting to ignore her bruises. Pain flared in her wounded back. Shaking and nauseous with shock, she threw up all over Jenny's cream shawl. It upset her. She would have to wash it, somehow. There were plenty of deep puddles around. She hesitated, watching the top of the steps, and when the ticket man didn't appear, she made herself climb up and snatch her dress, petticoats, and the black velvet pouch.

Dazed, she stumbled back towards the abandoned tin mine, hoping to find a way in. She followed the rusty fence down to where the path ended at a sheer granite wall built against the sea. The surf boiled on the rocks below, flouncing great glittering mops of seaweed. Cormorants sat on the highest rock, drying their sepia wings in the sunshine, their beaks lifted towards the sky.

There was no way in. Lottie walked back from the edge, her fingers trailing the cold wire netting. She felt suddenly feverish and wanted to curl up in a safe warm bed. She sat down on a ledge between two rocks. The rocks were warm from the sun, and prickly with gold and silver lichens.

I ought to put my proper clothes on, Lottie thought, trying to distract herself from the cloud of despair that had been waiting to swallow her up. She took off the shawl and rolled it into a bundle. The blue silk blouse felt kind against her skin, so she kept it on and pulled the petticoats and dress over it. The red velvet had dried stiff like cardboard in front of Jenny's fire, and the lace petticoats felt scratchy against her bare legs. Her feet were freezing cold and sore from running on the rough ground. She longed for the shoes and socks she had lost in the sea.

The thoughts about clothes seemed futile. The cloud of despair crept over Lottie as she leaned against the rocks. It was a cloud full of words. Tormenting words. Cruel reminders. *THIS IS NOT AMERICA* was the dominant phrase. It overwhelmed her with sadness and a sense of betrayal.

39

Lottie was eight years old, and more than anything she wanted her mother. Her mother had gone to America on a steam ship. Lottie had stood on the quay with her gran and both of them had cried, watching the ship until it was smaller than a bird, watching it confidently steaming out across that vast ocean, the sparkles dancing after it like mockery. When it had gone, and the steam was a smudge of cloud, and then a memory, Lottie had felt a chasm open up in her life.

'I can't take you with me, Charlotte.' Her mother's vibrant face had been sad and anxious before she boarded the ship. 'But I'll come back for you. One day. I promise.' The memory of that last hug still lingered like a scarf of chiffon around Lottie's shoulders. Her mother's expressive fingers twirling her hair, her mother's luminous eyes giving her a look intended to last, a look that would hold its sparkle for weeks, months, years, perhaps for ever in Lottie's heart. A diamond of a look. A look to sustain her through the hard times to come.

Lottie tried to comfort herself with the memory as she leaned her head against the rock, but she was shivering and wanting to go to sleep. Her eyes felt heavy, her skin clammy. She wanted some more of Jenny's elderberry cordial. She wanted her shoes and socks. And she didn't want to be in this place called 'S'nives'. Lottie had trained herself not to cry, but tears were painfully close. She shut her eyes, but was jolted awake by the rumble of cartwheels and the furry face and ears of a silvery brown donkey coming around the corner.

Lottie tensed, expecting it to be the man she'd seen earlier. She stared in surprise, first at the donkey's harness which was decorated with tassels of brightly coloured wool, and real flowers, marigolds and lavender stuck into his bridle. Bunches of mint and lemon balm hung from the sides of the cart. The aroma of dried herbs and the polish in the donkey's harness was oddly comforting to Lottie, and the donkey was looking at her with liquid brown eyes. She got to her feet. Why was this donkey apparently on its own ... pulling a cart with no driver?

Lottie had never been close to a donkey, but this one looked cuddly, and so ... she couldn't find a word. She felt the donkey actually wanted to love her. She walked up to him, thrilled when he stood still for her and rested his head against her body as if he saw her pain and wanted to offer his love in the form of a warm, furry head, soft rabbit ears, and the flowers in his bridle. She wound her arms around the donkey's head, burying her fingers in his lush fur.

'I see you've found a friend,' said a ringing voice, and the donkey pressed his head even closer into her body.

Lottie looked up into the fierce eyes of the most enormous woman she had ever seen. High cheekbones, a coil of snow-white hair, and a vast tent of a dress half covered by a gigantic apron, stained and puckered. Bare, freckled legs planted a long way apart, struggling to carry such a weight.

'Would you like me to take you home, young lady?'

41

The ringing voice reached Lottie through waves of dizziness. Her little hands clung to the donkey's fur, then let go as she crumpled like a rag doll, soundlessly, and lay on the cobbled road in a dead faint. The donkey lowered his head and pushed her gently with his velvety muzzle, but she didn't move.

'Oh dear, oh dear!' The woman struggled to get down close to the child's still form, and failed. So she stooped and picked her up, alarmed by the pale cheeks and closed eyes. Despite her blonde hair, Lottie had dark eyebrows and dark lashes. 'I know who you are. I know exactly who you are,' the woman said, 'and I'm taking you home.'

She placed Lottie on a rug in the back of the donkey cart and tenderly wrapped the fringed edges of the rug around her. She heaved herself up onto the driver's seat, almost toppling the cart with her weight, and picked up the reins. 'Giddy up,' she called to the donkey and set off in the rocking, rumbling cart through the narrow streets of St Ives, with the seagulls screaming overhead, and the wind doing its best to unravel the white coil of her hair.

Chapter 3

Nan

Arnie's grandmother reminded Jenny of a mountain. Her hips were so wide that when she sat down she was shaped like a pyramid. She lived in a dress of mottled blues and browns, and glints of purple came from the amethyst beads embedded in the folds of her neck. Her hair was a peak of white snow, the skin over her cheeks rough and glistening like a rock face. Her storm-coloured eyes missed nothing, and fixed Jenny with a confrontational stare.

The people of St Ives knew the old lady as 'Nan', for she had long ago buried her real name unceremoniously onto the compost heap in her garden. Nan seldom spoke, but when she did her voice would freeze a Labrador, turn a well-meaning man to stone, or fragment into a wheezy laugh that made the flowery dress wobble alarmingly and the rock-face cheeks crease into a smile.

Nan's knowledge of horticulture and folklore was legendary, and the folklore had split the family and caused Jenny to openly hate her. Nan wished she'd kept quiet about the stillborn baby, but apologies were not in her repertoire. Arnie was her favourite grandson. Nan had brought him up from the age of nine when his mother had died from smallpox, leaving Vic heartbroken and

43

alone. She'd been pleased, but slightly uneasy when Arnie had met and married Jenny, a feisty girl from Helston. Like Arnie, Jenny had lost her mother very young, and then her father had died in a mining accident.

When Jenny was pregnant with their first child, Nan had gone to visit, armed with a basket of broad beans from her garden. Her bones had chilled to the marrow when Arnie showed her the cradle he had made from elder wood. He was proud of the beautiful sheen on the light gold wood, smooth and polished, the inside cushioned with a crochet blanket Jenny had made in brand new white wool. 'It rocks,' Arnie said proudly and flicked it with his big fisherman's hand. 'It smells lovely too. It's elder wood, from that big tree they felled in the churchyard.'

'Elder wood?' Nan went pale. She had to tell him. He wasn't going to like it, but he was her grandson and he had to learn. Her voice came out louder and more critical than she intended. 'But ... elder wood! You must never, NEVER make a cradle from elder wood.' Nan pursed her lips. A mist of disappointment drifted over Arnie's devastated face. Nan felt pressure rising up through her chest and into her throat. It made her giddy. But she had to say it. She had to. 'You must burn it. Right now. Or the baby will die.'

The cradle had continued rocking on the slate windowsill as if it was laughing.

In the explosive silence, Jenny flew out of the kitchen, her eyes blazing. 'What a cruel, tactless thing to say, Nan. Arnie's worked hours and hours making it, and singing while he was sanding

44

it. A lot of love went into that cradle. And we're keeping it – and our baby's going to sleep in it. I don't care what you think.'

Nan tried to speak, but there was no stopping Jenny once she started a diatribe. 'How do you think that makes me feel? Saying our baby's gonna die when it's kicking away inside me – here, put your hand on me and feel it for yourself.' She patted her bump proudly, but Nan went rigid and backed away. 'How can you be so spiteful?' Jenny raged. 'You never liked me, did you? Just because I come from Helston.'

It wasn't true. Nan hadn't meant to be spiteful. She'd been doing her duty in warning them. To her, the old legends had power and wisdom. As for not liking Jenny – well, she'd tried, hadn't she? Nan looked at the broad beans, her eyes bitter, her cheeks taut.

'Don't you come here upsetting my family with your ridiculous superstitions, Nan.'

'I'm warning you – for your own good,' Nan said. 'That baby...'

'I don't want to hear it.' Jenny tossed her head. She grabbed the squeaky fresh bundle of broad beans from the kitchen table and flung them back into Nan's basket. 'You GO HOME and take your broad beans with you. You bigoted old witch.'

'You hot-tempered, insolent little hussy.' Nan's voluminous flower dress rustled and the willow basket creaked over her arm as she sailed out, her wide hips see-sawing, her chin high. Dignity was her suit of armour. But inside she burned with hurt, Jenny's shout stabbing cruelly at her heart.

45

To get upset over a few broad beans would seem ridiculous. So Nan kept quiet and retreated into the defensive shell she had built. Obviously Jenny could have no idea how much it hurt to have her gift flung back at her. Growing vegetables in a seaside garden wasn't easy and Nan had slaved through the seasons, planting shelter belts, tilling the gritty clifftop soil, saving seeds in brown paper bags. The lush green pods of broad beans were her pride and joy. Back then it was wartime and food was precious. Nan had picked the best of the crop for Arnie and Jenny, imagining them enjoying the nourishing meal. Her heart had trembled with pain as she struggled home with the rejected gift.

Nan had never gone back. Long years had passed since the stillborn baby. Arnie had taken Matt and Tom to see her, but Nan hadn't engaged with the two boys. Especially not Matt. Nan disliked him instantly. A spriggan. That's what Matt was. And the other boy, Tom, had looked at her with such enquiring candour in his eyes that Nan had shut down. She didn't do guilt. Her remedy was to become ever more reclusive, spending her days cultivating her garden and caring for her donkey and six cats. The animals met her emotional needs with their soft fur, their adoring gazes and unconditional love. And the plants rewarded her efforts with extravagant blooms, heady fragrance and produce that pulsed with the life force.

Nan only thought about the family on stormy days, indoors by the fire, turning the fading pages of albums, polishing wood and silver until everything flickered in the firelight. On the slate windowsill, Nan kept a telescope in a brown leather case. She watched everything that happened on Porthmeor Beach and the green cliffs of the 'Island'.

On the day of the shipwreck, Nan stayed in the window, watching the bodies being plucked from the sea. She recognised Arnie and Vic through the telescope. The courage on their tired, weather-beaten faces touched a forgotten place in her heart. She saw Arnie, and then Vic dive into the storm-flecked waves. Love, pride and guilt flowed through her veins in fierce, rapid beats.

When she saw them bringing Lottie ashore, Nan noticed the child's golden head moving as if searching for her lost parents. Then Jenny, running down the beach and gathering the ship-wrecked child into her arms with unhesitating compassion. Nan's whole world had changed in that moment. 'It's time,' she said aloud, to herself. 'It's time you went down and made your peace. St Ia has come again – from the sea.'

Matt was nine years old and very angry. The anger wouldn't leave him alone. It snapped at his heart and filled his soul with sadness. Matt didn't feel loved. 'Course I love you,' Jenny would say, but she didn't look at him the way she looked at Tom. The tone of her voice changed. When she spoke to Tom, her voice was warm and wel-coming. Matt wished his mum would talk to him like that, but she never did. There was always a sharp edge of disappointment in it for him.

Matt had hated Lottie on sight. It had been bad enough when Tom was born. Now this weird shipwrecked girl had invaded his home. Matt had never seen a girl like Lottie with such pale skin and pale hair, so much hair swirling around her, hiding her face. He didn't like the dismissive stare she'd given him, and the way her eyes had warmed to Tom's irritating friendliness. Intense jealousy had boiled in his mind when Arnie explained how Lottie had slept in their bed, in between HIS parents, when Matt had tried to creep in there on lonely nights and been pushed away. 'Get back to bed, YOU.' Not even honouring him with his name. YOU was such an insult. Like a slap.

So Matt made up his mind to hurt Lottie. He'd make her life hell. He'd tried to do it to Tom, pushing him over whenever he could get away with it, hiding his things, jumping on his sandcastles. A few times it had been satisfying, hearing his little brother's howl of pain, but as Tom grew older Matt found him infuriatingly placid, slow to anger and disarmingly kind. Lottie would be a much better target for Matt's grudge against the world. He knew, from playing with the local tribe of children, that little girls could be furiously indignant. Pure entertainment to Matt, a chance to stand there grinning and smirking. Their enraged crying painted a picture of his own inner pain, helping somehow to unlock it, release a bit of pressure. The recriminations didn't bother Matt. Bad was strong. Bullying was strong. And addictive. He felt no guilt.

'You stay here, Matt, and you, Tom.' Jenny had wagged her finger at the boys on the morning after the storm. 'I want that sand swept off the stairs. Put it in those two fire buckets in the yard.'

'But I want to see the wreck,' Matt protested, 'and help Dad with the looting.' He sidled along the wall to the door.

'Oh no you don't.' Jenny grabbed his thin arm, her fingers angry, her eyes fixing him like nails into wood. 'Someone's got to be here in case Lottie finds her way back. She's lost, Matt. She's in a strange place, she's lost her mum and dad, and her home, wherever it was. We've got to help her.'

'I haven't got to.'

'Yes, you HAVE.'

'Why?'

'Because I say so.' She looked in despair at her son's hardening stare. 'You stay here, Matt, or Daddy will deal with you. And you won't get NOTHING from the looting. Daddy and I, and Tom – and Lottie – will all be eating tinned peaches and you won't get any. So stay here and sweep the stairs.'

Matt shrugged. Jenny's words made him feel desolate, as if he couldn't go much lower. He sat down on the stairs, twiddling the hand brush Jenny had given him. All he wanted was to be out on the bright water, on his dad's boat, just the two of them. Arnie's boat was called *The Jenny Wren*, and Arnie had rescued her from a scrapyard in Hayle. Matt had proudly helped him to restore her, and together they had made her seaworthy again. Now *The Jenny Wren* was the brightest boat in the harbour with her coat of fresh paint in blue, white and yellow. She was a motorboat with a cabin and a big deck with room for Arnie's lobster pots and fish baskets. 'One day she'll be yours,'

Arnie had promised.

Jenny's angry voice carved into his dream.

'And don't just sit there ... SWEEP.' Jenny frowned at his insolent gaze. Tom was already eagerly sweeping sand, not getting much of it in the dustpan, but he beamed up at her. Jenny ruffled his hair fondly, and went out into the street, shutting the door behind her.

Matt remained sitting on the stairs, annoying Tom by beating out rhythms with the handle of his brush and with his bare feet. About an hour later, someone knocked at the door. 'I'll answer it, not you,' Matt said to Tom. 'I'm the oldest.'

He opened the door, and stood there, shocked to see Nan's storm-coloured eyes glinting down at him. Matt knew who she was, and he knew she didn't like him. It was mutual.

The silence simmered between them.

'Where's your father, boy?'

'Down 'Gwidden.'

'He's getting cargo from the wreck.' Tom's eyes gleamed with pride.

'And where's your mother?'

'Out, looking for Lottie,' Tom explained, while Matt hung his head and scuffed sand around the flagstone floor.

'Then you two boys go and get her,' Nan said. 'Tell her I've brought Lottie home and she's proper poorly. Have you got that?'

Only too glad to escape, Matt and his brother tore out of the house. Matt saw Lottie lying down in the back of the donkey cart, her eyes button black and still. It gave him goosebumps. Was she dead, he wondered? And was it his fault? Had his anger reached out and somehow cursed this pale child from the sea?

Nan took a metal bucket from its peg on the back of the cart and filled it with water from the street tap. She gave it to the donkey who drank noisily, sucking and shaking drops from his velvet lips. Then she tethered him to a ring in the wall and hung his canvas nosebag of meadow hay around his neck.

'Now then, young lady, let's get you sorted out.' Nan lifted Lottie from the back of the cart and carried her inside. 'Is this the right house?' she asked. 'Jenny's house?'

Lottie's eyes looked relieved. She nodded, recognising the black stove with its ornate brass and the reassuring curl of steam from Jenny's big oval cooking pot.

Nan put her in the wicker chair by the fire and the child just lay there like a rag doll, her eyes hungry for reassurance. Nan filled a cup with hot water from the kettle and took a small muslin bag from one of the capacious pockets of her apron. She sniffed it. Dried fennel and chamomile. She dunked it in the steaming water and added a spoonful of honey from the jar in Jenny's kitchen. 'Nan's healing tea,' she told Lottie, 'made from the herbs in my garden. You drink it.'

She watched, satisfied, as Lottie tasted it, then gulped it down, draining the cup, and snuggling deeper into the chair as if she wanted to sleep.

'You ain't very well,' Nan said. She pulled up a chair and sat close to Lottie, studying the expression in the child's eyes. *Grief,* Nan thought. *Deep, inexplicable grief.* Her heart went out to the little girl, so alone in the world, and so shocked. 'You'll get better, dear, when you've had a rest.'

But Lottie shook her head. She sighed deeply.

'You can tell Nan. Anything, anything at all.'

She waited while Lottie's haunted eyes searched hers, seeking answers to a queue of questions. 'Tell Nan,' she prompted, half-listening to the street outside, hoping Jenny wasn't going to come barging in. Nan felt she needed to bond with this intriguing child who looked so young and yet so old. Nan felt it was her, and not Jenny, who had the skills to find an answer to a question that was burning the child's soul. She leaned closer to hear the words.

'I don't want to be in S'nives,' Lottie whispered. 'I thought the ship was going to America.'

'America is far away – across the Atlantic Ocean,' Nan said. 'And who told you this was S'nives?'

'The stationmaster, and he laughed at me.'

'Well, he's wrong,' Nan declared. 'Now you listen to me, Lottie. This isn't S'nives. It's Saint Ives, and it's a special, magic place.' She lowered her voice, and Lottie's eyes fixed on her, listening. 'Its name comes from the sea, like you – only she arrived by magic. She floated on a giant leaf, all the way from the Emerald Isle where the fairies live. Before she came, this place was an ordinary fishing cove, but St Ia made it a magic place, full of light and flowers. She even found a well of crystal water. She taught people to find silver and gold.'

Lottie's eyes rounded. Her tight little mouth

relaxed into wonder, and Nan observed that she was fingering the black velvet pouch as if the contents might be a meaningful piece of jewellery. Nan lowered her voice to an enchanted whisper. 'Silver and gold,' she continued. 'At twilight when the sun and moon shine opposite each other across the water, you have to imagine you can float, like St Ia did, on leaves of silver and gold, and gather the jewels of the ocean. When you have them in your hand, you can go anywhere, even to America or China, or the land of ice and snow at the top of the world.'

Nan was enjoying herself. She'd often longed for a granddaughter to share her stories with. She sensed Lottie's need for deep, peaceful sleep to heal the trauma of the shipwreck and the grief of losing whoever it was she had lost. The fennel and chamomile tea was beginning to work and Lottie's eyelids were getting heavier. Hopefully she would drift into sleep and dream of St Ia and the silver and gold pathways of light on the water.

But, predictably, Jenny burst through the door, bringing in with her the wind and the soft eternal roar of the sea.

'Oh there you are!' She brushed past Nan in a swirl of skirt smelling of wet seaweed. Lottie's eyes flew open. 'Half the town's been out looking for you, Lottie.'

Lottie looked mutinous and sleepy. She turned her head away from Jenny and curled up in a ball.

'Let her be.' Nan put a restraining hand on Jenny's shoulder.

'What d'you think you're doing here?' Jenny gave her a look of pure hatred.

Nan's hand jumped back. She noticed Jenny was twitching with frustration. A time bomb, programmed to explode with relief at finding her lost child, relief which manifested as fury. Telling her to calm down would only ignite a second burst of rage. So Nan pursed her thin lips and stood there, looking down at Lottie.

Jenny interpreted the silence as judgemental. 'Get out of my home,' she hissed, pushing her face towards Nan. 'Go on. GO.'

Nan turned to granite. She turned away from Jenny, her head held high, her craggy jaw lifted to the light that streamed in through the open door. The curtain billowed into her face as if it wanted to give her a slap. She shoved it aside. She'd go home now and her cats would run to her with their tails up. She'd lead Mufty, the donkey, up the hill, and on the steepest part she'd walk behind the cart, pushing it for him, helping him as best she could.

Outside in the street, Nan was incensed to see Matt sitting on Mufty's back, bouncing up and down, with Tom watching gleefully. 'HOW DARE YOU,' she bellowed, and the women brushing the street froze like a game of statues. The boys' grins vanished and Matt got down, a ghost of an insolent smile in his eyes as he looked at Nan. 'That donkey is resting and having a meal,' she thundered as the boys scurried past her. 'How DARE you abuse an animal like that.'

Tom paused and looked up at her with clear, bright eyes searching into her soul. 'Sorry,' he lisped.

Nan gave him a frosty nod, and unhitched

Mufty from the ring in the wall. 'You tell your mother Lottie's got a fever.' She fished in the pocket of her apron and handed Tom another muslin bag of chamomile and fennel. 'Give her this. It's herb tea.'

She set off on the exhausting walk home, past St Ia's Well and up the hill. *I ought to go back,* she thought, a memory of Lottie etched into her tired old heart. *I ought to call the doctor to that child.*

Lottie heard the voices as if from a distance. She heard the crackle of the fire and the sigh of the waves, the cry of seagulls, and the crooning of the wind. She sensed the flurry of movement around her. Heavy skirts and boots. A smell of fish.

She opened her eyes, and found herself lying on a sofa in the window. The window had square panes and flaking paint, and in the top panes a slice of blue sky with racing clouds, a flicker of sunlight over the blanket Jenny had put over her. Now Jenny was looking down at her with anxious eyes, and beside her was a strange man smartly dressed in a waistcoat with brass buttons. He was holding Lottie's wrist and frowning at a gold watch attached to his pocket.

'Don't worry, Lottie – it's Doctor Tregullow,' Jenny said, and her face looked blurred. Lottie tried, but she couldn't keep her eyes open. She was aware of Matt and Tom nearby, trying to be quiet, whispering to each other. Then she slipped back into the dream. Or was it real? The violence of the shipwreck. The cries for help. The pain in her hands as she clung to the broken door. Then Nan, telling her about St Ia. Nan, giving her the sweet herb tea.

She cried out with pain when Jenny turned her over. 'You should see her back, Doctor. I put iodine on it, I didn't know what else to do.'

Lottie whimpered in protest. She didn't want anyone looking at the marks on her back. To be beaten was shameful. To remember those hard, cold eyes, the flared nostrils, the savage injustice of seeing avaricious glee in the smile of a person who was supposed to be caring for her. Hot stripes of pain had clung to her back as she ran alone through the night, a glimmer of hope in her heart as she saw the ship with its gangway still down on the quayside. The effort of standing up very straight and lying to the sailor who was guarding it. 'Excuse me,' Lottie had smiled her sweetest smile, 'I have to take an important message to my father. I know where he is. I'll be very quick.'

Without waiting for a reply, Lottie had marched confidently up the gangplank and onto the ship. 'She's sailing in ten minutes,' the sailor called after her, 'so get a move on.' It didn't occur to Lottie to ask where the ship was going. She assumed that all ships went to America when they sailed out west. She quickly found a hiding place, inside a coil of rope under a tarpaulin, a perfect shelter from the weather.

Excitement pulsed through her. She felt the ship dipping and rolling over the swell beyond the harbour, and she clapped her hands in joy. She'd done it! She snuggled down into her nest of salt-drenched rope, hearing rain pattering on the tarpaulin, and then wild splats of spray as the ship headed out into the gathering storm.

'Lottie!' Jenny was shaking her gently. 'Will you try to wake up, please? Doctor Tregullow wants to ask you some questions.'

Jolted out of her dream, Lottie felt bewildered and shivery. She looked at the two faces gazing down at her. The doctor's neat and serious face, and Jenny's rosy cheeks. Where was Nan? 'I want Nan,' she said. 'Nan looked after me.'

'Nan's gone home,' Jenny said. 'I'll look after you now.'

'Will you open your mouth, Lottie, please? I need to look at your throat.' The doctor peered into her mouth. He touched the sides of her neck, gently feeling her glands. 'Hmmm,' he frowned, then looked into her eyes. 'Who did that to your back, Lottie? Who beat you so badly?'

Lottie sank back into sleep. Her eyelids closed again to heavy darkness.

'Why would anyone beat a child like that?' Jenny asked, and the rest of her words blurred into a jumble. 'Lottie?'

'I was in the orphanage,' Lottie mumbled, 'and I let the birds out. I opened all the cages, and the birds were happy. They flew away, out of the window … but…' She sank deeper, into another nightmare. The voices of Jenny and Doctor Tregullow drifted away to the far edges of her consciousness.

'So she IS an orphan,' she heard Jenny say.

'She has got a fever,' Doctor Tregullow said, and Lottie heard the snap of his medical bag being closed, and the creak of his shoes. 'Keep her quiet, lots of drinks, and I'll come again in the morning to see her. I'll bring something for you to put on her back.'

'But, Doctor...' The cool of the sea wind brushed her hot cheeks as Jenny opened the door to let him out. 'We can't possibly pay you.'

'Don't worry, my dear. It was Nan Lanroska who sent me, and she's already paid me.'

The door closed and the footsteps walked away.

'Interfering old woman,' Jenny ranted, and Lottie sank deeper into a restless sleep, a sleep where storms raged and people argued.

'Nan was kind to Lottie.' Tom's bright voice was full of indignation.

'You hold your tongue. It's nothing to do with you what I think of Nan.'

'But why can't we go to Nan's house and see the donkey?' Tom asked, pouting. 'It's not fair.'

'Dead right it's not fair. Life isn't fair. So stop complaining. Lottie's proper poorly and we've got to look after her. She's a very sick little girl.'

Lottie lay there, listening, half awake and half asleep. *Is that me?* she thought. *A very sick little girl.* 'Am I going to die?' she asked.

Jenny came over to her immediately. 'Course you're not. We won't let you. You'll soon be better and running around again, and you're going to be our little girl.'

Comforted, Lottie gave in to the drowsy fever and closed her eyes again. She wished it was quiet. But moments later there was a new voice, new footsteps and skirts rustling. Someone new coming to stand by the sofa and look down at her.

'That's kind of you, Millie,' Jenny was saying, 'and it's beautiful. She'll love it.'

'Well ... poor little child. I knew you'd got her here and I didn't know what else to do, so I got me wool basket out and knitted it up. It only took me a few hours. Here you are, darling.'

Lottie felt something woolly and soft being pushed into her hand. She opened her eyes and saw a beautifully knitted doll, in a red dress like hers. The doll had long hair made from yellow wool. She had a pink face with a stitched-on smile and royal blue eyes with arched eyebrows giving the doll an expression of amiable surprise. She wasn't anything like the dolls Lottie had been used to. Hard, porcelain dolls with eyes of glass and hard little porcelain hands. This simple knitted doll felt squashy and friendly, like Nan's donkey.

'I made her for you,' Millie said. 'She's a cuddly friend for you to have in bed with you.'

'Thank you,' Lottie whispered, tucking the doll against her cheek.

The woman smiled down at her with happy, beaming eyes. 'I'm Millie,' she said firmly, 'Millie next door. And when you're better you can come in with me and I'll show you how to knit, and you can have toasted saffron buns for tea. How about that?'

Lottie didn't know what a saffron bun was, or if she wanted to learn to knit. But she noticed the way Millie's smile made lines radiate from the corners of her eyes, like sunrays. It made her want to smile back, and she did, before the fever swept her back into a dark, deep place.

'Where are you gonna put her, Jen?' Millie asked. 'You haven't got room for her have you? She can't sleep in with the boys.'

'She can,' Jen said. 'She'll have to at first.'

'You don't know what she's been used to.'

'It doesn't matter, Millie, as long as she's safe and warm.'

'But what about when she's growing up?'

'She's not gonna grow up,' Jenny said, 'if she doesn't come through this fever.'

Chapter 4

The Attic Stairs

Nan felt very alone as she hesitated in front of the door to the attic, an iron key in her hand. Supposing she fell on the steep narrow staircase? Who would know? And who would look after Mufty and her cats and chickens? Her shoulders twitched. She was cross with herself for worrying. *Get on with it,* she told herself, *and don't be ridiculous.*

The door to the attic had been locked for years. Ever since the rift with Jenny and Arnie. The attic was stuffed with memories, memories that hurt. Nan had forbidden herself to go up there, especially now her joints were painful, and she'd put on so much weight.

Two of her six cats sat, one on each side of her, looking expectantly at the attic door. They were brother and sister, Bartholomew and Bessie, both extravagantly fluffy, black and white and golden-eyed. Unlike the younger cats, they'd been in the attic years ago. A cat's paradise.

Nan looked down at their bright, wise faces. 'I suppose you can't wait to go up there.' She turned the key and eased the door open, breaking a spectacular cobweb with a soft tearing noise and the spiky shadow of an incensed spider running for cover. Mould and thick dust covered the steep stairs, and a lone woodlouse scurried out of sight. Dust motes danced in a shaft of morning sunlight from the gabled window. *Get on with it,* Nan thought again. She grabbed the rickety banister and hauled herself up, her big body brushing the walls both sides. The cats ran ahead of her, their paws pattering on the bare wood, and vanished into the spaces between the old furniture and boxes. Mice fled, squeaking, in all directions, one flying down the stairs between Nan's feet.

Step by painful step, she dragged herself up, not daring to stop in case she panicked, and worrying in a corner of her mind about how on earth she was going to get down.

Hendravean was a twin-gabled detached house standing alone at the end of Foxglove Lane. It faced east so in the morning its windows glared with reflected sunlight. Unlike most houses in St Ives, it had a huge garden encircled by a Cornish hedge smothered in wild flowers. The westerly gales tore into the back garden, and today there were still banks of cream-coloured seafoam from the storm. Nan could see them shivering and glistening in the sun, piled against the chicken house and the back of Mufty's ramshackle stable.

She paused by the attic window, her legs shaking, her breath panicky, her weathered fingers parting the cobwebs. It was reassuring to look down at her cultivated garden and see the chickens contentedly wandering and pecking, and the other four cats, all ginger, piled asleep on the seat against the shed. It calmed Nan down. Her breathing settled, and she found the strength to turn around and survey the dust-caked boxes, crates and furniture. The stacks of old pictures against the wall. The spinning wheel. The glint of a piano-accordion.

And the wardrobe.

She looked away. It was too tempting to unlock its creaking door and touch the taffeta and velvet gowns she had worn in her youth. Gowns with tiny waists and sweeping skirts, ruffled necklines and cuffs, now steeped in the scent of camphor. Nan remembered how desolate she had felt throwing the white mothballs in there like scattering marbles. *Get on with it,* she thought.

There was something in the attic that Nan wanted for Lottie. Arnie and Jen's Downlong cottage was small. Lottie would end up sharing a mattress with the boys, and Nan didn't think it was good enough for a shipwrecked orphan who looked like a princess. In the far corner of the attic was a bed, a special, treasured bed. Nan herself had slept in it as a child. She loved its ornate headboard, carved with twining leaves and woodland creatures, toadstools and the cheeky faces of Cornish piskies creeping through foliage. It even had the sun, moon and stars in the top corner. A bed to dream in. A perfect bed for Lottie. If only Nan could manage to drag it out of the attic, down the stairs and into the donkey cart.

It had been taken apart and stashed against the

wall, covered in a dust sheet. Nan's heart leapt with joy when she spotted it. But could she get to it? And would her wheezy chest cope with the dust? The air was heavy with it, she could taste it, and the two cats were inadvertently making it worse. They were belting in and out of the stacks of boxes, appearing momentarily, wild-eyed, and with a glaze of grey dust over their fur, only to vanish again into ever dustier spaces. The scrabble of their paws on the floorboards was comical and it made Nan smile as she edged her way towards the bed.

In one place the floor was littered with the discarded bright wings of butterflies and moths. 'Bats!' Nan said, aloud, and looked up at the rafters. Above her hung clusters of bats, upside down, like folded gloves of burnished suede, their tiny faces crumpled in sleep. A wasp flew close to Nan and she saw the glint of its wings as its yellow striped body passed through the shaft of sunlight. Frowning, she observed its progress across the attic. She didn't like wasps. Her skin chilled when she saw an enormous wasps' nest hanging, lantern-like, from the roof in the far corner. It was October, but she knew the wasps were still active. She could hear the low-pitched buzzing. There must be hundreds, even thousands of them in that huge nest. It made her task even more scary.

Nan had respect for all wild creatures. In fact, she often felt like a wild creature herself as she worked in her garden, a creature who had forgotten how to talk to other humans. Talking to bees and aphids and hedgehogs was easy and fun. Her self-imposed isolation had made her attempts at conversation sound fierce and abrupt. She had forgotten how to talk gently and kindly. Until she'd found Lottie with her arms round Mufty's head. A certain look in the child's eyes had touched a chord of abandoned tenderness in Nan's heart. She felt instantly connected and committed to this pale child with the stubborn, haunted eyes. Eyes that were ready for magic. For stories. For dreams and fables to help her grow and make sense of the world. All of which Nan could give her.

If it wasn't for that infernal woman. That Jenny. To get to Lottie, Nan would have to talk her way past, or over, or even through Jenny.

She squeezed between the back of the wardrobe and a wooden cider barrel which still retained a faint whiff of fermenting apples. Thinking she would have to make a gangway in order to drag the bed out, Nan gave the barrel a push. It toppled over with an alarming clatter. The noise made her heart race. She froze, then turned her head very slowly to look at the bats and the wasps' nest. Neither of them reacted, as if an old woman knocking down barrels was normal practice in their attic home.

Breathing hard, she finally reached the bed, and tugged at the dust sheet. It sighed and slid to the floor in a haze of dust. Nan felt emotional. She touched the green and white striped mattress. It was warm with her memories. It looked intact except for a small hole at the lower end with the stuffing bursting out. She examined the frame with its wooden slats and found some woodworm holes. *Vinegar,* she thought, *I'll fix you lot with white vinegar.*

The carved headboard had been tightly wrapped in oilcloth. Nan unpicked the knots and peeled back just a corner, and an old friend stared out at her. The carved badger peeping from curls of bracken. It looked fine. The oilcloth had done a good job and the wood still had a glow. It still felt alive. Nan smiled to herself as she ran her hand over it, remembering those pitch dark nights of her childhood. Touching the carved leaves and animals had been comforting to a child alone in the dark.

All she had to do now was drag it downstairs and load it into the donkey cart. First she struggled to undo the knots of rope and pull the mattress down from the wall. Then she heaved it towards the stairs, encouraged by the two cats who thought it was an excuse to go mad, pouncing and diving over the slowly moving mattress. More dust. Nan's breath wheezed and hurt, her cheeks flamed red with the effort.

She fetched the precious headboard, then the slatted base and the legs which were bundled into a canvas bag with various nuts, bolts and brackets. Once it was all stacked at the top of the stairs, Nan leaned on the windowsill trying to calm her breathing. She banged her fist on the window to force it open, its rotting frame shedding flakes of blue paint and a few splinters. The only people she could see were far away, fishermen spreading their nets to dry. There was no one nearby who would help her to get the bed downstairs. It seemed the whole town was still looting timber and boxes of goods from the wreck.

Nan thought maybe she could do it on her own if she fetched some rope from the garden shed. But first she must face the daunting task of getting herself down the steep stairs. She stood at the top, looking down, feeling the pain in her knees. She kept an eye on the wasps' nest, knowing the warmth of the morning sun would tempt them out. Already a number of the striped yellow insects were zigzagging around the rafters. She would have to move carefully, not drawing attention to herself. If just one wasp came close and she swatted it, the whole nest would be summoned to attack her.

Leaning heavily on the banister, Nan took the first painful step down. Then another. And another, her breath fast and shallow, fighting the fear. A bead of sweat trickled out of her hair, and her knuckles looked blue as she clung to the rail. A sharp pain stabbed her left knee, like bone rubbing against bone. Nan gritted her teeth and forced her foot down onto the stair. *You can do this. You can,* she thought. Her knees were weak but her grip was strong, so strong that the banister cracked and tore away from the wall. Nan cried out as she fell forward, banging her head on the wall. Knocked unconscious, she bumped and slid down a few steps and then her huge body came to a halt, wedged awkwardly in the narrow stairwell.

The sky darkened and clouds rolled over the sun. Hailstones stung the roof tiles and hissed along Foxglove Lane as if the weather rumbled out a warning of imminent death. Down in the garden a pair of foxes came, ginger-eyed and swift, over the Cornish hedge, caught one of Nan's speckled chickens and dragged it, squawking, over the wall and away into the bracken-covered cliffs.

Jenny was terrified Lottie would die. She'd sat all night with the feverish child, sponging her hot face with a flannel dipped in cold water. Now and again Lottie had something to say, looking at Jenny with bright, dilated eyes. 'I wanted to go to America,' she said, more than once, and, 'I let the birds out and I'm glad I did. They flew away out of the window and then...'

'What birds?' Jenny asked, but Lottie's eyes were closed again. In the morning, when Doctor Tregullow came, Lottie wouldn't answer any of his questions but she let him dab some tincture on her back. 'It might sting,' he said, 'but it will make it better. You go back to sleep now.' And Lottie did, curled on her side, her face turned towards the open window and the cool breeze from the sea.

'I suppose you've got no suitable clothes for her.' Doctor Tregullow looked over his glasses at Jenny.

'No. Nothing.'

'Would you like my wife to run her up a couple of dresses? She's got plenty of fabric, old curtains and that sort of stuff. She likes sewing, and it won't cost you anything.'

'Yes please,' Jenny nodded, feeling tears pricking her eyes.

'And you should get some sleep yourself,' he added, folding his stethoscope into his medical bag. 'You look tired.'

'I can't. Look at this heap waiting for me. It's Monday.' Jenny showed him the mounds of washing piled on the scullery floor. Some women had already done theirs and strung it across the street to dry in the sun and wind. Earlier, a hailstorm had hissed over the cobbles, leaving globular clusters of ice along the base of the wall.

Once the doctor had gone, Jenny made herself a cup of strong tea and went back to sit with Lottie. She was glad the boys were in school. It had been a fight to get them to wear shoes and socks that morning, and Tom had cried loudly because his shoes were too tight. He was growing so fast and Matt's hand-me-downs were often not big enough.

Lottie would need shoes. Smart girly shoes. And she needed a proper bed. Jenny sat worrying about how to afford them for her. She already loved the brave little girl and didn't want to let her down. 'I'm here with you. Don't worry,' she kept saying when Lottie woke up.

Arnie had come downstairs at first light and sat beside her, a tray of tea and saffron buns between them.

'I can't make sense of anything she's saying,' Jenny said, glad of the hot tea steaming between her hands.

'It will all come out in time,' Arnie said wisely, 'just let her be. And you get some sleep, Jen.' He'd given her a cuddle, slurped his tea, and gone to get his boat ready for a day's fishing.

'When you come back we'll unpack the boxes,' Jenny called after him, looking at the stack of rough wooden crates from the wreck. She thought some of them had tinned food in them. She could see labels hanging, soaking wet, from between the slats, in a mess of wet straw and fronds of seaweed. The boxes loomed in a toppling tower in the back yard where Arnie and Vic had dumped them, leaving a trail of seaweed and straw through the living room. Normally Jenny would have cleared it up, but now she just ignored it. She wasn't going to leave Lottie.

The day passed and squares of sunlight moved out of the scullery and across the living room floor, mellowing to a deep rose pink as the sun set. The boys came home from school, and still Lottie was feverish, her small face troubled, her breathing rapid and shallow. 'You LEAVE HER ALONE,' Jenny said fiercely to Matt and Tom who wanted to wake Lottie up and talk to her. 'She's very ill. She might have something infectious and we don't want you catching it.' She sensed the boys felt miffed. She held out a hand to them. 'You don't have to be jealous. I don't suddenly love Lottie more than you. I just need you to be good while she's ill.'

Matt gave her a sullen, chilling glare, and Tom looked at her sorrowfully like a spaniel.

'Go upstairs and play marbles,' Jenny said and they did. She sighed with relief when she heard the marbles rolling noisily over the floorboards. But before long the two boys were playing *Shipwreck*, bouncing on the mattress and fighting. Predictably it reached crisis point with Tom crying, a loud, nasal, echoing howl.

Lottie tried to sit up, her eyes black and bright with alarm.

'It's all right, Lottie. It's just Matt and Tom. Don't take any notice.' Jenny smoothed the child's hair back from her hot face. She comforted Tom who came downstairs and wanted to sit on her lap and cry. She was glad when Arnie finally came home and put the boys to bed. The low rumble of his voice reading them a story seemed like a blessing to Jenny. To have a husband who loved his family enough to put them first, even when he was tired and hungry.

'She's not getting any better,' she told Arnie when he came downstairs.

He stood looking down at Lottie, and touched her face gently. 'Hmmm, she is hot. She's burning up.'

'Should we call the doctor again?'

'I don't know. If it was Matt or Tom we'd trust they'd come through it. But we don't know what illnesses Lottie's had – and she has just survived a shipwreck. She was icy cold and scared.'

'I'm trying to get her to drink, but she won't,' Jenny sighed. 'I just don't know what to do.'

'Nan would know,' Arnie said, then held up his hand when he saw fire in Jenny's eyes. 'All right. All right – I won't mention her again.'

'I do NOT want that cranky old woman interfering. And I don't want a quarrel with you over it.'

Arnie's jaw stiffened and a muscle twitched in his cheek. His eyes looked hurt under their long lashes. He loved Nan dearly. He'd grown up at Hendravean, his life enriched by Nan's love of folklore and music. She'd been strict but he'd soon discovered that inside her hard shell of eccentricity and power was a sensitive soul with a heart of gold. He knew she loved him, and he was saddened by Jenny's unforgiving attitude. To keep the peace at home, Arnie had to visit his nan by stealth. He felt his boys were missing out on the influence Nan could have given them. He hoped it might change now Lottie had come into their lives.

'She's trying to talk.' Jenny turned back to Lottie, her gaze tender again. 'What is it, Lottie? You can tell me. I'm here... I won't leave you.'

The bright black eyes stared up at them in the candlelight. 'Is Nan coming back?' Lottie asked.

Arnie and Jenny looked at each other. 'Not tonight,' Arnie said. 'She's got six cats and a donkey and some chickens to look after.'

'I gave the donkey a hug,' Lottie said, 'and he loved me. I wish he was my donkey. I want to see him again. And I want to see Nan again. She was kind to me, and I like her.'

Arnie looked at Jenny in silence, and behind his silence was a secret smile. Behind Jenny's silence was a stubborn wall of resistance, a wall stronger than granite.

Delivering milk in St Ives was no easy task with a pony and cart because of the steep hills. Les Pengellan had worked out a route from his farm zigzagging down the narrow streets, always parking the pony on the level. The cottages in very steep streets had to be done on foot by him and the boy, each carrying a basket clinking with heavy bottles of milk. They'd start at the top and work downwards, one each side of the road, so that they carried the weight downhill, never uphill.

One of the first calls of the day was at Hendravean, Nan's house at the end of Foxglove Lane. The lane was smooth enough for the pony to trot smartly along between the high banks of gorse and bracken. At this time of the year the sun would be rising over the vast bay of Hayle sands, just as it was that Tuesday morning.

Les parked the pony in Nan's gateway and walked up the garden with her bottle of milk, setting it down in the corner of the doorstep, covering it with a piece of slate to stop the cats getting into it first.

'That's very odd,' he said, aloud, frowning as he saw Monday's bottle of milk still there under the slate. 'Gone sour.' He sniffed it and debated whether to tip it away. Better not. Nan might tell him off in her strident voice. He looked up at the house and was surprised to see one of the attic windows swinging open. Scanning the garden he noticed the mess of speckled feathers on the lawn. 'Foxes,' he muttered. It wasn't like Nan to let that happen. Usually she was out working in her garden early in the morning, in all weathers, or she'd be vigorously grooming the donkey. Mufty was still in his stable, looking out and kicking the door with his hoof. Something was wrong.

Mindful of his pony waiting patiently in the gateway, Les shrugged and walked away. He didn't want to intrude. He'd tell someone. Arnie, if he could find him. He glanced down towards the bay and saw a number of fishing boats going out, silhouetted against the light of the morning sea. The church clock struck eight. He had to finish his delivery round and hurry home to get the cows in and milked, the glass bottles washed and ready for the next day. He had no spare time at all. And anyway, it was none of his business.

In the night there had been a sudden change in Lottie's condition. At three o'clock in the morning she'd sat up and asked for a drink, then said she was hungry. Jenny had made her a bowl of hot oat porridge with golden syrup swirled into it, and some creamy milk. Lottie had eaten it daintily and scraped every last bit from the bowl. She'd snuggled down under the blanket on the sofa and gone straight to sleep, peacefully. The fever had gone. Jenny touched the child's brow and it was cool, her breathing normal.

Relieved, Jenny collapsed into the wicker chair and fell into an exhausted sleep. She half-heard Arnie giving the boys their breakfast and the fierce whispering he was doing. 'Don't let's disturb Mummy. She's VERY tired.' Smiling to herself, Jenny dimly heard their feet running past the window and felt Arnie kiss her tenderly. His clothes smelled of fish. 'I'm taking the boat out whilst the sea's calm, Jen. I'll be out all day. Love you.'

'Love you too,' she muttered and went back to sleep. She slept on and so did Lottie through a blissful hour of early morning, of sunlit streets and a calm, silk sea. Even the seagulls were quiet, gathered in the shallow streams of the ebbing tide, fluttering and bathing and preening their feathers.

Grateful for the restorative sleep, Jenny dozed pleasantly, aware of her need for a bath and a change of clothes. That would have to wait until early evening when Arnie would fill the tin tub for her, bringing in bucket after bucket of water from the street tap. Then a kettle full of hot water, a block of yellow Sunlight soap and the bath was ready for her in front of the fire. For her first. Then the boys. And Arnie last, and she'd relish the gleam of his lean, muscular body in the fire-light.

It was a beautiful morning, the sea shimmering, the town settling back into normal life after the storm. Jenny longed to go out. She looked down at Lottie, still fast asleep with Millie's knitted doll tucked against one cheek. *Perhaps today will be better,* she thought, *and I can spend some time with Lottie, make her feel at home.*

She opened the door to take the milk in and was surprised to see a note wedged under the bottle. She pulled it out. It was hard to read, scrawled in pencil on an opened-out cigarette packet.

'SOMETHING IS WRONG UP AT NAN'S PLACE. YESTERDAY'S MILK NOT TAKEN IN. ATTIC WINDOW OPEN, AND DONKEY STILL IN STABLE. THOUGHT I SHOULD TELL YOU.

LES PENGELLAN'

Jenny immediately felt guilty. She had told Nan to go away, and Nan had brought Lottie home, and called the doctor, AND paid him. But so deep was her hatred of Nan that Jenny quickly

74

stuffed the guilt into a far corner of her mind. She carried the milk, and the note, into the scullery and looked at the piles of washing. She must stoke the fire, and make pasties, and clean the straw and seaweed from the floor. She wasn't responsible for Nan. *Let the old witch sort herself out,* Jenny thought, allowing rebellion to burn through her mind. *Why should I go running up there just because there's a window open?*

She worked doggedly, filling the washtub, rubbing the sheets vigorously over the washboard, then wringing them through the mangle, the water streaming onto the stone floor, and the flattened sheet emerging arched and stiff. A depressing task. No matter how hard she worked, the thick linen still looked grey and retained an undefinable odour. She hung them across the street on a line she shared with Millie and stood for a moment, drying her sore red hands on her skirt, enjoying the sun on her face.

She turned to go back in and was astonished to see Lottie standing at the sink, her small arms pounding the pile of socks and shirts in the soapy water.

Jenny was going to shout at her but Lottie gave her a heart-melting smile. Her eyes looked blue again, and confident.

'I'm going to help you,' Lottie announced, squeezing the water from a pair of Arnie's socks. 'I know how to do washing,' she added, 'I did it in the orphanage.'

Jenny gulped. The thought of Lottie's tender little fingers getting caught in the mangle was alarming but she didn't want to crush the child's obvious pride in her ability to help. 'That's kind of you, Lottie. We'll do it together,' she said, and another smile flashed up at her.

'You're doing a good job. But I shall do the mangle. We'll have it done in no time with you helping. Then we'll have a cup of tea with my ginger biscuits.'

A sudden glow of harmony shone over the two of them, working together, Lottie again wearing the blue silk blouse, her feet bare, her hair hooked behind cute little ears, her soft round cheeks still pale.

'How old are you, Lottie?' Jenny asked curiously.

Lottie took a deep breath. 'I'm eight,' she announced, 'and a half.'

'So when is your birthday?' Jenny was surprised. She'd assumed Lottie was about five.

'On the eighth of May.'

'Oh – a summer birthday, eh? The eighth of May is a special day in Cornwall,' Jenny said, smiling. 'It's Helston Flora Day. And because I was born in Helston I'm allowed to wear a really pretty dress and a hat, and we dance through the streets, all the morning, and the Helston Silver Band put on their best suits and march along with a big boomy drum playing *The Furry Dance*.'

'*The Furry Dance?*'

'I'll teach it to you later,' Jenny promised, turning the handle of the mangle, 'and on your birthday you shall wear a pretty dress too, and we'll all go to Flora Day ... on the train.'

'What does Flora mean?'

'Flowers. The whole town is decorated with

bluebells and lily-of-the-valley, and the scent is wonderful.'

Lottie looked pensive. Her eyes examined Jenny's soul. 'We could go in Nan's donkey cart,' she said brightly. 'Nan decorates it with tassels of wool, and bunches of herbs, and the perfume keeps the flies away from Mufty. She told me what they were – mint, sage and chamomile, and elder leaves, and lemon balm.'

'Fancy you remembering,' Jenny said, astonished to find Lottie so articulate. 'But it's a long time until May. We've got winter to come, and Christmas...'

'I'm going to make Nan a Christmas present. And one for Mufty.' Lottie's eyes shone. Then, without warning, her expression changed to a horrified frown. She ran to the sofa and seemed to be searching for something. Her face crumpled, and she walked slowly back to Jenny, as if in a nightmare.

'What's the matter?' Jenny asked, alarmed.

'My black velvet bag. I've lost it.' The words tumbled out and with them came the tears. For the first time since the shipwreck, after all she'd been through, Lottie was sobbing inconsolably. She curled up in a ball and let Jenny hold her close, both of them smelling of washing soda and steam.

'I must have left it in Mufty's cart,' Lottie wept. 'I've got to find it. Where does Nan live?'

Jenny battled with herself. She felt it was a plot being masterminded by some well-meaning celestial committee. Pushing her towards Nan's place. She couldn't let Lottie go on her own. 'How about if Arnie takes you up there in the morning?'

Lottie's distraught eyes looked up at her, the sunlight from the window making the tears sparkle along the curve of her eyelashes. 'No. No ... you don't understand,' Lottie sobbed, but she straightened her back, quickly regaining her composure. 'I must go IMMEDIATELY. Will you please tell me where Nan lives? Or I shall go out by myself and ask someone.'

A very determined little madam, Jenny thought. *Now what am I going to do?*

Chapter 5

A Cat in the Window

Jenny felt proud of Lottie as they walked through the town in the afternoon sunshine. Lottie didn't exactly walk. She floated, with her beautiful hair flowing down her back and her head held high. People turned to look at her curiously. The child from the wreck. Who was she? Whoever she was, Lottie had presence and grace.

Calming her down had been easy compared to the battles Jenny was used to with the boys. It had begun with Jenny finding her a pair of shoes. 'You can't walk all the way to Nan's place in bare feet,' she explained, opening the lid of the settle again. Down in the bottom corner in a brown paper bag were her own favourite shoes and socks from childhood. 'I wore these for my first ever Flora

Day dance,' she sighed. 'I wanted to keep them nice, for ever, as a happy memory. But you can borrow them, if they'll fit you.' It was hard to give them to Lottie. But the look of wonder and gratitude on the little girl's tear-stained face made it worthwhile.

'They're LOVELY.' Lottie stared at the shoes in amazement. 'I've never seen shoes with pretty flowers on them.' She fingered the woollen flowers threaded over the strap, colours still bright on shiny black shoes.

'My mum made the flowers. She crocheted them.'

Lottie's mouth fell open. 'She's clever.' Then she looked deeply serious. 'Is she dead now?'

'Yes, I'm afraid she is,' Jenny said, and they were both silent for a moment of empathy. Lottie pulled on the clean white socks, then slipped her feet into the shoes.

'They fit me!' She deftly fastened the buckles. She skipped around the living room, her slim legs elegant in Jenny's Flora Day shoes. 'I LOVE them.' She flung her arms around Jenny. 'Thank you ... and ... I won't get them muddy. Can we go to Nan's place now?'

Jenny eyed the half-finished pile of washing and decided to leave it. She was glad to see Lottie better after the fever. She told Millie where they were going and asked her to be there for the boys when they came back from school. Millie was pleased to be asked. She beamed at Lottie. 'I'm glad you're better, my love. Look at your pretty shoes!' Then she looked knowingly at Jenny. 'I thought you said you'd never go to Nan's place. How come? Buried the hatchet, have you? About time.'

Jenny's cheeks flushed. 'I had a note from the milkman. He thought something was wrong up there. And Arnie's gone all day, with this late tide.'

Millie frowned. 'I'll come with you, Jen, if you like – but I'm slow going up that hill. What if it's something you can't handle? Nan is a heavy woman.'

'Thanks, but no, we'll be fine.'

The truth was that Jenny wanted Lottie to herself. She hoped Lottie would tell her what had happened, how she came to be on a ship. Everything she'd said so far was like a jigsaw with pieces missing. Why did she keep asking about America? Who had beaten her? And how had such an articulate, well-dressed little girl ended up in an orphanage – and then on a ship?

At the edge of Downlong, the green turf and rocks of the 'Island' stretched away between Porthgwidden Cove and Porthmeor Beach. 'Is that the ship I was on?' Lottie asked, and suddenly the bright energy seemed to be draining out of her. She leaned her head against Jenny's skirt. 'I'm dog tired,' she added.

'Yes ... that's the ship – or what's left of it,' Jenny said, and a shiver passed through both of them as they saw the blackened hulk of the ship, looming at a crazy angle, on the rocks. 'If you're tired, we could sit and have a rest.'

'But not here,' Lottie said. 'I don't like seeing the broken ship.'

Jenny led her over the saddle of turf that connected the 'Island' to the town, and they sat on a bench overlooking Porthmeor Beach. Behind them loomed the massive drum of the gas works, the circular railings at the top covered in sparrows, crows and seagulls. Next to it was the hillside cemetery, the gravestones facing the western sea. The waves were perfect, rising out of a tranquil sea in gleaming semicircles, the surf peeling away from translucent curls of jade. Beyond the 'Island', the afternoon light turned the rising waves to indigo, the horizon a sharp line as if drawn along a ruler with a crayon. Jenny watched Lottie's eyes and sensed the question coming. 'Is America out there?'

'Yes.'

'How far away is it?'

'A long way.'

'But HOW far? How many miles?'

'I don't know. You'll have to ask Nan,' Jenny said, and immediately regretted it. Her mind had been figuring out how to avoid seeing Nan. They'd sneak into the garden, search the donkey cart, and once the velvet bag was found, they could quietly leave. She'd tell Lottie Nan was asleep. *Liar*, she thought uncomfortably, *and you're a coward, Jenny Lanroska.*

'Why am I so tired, Jenny?' Lottie asked.

''Cause you've been poorly. And you've had a proper upset too.'

'Where is Nan's house?'

'It's that one, all by itself.' Jenny pointed to Hendravean, thinking how grim the big house always looked with its gabled windows.

Lottie stared. 'There's a cat in the window.'

'So there is.'

'Will he let me stroke him?'

'I expect so.'

'I've never stroked a cat. Never in my WHOLE life.' Lottie jumped up with new energy. 'Come on.'

They walked on along Porthmeor Road. The cat in the attic window disturbed Jenny. The attic windows had never been open before. Surely Nan hadn't tried to go up those steep stairs by herself? What could have happened? Jenny felt a shudder of nerves deep in her gut. She wished she had let Millie come with her.

'What a funny road,' Lottie remarked as they turned in to Foxglove Lane. 'It's got walls covered in grass.'

'Cornish hedges,' Jenny said. 'You wait 'til spring. It'll be covered in primroses. And it's a lane, not a road.'

'I've never been along a lane. I lived in a big city.'

'Where was that then?' Jenny asked, but Lottie went quiet, trailing her fingers over the cushiony grasses and thrift.

The gate to Hendravean was open. As soon as Lottie saw Mufty's face looking out of his stable, she was gone, running across the yard, the donkey watching her eagerly. Jenny glanced up at the attic window and saw the cat, Bartholomew, checking her out. With an echoing meow, he quickly disappeared from the attic window and reappeared from the scullery window. He trotted over to her, meowing, and within seconds all six cats converged on her, weaving around her ankles with their tails up.

'Mufty is extremely hungry,' Lottie called in

her clear voice. No chance of Nan not noticing them now. Then Lottie saw the cats and squealed with excitement.

'Gently, gently. Don't run at them,' Jenny said, 'or you'll frighten them.'

Lottie slowed down to a theatrical creep, and Bartholomew made a beeline for her, his magnificent tail waving. The look of pure joy on Lottie's face touched Jenny's heart. 'What's he doing?' Lottie asked. 'He's making a snoring noise.'

'He's purring. That's 'cause he likes you,' Jenny said. To her it was obvious the cats were hungry. She looked at the silent house and went cold with fright. She wanted to turn and run. *Why me?* she thought.

'He's so fluffy and soft. I love him.' Lottie looked up at her with shining eyes and, for the first time, Jenny heard her giggle when Bartholomew brushed his whiskers against her bare legs.

'You stay in the yard and look for your bag, Lottie,' she said. 'I'll go and see if Nan is there. She might be asleep.'

'All right.' Lottie was so entranced by the cats that she hardly noticed Jenny.

Jenny felt caught between a horde of starving animals, a shipwrecked orphan, and an old woman whom she hated and who might be horribly dead inside that frowning house.

The front door looked reassuringly homely, a whiff of polish coming from its timber. Jenny could see her reflection in the round brass door-knob. She turned it and the door swung open. 'Are you there, Nan?' The air glistened with the scent of blackberry wine. 'Nan?' Jenny walked in, the quarry tiles clinking under her feet. Bunches of dried herbs hung from a beam, brushing the top of her head, and releasing tangy aromas of rosemary and mint. An enormous mirror gleamed on one wall, surrounded by fading rosettes Nan had won for her flowers and preserves. Horse brasses shone from the panelled oak walls, and brown and white porcelain horses cantered across the sheen of a rosewood sideboard. Everything seemed to have a listening presence, eyes of china and brass watching Jenny.

The kitchen door was open. Jenny found herself creeping on tiptoe. She peeped in, startling a bunch of mice who were on the table tunnelling into a stale loaf of bread, the crust spotted with blue mould. She walked into the scullery where Nan had been bottling pears and making wine. The garden door was wide open to a tangle of foliage and a glimpse of colour in the flowerbeds beyond.

Jenny went back to the bottom of the stairs and shouted. 'Nan? It's Jenny. Are you all right?'

Silence. She listened intently, and then heard something that sent a chill crawling up her spine. Breathing. She could hear someone breathing, faintly, and wheezing. *Nan must be ill in bed*, she thought, and jumped as Bartholomew shot past her and ran upstairs. Jenny was afraid of Nan and she was tempted to turn and run back into the sunlit yard and the simple joy of seeing Lottie playing with the cats in the sunshine.

She made herself go upstairs. The landing had four doors, one of them open. Jenny could see a four-poster bed covered in a massive crocheted blanket of jewel-bright colours. The bed was empty. *Where was Nan?*

She called out again. 'Nan? It's Jenny.'

A creak came from the attic stairs, and the voice she had dreaded hearing bellowed through the house:

'O MAGNUM MYSTERIUM.'

Jenny froze. *The woman's gone mad,* she thought, *she's spouting Latin!*

It was followed by a wheezy laugh.

'Pardon?' Jenny headed for the attic stairs, shocked to see Nan wedged halfway up, her face crinkled with laughter, but her eyes, usually so fierce, were the eyes of a frightened, lonely old woman. 'Oh Nan,' she said kindly, 'did you fall?'

'Of course I fell. Why else would I be stuck here? Stuck. That's what I am.'

Jenny started up the stairs, but Nan shouted at her in the wheezy voice. 'No. Go back, you stupid girl. If I fall we'll both get hurt.'

'But...'

'But me no buts – Jenny. You go and get help. Arnie and Vic, or the coastguard, or somebody – or even the fire brigade. It'll take an army to get me out of here.' Nan began to laugh, her big belly shaking the staircase, and the laughter seemed precarious as if it could quickly switch over to crying.

'How long have you been there, Nan?'

'All day and all night.'

'You must be cold.'

'Of course I'm damned well cold. The damned stove has gone out. And the damned chickens

85

haven't been fed.'

'Don't worry, Nan. I'll see to it all,' Jenny said, feeling compassion at Nan's obvious distress. 'Don't you even try to move. I'll fetch you a rug and a drink. Then Lottie and I will feed the animals and light the stove. Then I'll get help.'

Jenny went back to the bedroom and dragged the crocheted blanket from the bed. She filled a cup with water from the big jug on the marble washstand. A small bottle of brandy was on the bedside table so she picked that up too and hurried back to the attic stairs. 'I'm coming up whether you like it or not,' she said, and saw relief in Nan's eyes, even a flicker of gratitude. 'There you are.' She tucked the blanket over and around Nan as best she could. 'Are you hurt?'

'Yes, of course I'm hurt. I fell down these infernal steep stairs.'

'Well, let's hope nothing's broken and it's just bruises,' Jenny said. She half-wanted to apologise for the way she'd spoken to Nan earlier but her anger was still there, like a stone wall. 'What was it you said first?' she asked. 'O mag – something?'

'O Magnum Mysterium,' Nan said, and her storm-coloured eyes were looking right into Jenny's mind. 'It's Latin – you wouldn't know, would you? It means *Oh great mystery.*' Her voice became a wheezy whisper. 'God works in mysterious ways, Jenny. I lay here praying and praying for help. And what does God do? He sends my deadly enemy to help me!' She burst into another volley of laughter, spilling some of the water over her bristly old chin.

Lottie put her foot on one of the wooden wheel spokes and scrambled into Mufty's cart which was parked in the yard. The black velvet pouch was wedged between two baskets, and she retrieved it quickly, a lump in her throat. She took a deep breath. No need to cry. She inspected it, feeling the familiar contents through the worn velvet. Her fingers pulled at the drawstring. The knot was still sealed. Lottie had done it herself with a drop of red sealing wax held over a candle flame. It was safe. Her heart beat a little faster, remembering. No one, not even Matt, could undo the knot, and she'd keep it that way. The animosity in Matt's eyes had registered in Lottie's sharp mind. Fear and challenge knotted together as tightly as the drawstring.

Jenny had given her an apron to wear over her red dress. Lottie tucked the velvet bag into its deep pocket, and climbed down from the cart, knowing exactly what she was going to do next. She gave a little skip of excitement.

Next to Mufty's stable was a sweet smelling shed stacked with bales of meadow hay and hessian sacks of grain. The door was open and a flock of chirruping sparrows fled past Lottie with a burr of wings, their bodies fat with the corn they'd been feasting on. Lottie went to one of the bales of hay and grabbed an armful, enjoying the honey-sweet scent. She took it to Mufty who was waiting, his eyes bright in his furry face. 'Here you are, Mufty.' She stood on tiptoe and pushed the hay over the door, happy to hear the donkey munching and rustling.

Back in the shed, Lottie surveyed the hessian

sacks. She read the black lettering on them. Whole oats. Bran. Corn. That was it. Corn! She went to the open sack and plunged her small arms deep into the glistening grain. She couldn't resist playing with it, smiling as it streamed through her fingers. Then she found a metal bowl, scooped corn into it and took it out into the sunshine.

Lottie had never seen a real chicken, only pictures of them in books with smiling women scattering corn on the ground. The women and the chickens glowed with happiness. To Lottie it was like a dream coming true as she stepped outside with the bowl of corn and chickens came belting towards her from all directions, their scaly legs taking huge strides. Giggling with joy, Lottie hurled arcs of corn into the light, some of it raining down on the chickens' plump backs. A feeling of peace settled over the yard as the chickens pecked busily at the corn, beaks to the ground, stubby tails pointing at the sky. A cruising seagull tried his luck at pecking corn and was swiftly evicted by the cockerel who flew at him like a dragon, colours gleaming, a hooked beak breathing puffs of fire. *I fed the chickens*, Lottie thought, ecstatically, *it's the BEST thing I've ever done, in my whole life.*

A twinge of pain from her back reminded her that what she saw as joy was so often regarded as a punishable crime by the adults. Would Nan be cross? Or Jenny? Lottie glanced at the house. Nan and Jenny were her friends. Only Matt, and the orphanage women, had felt threatening.

Lottie leaned against a sunny wall, watching the chickens and the flock of sparrows until they had eaten every last morsel of corn. The chickens waddled away, except for one, a motherly, amber brown hen who meandered close to her and sat down, her bright eyes looking at Lottie. Spellbound, Lottie reached out and touched the sheen of her back, marvelling at the warmth of it while the chicken made conversational crooning noises in her throat. 'Can I pick you up?' she asked, and stood up, working out how to peacefully pick up a bird who looked too full of corn to move.

Experimentally she slipped her hands under the warm body, one each side, and was thrilled when the hen didn't move but allowed herself to be picked up. She nestled contentedly into Lottie's arms, even tucking her feet up out of the way. The crooning sounds deepened, and so did the awe Lottie felt at cradling this soft shell of warm feathers and friendliness. She carried the chicken towards the house, proud of herself, wanting to show Jenny and Nan that she was holding a chicken. A glow of importance hovered over Lottie's life.

'Put that chicken down this minute.' Jenny whirled out of the house, hot-cheeked and frowning. 'We've got to help Nan. She's fallen down and she's stuck on the stairs. She can't move. PUT THE CHICKEN DOWN.'

Lottie bit her lip and did as she was told, sad to see her new friend walking away, her moment of glory deflated.

'Look at you! Covered in hay. What have you been doing?' Jenny picked bits of hay from Lottie's hair and clothes. 'What's this in your hair? Corn?'

Lottie looked dejected. 'I fed Mufty. And the chickens.'

Jenny's face softened. 'Good girl,' she conceded. 'But now, we must get help for Nan. I'm going to run down to the harbour and see who I can find.'

'Can I stay here?' Lottie asked. 'I could make Nan a cup of tea. I know how to make tea.'

'The stove's not lit. When we've lit it you can make tea, Lottie. You can stay here if you promise not to run off again; just stay in the yard.'

'I shall go and talk to Nan.'

'I don't think that's a good idea.'

'Why not? Nan likes me.'

Jenny looked perplexed. 'If you must. Look, I can't stand here arguing, dear. You be a big girl. Be sensible. And I'll be back soon. All right?'

'All right, Jenny.'

Lottie stood up on the wall and watched Jenny's head bobbing as she ran down Foxglove Lane. She thought about Jenny's eyes. Kindly eyes, ready to laugh and sing, but today her eyes were overloaded with too many sparkles, not all of them friendly. Lottie felt older and wiser than Jenny but there was no way of expressing such a thought. In her short life Lottie had learned some hard lessons. How to survive the worst kind of emotional trauma – by herself – and through it all she'd learned to hang on to inner happiness, tenaciously, just as she'd clung to the broken door on the stormy sea.

She studied the view of the little harbour town that was to be her home, and liked the way the cottages nestled into the hillside. She liked the way the church tower sent the sound of bells chiming across the water. She liked the immaculate, confident seagulls that hung on the wind, their stillness as they perched on the harbour wall, looking at her with one bright golden eye, and their wild, exultant voices. She thought St Ives looked like a fairytale town in a story book. But most of all she liked Nan and her charismatic donkey cart. She wanted more and more of Nan's stories about Saint Ia and the sun and moon shining across the water.

In the distance she could see Jenny running towards the harbour. *I'll go and talk to Nan,* Lottie thought, and she ran to the house door which Jenny had left open. She peered inside. A glimmer of metal shone from the top of the rosewood sideboard, a round brass gong hanging from a polished pedestal. A drumstick with a soft ball of a head lay beside it. Lottie's fingers quivered with temptation. A gong! Why did Nan have a gong? Did she bang it, just for the fun of hearing the sound reverberate through the house? Or did she use it to call people in?

Lottie reached out and picked up the drumstick. It smelled musty. Silence glistened in the shaft of sunlight, expectantly, as if silence was a person waiting to come alive, waiting for the gong. Jenny had said Nan was stuck on the stairs, but the staircase was empty; a crimson carpet with patterned borders covered the middle of it, pinned there with bright brass stair rods. What would happen if she banged the gong? Lottie didn't want anything to happen, but she longed to experience the delicious power of wielding the drumstick and sending the sound echoing through the empty house and out over the cliffs and the rocks, into the streets of St Ives.

No one was there to punish her. No one would see her. So ... why not? Lottie gave the gong an experimental tap. It made a muted hum, and a whisper rippled into the herb-scented caverns of Nan's house. Nothing happened. Excited, Lottie swung the drumstick and hit the gong harder. The sound trembled like a cry in the wind, dying away to a sigh and vanishing into doorways and shelves of bottled pears.

Harder, Lottie thought, and swung the drumstick outwards. But before she could make the magnificent satisfying sound, a voice bellowed down the stairs, and it was chillingly different from the voice Nan had used to tell her the story of St Ia.

'WHO is down there meddling with my things?'

Lottie's arm jumped back, dropped the drumstick, and knocked over one of the china horses. It crashed to the floor and broke into two pieces. Lottie's heart thudded as she stared at the hollow fragments of china. She felt more frightened than she'd felt in the shipwreck. Petrified, she stood perfectly still in the hall, and the voice boomed out again.

'Who is down there?'

The grandfather clock in the hall ticked into the silence, each tick like the sucking in of a breath.

What should she do? Lottie thought of her mother then, a clear picture of those tormented eyes set in a face ruled by encrypted grace. She remembered the time when her mother had broken a Crown Derby teacup at Lady Rees Evans' tea party. 'I'm SO sorry. Clumsy me! I'm afraid I've broken one of your beautiful cups'. Lottie had watched the red flush creep up Lady Rees Evans' hollow cheeks, and creep back again as her mother turned on the charm. It was all about courtesy and control. 'You could do the same, honey,' her mother had said later. 'You make a mistake – you deal with it straight away. Otherwise it blows up like a black cloud over your life.'

Lottie's eyes burned. She picked up the two halves of the china horse and carried them upstairs. Bartholomew escorted her, his tail waving importantly, and, not knowing what she was going to find, Lottie followed him to the attic stairs.

Nan was still wedged halfway up. When she saw Lottie, her glare changed to a smile.

'I'm so sorry. Clumsy me. I wanted to bang the gong, and I accidentally knocked the china horse over – and ... it broke.' Lottie held out the two hollow pieces.

The seeds of a smile twinkled in Nan's eyes. 'Give them to me.' She took the two halves of the broken horse in her fruit-stained hands.

Lottie wanted to turn and run but she made herself keep still. Standing close to Nan felt better than standing alone in the hall. 'But,' she added, 'I don't think I deserve to be beaten.'

'Beaten?' Nan looked puzzled. 'Of course I wouldn't beat you, child. Whatever gave you that idea?'

Lottie shrugged, her eyes roaming over the colours of the blanket.

'I expect it could be mended.' Nan tried to fit the two pieces together. Then she lowered her voice to a whisper. 'You know what? I never liked this particular horse anyway. We'll put it out in the barn and I shall make it into a flowerpot.'

'How?'

Nan smiled and handed the china back to Lottie. 'You'll see. Now you go and put them in the barn next to Mufty's stable, and when I'm better you can come and help me. All right?'

Lottie nodded.

'And while you're out there,' Nan added, 'you can open the lids of the nesting boxes inside the chicken house and see if you can collect some eggs. Take a basket from the kitchen.'

Lottie felt like a candle that had just been lit. She skipped downstairs, through the bedroom and down the main stairs, only to meet Jenny coming with Vic and another man.

'Hello, Princess.' Vic looked at her curiously. 'All dried out now, are you? Last time I saw you, you were like a drowned rat.'

'How did that happen?' Jenny eyed the broken china horse in Lottie's hand.

'It was an accident,' Lottie's eyes were calm and very adult, 'and I've dealt with it.'

Chapter 6

The Sole Survivor

'I don't want that worm-infested rubbish in my house.' Jenny stood in Nan's garden, hands on hips and two spots of angry colour on her cheeks.

Arnie continued loading the bed onto his hand-cart in obstinate silence. The precious headboard was in, and the bundle of slats. He tied the green and white mattress on top, winding a rope around it.

'That rope is wet, Arnie, and it stinks of fish,' protested Jenny. 'And look at that fusty old apology for a mattress.'

The obstinate silence darkened. Arnie tugged at the rope, refusing to look at Jenny, a tactic which she found infuriating. 'Will you LISTEN to me, Arnie?' She grabbed his sleeve and shook it.

'I'm listening. Can't help hearing when you shout like that.'

'I'm not shouting. I'm trying to get this into your thick head. I don't want Nan's fancy bed. And I don't want her brainwashing Lottie with her stupid folklore.'

Arnie continued tying the knots. 'I thought you wanted the best for Lottie.'

'I do, of course I do. But we could make her a bed. You've got enough wood stacked in the yard.'

'What's wrong with this bed?'

'It's ancient. It came out of the ark. And it's HERS. We'll be for ever beholden to Nan for it. She's only doing it to get her oar in. It's bad for Tom and Matt if Lottie gets spoilt. It isn't fair.'

'Lottie needs a bed, Jen.'

'But not a bigoted old grandmother to go with it. Why should Nan be let back into our family just because of a shipwreck? We've had nothing to do with her for years – eight years, Arnie. I know you've been visiting her and taking Matt and Tom, but the boys don't like her. She's intimidating and cranky, and she doesn't like them either – especially Matt. You should support me – not side with her.'

'I am supporting you.' Arnie's voice was suddenly, frighteningly loud, like a whip cracking. He was looking at her now, as if he didn't like what he saw, the weather-beaten skin on his cheeks drawn into taut hollows. 'I'm up here, loading Lottie's bed, when I should be out there fishing.' He glanced at the sunlight sparkling on the waves. 'And whether you like it or not – Jennifer – I love Nan. She's been good to me, and she'll be good to Lottie, if you give her a chance, and the boys. I don't know what gets into you. Why can't you forgive and forget, and stop being so spiteful.'

Jenny had spent the last week loving and caring, and worrying about Lottie. To be accused of being spiteful was an unbearable insult, especially from Arnie, who had shouted it all over St Ives. She felt abused and infuriated. And the way he'd called her 'Jennifer', with such cold dismissive anger. She was his WIFE – wasn't she?

96

Not just his wife, but the mother of his boys, his housekeeper, cook, slave, washerwoman, and devoted, adoring defender.

'You're being unreasonable, and childish,' he added.

Jenny exploded. She screamed at Arnie and tears of exhaustion raged down her cheeks. She seized the bag of clean linen Nan had given them, wrenching it out of the cart and sending it flying across the garden. Too late, she caught a glimpse of Lottie standing in the doorway, looking shocked and scared, a ginger cat in her arms with its tail hanging down over her body. Jenny hadn't wanted Lottie to witness her row with Arnie. She wanted Lottie to feel loved and secure.

It wasn't going to work.

'I'm going home,' she yelled, 'and packing me bags, Arnold Lanroska. I've had enough.'

She managed not to run. She swept along Foxglove Lane, her chest burning, as if she carried a scorching lump of pain lodged inside her. She felt its flames dying down with every distancing footstep. Her feet seemed to have a mind of their own. Instead of heading for home, they were taking her towards the station. *I've got no money,* Jenny thought, *no money for a ticket, and no bag to pack, and not much to put in one, and Arnie knows I don't mean it anyway.*

She got as far as the church and stopped, leaning against the porch, tempted to go inside but not wanting the vicar looming over her. What she needed was the peace it offered, peace from the babble and energy around the harbour, the group of stooping women gossiping as they packed fish, the men sorting lobster pots and nets, shouting and laughing from the decks of boats. Inside the church there was always a light burning in a red glass, and a scent of incense. A memory.

Jenny sat down on the steps, aching as she remembered their wedding: Arnie, turning to gaze at her with love and pride in his eyes; his craggy, fisherman's hands awkward as he slipped the ring onto her finger. Where were those smiles now? Could smiles blow inland and vanish like the weather? Were they meaningless magic? Smiles ready to mature into judgemental glares, waiting gleefully for her to turn into a downtrodden, downhearted fishwife, her young hands roughened with endless washing, fire-stoking, baking and making do. Waiting for her children to drain the sparkle from her eyes. *Matt,* she thought, *Matt did that.* Jenny hadn't been ready for him, and the birth had torn the life out of her. Instead of bonding, she had wanted nothing to do with the screaming kicking baby, the baby with black, malevolent eyes. And she'd hated herself for it.

When Tom came it was quite different. He'd been sweet and placid. Adorable. The powerful mother-love, on hold since the stillborn baby girl, flooded back and Jenny felt Tom had somehow rescued her from what felt like a mine shaft, his dancing eyes and limitless smile leading her back into normal life – Flora Day life where every day was a day for dancing and singing and being her normal, happy self.

Her normal, happy self. The thought made Jenny lift her face to the sun again, and it calmed her angry, painful breath. Had she really screamed at

Arnie like that? And was there a way back? He wanted her to accept Nan back into their life. But she couldn't. She just couldn't.

It would be hell if she did, and hell if she didn't.

'I'd like to see the boys again,' Nan said, sipping the cup of tea Arnie had made for her. It was late afternoon, and she was feeling better after her rescue the previous day, and a good night's sleep. She was thankful to find she hadn't broken any bones but had just a few bruises, including the one on the side of her head. Her own herb tea had soothed the pain. 'I don't need medicine,' she'd declared when Arnie suggested the doctor. 'I make my own. It's all out there, in the garden. I could give Jenny a remedy if she'd let me.'

'She won't,' said Arnie briefly.

'She's got a bee in her bonnet,' Nan said.

'She has,' agreed Arnie, 'but she's tired – she's been nursing Lottie day and night since the shipwreck. It's a week ago now.'

'Where's Lottie now?' Nan asked. 'You need to keep an eye on her, Arnie.'

Arnie glanced out of the window. Lottie was brushing Mufty who was tied up outside his stable. 'She's happy out there grooming the donkey.'

'She's a very intelligent little girl,' Nan said. 'How much do you know about her?'

'Not much. She's eight years old. But how she came to be on a cargo ship is a mystery.'

'Where did the ship come from?'

'I dunno – Cardiff maybe – or Swansea.'

'But she's not Welsh,' Nan said. 'She doesn't

99

have a Welsh lilt to her voice.'

'She speaks posh,' Arnie said, 'and that won't go down too well in St Ives. Judging by her clothes she's come from a rich family.'

'Hmm – aristocracy,' Nan said. 'What WAS she doing on the ship?'

'We think she was running away. Poor little mite, she's been beaten, Nan, savagely beaten. Jen put iodine on her back – it looks bad.'

'Oh dear.' Nan looked shocked. She lowered her voice to a whisper. 'You should keep quiet about it. Otherwise word will spread and the person who beat her will come looking for her when news gets out about the ship. Was she the sole survivor?'

'We thought we'd got them all out of the water. But apparently there was one missing, presumed drowned. He'd have had no chance in that sea. Eventually the body will be washed ashore, somewhere along the coast.'

Nan looked thoughtful, sipping the last dregs of her tea. She put the cup down and fingered the amethyst beads around her neck. 'I believe...' she began, and hesitated, put off by a sudden flash of scepticism in Arnie's eyes. *Say it anyway,* she thought. 'I believe Lottie was sent to us, like a gift. Like St Ia. Like St Ia, Arnie.'

Arnie managed an impartial kind of grunt, but Nan didn't miss the spark that floated through his eyes. She looked fondly at his long eyelashes, his handsome Cornish profile, the lean, strong bulk of him cramped in a chair too small for him. She reached out and patted his knee. 'Don't let Jenny drive you out of yourself.'

He frowned. 'What do you mean?'

'You KNOW what I mean.' Nan tried to get eye contact, but Arnie's gaze slipped away like a fish escaping through the water. 'Didn't I tell you? A Helston girl is different from a St Ives girl. Helston's inland – and it's soft. They've got flowers, like we've got pilchards. Jenny's had a different kind of life – and Lottie – well, we don't know, do we? But I would say Lottie's come to you as a blessing – whereas Jenny...' Nan's voice stopped like a bird flying against glass. She saw a warning twitch in Arnie's jaw. Nan knew life wasn't easy for her beloved grandson. She'd observed Jenny screaming at him and storming off, and she'd watched him wearily pick up the bag of linen and pack it into the cart. Then she'd seen him take Lottie over to Mufty's stable, lead the donkey out and tie him up, all the time talking to her. A smile lit up Lottie's face when he handed her a brush and showed her how to groom the donkey's coat. Halfway across the yard Arnie looked back at her and called, 'Don't brush him so gently. He's not a butterfly. Lean into it. Press harder – he'll enjoy it more.'

Nan realised Arnie had shouldered the pain and hurt of Jenny's tantrum, and successfully distracted Lottie from worrying about it. 'I'm going to help you, whether Jenny likes it or not,' she assured him. 'Lottie can come with me to the nut grove at the weekend. It's time we did the picking.'

'She'd like that – she probably doesn't even know what a hazelnut is. Jenny gave her one and she didn't know what to do with it. But...' Arnie turned his eyes to look at Nan, his brow etched with thought, '...I think the boys should go too – they'll soon be jealous and start playing up if Lottie gets all the treats. That is – if you can handle Matt and Tom.'

A wicked smile creased Nan's face and she gave a wheezy laugh. 'Handle them? Me? Those two little toads won't dare step out of line with me.'

'But I've never been to school.' Lottie clung to Jenny's hand, staring into the classroom. It smelled of sharpened pencils and floor polish.

'You didn't tell me,' Jenny said. 'So how did you learn to read so well?'

'I had a tutor. Miss Morgan.'

'Right – well, you'd better tell the teacher that.'

Lottie didn't feel like herself at all. She was wearing a dress made for her by the doctor's wife from a brown and white curtain, and a biscuit-coloured apron over the top. On her feet were Jenny's Flora Day shoes, without the crocheted flowers. 'But why?' Lottie had pleaded. 'Why can't I keep the flowers?' To her it was a tragedy, a dumbing down of the happiness and dancing those bright little flowers had represented. It made her think school would be colourless and grim.

She looked at the silent children sitting in twos at wooden desks, aware of them staring back at her. One girl who sat on her own at the back gave her an open, friendly smile. She was a big girl with an aura of power, her hair tossed back, her eyes searching for mischief. 'What's your name?' she hissed. 'Mine's Morwenna.'

David Merryn swung round from writing on the

blackboard, a stub of chalk in his hand. He took a cane from the top of his desk and rapped it on the wooden lid. A pulse of fear rippled through the children, and especially through Lottie. She didn't want to be there. She eyed Morwenna who now had her head down, pretending to read the book on her desk. Lottie could see it was upside down. She let go of Jenny's hand, went over to Morwenna, and quietly turned the book the right way up. Their eyes met in a moment of empathy.

'Ah – Mrs Lanroska. This must be the orphan from the wreck.' David Merryn's mirror-bright leather brogues squeaked across the floor. Lottie looked up at him, thinking he resembled a marionette, a set of bones strung together and covered in tweed.

'That's right, Mr Merryn. Her name is Lottie.'

Annoyed by his loud voice and attitude, Lottie went back to stand beside Jenny. Mr Merryn's keen eyes glinted down at her, a lock of hair flopping over his brow, a bead of sweat trickling past his left ear.

'She hasn't been to school before,' Jenny said, and lowered her voice to a whisper. 'Private tutor at home.'

'How old is she?'

'Eight.'

'Can she read and write?'

'Very well.'

'Hmmm.' Mr Merryn's eyes assessed Lottie from her Flora Day shoes to the green satin ribbon Jenny had put in her hair. 'You sit down there, Lottie, next to Morwenna. I'm afraid she's a bad girl.' He steered Jenny towards the door.

'Leave her with me. If she's good, she'll be happy here and learn. If she's not – then she'll end up like Morwenna Bartle. Sit down, Lottie.'

Lottie opened her mouth to say she didn't want to sit down, but caught the look in Jenny's eye and changed her mind. She didn't fancy sitting next to Morwenna but she managed to do it, perching on the end of the bench, her eyes fixed on Jenny, hoping to convey a silent, desperate message: *Don't leave me here – please.*

Jenny's eyes were wide open and she was whispering to Mr Merryn, something about Morwenna.

Don't leave me here – please, Lottie sent the thought again, but Mr Merryn firmly guided Jenny to the door, and held it open. 'You can leave the discipline to me, Mrs Lanroska. Goodbye now.'

It was a defining moment in Lottie's life. *I'm on my own again,* she thought with a touch of defiance, watching the last corner of Jenny's skirt disappear through the door. *Shipwrecked. This time in a classroom.* Her eyes strayed to the cane which Mr Merryn was absently tapping against his bony thigh. He crossed the room on loud feet and opened a lopsided cupboard.

'Come here, Lottie.'

Lottie froze, and Morwenna gave her a shove. She found herself walking up to Mr Merryn with her heart beating furiously. He handed her two brand new smooth exercise books, one marked *ENGLISH* and the other *ARITHMETIC*. Then he gave her a dark red pencil with somebody's teeth marks at one end, a rubber with grubby corners, and a cracked wooden ruler.

Lottie accepted them numbly, remembering her old schoolroom at home, and the lovely tin of sharpened Lakeland pencils in bright colours, and the black Waterman fountain pen she'd been learning to use. She remembered the kindly face of Miss Morgan and how patiently she'd taught her to read and write. Another face floated into her memory. A vivacious, encouraging face, ready to laugh and enjoy life. Her mother.

But that was – before.

'You can choose a book to read, from the shelf,' Mr Merryn said. 'Be quick, and put it inside your desk. We're going to do English now.'

Lottie glanced at the embossed spines of the books, mostly a dull red or a faded blue. She would have liked to browse, but quickly chose *BLACK BEAUTY,* and sat down next to Morwenna, keeping her distance, alarmed at the way the girl had shoved her.

Mr Merryn turned his back to write on the blackboard, and immediately the children's heads turned to stare at Lottie. She stared back, defiant, curious, her gaze drawn to a neat, small girl with kind eyes. She looked serious and focused. Lottie wished she was sitting next to her instead of big, wild Morwenna.

'Stop staring at Lottie.' Mr Merryn swung round. 'You can make friends with her at play-time. Now...' He pointed at the words on the blackboard, 'you will write *COMPOSITION,* and the date, and the title. Who can read the title? Yes – Natalie.'

The small girl with the kind eyes stood up

smartly and read the title in a clear voice, '*AN INTERESTING JOURNEY*.'

'Thank you, Natalie.' Mr Merryn's eyes twinkled fondly at Natalie. 'An interesting journey – I'm sure you can all think of a journey you have been on – in a horse and cart, or a train, a boat, or even a ship.' He looked directly at Lottie, and she understood instantly what he was trying to do. Had he chosen that title especially for her?

'You may begin.'

There was a flurry of movement, a whisper of small hands smoothing the next clean page of exercise books, a rattle of pencils, then an industrious silence. Lottie glanced at Morwenna who was struggling to copy the date and title from the blackboard, her pencil stub clutched awkwardly in her left hand.

'Morwenna Bartle.' Mr Merryn crossed the room, brandishing a ruler, his eyes triumphant, like those of a fox pouncing on a rabbit. 'Wrong hand. Again! You will write with your RIGHT hand – how many times must I tell you?' He aimed a swipe at Morwenna's hand, but she whipped it away and the ruler hit the desk with a crack. 'And don't you dare glower at me like that.'

Morwenna changed the pencil to her right hand, gripping it even tighter, her face hot with fury. An enormous tear plopped onto her book. Lottie looked at her sympathetically.

'Just ignore her, Lottie.' Mr Merryn's hard stare softened a little as he looked at Lottie. 'Morwenna Bartle is a bad girl, and a dunce. You get on with your own work.'

He walked away and lit a cigarette, inhaling

deeply, sending blue smoke curling into a shaft of sunlight. Lottie felt she couldn't begin until Morwenna was calm. She waited until Mr Merryn turned his back, then she leaned over and wrote the date and title in Morwenna's book, in her best writing. The girl looked at her in disbelief. 'Thanks,' she mouthed, and a bond was forged. Forever friends.

Chapter 7

The Maiden's Tears

Lottie followed Nan along the wooded path to the nut grove. To her left, the sea twinkled beyond the trees and to her right the green woodland twilight glimmered with mosses and ferns. Lottie had never been in a wood. She'd only seen pictures of woods in a book of fairy tales, and this was so different from a paper wood. This real wood was sensual. It crackled and sighed. It smelled earthy and ancient. It invited her to touch and feel, to poke a finger into a cushion of moss and experience the deep, damp softness of it, to skim her hand through curtains of foliage, to discover a clump of fungi burnished gold by a sunbeam.

'Mushrooms!' Lottie cried, excited, and touched one of the domed heads. It felt smooth as skin.

'No, those are toadstools, Lottie,' Nan explained. 'Don't even touch them. They're poisonous.'

Lottie looked at the tiny, umbrella-like fungi in awe. 'Where did they come from?'

'They grew, in the night. From spores.'

'Where did the spores come from?'

'From older toadstools.'

'What does a spore look like?' Lottie examined the ground under her shoes, hoping to find one.

'They're invisible,' Nan said. 'They're smaller than a dot on a piece of paper. The wind blows them around. We're probably breathing them in right now. Something's making me wheeze.' She sat down heavily on a tree stump. 'I need to rest for a minute.'

'I'll stay with you, Nan.' Lottie leaned against Nan's comforting bulk, and listened to the steady thump of the old lady's heart, and the high-pitched wheeze of her breath. It didn't sound right. Lottie had heard that kind of breath before, in her old life, when she'd sat beside her gran, for the last time. Her gran had been little, half the size of Nan, but brave and bright like a robin. Lottie had watched the light in her eyes go out, like the flame of a candle stub. Suddenly, where light had been, there was blank, black stillness. Nothingness. It had happened so fast that Lottie hadn't even seen the last wisp of Gran's presence vanish into the air.

'Don't you fret about it,' Nan said, sensing the child's anxiety. 'It's only my wheezy old chest. I'm not going to die. I'm going to be around to see you grow up.' She gave Lottie a pat on the shoulder and pointed into the tangled twigs of a hawthorn tree. 'Look – see that bird? Oh, what a little gem.'

In a moment of shared magic, they watched a tiny, mouse-like bird hopping around in the prickly branches, its stubby tail up, its bright bead of an eye winking as if it knew they were there and wasn't afraid.

'It's got a yellow stripe on its head,' Lottie said, fascinated by the bold little creature.

'It's a goldcrest,' Nan said. 'There's plenty of those around here.'

'A goldcrest.' Lottie searched her mind for a word to describe its wonder. 'It's exquisite,' she announced, relishing every syllable, her eyes firing the word into Nan's astonished expression.

'You DO know some long words,' Nan remarked. She got to her feet again and picked up her basket. 'Now where are those boys? I hope they're not going to be an infernal nuisance. I can hear them up there somewhere.'

Matt and Tom had been good on the train trip to Carbis Bay, both appearing intimidated by Nan. They'd walked quietly on the coastal path to Carrack Gladden, until it wound into the trees. The woods seemed to incite a kind of madness in them, and they'd gone crashing into the undergrowth, armed with an enormous stick each, thrashing at ferns and invisible tigers, shaking storms of red berries from the hawthorn trees. 'Little toads,' Nan had muttered.

She and Lottie climbed on, up the rocky path with sunlight flickering over dry brown earth and drifts of fallen leaves. The boys were whooping and yelling, both at the top of an ancient curly oak tree. 'I can see the lighthouse,' Matt shouted, and his hot face glowed down at Nan and Lottie,

109

'and the Carn Brea far away.' Lottie stared up at him through the branches. Matt had his cap on backwards, with some feathers stuck under it, and the branch he was sitting on looked too thin to take his weight. He didn't seem to care but sat there grinning down at Lottie. Tom was further down, clinging on, his plump legs hunched and covered in scratches, his lip quivering.

'Can't you get down, Tom?' Lottie asked, and he shook his head miserably. 'Yes, you can. Just go slowly, and think before you move.'

'Good advice.' Nan looked at Lottie approvingly.

'I want Daddy,' Tom said.

'Daddy is busy. We can't go all the way back to St Ives. You get yourself into a pickle, you get yourself out,' Nan tutted and stood up, brushing twigs from her skirt.

'Why don't you climb up here, Lottie?' Matt called.

Lottie shook her head. She'd never climbed a tree and didn't fancy trying.

'I DARE you,' Matt shouted. 'Cowardy custard.'

Lottie turned her back on him, her face flushed. She knew what 'Cowardy custard' meant from the books she had read, but it was the first time anyone had called her that. She began gathering acorns from the woodland floor. 'Those aren't hazelnuts,' Matt yelled down. He gave a horrible laugh. 'Don't you even know that? Townie.' He tore an acorn from his branch and chucked it down at Lottie. It hit Nan on the cheek.

'Right.' Nan pursed her lips, and turned her

back on Matt. 'Come along, Lottie, and Tom. We'll go on and enjoy picking hazelnuts, and we'll leave that rude little boy in the tree. Perhaps the crows will get him.' She swung her basket over her arm and walked on.

Lottie waited for Tom who was scrambling down the tree. She wasn't sure he could manage. He was only five and she thought he looked scared. On the lowest branch he hesitated, then jumped, landing with a thud. 'You're a good climber,' Lottie said, noticing Tom was trembling from the effort of overcoming his fright. He rubbed at a graze on his shin, and pulled a twig out of his unruly slab of hair.

Obviously keeping up with Matt was too much for him, and he seemed glad to take Lottie's hand and walk beside her, his sleepy eyes looking up at her adoringly. 'You're like my big sister,' he said, and Lottie felt proud. Being a big sister appealed to her. She already felt responsible for Tom and, surprisingly, for Matt. She didn't think it was right to go off and leave him up there in the curly oak tree. What if he fell? She worried about him and listened for him to be following. He soon was, begrudgingly, kicking leaves and swiping stinging nettles with his stick.

Nan was ahead of them, deep in the nut grove, her bulk half hidden by the papery leaves of the hazel trees, her stout arms reaching up to pick the hard, shiny nuts in their feathery green cups. She didn't look round to see if Matt was there, but went on filling her basket.

'You lot pick them up from the ground,' she said. 'I can't bend down to get those.'

The four of them gathered the abundant hazel-nuts in an industrious silence, broken only by a steam train powering through the cutting nearby.

When the baskets were full, Nan led them down a steep path to a rocky hollow where the grass was rich and moist. She sat down on a flat rock, next to a spring that bubbled up from a deep round hole. It was surrounded by weathered stones and festooned with vivid green delicate ferns. Nan looked at them for a long time in silence, running her rough old fingers through the arching fronds. Lottie copied her, enjoying the airy lightness and magical fluttering of the ferns. 'What are they?'

'These are rare, very rare Maidenhair Ferns,' Nan said, her voice quiet and full of mystery. 'Never pick them. They are special.' She looked upset. 'People used to try to dig them out of the stone and take them home to plant in a pot. Wicked thieving. WICKED.'

The three children stared at her, mesmerised by the sudden change in Nan's voice and the look in her storm-coloured eyes. It was spooky. Lottie sensed a story brewing in Nan's mind, a story waiting for a captive audience. It had such power that even Matt kept still, crouched on the rock, his eyes fixed on Nan.

'This was once a Holy Well,' she began in a hoarse whisper. 'The Holy Well of Carrack Gladden. I shall tell you the legend – it's sad – and it's beautiful – the legend of the Maiden's Tears.'

Jenny was enjoying her Saturday morning without the children. She loved the sound of Arnie and Vic whistling and chatting as they worked upstairs. They'd put Lottie's bed together, and now they were building a partition out of driftwood planks to give Lottie a tiny bedroom of her own. The room had two windows, one front and one back, and Lottie was to have the back one with its view down into the yard and across the rooftops. A wedge of dark blue, sparkling sea was visible, and Millie next door had a garden with a palm tree she was proud of, its blade-like leaves vibrating in the wind. In the cleft between two of the rooftops was a well-established seagulls' nest. Jenny thought Lottie would enjoy watching the devoted pair of herring gulls raising their young in the spring. Along the cottage walls, under the eaves were the cup-shaped nests of house martins, and on the north side of the yard the eaves were occupied by a colony of sparrows. It was part of life in St Ives, a life shared joyfully between birds and humans, and the many cats in the town.

Today Jenny was happy to have Mufty tethered in the yard, with his hay net and bucket of water. Mufty had been led through the cottage, leaving his cart, loaded with Lottie's bed, parked outside in the narrow street. Mufty was good company, always ready for a cuddle and a few treats. 'You're a good friend, Mufty,' Jenny said, fondling the donkey's long fluffy ears as he munched the carrot tops she'd given him. 'It is a pity Nan is so difficult. If only she just listened, like you.'

Jenny had made an effort to hide her vengeful feelings about Nan, especially when she'd seen how excited the children were about going to the nut grove with her. She was looking forward to seeing Lottie's face when she discovered the bed and, she had to admit, it was the perfect bed for a little girl. She sighed, and went inside to iron the bed linen Nan had sent down, finding it incredibly white and scented. Little muslin sachets of pot pourri and lavender kept dropping out from the pile. *She makes her own,* Jenny thought in awe. She was sniffing the perfume when someone rapped on the door. Jenny tensed. Most of her visitors were friends who just walked in. This had to be someone official, maybe threatening to take Lottie away.

She opened the door suspiciously, and was surprised to see Lottie's teacher, David Merryn, standing there with a book in his hand. Her eyes rounded. 'Mr Merryn!'

'Good morning, Mrs Lanroska.' He touched his cap. 'Excuse me calling like this on a Saturday, but I felt you had to see Lottie's English book. May I come in?'

'Yes, of course.' Jenny felt her heart racing as she stood back to let him in. *What has Lottie done?* she thought, bracing herself for trouble. *It has to be that Morwenna Bartle's fault.*

David Merryn stooped to get his head under the tiny cottage door. His eyes darted around the room, looking at the trail of hay and bits of mud Mufty had brought in.

'You'd better sit down.' Jenny showed him the wicker chair, but he chose to pull out a chair and sit at the table. He put two books down in front of him. One was *BLACK BEAUTY* and the other Lottie's English book.

'Are the children here?' he asked.

114

'No, they've gone nutting.'

'And is your husband in?'

'Yes, and his dad. They're upstairs building a bedroom for Lottie.'

'I think your husband should be here too. Can he spare the time?'

Even more alarmed at his serious tone, Jenny called up the stairs, and Arnie's head appeared. 'Can you come down – we've got Lottie's teacher here. He says it's important. Vic had better come too.'

Arnie and Vic clattered downstairs in their work boots, their clothes covered in sawdust, sleeves rolled up, and their eyes full of life and light. Jenny felt better immediately, and the four of them sat round the table.

'So what is it, Mr Merryn?' Jenny asked.

'You can call me David.' He took his cap off and put it on the table. It looked uncannily clean, and so did his hands as he carefully opened the smooth light green exercise book. 'I ... must explain,' he hesitated, his eyes nervous behind the round spectacles he wore. 'You see, I took the children's books home to mark as I always do. Lottie has survived that dreadful shipwreck, such an ordeal for an eight-year-old. I didn't expect much from her, but for composition I chose the title of *AN INTERESTING JOURNEY*, thinking it might encourage her to write about her experience.' He paused, looking round at the three attentive faces as if they were a class of children. 'I thought Lottie might manage to write a few lines – most of the class do one or two pages. I walked around, supervising them, and I noticed

Lottie was working very hard. She wrote faster and faster, and never looked up from her book once – page after page – she just kept going as if her life depended on it. To be honest, I anticipated an illiterate mess, but when I opened her book I was astounded, and so moved.'

'Why? What's wrong with it?' Jenny snapped, wishing David Merryn would get on with it.

'Nothing – nothing at all, Mrs Lanroska. Don't look so worried.'

He's human, Jenny thought, catching the same glint of surprise in Arnie's eyes.

'Lottie has written five pages,' David Merryn continued, 'in excellent handwriting and only a few spelling mistakes. But – what she's written is so important, and it truly touched my heart, as it will touch yours. I felt I had to come straight round and see you. I'm glad you were in, and it's good that Lottie is out.'

'Let's have a look then,' Jenny said, eyeing the book still closed under David Merryn's chalk-ingrained thumbs.

'But I must just tell you...' he continued, hanging on to the book, 'when she finished writing, minutes before the bell for playtime, Lottie put her head down on the desk and wouldn't move. I had to pull the book out from under her arms. She wasn't crying. She just seemed – frozen. She wouldn't go out to play. She wouldn't move, and I didn't think I should force her. I tried to get her to talk to me, but she seemed locked into herself, if you know what I mean.'

Arnie nodded. He looked at David Merryn from under his long eyelashes. 'We do. Don't we,

Jen?' He held out his hand for the book, opened it, and gave a low whistle of surprise. 'She can write better than I can.'

He put the open book between himself and Jenny, and Vic got up to read it with them. Their three heads bent over Lottie's neat, rounded script. The sound of the sea sighed through cracks in the window panes, and the eternal anthem of seagulls echoed from the harbour.

David Merryn cleared his throat, breaking the pool of silence as Arnie turned the last of Lottie's five pages, to where she'd written *THE END* with elaborate scrolls on the letters. 'I think,' he said, 'that this could one day be a very important document.'

'Before I tell you the legend,' Nan reached down and dipped her hand in the well water, 'you must make a wish, because this is also a wishing well.' The water sparkled as it ran through her fingers, and the sun lit the brown freckles on the back of her hand. 'BUT...' she added forcefully, 'you must make the wish in silence. Don't tell anyone, and don't speak the words aloud, or the wish won't come true.'

Lottie knew immediately what her wish would be. She scooped a palmful of the ice-cold water and closed her eyes tightly. *I wish my mother would come back from America and find me.* The water felt alive in her hand and she let it trickle back into the well. She imagined the handful of water carrying her wish through the deep blue ocean, all the way to America. The silence hung in the air above the well. Lottie opened her eyes to check

Matt and Tom were still there. Both boys were uncannily still, like time's forgotten children in a painting behind thick glass. Nan seemed to have cast a spell on the three of them, and her eyes were firmly closed, intensifying the strange power she had, as if nobody would dare to move until her eyes flickered open.

The sound of the well water was intimate, like tiny bells being inhaled by the whisper of waves along the shore of Carbis Bay. Today the sea was a dark Prussian blue, and Lottie noticed a bird out there behaving oddly, its sleek body lit lemon-bright as it folded its wings and dived, arrow-fast, vanishing into the water. Just as Lottie became convinced it had drowned, it reappeared in the sky, flexing its black-tipped wings. And again, the lemon-bright, spectacular dive into the water. Lottie longed to ask what kind of bird it was, but Nan's eyes were still closed.

Finally Nan opened her eyes, and the storm shadow had gone. Her eyes glistened with mysterious light, and she clasped her freckled hands together as if they were a book. Lottie somehow knew that when she began to tell the legend, her hands would open and let the story flow out into the silence.

'A long, long time ago,' Nan began, 'not hundreds, but thousands of years ago, a maiden and her lover came walking, hand in hand, through the nut grove.'

Matt tried a discreet smirk at the word 'lover', rolling his eyes, and one side of his mouth twitched. Nan zapped his lopsided grin with a glint in her eye, and a pause just long enough to refreeze him, effortlessly.

'The maiden had long golden hair, like Lottie,' Nan said, and Lottie instantly identified with the maiden, visualising a cream silk dress, a tiara made from flowers, and Flora Day shoes. She saw her drifting through the nut grove, her dress rippling in hazy sunlight. The man would look like Arnie, tall and broad-shouldered, with soulful, confident eyes under long lashes. He'd be dressed like a prince.

'They loved each other very much,' Nan continued, 'and the maiden dreamed of their wedding day and how happy she would be. She thought her life was perfect. She believed nothing could ever go wrong. She trusted her handsome man, and when he said he wanted a swim in the sea, she let him go. While he was gone, the maiden explored the clifftop paths. It was early summer and she was happy to be picking flowers in the hot sun. There were sea pinks, bluebells and moon daisies. She added pink campion, sheep sorrel and ferns. Then she pulled the white ribbon from her golden hair and tied it tightly around the flower stems to make a bouquet fit for a bride. But as time passed and her lover did not return from his swim, she grew worried. She came to sit by the wishing well, on this very stone.' Nan paused to pat the lichened stone she was sitting on, the folds of her green and purple dress brushing the lush grasses. The mood of the listening children shifted into sorrow as they sensed impending tragedy, and a note of foreboding rang in Nan's voice. 'The maiden sat gazing out to sea for many hours, until the sun turned scarlet in the

119

west. Still he did not return and, as the sun set over the western sea, the maiden was distraught. She knew her lover had been drowned. The sea had taken him.'

Nan paused again, to allow the voice of the wind to speak in a great breath that swept through the dry ferns, the gorse and the fluttering yellow leaves of the nut grove. It unravelled a strand of Lottie's hair and left a tiny ripple of silver on the surface of the well pool.

Then she continued. 'Grief-stricken, the maiden took her bouquet of flowers and flung it over the edge of the cliff as a token of her love. She heard the sea suck it away, and the seagulls cried for her, and the wind moaned in sympathy. As twilight came, and the evening star shone bright in the west, the maiden sat weeping. Her tears dripped into the waters of the well. Her tears never stopped. They filtered down, through the rocks, and carried the seeds of the Maidenhair Fern down, down to a dark cave on the sandy shore. The ferns grew in the rocky walls of the cave, and even to this day the maiden's tears drip from the fronds of fern, and when the sun sets, the light turns them to drops of silver and gold.'

'Like diamonds?' Lottie whispered.

'Like diamonds.' Nan's hands came back together. The story was over. The book closed. The shockwaves settling.

Lottie held on tightly to the black velvet bag deep in her apron pocket. *Diamonds,* she thought, *tears of stone.* The story was devastatingly true. Her mother might never come back. She would have to be a Lanroska. A broken-hearted Lan-

120

roska. Nan was looking at her enquiringly, as if she could see right into Lottie's heart.

'Stupid maiden,' Matt said, and the atmosphere changed instantly. Nan shut her eyes and pinched the top of her nose as if she couldn't bear to look at Matt.

'No she weren't.' Tom gave Matt an angry push.

'Don't you DARE fight!' Nan snapped. She reached for the deep willow basket full of hazelnuts and heaved herself up, her eyes scanning the beach. 'The tide is going out, so we shall walk back, up this path and through the nut grove. We'll have our picnic on the beach. I'm not going to let you go looking for the fern cave. It's too dangerous for children.'

Chapter 8

'That Man Is Watching You'

Matt knew the one way to seriously upset Lottie was to pinch the black velvet bag she guarded so fiercely. He awaited his chance, watching her as she darted around helping Jenny, helping Tom with his reading, walking to school with Morwenna. He watched with jealous eyes as Lottie bewitched Arnie with her engaging smile and her bright, confident chatter. Lottie had taken a big slice out of Matt's life. Even his bedroom had been cut in half to accommodate Lottie and her grand bed, leaving him and Tom too close together, their mattress covering most of the floor, taking away their play space.

He didn't dare carry out his plan at home. Lottie would get all the sympathy and attention while he got the blame. It wasn't fair. Matt smouldered, eyeing Lottie and sending her bad thoughts and dark, dark wishes in the privacy of his mind. His chance came on a sunny afternoon when the three of them were out on the cliffs after school. It was April, and the cliffs beyond Porthmeor were cushioned with sea pinks, the sea covered in sparkles, the air still and drowsy.

'I'm going to sleep in the sun,' Lottie announced, 'and my pillow is made of sea pinks. Do not disturb me.' She stretched out, on her back, and Matt could see the bump of the black velvet bag in her apron pocket. Tempting.

He loitered, pretending to engage with Tom who was investigating an ants' nest, cutting it into slices with Jenny's bread knife to see what the ants were doing.

Lottie woke up immediately and clutched her empty pockets, uttering a cry of rage. 'You beast, Matt. Bring that back. Give it back. Give it back.'

Relishing her distress, Matt danced around on top of the rock, waving the black velvet bag, tantalising Lottie. What was inside? He picked at the knot but it was too tight. He'd cut it open and find out. Whatever was in there felt knobbly and hard, like beads with sharp points. A necklace. Or a locket. He'd get the bread knife from Tom, cut the bag open and find out.

Matt assumed Lottie wouldn't be able to climb

up on the high rock, but he was wrong. She lifted up her skirt and charged across the grass, tagging Tom on the way. 'Matt's got my bag.' Tom threw her a bewildered glance and carried on observing the ants' frantic efforts to rescue their cream-coloured eggs and reconstruct their complex home.

'Give that back, Matt,' Lottie yelled. 'You'll be sorry if you don't.'

'I'm going to open it!' Matt chanted, enjoying himself.

'Don't you DARE. It's MINE.' Lottie looked up at him, her cheeks glittering with tears of fury. She seemed completely distraught and when Matt didn't respond, she started to climb the sheer face of the granite rocks. Matt hesitated. What if she fell? He would get the blame. But did he care? No. He was going to maximise the supreme moment of glory he had made for himself. Lottie's small fingers clung to the rock, her slim shoes slipping perilously. She was breathing hard, but getting there. Laughing cruelly, Matt moved on, higher and still higher to the mighty block of weathered granite, the 'giant's head' which towered over the sea, a steep glistening rock face dropping vertically down to the water. It was a storm wall, pounded by clouds of spray from the Atlantic. Today the sea was quiet, and Matt looked down at its mirrored flickering. The ocean floor glowed deep down in the clear water, like a garden with mops of sea-weed and sea anemones in rich wine reds and browns. A large spider crab was clambering side-ways across the sand.

Silhouetted against the shining sea, Matt held

up the black velvet bag, and dangled it over the water. 'I'm going to drop it,' he chanted.

Lottie's fingers and toes burned with the effort of clinging to the rock face high above the turf. She was stuck. With her cheek pressed against the lichened granite, she thought it through. Matt was bluffing. He wouldn't dare to throw her bag into the sea. If he did, Arnie would make him dive down and get it back. For some reason Lottie couldn't fathom, Matt was trying to hurt her. Why? She'd seen the way he looked at her sometimes, and if she was brave enough to look back, deeply, into his eyes, beyond the hatred there was sadness.

Her greatest fear was that Matt would find a way to open the bag and take out the very private contents. The thought of his grubby, meddling fingers holding it was a violation of her right to keep a secret treasure from her old life, a treasure her lost father had touched. If Matt threw it in the sea, Lottie felt her whole life would be ruined. She had to make a decision. Whether to let go and fall back into the cushions of sea pink, or to climb up there and confront Matt.

A loud yell from Tom made her let go and slide down into the soft springy turf.

'I've found the Queen Ant!' Tom's voice was a shriek of joy. 'You've got to see her. Come quick. QUICK, Lottie.'

Lottie rolled her eyes, imagining an ant with a crown on her head. She sensed Matt hesitating, disempowered by his brother's small drama, and by Lottie turning her back. She went to Tom who beamed up at her, and pointed to an extra large ant crouched in a chamber, not doing anything, just sitting there while ants scurried madly around rescuing eggs from the demolition site Tom had created with the bread knife. 'That's her – in there, Lottie,' Tom whispered, his voice hoarse with awe.

'But, Tom...' Lottie studied the radiance on his chubby face. She was lost for words. She identified with the plight of the Queen Ant. A secret, violated. 'That's so unfair. Those poor ants, Tom. Look at the home they've made – all those tunnels and rooms – and you come along with a bread knife and chop it to pieces. It's like a war, Tom, and those ants are soldiers, trying to save their city.'

Tom looked crestfallen. The bread knife fell glinting onto the grass.

'You wouldn't like it if you were an ant,' Lottie said, and she helped him put the slices of turf back together, patting it into place. 'There, it's all mended.'

'They've stung me, Lottie, all up my arms and legs. And don't tell Mum I've got the bread knife. I want to go home now. I don't feel well.'

Lottie put her hand on Tom's brow. 'You're too hot. It's just excitement.' She took his hot little hand in hers.

'I got stung all over,' Tom said, showing Lottie the skin on his arm, now fiery pink and bumpy.

'We'll go home,' Lottie said, 'but first I've got to climb up there and persuade your tiresome brother to give my bag back.' She looked up at Matt, alarmed to see him trying to pick the knot open on her precious bag.

'Nan's coming,' Tom said, and he let go of Lottie's hand and ran to meet Nan who was plodding across the grass towards them, a reassuringly bulky figure, still in her blue and white dress, a wide-brimmed straw hat shading her face.

Nan ignored Tom, glanced fondly at Lottie, then glared up at Matt with fierce eyes. 'Get down off that rock, Matthew Lanroska.' The shout came from her belly, and it made Lottie jump and Tom cry. Even the flock of screaming seagulls went suddenly quiet, dropping down to sit like statues on the rocks below the cliff.

As the shout travelled on across the bay and disappeared into the sand dunes of Hayle Towans, Lottie enjoyed watching Matt scrambling down, his eyes guilty. She sensed his bones trembling as he stood in front of Nan.

'Give that back,' she thundered, and Matt chucked the black velvet bag at Lottie's feet, his thin shoulders arrogant, his eyes empty and lost.

'Say you're sorry,' Nan bellowed, and Matt mumbled something that sounded like 'sorry', his words shivering in the light.

Lottie picked up the black velvet bag, glad to have it back intact but wishing it didn't have the feel of Matt now ground into the fabric. At the same time, she felt an odd sense of compassion for Matt. He wanted glory, and he ended up with humiliation.

'And what have you been doing with that?' Nan turned her attention to the bread knife in Tom's hand. 'And look at the state of you.'

Tom gave her a disarming grin. 'I investigated an ants' nest,' he said proudly and his eyes shone. 'I found the Queen Ant.'

126

'Did you indeed?'

'But we put it all back,' Tom said. 'Lottie helped me. Didn't you, Lottie? Lottie's my big sister now.'

Nan didn't answer. Her eyes gazed at the sea. The three children stared at her, mesmerised by the way her expression suddenly changed from anger into magic. Now Nan spoke in whispers. 'That's why. Why the dolphins are coming. It's the web. The web of life.'

As she spoke, a wild music came from the calm sea, a high-pitched, ethereal, wordless song pitched at the far end of human hearing. Then splashes, not from waves but from huge dark curling dolphins, hundreds of them, leaping and blowing.

'What are they?' Lottie's eyes rounded. She could feel the power and energy of those leaps.

'Dolphins,' Nan whispered. 'Watch carefully and you will see whether they are smiling.'

'Smiling?' The three children watched intently. Lottie could see the dolphins' faces in the split second when they were in the air, and she felt they were seeing her, looking at her, looking into her very soul. Those flashes of time seemed to expand and last just long enough for her to feel the dolphins knew her, knew who she really was. Charlotte. Every leap and every splash whispered her name. Lottie muttered the name to herself, but the sound of it sapped her confidence.

Nan looked down at her. 'Were you going to tell me your real name?'

'No. Never.'

Together they watched the dolphins speeding

127

away towards Godrevy. Nan tapped Tom on the shoulder and turned him round to face her. 'Now listen to me, young Tom, and you, Matt. You must never, NEVER upset the ants. Some of these ant hills are centuries old. They are like ancient cities. The ants are intelligent and telepathic with other life forms. No wonder they stung you.'

'But I wanted to see the Queen Ant,' Tom protested.

'I'd like to see the Queen Ant,' Nan said fiercely. 'No, don't show me. Put that bread knife away. What the Queen Ant is doing is none of our business.'

'He cut the ant hill into slices,' Matt added.

'Then you should have stopped him. You're his big brother. Now you remember – never upset the ants or the spriggans will get you. You're interfering with the web of life. Those dolphins picked up the ants' distress and came to empathise.'

'How could they?' Matt asked, sceptical.

'Sonar,' Nan said. 'It's a language – a language without words – and it can travel far across the world.'

'To America?' Lottie asked.

'Even to America.'

'Mum says Lottie's not to talk about 'merica,' Tom said, his eyes serious. 'It makes her sad.'

'Why's that, Lottie?' Nan asked.

'I don't know where America is.'

'Right.' Nan picked up her basket of herbs. 'You boys go home and tell Jenny that Lottie's with me for an hour. I'll give her a nice tea, and we'll get my globe out of the cupboard and find America.'

'Can't Matt and me come and have tea?' Tom

asked forlornly.

'Certainly not. I don't give my saffron buns to boys who tease girls and cut up ants' nests.'

Matt glowered at Nan, but couldn't match the cold stone stare she was giving him. With an arrogant twist of his thin shoulders, he turned and headed home, doing a rollicking walk, a way of making his back look defiant. Tom stood there, hot-cheeked and tearful, rubbing the ant stings on his legs. His brother didn't want him, and neither did Nan. 'I wanted to go with Lottie.'

'He's not very well.' Lottie put her arm around Tom and smoothed the hair away from his brow. She smiled into his unhappy eyes and felt him drawing the smile into his heart as if she was the only person who cared for him. 'You go home, Tom. It will be all right, and I won't be long. Wash the bread knife in the sea and put it back in the kitchen when your mum's not looking.'

They watched Tom trudging down the path to the beach, then running as if he'd suddenly found his energy on the glistening sand, energy that drew him to the foaming edge of the Atlantic.

'You're a good big sister,' Nan said, 'but Matt bullies you. I can see that.' She pointed to the black velvet bag still clutched in Lottie's hand. 'Why don't we find a hiding place for that? Then you wouldn't have to worry about it. I've got a secret cubbyhole in my bedroom wall. It's got a little door with a key, and it's hidden behind a mirror. We could put it in there and lock it, and you can keep the key – for ever.'

'I'd like that.' Lottie slipped her small hand into Nan's hand, comforted by the reassuring, rough kindness of it.

'But you ought to tell me what's inside the bag, didn't you?' Nan asked. 'Is it valuable?'

Lottie thought about the secret thing in the bag, the way it twinkled with blue-white points of light, the way it felt hard and cool and mysterious. She longed to see it again, to open the bag and let it slither out into the light, its sparkle reflected in Nan's look of amazement. In her heart, Lottie yearned to tell Nan its story, and its destiny. *I am strong,* she thought, and shook her head. 'I shall never tell anyone,' she said firmly. And, not for the first time, she felt the pain of her own strength, hurting her, like a tight band around her temples and down the back of her neck. 'I've got a headache.'

Nan tutted. 'Willow bark tea with a spoonful of honey. Come on.'

That first summer in St Ives was a happy time for Lottie. Arnie and Jenny managed to legally adopt her, and she loved her new identity as Lottie Lanroska. No need now to reveal her true name. With the black velvet bag and its contents safely hidden in Nan's secret cubbyhole, Lottie felt liberated. Her only responsibility was to be a sister to the two boys – her brothers now. She took the role seriously. Tom was easy. He adored Lottie and would do anything to please her. Sometimes he just sat gazing at her, thinking she was like a beautiful seashell, all curly and fragile, her skin golden and the top layer of her honey-coloured hair bleached flaxen from the sun. He admired her agility, the way she would balance perfectly on a rock or a wall or leap over a pool in the sand. He loved her to read him stories and help him with his school work. It was Lottie, and not the school, who taught Tom to read and write. Without Lottie, Tom would have quickly given up and retreated into apathy at the back of the classroom.

Matt was both an annoyance and a challenge to Lottie. From the start it was a power struggle. He didn't want to admit that Lottie was in charge. Only in moments of extreme frustration did he discover a tiny nugget of peace, the peace that came from letting go of the struggle and allowing Lottie to take over his life.

The only disappointment came on Lottie's ninth birthday. Jenny's promise to take her to Helston for the Flora Day didn't happen. 'We haven't got enough money to go,' Jenny explained as they looked longingly at the poster advertising a charabanc outing to Flora Day. 'I'm meant to go every year. But I can't.' She looked sad. 'I should be dancing in the midday dance. I miss it. But next year I'm going to go flower picking in March and earn some money for us to go.'

'Doesn't Daddy catch enough fish?' Tom asked.

'Not always – but that's not his fault,' Jenny said. 'And when he does there's something more important to spend it on, like new shoes.'

The children ran wild in and around St Ives, racing up and down the endless flights of granite steps and narrow alleyways. They were forbidden to play on the harbour beach at low tide as the sand was black with coal dust from the coal ship which came in from Swansea. And Jenny didn't like them to go on the 'Island' which was covered by ramshackle sheds and allotments, and grazed by an assortment of goats, horses and cows. So the children played around the rocks and pools at the far end of Porthmeor, and built dens out at Clodgy, in between the giant stacks of granite.

Morwenna tagged along with them in bare feet and a raggedy pale blue dress. She and Lottie were good friends, much to Matt's annoyance. Morwenna struggled at school, but out in the streets and on the beaches she was sharp and observant, always knowing when the tide was coming in or if the cliff was too crumbly to climb. It was Morwenna who alerted Lottie to a new kind of danger, on a sun-soaked Saturday in July.

'That man is staring at you, Lottie,' she whispered, cupping her hands over Lottie's ear.

Lottie looked at her in surprise. 'What man?'

'That artist.' Morwenna pointed to a bearded figure hunched over an easel uncomfortably close to where they were playing. 'Do you know him?'

'No. I don't know anyone,' Lottie said, and she looked directly at the man with her intelligent dark blue eyes, unafraid, assessing him. 'He looks like that because he's drawing,' she told Morwenna. 'Artists are always squinting and holding up pencils.'

'But, Lottie ... he's leering at you as if ... well, you know what I mean,' insisted Morwenna.

'No, I don't know what you mean.' Lottie went on arranging shells and pebbles on a mound of damp sand. 'I'm making a shell garden. You can do the edges. Use the blue mussel shells.'

'But, Lottie ... that man is still watching you. Men look at my mum like that and next minute they're in bed with her,' Morwenna giggled. 'We should go home.'

Lottie frowned. A vague memory teased the fringes of her mind. She squatted down in the sand and started making a flower from the tiny conical limpets she had gathered from the high tide line. They had beautiful sunray patterns on them in browns, blacks and soft reds and yellows. 'I'm not going to let a silly old artist stop me making this garden.' She carried on working in the sunshine, enjoying the way the sand sparkled with grains of crystal. Above her in the summer sky, the sand martins dived and swooped into their holes in the layer of clay at the top of the low cliff. Tom was lying on a rock, watching them intently, while Matt was digging furiously with a blade of slate, making dams in the stream.

Tom heard what Morwenna was saying, and he kept a discreet eye on the artist. Morwenna was right. The man was indeed watching Lottie, a glint of narrowed, indigo eyes staring at her, then drawing, his pencil flickering over the paper in swift strokes. Then he'd pause, look at his drawing, and stare again at Lottie. A shadowed smile lurked inside his wiry grey beard.

He put his pencil behind one ear and stood up. He stepped back, squinting at his picture. He took a few, eager steps towards the girls as they squatted in the sand making their shell garden. And again, he stopped, and he stared.

Lottie had her back to him, engrossed as she worked her way around the shell garden. She frowned at Morwenna who was nudging her. 'I shall not be distracted from making my garden.'

133

A crack in Lottie's world opened up when the bearded man called out to her.

'Charlotte?'

His voice was gentle, but Lottie reacted as if she'd been stung by a hornet. She swung round, a few precious seashells scattering from her hand, her heartbeat suddenly wild and insistent. She stared at the artist, trying to see the face inside the wiry mass of beard.

'It is Charlotte, isn't it?' he enquired.

Lottie froze. Something inside her panicked and broke apart. *I'm not Charlotte now. I'm never going to be Charlotte again. Never.* The thought razed through her like rope.

The man lowered his gaze to get eye contact with her. 'Charlotte.' His eyes shimmered with excitement.

Lottie fled, up the sandy slope from the beach and into the streets of Downlong. Morwenna scurried after her, hitching up her ragged blue skirt and giggling. The sand garden was left to collapse into the foaming edge of the rising tide.

Tom rolled over and got up. He stuck his chest out and confronted the man. 'You leave her alone, mister. She's not called Charlotte, and she's our big sister.' He picked up a granite pebble. 'If you don't go away I'll get my dad and my grandad on to you and they're proud Cornish fishermen.'

The artist held up a bony hand. 'No need to throw stones, young man.'

Matt looked up from masterminding his dam in the stream and saw Tom with the pebble in his hand. He bounded over to him. 'What's the matter?'

'He was leering at our sister. Morwenna said he was.'

Matt didn't know what leering meant. He saw it as an excuse to get at Tom. He wrestled the pebble out of Tom's hand, pushed him over in the wet sand, and quickly sat on top of him, enjoying the look of fury in Tom's eyes. 'Daddy said we're not to throw stones at the artists.'

'I weren't gonna throw it.' Tom pushed back at Matt with every fibre of his being. 'Get off me.' He bucked and struggled but Matt ground him into the sand. Tom clawed at a pebble and hit him on the head with it.

'Right, you're gonna get it now.' Matt's fists pummelled Tom's chest. He rolled him over and pushed his face into the sand until Tom could hardly breathe and blood was oozing in tiny beads from where a fragment of shell dug into his cheek. Tom's howl of pain was music to Matt. He wouldn't stop until his brother was limp and begging for mercy. And it was all Lottie's fault. For being there.

At the top of the beach, the bearded artist was packing up his gear, carefully tucking his sketch of Lottie into a leather portfolio, his name, John De Lumen, embossed in gold letters on the side. He took a gold watch from his top pocket and looked at it. Time to head back to the station. Time to leave beautiful St Ives and catch the train back to London.

Leaving the boys wrestling on the sand, he allowed himself one last gaze at the white lace of the incoming tide, and at the poignant image of Lottie's shell garden crumbling under a long

135

tongue of surging foam. *He had her,* John De Lumen thought joyfully. His swift, confident pencil had captured the likeness of the most beautiful child he had ever seen. He would go home to his studio in London, pin the sketch on the wall, and begin an oil painting of a sun-kissed little girl innocently playing beside the vivid jade and silver ocean, her hair tumbling around her very distinctive face. Charlotte. It had to be her. Someway, somehow. He would call the painting *Discovering Charlotte*. It was to be his best painting, and he imagined it hanging in a gallery, people standing in front of it, tasting the sea salt, sensing the ripple of the child's hair, looking deeper, seeing the blend of innocence and wisdom in her dark blue eyes. He visualised the art critics and the reviews.

John De Lumen walked away in long strides, his easel under one arm, a cluster of seashells jingling in one pocket of his tweed jacket. Oh yes, *Discovering Charlotte* was a painting with a very special destiny.

Chapter 9

Flora Day

It was the night before Flora Day and Lottie was awake, listening anxiously to the row going on downstairs. She sat up in bed, in the dark, leaning her cheek against the carved wooden headboard. It comforted her, just as Nan predicted. She trailed her fingers over it and found the squirrel, smiling as she touched the bushy tail and remembered when she'd seen a red squirrel in the nut grove, his exquisite little hands curled around a hazelnut. A real squirrel so intensely alive that his lithe body twitched and pulsed, the tufts of fur in his ears so fine, like a dandelion clock ready to blow away.

Her bedroom was completely dark except for the window, open to the phosphorescent light of the summer moon on the sea. Lottie smoothed her hand over the carved leaves and branches until she touched the owl. A wise old owl. Wisdom was what she needed right now, on the eve of her tenth birthday. Wisdom to understand why Jenny and Arnie were quarrelling downstairs, their voices hissy, the anger muted as if they didn't want the children to hear. But Lottie's sharp hearing picked up every single word.

It was about Flora Day. Jenny would be dancing with another man, called Troy, and Arnie didn't like it. 'I'd be proud to dance with you, Jen,' he said. 'It's not fair. You're MY WIFE.'

'But you can't. You weren't born in Helston.'

'And Troy was?'

'Yes, he was. You know that already, Arnie. Why have I got to explain it to you all over again? We have this argument every year. You're just jealous.'

'Dead right I am. Why should he be dancing round Helston with you when I'm out there fishing and trying to make money?'

'You could come with us.'

'No thanks. I don't want to stand there and see MY WIFE dressed up like a doll and dancing

137

with some idiot in a grey top hat. He's got more money than sense if he can take a day off. And if I saw him with you – looking down the front of that revealing dress, I'd ... I'd smash his head in.'

There was a bang which Lottie knew was Arnie's fist thumping the table. 'I don't want you to go, Jen.'

'It's my culture and my birthright. You can't stop me, Arnie. Flora Day is in my blood. And it's Lottie's birthday.'

'That's nothing to do with it.'

'Yes, it has. She's been looking forward to it. And she helped Millie make the dress. Have a heart, Arnie. Lottie's a lovely little girl and she helps me with everything. She deserves a day out – and so do I, Arnie Lanroska. So stop trying to keep me prisoner.'

Lottie sighed, moved by Jenny's description of her. But it was bittersweet. The hissed words were like a huge eggshell downstairs and it was cracking open, releasing something ugly and threatening. Resentment, anger, jealousy. A power trio all too familiar to Lottie. Nan described jealousy as the 'green-eyed monster'. Like the man who had beaten her. A monster with a black hole where its heart should be. Lottie didn't want that to happen to Arnie. She loved Arnie, and she loved Jenny. She debated whether to go downstairs and tell them both to shut up.

There was a nasty, fracturing silence after Jenny's words. Then Arnie said, 'Ouch.'

'What d'you mean – ouch?'

'Ouch – that ... hurt.'

'What hurt?'

138

'You.' Arnie's voice rang with pain. 'You thoughtless bitch. Saying I keep you prisoner when I work my guts out trying to keep a roof over our head. It's not easy, Jen. I don't even like fishing. It's all there is here in St Ives after the mine closed. I was a tin miner and proud of it.'

'Don't give me the hard luck story. Do you think I like the work I do? Day in, day out? And don't you EVER call me a bitch, Arnie Lanroska, or I'll be one.'

Lottie heard the crash of a chair being shoved back.

'That's right. Go on,' Jenny yelled. 'Walk out like you always do. Run away. Go on. Go. Go then. See if I care.'

A door slammed and Lottie heard Arnie's boots scuffing the sand-glazed cobbles as he strode away, his footsteps vanishing into the dark town. The church clock chimed its chimes across the water. Ten o'clock.

Where would Arnie go? Lottie thought about Arnie out there in the night. Without a lantern. She got up and padded downstairs in her white cotton nightie.

Jenny was in the wicker chair, darning the holes in the elbows of Matt's navy-blue jersey. She looked up at Lottie in the candlelight, her eyes troubled. 'You should be asleep, Lottie. What's the matter?'

'Where's Arnie going?'

'You don't miss much, do you?' Jenny sighed and slipped her arm around Lottie, pulling her close. 'Don't you worry about Arnie. He'll go down to Vic's place, or go to the pub.'

'I want him to be here in the morning when it's my birthday,' Lottie said. 'I never had a daddy before.'

'Oh, he'll be back, don't you worry, Lottie, but he might be in bed asleep when we get up. I'm going to sleep on the sofa so that I don't disturb Arnie when we get up at five o'clock to catch the charabanc to Helston. It's exciting. Your first Flora Day – and your birthday.'

Lottie leaned against Jenny, her mind brimming with questions. 'Why can't Arnie come with us?'

'He could. But he won't. Too much work to do.'

'But the east wind is blowing,' Lottie said.

Together they listened to the easterly gale out there in the night, driving robust waves into the normally tranquil harbour, making the boats rock wildly and tug at their mooring ropes.

'We should go out and get Arnie back,' Lottie said passionately.

Jenny pursed her lips. 'No, Lottie, don't be silly. You go back to bed. Now.'

'I wish I wasn't a child. I wish I was grown up so that you'd listen to me.'

'Well, you'll be a year older – in the morning. Go back to bed or we'll all be tired and grumpy. Arnie can look after himself.'

Lottie sighed loudly. She peeped into the kitchen to smell the apple and cinnamon pasties wrapped in greaseproof paper and packed in a basket on the table, a picnic breakfast to eat on the journey. She wanted to steal one and take it to Arnie wherever he was, out in the lonely night.

'Lottie!' Jenny's voice was a low, warning growl.

'All right, I'm going back to bed. If I MUST.'

Arnie stood at the bottom of Bunkers Hill, trying to make a decision. He could hear the waves slamming against Smeaton's Pier and pouring down the other side. The breath and hail of the spray, the groan and creak of the boats. Had he tied *The Jenny Wren* securely? He was sure that he had. But something niggled in his mind. A frayed rope, a rope he should have replaced. What if he lost the boat? No boat, no job.

Right now, the boat was way down his list of priorities. Jenny was at the top. Jenny, and his home and family. The light in his children's eyes when they ran to welcome him home. His home wasn't beautiful. It wasn't clean. But it was wonderful. His home steamed with baking pasties and lavendered laundry. His home flickered with friendly lights, candles and reflections of candles. His home was peaceful when the children were sleeping, their still cheeks glowing from days of playing in the sun. His home wasn't far away, but Arnie felt far away from it. He felt he was losing everything he deeply treasured.

And it had begun with the dress.

For weeks, Jenny's Flora Day dress had been hanging in a corner of the living room, its beads winking in the candlelight and sparkling in the shafts of morning sunlight. Arnie was in awe of THE DRESS, afraid he might touch it with his dirty hands, or tip creosote on it. Even the boys walked around it in a wide circle, eyeing it respectfully. Only Jenny, Lottie and Millie were allowed to do mysterious things to the cloud of peach organza, stitching it and smoothing it. Beads rolled across the floor, and he had to pick his way round them and over them, in case his size ten boot might crack one of the hallowed gems.

It was as if THE DRESS had flown in through the window like a giant butterfly and pitched there in Arnie's home. Not to be disturbed. A dress in hibernation. And tomorrow THE DRESS was to fly out into the sunshine, on Jenny, on Jenny's curvy body. To dance in another man's arms.

It was more than Arnie could bear.

Standing in the cold east wind at the bottom of Bunkers Hill, he felt rebellious. Then guilty. *Matt is like me,* he thought. *I've passed it down to him – the sins of the father.* Above the roar of the waves, the sound of laughter and singing drifted from the Sloop Inn. The money in Arnie's back pocket burned. He'd spend it. That's what he'd do. Drink. Drink through Flora Day until it was over.

At five minutes to seven on the morning of the eighth of May, the little town of Helston hummed with anticipation. Meneage Street and Coinage Hall Street were lined with crowds of people, the excitement rippling above their heads as they waited against the sunlit walls. Bluebells and bunches of fresh green foliage hung from doorways and windows, the air heavy with their scent, and the sweet perfume of the tiny corsages of white flowers that everyone was wearing. 'Lily-of-the-Valley,' Jenny explained as she pinned one to Lottie's dress. 'You've got to wear one – and you boys. It's traditional. Men wear it on the left,

142

flowers pointing up, and ladies wear it on the right, flowers pointing down.' Lottie was mesmerised by Jenny's dress, a swirl of peach organza with crimson silk roses sewn amongst the ruffles of the skirt. Beads sparkled around the neckline and along the sleeves. Her wide-brimmed hat was trimmed with moon daisies, campion and cowslips, with a peach-coloured ribbon fluttering in the haze of the morning sun. Jenny looked radiant and Lottie couldn't wait to see her dancing. 'Not yet,' Jenny told her. 'First we've got the children's dance, then the Hal-an-Tow.'

'I like the Hal-an-Tow,' Matt said. 'It's scary. You'll be scared, Lottie. There's an enormous dragon.' He thrust his face close to her, his eyes bulging, wanting to frighten her.

'It's not a real dragon,' Tom said. 'It's made of cardboard painted red, and I'll look after you, Lottie.'

'I know the legend of the red dragon,' Lottie said. 'Nan told me.'

Jenny rolled her eyes. 'Tell us then, Lottie, as it's your birthday.'

Lottie beamed, and lowered her voice to a mystic whisper, the way Nan did. 'Centuries ago,' she began, 'a ball of fire fell out of the sky and landed in Helston, in Angel Yard, and people were terrified. They thought it was a red dragon. But it turned out to be an extremely large stone, and they cut it up and used it to build the wall of the Angel Pub.'

'What nonsense,' Jenny smiled.

'But it could be true. Nan said it might be a meteorite.'

'What's that?'

'A stone that falls out of the sky.'

'Shh!' Jenny whispered, her eyes fierce under the pretty hat. 'We've got to listen for the drum.'

The silence intensified as the hands of the town clock moved towards seven o'clock. The clock seemed to take a deep metallic breath before chiming. Seven o'clock. On the eighth of May. Lottie's birthday. She loved the sky blue dress Millie had made for her birthday. But she felt disappointed too. She'd begged Jenny to let her dance in the children's dance, but Jenny stood firm. 'No, you can't. Only children born in Helston are allowed to do the Furry Dance.'

Lottie felt like making a huge fuss and saying she didn't agree with those Cornish traditions, but she made herself keep quiet. The excitement of getting up early, at 5 a.m., dressing up and climbing aboard the charabanc in Royal Square. The thrill of whizzing along the flower-filled lanes, singing and laughing, with lofty foxgloves nodding down at them. The billows of pink campion, yellow hawkbit, and the sweetly scented green flowers of Alexanders. The charabanc rattled on over the high granite moors of Carnmenellis then plunged down towards Helston's softer wooded landscape, the lanes hazy with pollen, the woods carpeted with white wild garlic bells and bluebells. Lottie had never seen so many flowers. Inland Cornwall in May was richer in magic than any of the fairy tales she had read, and now her mind glimmered with the stories Nan had told her. Stories not in books. Stories falling through generations like huge sparkling raindrops.

While they waited in the humming silence Lottie studied Jenny's face, her small nose and determined chin, the sheen of her perfect skin under the glow of the wide-brimmed hat. *It was a pity Jenny was forever saying no,* Lottie thought. And Jenny had said an extra loud 'No' when she'd asked if Morwenna could come on the trip. 'She's trouble. Comes from a bad family. And why should I pay for HER to come?' Lottie came close to shouting at Jenny but she knew it wouldn't work. Jenny's words were final. But still it was disappointing. The two girls were firm friends now and Lottie didn't understand why Jenny seemed to actively hate Morwenna. It was the same with Nan. Jenny did tolerate her but she wasn't going to let Nan into her heart, and preferably not into her home either. Nan just laughed, pretended she was too tough to care what Jenny thought, and came anyway, filling Lottie's life with a cornucopia of herbs and cats and stories.

The clock struck seven and deep in the heart of Helston a diminutive man in a blue uniform stood poised behind a massive drum, his elbow quivering with excitement as he hit the first beat with the force of an old tin miner wielding a pickaxe. The boom reverberated through the town, making Lottie jump. She was leaning against the window of a draper's shop and she felt the glass vibrate. One. Two. Three. Four. The thump relentless, like a heartbeat, and behind the drum the Helston Silver Band blared out the lilting tune of the Furry Dance.

'They're coming.' Jenny's whisper was electric.

'Don't cry, Jenny.' Lottie noticed a tear trickling

145

from Jenny's eye.

'You let her cry,' Millie said wisely, her face with its sunray wrinkles smiled down at Lottie. 'Them's 'appy tears. Tears fer comin' 'ome.'

Matt and Tom darted into the road to watch the band marching up Coinage Hall Street. Jenny stiffened. 'Get back here and behave, the pair of you.' They slunk back, Matt scowling. 'Don't make me wish I hadn't brought you,' Jenny said. 'You behave properly or we won't go to the market.'

'No toffee apples,' Millie warned.

The band marched past and Lottie experienced the power of the big drum running through her like a shiver. Behind the band came a long line of children dressed in white with flowers in their hair, dancing in pairs, a boy and a girl. Lottie was envious. How romantic to dance in white in the early morning with everyone clapping and cheering and waving the flag of St Piran from high windows above the shops. Her feet itched to dance as if her new shoes were alive with the memory.

The line of children danced into open doorways, around kitchen tables and back gardens and out again, weaving loops of joy as if stitching the town of Helston together for all time. The procession disappeared around the corner and up Meneage Street, the thump of drum fading, the notes of the Furry Dance lingering like glow worms in the twilight.

Jenny trembled with emotion. She opened her arms and drew the three children close like baby birds nestled in the peachiness of her dress. 'Shh,' she whispered, 'be very quiet now and listen for

146

the Hal-an-Tow.'

Another silence frowned over them as if it came from the sky which was now a translucent grey. Heavy drops of rain began to fall. Jenny looked up in disbelief. 'It NEVER rains on Flora Day. NEVER.'

The five of them huddled together under Millie's massive umbrella. It had a hole in it and a smell of lobster pots and moss. Lottie watched the splodges of rain mottling the cleanly swept street and pressed close to Jenny, trying to gather the ruffles of her dress under the umbrella. She remembered what Nan had said about the Hal-an-Tow. It was the dark side of Flora Day. She wanted to tell Jenny. But Jenny and Millie were alert again, listening, their eyes gazing down the street.

The rain pelted on Millie's umbrella, and stopped abruptly like a wave of applause. Even the sky seemed to be listening. Then, from the valley of the Cober River came a new, unearthly sound. An eerie whistling. Matt threw Lottie an intense look, a look that said he wanted her to be frightened.

The whistling never stopped but grew louder, and a rustling sound and a howling sound surged out from the steep narrow alleyway and into Coinage Hall Street.

Lottie sidled close to Millie who looked down at her with reassuring eyes. 'It's all right, me little 'un. 'Tis just pretend.'

But the approaching Hal-an-Tow was terrifying to a child. To Lottie it looked like a mad, whirling, angry forest invading the town; the whistling

147

and rustling was like the storm wind overturning her safe ship. She made herself stand still, comforted by Millie's slow heartbeat in her left ear. She imagined herself as an ice fairy in her blue dress, frozen and untouchable.

The whistling branches with green human legs danced up the street, swishing bunches of foliage along the ground, over the walls and into the air, elm leaves, willow whips and fans of sycamore. The actors, or Mummers as Jenny called them, wore raggedy clothes and hats stuffed with foliage. As they came closer, Lottie was relieved to see they were human, with very human eyes flashing from gleeful faces. They were blowing tin whistles and elder flutes and some had tambourines, adding to the din. The town of Helston stood still in shock, even though it had seen it all before, the crowd joining in the whistling with enthusiasm.

Tom and Matt were jumping up and down, letting out bloodcurdling howls, their eyes shining.

'Let 'em go mad,' Millie said, putting a restraining hand on Jenny. 'It won't 'urt 'em.'

The Mummers stood in a circle, their branches held high, guarding the space as a band of folk musicians came, playing the Furry Dance on a variety of flutes, fiddles and drums. There was booing and whistling as the towering red dragon did its gyrating dance in the middle of the circle. Then cheers as the avenging knight fought and killed it with a remarkably realistic sword.

'There you are. Light triumphs over darkness,' Jenny said, looking at the boys with wide, bright eyes. 'It always does. Every year. In Helston it does anyway.' She looked up at the gathering rain clouds. 'It's my turn next – and I might have to dance in the rain.'

'What will you do if your lovely dress gets wet?' Lottie asked.

'Carry on dancing – and smiling,' Jenny assured her. 'Even if I look like a dishrag, I've got to carry on.'

Millie chuckled. 'Well the flowers on yer 'at will be 'appy.' She laughed heartily then pointed to a man in a grey top hat who was striding towards them. 'Is that 'im, Jenny?'

Jenny glowed. She waved and twirled her dress. 'That's my dancing partner – Troy. We've done the midday dance together for years.'

Lottie looked dubiously at Troy's fleshy pink smile. Last night's argument between Jenny and Arnie still haunted her. The boys had slept, but Lottie had listened, miserable and anxious. Was Arnie right? Should Jenny really be dancing through Helston with another man – a man who Arnie apparently hated? Troy looked confident and smart, but his jacket smelled of beer. She backed away when Jenny tried to introduce her. 'Our new adopted daughter, Lottie – from the October shipwreck. Don't be shy, Lottie. Shake hands nicely.' But his hand was too hot, and too squeezy. Lottie set her face and twisted out of reach. The boys stood back too, looking at each other.

It felt wrong to all three children. Their faces were anxious and very serious as they watched Jenny go swanning off with Troy, her flower hat

149

bobbing, her mane of hair defiantly swinging.

'Well, don't look so po-faced!' Millie teased. 'You lot cheer up and let yer 'ardworking mother enjoy 'erself fer a change.'

A rumble of thunder growled from the darkening sky. The eerie whistling began again as the Hal-an-Tow moved on to perform further up the street.

'I wish our daddy was here,' Tom said soulfully.

Back in St Ives, Nan sold the last of the herb posies from her basket. The east wind had dropped, the sea was calming down, and the May sunshine was too hot for her to tackle the walk up Porthmeor Hill. She sat down on a stone ledge to rest and count her money. One pound, fourteen shillings and sixpence. Enough to buy Lottie a birthday present. Coloured pencils in a tin were what she wanted, and Nan had seen some in the Post Office. Then she planned to go home and make Lottie a birthday cake with butter icing and glacé cherries. She'd take it down to welcome the family home from Flora Day. She hoped they'd ask her to stay and play the cottage organ and have a sing-song.

Most of Nan's dreams were focused on Lottie. She knew Lottie was bright, and David Merryn wanted her to take a scholarship and get into the grammar school. Nan planned to start teaching her music, and botany, and show her how to make pot pourri and willow baskets.

Her dreams were interrupted by an urgent bell, ringing fast and continuously. A noisy motorcar came rattling along Wharf Road, *much too fast,*

150

Nan thought, appalled. And why the bell? What was going on? Then she saw the notice on the bonnet of the car. *POLICE.*

Wharf Road had only recently been built to create a promenade for visitors. Artists from 'up-country' had started coming to St Ives and setting up their easels along the edge of the new walkway, much to the annoyance of the fish packers and net makers who assumed the new space was for them. *If someone was in trouble with the police, it would be one of those visitors,* Nan thought, *not a Cornish person.* She watched the police car and saw two helmeted policemen get out, brandishing notebooks. One of them carried a coil of rope which he stretched across the entrance to Smeaton's Pier, and he stood in front of it, stopping people going down there. The other one went to a crowd of locals who were gathered, looking down at something on the ground.

Nan overheard two women talking close to her.

'Apparently they've pulled a body out of the water.'

'Dead?'

'Looks like it. Must have been swept off the pier by those big waves in the night. Some poor visitor who doesn't understand the ways of the sea.'

'No – they say it's one of the fishermen, a man in a navy-blue jersey. A young man.'

Nan clutched her basket tightly. She blanched with shock. It couldn't be. No, it couldn't be Arnie or Vic. Could it? Surely not. They were life-boat crew, strong swimmers, respected knowledgeable men. It couldn't, shouldn't happen. Nan's skin went cold from the soles of her sandalled feet to the roots of her silvery hair. She felt numb and faint as if she was going to pass out. She clasped the bone handle of her walking stick and took some deep breaths. She told herself not to panic, not to get in such a state when she didn't know the truth.

Intending to go over to Smeaton's Pier and find out, Nan struggled to stand up, and sat back down again when she saw Vic. He was walking between the two policemen, shaking his head, his face white and drawn. Nan got up and hurried towards him.

'Mother!' Vic looked at her with tormented eyes, his cheeks moon-pale, his smile gone as if it had never existed.

It was then that she knew.

'Arnie,' she whispered. 'It's him, isn't it?'

Vic closed his eyes and nodded.

'NO!' Nan's voice, and the terror in her eyes filled the busy harbour and everything stopped. Time stood still. 'Not my Arnie – my grandson – I loved him – I … I brought him up.'

It was more than Nan could take. She fell forward, her stick flying one way, her basket the other. She saw Vic's face, spinning with the sky and the boats as she crashed onto the windblown sand at the side of an upturned dinghy. She clawed at the side of the boat, then let go and lay still.

'Oh God – not you as well, Mother.' Vic ran to her, and Nan dimly registered the smell of oil and fish on his clothes. Dimly. Until there was nothing.

High above the harbour, down the steep hill

152

from Carbis Bay, the charabanc came chugging home, full of singing, happy people, flushed and windblown from their day out. Tom fast asleep in Jenny's arms, Matt and Lottie still singing the Furry Dance.

Chapter 10

The Queen of St Ives

Jenny and Lottie were in high spirits as they left the charabanc and skipped through Royal Square with Millie and the boys following, singing the Furry Dance and jingling the tambourines which Troy had bought them in the market. In Jenny's bag were two mysterious hairy coconuts that Troy had knocked down on the coconut shy. They couldn't wait to taste the sweet milk inside and munch the chunks of white nut. Arnie would saw the coconuts open, Jenny promised, and the empty shells could be used to make music.

It had been a wonderful Flora Day. Jenny felt alive again and despite her aching feet, she still wanted to dance. Dancing through St Ives in her gorgeous dress with Lottie whirling and smiling beside her, Jenny felt proud, and conspicuous. She hoped Arnie would be waiting on the door-step. She was surprised when the people she met turned their heads away from her smile.

'They'm jealous. Take no notice,' Millie declared.

Something felt wrong. The seagulls were oddly silent, the sky a violet grey, the air humid and thundery. The doors of the terraced cottages were shut, the window panes glimmering with subtle movements of curtains and faces bobbing out of sight as Jenny and her family danced homeward.

'Shame on you, Jenny Lanroska.' Maudie Trip-coney stood at the top of well-scrubbed granite steps, a polishing rag in her hand.

'You should've come with us,' Jenny taunted, flashing a smile as she swung past, her dress brushing its beaded skirts along Maudie's wall. 'You don't know what you're missing.'

Thunder growled around the bay and coppery lightning flickered over a gloomy ocean, gilding the little fleet of Seine boats heading home to the harbour.

'You've got a shock coming to you, my girl.' Maudie's shout unfurled and reached into Jenny's heart as she danced.

Nearly home, and her feet were faltering, her skirt hanging limp. *Something's wrong,* she thought, surprised to see Vic waiting on the doorstep. The boys ran to him bright-faced with their tambourines, but Vic didn't smile. His face was deathly pale, his eyes dark like troubled water. He didn't smile at Lottie and call her Princess. He didn't want to hold the coconut Tom took from Jenny's bag. He didn't speak. Couldn't speak.

Jenny stared at him, and so did the children who had never seen their grandad without his welcoming smile and the twinkle in his eyes. 'What is it, Vic? What's wrong?' Jenny's voice trembled and rain began to fall in huge, ponderous teardrops, splashing her hot skin. A lone seagull on the roof lifted its head and sent a rhythmic, anguished cry echoing through the cobbled streets.

Vic held the door open. 'Best come inside, out of the rain.'

The boys darted in. 'Nan's here!' Tom yelled.

Lottie's eyes shone. 'Let's show her the Furry Dance.'

'Not now,' Vic said in a strange voice. 'You children sit on the sofa and be quiet.' He looked at Nan. 'Should we send the children upstairs?'

Nan shook her head. 'They've got to face it. We all have.'

'Nan's crying!' It was Lottie who noticed the old lady's red-rimmed eyes. She ran to comfort her, taking out the embroidered hanky Jenny had given her for Flora Day. She dabbed the tears from Nan's papery cheeks.

'Oh, Lottie. Poor Lottie,' Nan said in a husky voice, and a few sobs rocked her big body. 'After all you've been through. Now this.'

'Now what?' Jenny looked from one to the other, not best pleased to find Nan sitting in Arnie's leather armchair. 'What's happened?'

'You sit down, Jenny.' Vic led her to the wicker chair, moving gingerly as if he had suddenly aged in one day. He looked at Nan. 'I can't tell her.' He broke down, holding his head in his hands and slumping onto the wooden stool. Outside, the rain lashed the streets, filling the cottage with whispers. Vic's knees were shaking violently. He reached for Jenny's hand and held it tightly, looking into her eyes. 'Arnie,' he croaked. 'We've

155

lost Arnie. My best, best boy … my boy…' and then he cried, unashamedly, sobbing great gasping sobs, unable to stop.

Horrified, the children froze on the sofa.

'What do you mean? Lost him?' Jenny's eyes rounded with alarm.

'He's gone. Dead. They pulled his body out of the harbour.'

'Dead?'

The word filled the cottage. It silvered the raindrops on the squares of glass. It rang through the iron stove. It soaked into the granite walls. It grew like a cumulonimbus, engulfing Jenny's home, crushing everything under its weight. And it wouldn't leave. It was there, in the cottage, there to stay. DEAD.

'NO!' Jenny screamed. She ripped off her Flora Day hat and flung it spinning into a corner. She tore at her carefully pinned hair, ripping it loose, sending pins tinkling over the stone floor. 'No, no, no … not my Arnie.'

Tom stood up. 'My daddy's not dead,' he announced. 'My daddy is out fishing.'

Nobody spoke. Lottie drifted around, picking up Jenny's hat, gathering the scattered hairpins. She rescued Tom from his stance in the middle of the floor and took him back to the sofa.

'How could this happen?' Jenny asked. 'Arnie was a strong swimmer – how COULD it happen to a member of the lifeboat crew? When he's saved so many lives?'

Vic held on to her hand, trying to calm his breathing. He managed one word. 'Drunk.'

'Drunk?' Jenny was appalled. 'What was he

thinking of?'

Vic collapsed again, shaking his head and weeping in great lurching sobs. Jenny leaned her cheek against his shoulder, her arm around his back, shocked to feel the heat and power of his grief. Nobody had ever seen Vic cry like that. Strong, dependable, brave lifeboat men didn't show their feelings. 'It's me who should be crying, Vic,' she said, feeling the shock creeping over her skin, like the tide cooling the warm summer sand. She couldn't cry. Not with the three children sitting there with terrified eyes. 'Go upstairs and play marbles,' she said, but none of them moved. 'Will you GO UPSTAIRS.'

'Let them stay,' Nan said. 'They're not babies. They need to know the truth.'

'Don't you tell me how to raise my children.'

Nan's eyes glittered with fury. She let go of her pent-up feelings, hurling bitter words at Jenny's shocked face. 'It's YOUR fault,' she cried. 'Arnie was my grandson, my best grandson. You've done this to him, you shameless hussy. Going off to Helston dressed up like a dog's dinner and dancing with another man. Arnie loved you – God knows why – but he did, and he was jealous, of course he was. But no – you wouldn't listen to him, would you? So what did he do? What any man would do – went to the pub and got drunk, trying to drown his sorrows. Broke his heart, you did – broke his heart. It's your fault he's dead.'

'Not in front of the children, Mother,' Vic pleaded.

The silence boiled as Jenny turned on Nan, her face ashen. 'Get out of my house,' she yelled,

157

'and don't come here ever again. I've got enough to deal with, without your spiteful tongue.'

'Jenny – now is not the time for this feud,' Vic said. 'Mother can't walk home tonight in this rain. She's suffering from shock – we all are – and you are going to have to cope with being a widow, with three youngsters to raise. You need all the help you can get.'

Jenny gripped the arms of the wicker chair and looked at Vic, who seemed to have found his quiet strength again. She still couldn't cry. It hadn't sunk in yet. Thoughts flew wildly through her mind like trapped birds. An absurd, taunting memory of dancing with Troy, the radiance on his face. The look in Arnie's eyes when he'd begged her not to go. The last words she'd spoken to him. She hadn't told him she loved him. She hadn't said goodbye. Arnie had been taken from her. So cruelly. Who would hold her in the night? Who would love and inspire her children? How would she manage? And how would she cope with the paralysing grief which was now rolling over her like the incoming tide. Unstoppable.

'It's not true, is it, Lottie?' Tom said in a very audible whisper, looking up at Lottie.

'I think it's true.' Lottie looked at him kindly and held him close, her arm around his shoulders. Tom leaned against her, his eyelids heavy as he processed her reply. Matt was hunched on the arm of the sofa where Lottie couldn't reach him. He looked desolate and alone, detached, floating further and further away in a bubble of sorrow.

Jenny looked at her three children. *They haven't got a daddy,* she thought. Compassion fired up her

158

courage and she went to them, crossing the room in her peach organza dress, and squeezed herself onto the sofa. She held out her arms, and hugged Lottie and Tom in a tight little knot of grief and love. 'It's gonna be hard,' she said. 'Very hard. But you've got me, and we must stick together. Together we're strong.' She looked at Matt, but he didn't move from his lonely bubble. Suddenly he swung down from the sofa, without looking at anyone, and stumbled out, into the rain. He slammed the door so hard that the china jingled in the kitchen. His footsteps melted into the thundery evening.

'Matt!' Jenny cried.

Vic held up his hand. 'Let him go, girl. Let him deal with it in his own way.'

'You're going to have trouble raising HIM without a father,' Nan said.

Jenny let that remark pass, and focused on comforting Lottie and Tom. She'd find the fire to confront Nan on another day. Not now when she felt shocked and beaten. Being a mother mattered more. Questions queued in her mind. What had happened to Arnie? Where had they taken his body? Who had found him floating in the harbour?

But before she could begin to ask them, something happened outside on that thundery evening in May. An almighty reverberating boom rocked the little town of St Ives. The sound crackled along the harbour and circled the bay, dying away into a rumble. Seconds later another boom, exactly the same.

'That wasn't thunder.' Nan sat up very straight.

'That was the call-out maroon.'

Vic had already jumped to his feet. 'I've got to go.'

'You're not in a fit state to go out,' Nan said.

'Course I am. D'you think Arnie would want me to sit here? I'm going.' Vic was already on his way out.

'Take Arnie's oilskins,' Jenny said.

Vic shook his head. 'I couldn't.'

Tom started to howl. 'I don't want Grandad to go.'

'Don't be such a baby,' Nan said. 'Grandad is a proud Cornishman. He's going to help man the lifeboat. There's a ship out there in distress.'

Tom howled louder than ever. Finally it was too much for him.

'I'll put him to bed and read him a story,' Lottie said. She was remarkably calm.

'That's my girl.' Jenny threw her a look of gratitude.

Vic turned in the doorway. 'Whether you like it or not, Jenny, Nan has got to stay here until morning. She's had a fall, and a terrible shock. You keep the peace. Keep the peace – both of you.'

Jenny and Nan eyed each other uneasily as Vic went out. They listened to his heavy footsteps running down to the harbour.

'And by the way, it's my birthday,' said Lottie, 'but it doesn't matter.'

John De Lumen set up his easel on the edge of Wharf Road. He wanted to paint the harbour in the morning sun at high tide when the water

160

lapping against the wall was a mysteriously jewel-bright green. The colours of the granite and the boats were warm and earthy against the sea, and the sun shone silver through the wing feathers of the herring gulls. After the long winter in London, he enjoyed just being in St Ives, in the clear, clean air. Today was the last day of his holiday, and there had only been one disappointment. He hadn't seen the child. He was still working on his oil painting, *Discovering Charlotte,* and one more glimpse of her would have helped to refresh his memory. But perhaps she didn't live in St Ives. She could have been on holiday on that hot day in July.

As he unpacked his watercolours and brushes, it occurred to John De Lumen that there was something uncannily different about the place. Stroking his beard, he gazed around to try to identify the change, and realised the harbour was unusually still and quiet. The boats rocked gently on the tide, but not one of them was in use. The two piers were deserted. No fishermen mending nets or sorting lobster pots. No voices calling to each other. No whistling. No laughter.

He picked up his favourite brush and smoothed it between finger and thumb. He dipped it in Cerulean Blue intending to begin painting the sky and as he did so, the church bell began to toll, a rhythmic, muffled tone singing softly over the water. Outside the lifeboat house, a group of men was assembling, not talking but silent, their tanned faces serious. They looked like fishermen but wore suits and black ties. Without fuss they arranged themselves into three rows in a crescent

161

shape, all standing proudly with square shoulders and strong faces looking up Wharf Road.

'Excuse me, sir.'

Startled to be tapped on the shoulder by a policeman in a helmet and black cape, John dropped his paintbrush, leaving a daub of Cerulean Blue on the pavement.

'Would you mind moving, sir? You can't paint here until later today. There's a big funeral in St Ives.'

'Yes – yes, of course.' John quickly closed his paint box and bundled everything into his bag. 'Who is it? A local person, I suppose.'

The policeman lowered his voice. 'A tragedy for St Ives, sir,' he said. 'A young man, one of Cornwall's best lifeboat crew – died in tragic circumstances – a family man, loved by everyone.'

'I'm so sorry.' John folded his easel. He noticed people waiting outside their doors along Wharf Road. 'If I stand quietly over there and pay my respects, will that be all right?'

'Yes, sir. Thank you. You can come back and paint your picture later today.'

John crossed the road and tucked himself into a shop doorway. He hadn't planned to be watching a funeral. He could have moved on to paint somewhere else. It was just a gut feeling that for some reason he had to be there and watch this Cornish funeral. Part of life's rich tapestry, to an artist. And a memory to take back with him to London, a reminder of the close and loving community found in these Cornish towns. So he stood still to watch, dispassionately, not expecting to become emotionally involved.

Wharf Road was clear, swept clean by many brooms in the night, and the ceremony began, for John De Lumen, with a single comment from a woman who stood nearby. 'They'm comin'.'

Everyone stiffened and turned to look expectantly at the group of men gathered outside the lifeboat house. John De Lumen's mouth fell open as the St Ives Male Voice Choir began to sing, deeply, from the heart and from the belly, in flawless harmony. Their power filled the harbour from West Pier to Smeaton's Pier with a quality of sound John had never heard before: a ringing, compellingly human music. It moved him profoundly. He knew the hymn tune. The words reached his soul in well-remembered phrases: *A thousand ages in thy sight – are like a moment gone* and *Time like an ever rolling stream – bears all its sons away.*

There was a moment when the choir, the bell and the seagulls were in balance, and the intensity was like a clarion, a warning of the grief to come. It was joined by the clop of horses' hooves and the slow procession appeared at the far end of Wharf Road. First came a flagbearer dressed in Cornish tartan solemnly carrying the flag of St Piran, then the two black horses, walking so carefully, their coats shining in the sun, a plume of black nodding on each head. They pulled a wagon with the coffin draped in the RNLI flag and surrounded by flowers in RNLI colours of orange, indigo and white.

John watched it passing, a lump in his throat, a sadness surfacing from way back in his life. He was unprepared for what he saw next. Behind the

163

coffin came three children dressed in black, two boys with their heads bowed, and a little girl walking between them, a black veil covering her small face. She walked with grace and courage and as she passed close to him, John saw the tumble of blonde hair swinging down her straight back. Charlotte! *A child of tragedy,* John thought, and it added poignancy to his painting. It would be in her eyes. He longed to talk to her but now she seemed even more remote from him than she had on the beach. He hoped that sunny summer day was locked into little Charlotte's heart to help her through this tragedy.

Behind the children came a woman, all in black, walking alone, her pretty face unreadable under the black veil. Obviously the widow, tragically young. What did the future hold for her now? A grim time of raising three children, alone, and in poverty.

Next came a donkey cart, the donkey led by a man whose deeply tanned face looked swollen, his eyes red-rimmed from grief. The donkey plodded dutifully, its long furry ears pricked as if doing its best under the circumstances. A name was on the brow band of the bridle. *Mufty.* Sitting on the donkey cart was a silver-haired lady in a magnificent black velvet cloak which covered her huge body and sashayed over the edges of the cart. She wore a broad-brimmed hat with a black veil. The grandmother. She turned her head and looked directly at John, her eyes fierce, looking him up and down as if she thought him an impostor, an 'Emmet' who had no business gawping at this Cornish funeral. The sun flashed on a set of

164

purple beads around her throat. A formidable lady. One who could freeze the roots of his hair with one imperious glance.

The male voice choir began a new hymn, the fisherman's hymn, *Eternal father strong to save*. And behind the donkey cart the crew of the lifeboat marched in their oilskins and sou'wester hats, each carrying an upright oar. It made an impressive statement. John became more and more deeply moved, overwhelmed to see the entire population of St Ives following in their best, blackest of black clothes, and all of them singing the hymn. It resounded from the cottage walls and the harbour with a great roaring, earthy, emotional song.

So much love. For one young fisherman.

John found himself swept along, carrying his gear, wanting to follow, to be part of this close community, to be there inside the church of St Ia, hidden in a stone corner, watching Charlotte in her hour of grief. Learning more about her strength and beauty, and her vulnerability. Coming closer to solving a mind-haunting mystery that had caused him to swap his comfortable predictable world for the life of a struggling artist.

The tolling bell and the singing stopped as the cortege reached the open doorway of St Ia's Church. The seagulls took over with a symphony of screams, their orange beaks and white wings colouring the sky. The crowd waited respectfully, watching the coffin being unloaded onto the pallbearers' shoulders. A whiff of incense uncurled from the candlelit interior and sombre organ music rolled over the stone floor and out into the town. John stared at the straight backs of the mother and her three children. He watched the grandmother being helped down from the donkey cart in her voluminous cloak.

Suddenly there was a commotion at the church door. The coffin had gone in and the mother gently ushered the children to follow it inside. The older of the two boys hesitated.

'I'm not going in there,' he shouted at his mother, and he tore his arm from her grasp and ran, dodging wild-faced between the waiting crowds. The mother gave an anguished cry, 'Matt!'

'Let him go.' The grandmother's voice echoed louder than the male voice choir, the purple beads glinting around her throat, sending a ripple of servitude through the long queue of mourners. Nothing happened until she turned in a swirl of black velvet and continued on her way to the church door. *The Queen of St Ives,* John thought, awed. He hoped he would never come face to face with her. Another more reckless creative part of his mind imagined a painting of her.

Someone had managed to grab the boy who had run away. Another substantial Cornish woman. 'Shame on you, Matt Lanroska,' she shouted. 'You get back in that church before I give you a good hiding.'

But Matt struggled like a wild cat. 'Get off me. It's none of your business.' He kicked at Maudie Tripconey's swollen ankles. Then he spat at her disapproving face, ripped his arms free from his sleeves and escaped, leaving Maudie holding his jacket and tutting. He ducked under the barrier and fled onto West Pier, expertly dodging in and out of the stacks of lobster pots. This time it was the policeman who strutted after him.

What happened next took John's breath away. At the end of the pier, Matt stripped off most of his clothes revealing a suntanned wiry body. The policeman broke into a heavy run. 'Don't do it, lad.' Matt looked back at him, then he jumped, out into shimmering space and plunged like a gannet down into the deep water.

Had it not been for her grief, Nan might well have felt like the Queen of St Ives, for she had masterminded the funeral of her beloved grandson. She paid the undertaker after breaking into the substantial roll of cash she kept in an earthenware jar in the larder. It was her rainy day money, never to be squandered, but kept craftily hidden under a pile of grain. The undertaker's eyes had popped with surprise when she'd counted out the wad of pound notes, sending beads of pearl barley bouncing over his dark oak table. Many of the flowers had come from her own garden, mostly marigolds, moon daisies and calla lilies, but she had bought some from a florist, and a pair of damask curtains provided the royal blue background cloth. She'd sent Vic to organise the male voice choir, choose the hymns and arrange for Wharf Road to be swept clean. It had all gone smoothly, but what Nan hadn't expected was the way the entire town had downed tools and shown their quiet love and respect for Arnie's life. Nan felt emotionally overwhelmed by it. She would behave impeccably. With the dignity of a queen. But it was hard. The music. The flag of St Piran.

167

The bell tolling. The memory of Arnie's soulful eyes, those long lashes, that knowing smile, carried in her heart, now and forever.

Fury burned around the edges of Nan's grief and every time she thought it was under control, a new spurt of flame would burst out. She was furious with Jenny from the start. Then incensed with Matt's behaviour.

When Jenny insisted on disappearing to search for Matt instead of going into the church hall where the wake was to be held, it added another spike to Nan's seething resentment. She held it all in, sitting in the far corner of the hall in her black velvet cloak, trying to be civil to those who were brave enough to talk to her. Nan was proud of Lottie, very proud, as Lottie glided around with plates of biscuits and cakes, her sadness neatly hidden under a bright face and an appealing charm. Nan was even a little proud of Tom who looked wise and composed as he followed Lottie with his tray of sausage rolls.

For Jenny to miss the wake seemed outrageous and unacceptable to Nan. Jenny was out there in the May sunshine in her black mourning clothes, obsessed with finding that evil little boy. *Let him drown*, Nan thought. *And her as well.*

It was one of those rare days when St Ives was blessed with a calm sea lapping gently at the harbour wall, a lagoon of jewel-green water reflecting the palaces of cloud, the huddle of cottages and the masts of boats. The Atlantic in healing mode.

The water wrapped itself around Matt like cool

168

satin, supporting him as he floated on his back, looking up through the lustrous air at the sky. 'I'm down here, Daddy,' he murmured. 'Can you see me, Daddy? Are you there?'

Matt felt better in the water. It seemed to talk to him. 'Trust and let go, and I will carry you,' it said. The water protected him from the endless criticism and condemnation. Nobody liked him. And it hurt. It chipped away at Matt's plan for his life, relentlessly, so that hardly any of it was left. His plan was like a letter of truth with burning edges. Only the middle was still readable, a mere fragment of his dream.

Arnie had taught Matt to swim; how to swim safely and creatively, how to swim for survival, and how to swim for pure joy. He'd taught him how to read the sea's moods and currents, where and when to swim in and around St Ives.

It was May, and the sea was still cold. He mustn't stay in too long. Matt looked back at West Pier and saw the policeman standing there holding a red and white lifebuoy ring. 'Are you all right down there, lad? Want me to come and rescue you?'

'Course I'm all right. I can swim,' Matt called back. He rolled over like a seal and did a fast, smooth front crawl, heading for the boats. Soon he would be hidden from the policeman, and from the world. He swam between the boats, awkwardly avoiding the anchor ropes and when he found *The Jenny Wren*, he climbed aboard. 'I'm here, Daddy. I'm in your boat.'

The one place where Matt felt at peace was on the deck of *The Jenny Wren*. Inside the cabin, with

169

the May sunshine softly warm on the wooden seats, Matt felt drowsy, wanting to sleep as a way of switching off the stress. He curled up in a corner, his head on an old tapestry cushion Arnie kept there, hoping the gentle swell would rock him to sleep, knowing he was safely hidden. The singing inside the church and along the quay was loud enough to come floating over the surface of the water, reaching into the boat, as if pursuing him. Matt pressed his hands over his ears and stared out at the dazzling water beyond the harbour. He couldn't sleep, but he could dream.

His dream was a memory of a time when Arnie had taken him out on the boat, into the wide expanse of the bay. Instead of fishing, Arnie had talked, his voice quiet, his eyes peaceful and kind. It was one of the few times when Matt felt loved. 'One day, this boat will be yours,' Arnie promised.

'What about Tom?' Matt had asked.

'Tom's just a baby. You're my firstborn son, Matt, and you're important to me.'

Arnie explained about the tides and currents of St Ives bay. Where and when it was dangerous. Why the Hayle River turned the sea red. Where the seals lived, and how the cormorants caught their fish. He'd let Matt have a go at steering the boat and taught him how to bring her safely back into the harbour.

Those times were precious to Matt. He almost felt Arnie was in the boat with him now. He wasn't in that coffin inside the church. He was out in the light. Just him and Matt. And the words he'd spoken were woven into a shining cloak swirling around his shoulders. *The Jenny Wren* was his boat now. His own boat, and his sanctuary from the world.

Chapter 11

Caught in the Conflict

'You can't SELL Daddy's boat.' Matt's eyes were savage with pain as he looked at his mother.

Lottie sighed. Caught again in the conflict. Her peaceful, secure new life had come to an end on the day Arnie died. Today, on the first day of the summer holiday, it was raining, the rain driving sideways in from the Western Sea in densely packed needles of silver, and the colours of the cobbles glowed in the wet streets.

'I can sell the boat,' Jenny said. 'Sell it, or we don't eat.'

'But Daddy promised it would be MY boat when I grow up.'

'Well, you won't grow up at all if we don't get some money in for food.' Jenny looked at him fiercely. 'Stop making trouble, Matt.'

'How is that making trouble?' he asked. 'Remembering what Daddy promised isn't making trouble. Is it, Lottie?'

'Don't drag Lottie into it,' Jenny snapped. 'Where do you think I'm gonna get money from? Eh?'

'You could get a job,' Matt said sulkily.

'And who would look after you children? And do the washing?'

'We don't need looking after,' Matt argued. 'Do we, Tom?'

Tom looked up from making a model cart from matchboxes. 'Yes, we do. I want Mummy to be at home. Why don't you do what Nan does, Mummy? Nan sells flower posies and herbs.'

'Don't tell me what she does,' Jenny ranted. 'And Nan has got a garden and we haven't. Anyway, I don't know how to grow plants.'

'Nan would teach you,' Lottie said brightly. 'She's teaching me.'

'THAT WOMAN is not gonna teach me anything. I don't care if she knows how to make solid gold bricks. I don't want nothing to do with her.' Jenny frowned at Lottie who was making pompoms from wool and old cardboard milk bottle tops. 'And what d'you mean, she's teaching you? I told you not to go up there, Lottie.'

'She went up there yesterday,' said Matt gleefully, 'and the day before – and the day before that.'

Lottie felt her face going red. She continued winding the skein of yellow wool through the hole in the centre of the bottle top. It was true. She had been going to see Nan as often as she could, letting Jenny think she was out playing or out with Morwenna. After Arnie's death, Jenny had forbidden her to visit Nan. Shocked and disappointed, Lottie had kept quiet and done it anyway. She loved Nan, and Nan loved her. She knew that. The visits were precious times for Lottie. Nan was teaching her about herbs and

172

flowers, how to make jam from fruit, how to care for the animals, and now music: how to read music and play it on a wooden recorder. Nan had promised to teach her to play the piano accordion when Vic could bring it down from the attic, and when Lottie was strong enough to hold it. On wet days, Nan took out the photo albums and showed her pictures of Arnie as a little boy, or they would read together from Nan's extensive library.

'Is it true, Lottie?' Jenny asked sharply.

Lottie stopped threading the yellow wool. She didn't like having to tell lies. So she kept quiet.

'Lottie?'

Silence.

'Look at me will you?' Jenny's eyes always seemed to be angry since Arnie died. Lottie didn't like looking into them any more. She actually felt she had lost Jenny as well as Arnie. Jenny banged a fist on the table, making Tom's matchbox cart topple over. 'Will you answer me, Lottie?'

Lottie shook her head. She stared at the ribbons of rain pouring down the window.

'Answer me. Have you been going up to Nan's place or haven't you?'

Silence.

'Yes or no?'

Lottie was aware of Jenny burning a path to her secret life. But she didn't feel like a vulnerable ten-year-old. Oh no. Lottie felt like a grown woman, a woman with rights to a life of her own.

'Yes,' she said, looking steadily at Jenny. Beside her, at the table, Tom twitched with anxiety.

'Yes? Is that all you have to say?'

Lottie just looked at her.

'How dare you disobey me?' Jenny was pumping herself up for one of her rages. Rages ten times worse since Arnie died.

Tom froze, looking at her beseechingly, a half-glued matchbox gripped in sticky, industrious fingers.

'I want an explanation, Lottie.'

Lottie thought carefully. Finally she said, 'I'm not going to stop visiting Nan. I have a right to a life of my own. And there's nothing more to say.' She picked up her wool and went on threading the pompom.

'You little MADAM.' Jenny raised her hand to slap Lottie, changed her mind and hit the table instead.

Lottie managed to keep still, trembling inside, her beautiful dark blue eyes inspecting Jenny's hidden soul. She longed for Arnie to come and make everything right. Her memory of him was vivid. The love in his eyes as he'd rescued her from the sea. His quiet voice explaining things to her. The way he calmed Jenny down and made her laugh. The way he'd sprawl in the middle of the sofa with a story book and the three children snuggled round him. The way he'd taught her to swim on Porthminster Beach. She missed him. It hurt, along the rims of her eyes and into her hair like a tight cord drawn around her head.

It wasn't Lottie who broke down, but Tom. 'You're not to hit Lottie, Mummy. It's not fair.' He swept the matchbox cart onto the floor, put his head down on the table and howled unashamedly. 'I want Daddy. Why did our Daddy die?' He looked up at Jenny, the question fathomless in his eyes.

Lottie stared at Matt who was sitting on the stairs, endlessly bouncing a ball he'd made from rubber bands he'd collected since he was five. She didn't want Matt to upset Jenny even more with one of his knife-edged remarks. Matt thought he owned the answer to Tom's question. He blamed Jenny for Arnie's death, and told her so at every opportunity.

Jenny went to the sofa, her face pale and desperate. She held out her arms. 'Come here, Tom – and you, Lottie.'

Lottie picked up the matchbox cart and arranged it considerately on the table. She put her arm round Tom and steered him to the sofa. He curled up between her and Jenny, his loud crying diminishing into sobs and sniffs.

'And you, Matt,' Jenny said hopefully.

Matt wavered, then hardened his stare, shoved the rubber ball into his pocket and stomped upstairs.

'We've got no money,' Jenny said in a low voice, her arms around Tom and Lottie. 'We've got to stick together, not fight.'

They clung together, letting the pain settle, listening to the rain, and the sound of Matt slamming around upstairs. He was dragging furniture across the floorboards and there was the sound of a bucket clanking. Then he came running down the stairs.

'The roof's leaking, Mummy. It's coming through the ceiling in your bedroom – in two places.' He grabbed a white enamel bowl from the kitchen and ran back up the stairs with it. They all followed him up and stared into Jenny's bedroom at the rainwater pouring in through a sagging hole in the ceiling.

On that night of relentless rain, Jenny bedded down on the sofa, sleeping in deep dreamless interludes and waking to the muted glow from the stove and the deafening roar of her worries. Several times in the night, she heard Matt get up to empty the rainwater from the bucket. She heard his bare feet struggling with the weight of it, then the battle with the broken window catch and the clank of the bucket. He was emptying the water down into the street, and she heard the slap of it landing, then the gleeful ring of drips leaking into an empty bucket. *Matt is being responsible for once,* she thought in surprise. In the morning she'd say thank you and give him a cuddle, if he'd let her. Matt had offered to run down to his grandad's cottage at first light and ask for help before Vic set out in his fishing boat. *Matt CAN be helpful,* Jenny thought. She pictured the leggy, resentful boy he had become, and winced with remembered hurt from the times he'd yelled, 'I hate you,' or 'It's YOUR fault Daddy died.'

Matt, and the leaking roof were just some of the problems stacking up in Jenny's life. Without Arnie she felt like half a family, the weakest half. Every day, every hour she was making terrible mistakes. Shouting at the children. Bursting into tears. Losing her temper. Making a mess of everything she tried to do. Extreme grief seemed like a demolition gang, knocking down a different bit of her every day, leaving her to find her way through the rising dust cloud. Nobody talked to her about Arnie. Even Millie seemed to be avoiding her. And Vic was too hollowed out by his own grief, and his need to pretend he was cheerfully coping.

Today she had come perilously close to slapping Lottie, something she and Arnie had pledged never to do. It had taken little Tom's open-hearted distress to bring Jenny home to her true self. At times she realised the three children were carrying her. Loving and accepting her as she stumbled blindly through the day, burning their meals, ignoring their cries, pushing them out to run wild in St Ives, not knowing or caring where they were or who they were with. Jenny had given up trying to ban Morwenna, sensing she and Lottie were close friends.

It was Vic who talked Matt through the business of selling *The Jenny Wren*. At seven o'clock the following morning in clean, forgiving sunshine, Vic was up on the roof, fixing the leak, and he took Matt up there with him. 'You can't use your Daddy's boat 'til you're fourteen, Matt,' Jenny heard him say. 'We can't leave the boat to rot – because it will rot. A friend of mine, Terry – you know Terry – he wants to buy it. He'll look after it – and when you're fourteen maybe we can buy it back for you.'

'But it's still not fair,' Matt said. 'Daddy wanted ME to have it – so I should have the money for it, shouldn't I?'

'Life isn't fair,' Vic told him, and Jenny could hear the crunch of slate tiles as he wedged them into place on the roof. 'You wouldn't walk round with a big bag of money while Tom and Lottie and your mum are starving, would you?'

'No,' said Matt, after a pause, and what he said next chilled Jenny to the bone. 'I'd share it with Tom but not with HER.'

'Who d'you mean? Lottie?'

'No – Mummy. It's her fault Daddy got drunk and drowned. She betrayed him.'

'No – no, lad – she didn't.'

'She DID,' insisted Matt. 'She made Daddy jealous 'cause she was dancing with Troy, and she knew he was jealous but she still did it. I hate her, Grandad. I hate her.' A fragment of masonry came whizzing down and crashed into the street. 'I wish that was HER head.'

'If you're going to throw stones, I won't have you up here helping me,' Vic said firmly, his voice quiet. 'You go down my ladder and pick up every single bit of that piece of tile, and bring it back up here, right now. No messing.'

Matt did climb down, with a very red face. He glanced guiltily at Jenny who was on the doorstep, picked up the fragments of tile and climbed the ladder with the same reckless, careless confidence as Arnie had always shown.

'Now you've gotta change your attitude...' Vic began, but Jenny couldn't bear to hear any more. She went inside, took Arnie's coat from the back of the scullery door and held it to her face. 'I loved you, Arnie – I adored you,' she wept, letting the tears soak into the oily, salty old fabric of the coat that felt like Arnie. She tasted the bitterness of being hated by Arnie's firstborn son. She'd wanted so much to be a mother, but it had been harder than she imagined. Harder – and now impossible. What would she do when the money from the boat ran out? By then it would be winter, and the children would need new shoes and warm coats. And decent meals.

Pull yourself together, Jen, she told herself, replacing Arnie's coat on the door. She stoked the fire and added some of the coal scavenged from the harbour beach. Once a week the coal ship came in from Swansea, laden with silvery black Welsh coal. As each sack was unloaded and carried up the granite steps to the horses and carts waiting on the pier, plenty of it got spilled, ending up on the sand against the harbour wall. Unbeknown to Jenny, the St Ives coalman had seen the Lanroska children gathering it into sacks and dragging it home with black hands and legs. He knew they were Arnie's children, so he was extra careless with the coal, 'accidentally' letting the sacks topple and drop some sizeable chunks.

On the following Tuesday when the children arrived home with bags of coal loaded into Arnie's driftwood cart, Jenny made sure she met them at the door. The two boys looked like chimney sweeps, their eyes sparkling from sooty faces. Only Lottie managed to keep reasonably clean but her hands and feet were black, and there were smudges on her pinny.

'You're not coming in here,' Jenny said, heartlessly but with a touch of humour. 'You go in the sea and get clean – go on – down Porthminster – and don't come back 'til you're clean.'

'But I'm hungry, Mummy.'

'And I'm tired.'

'I don't care,' Jenny fired back. 'You can't eat

with hands like that. You'll be eating more coal dust than bread. And while you're gone I'll be getting dinner ready.'

'What is it?'

'Star-gazy pie.'

'Again?'

'Yes – again, Tom. Pilchards are all we've got. Now will you GO and get clean, or do I have to chase you down the road with me rolling pin?' Jenny reached for the wooden rolling pin which was on the scullery table. Her eyes twinkled with a rare moment of fun and the three children ran off, giggling. Jenny sighed, her smile vanishing, the glint of humour misted over like an island in a storm. She wheeled the precarious cart through the cottage to the yard and tipped the scavenged coal into the outhouse. It was enough for about three fires. And then what? How would they live and keep warm through the winter when westerly gales buffeted the streets, when the hail stung your face and the salty wind burned your eyeballs. Endless days when the fishermen couldn't go out and there were no more pilchards, and no fuel to light the stove. No hot drinks and no cooked meals.

Her boys were tough and used to those dark winter days of blankets and candles. Jenny worried about Lottie. She wanted Lottie to be radiant, the way she'd looked when Arnie was alive, not thin and haunted as she looked now. *I could lose her,* Jenny thought, remembering how ill Lottie had been after the shipwreck.

'You all right, Jen?' The door opened and Millie came in with a tray of pasties and a fruit cake she had made. 'I thought you could use these up. I made too many.'

'Oh Millie.' Tears welled in Jenny's eyes. She suspected Millie had made them on purpose and was offering her a face-saving way of accepting them. 'Course I can. The children will love them – and CAKE! Will you stay and eat with us?' She gave Millie a hug. 'You've been such a good neighbour.'

Millie sat down at the table. She looked uneasy.

'Something's up?' Jenny said, concerned.

'Well … yes. I've got summat to tell you, Jen.' Millie's merry eyes looked doleful, and she was pulling a long cream-coloured thread from the bodice of her apron, winding it around a flour-ingrained finger. 'I feel bad – leaving you on your own, things being as they are, but I gotta go an' live in Penzance. Me sister's on her own like me and she's crippled with arthritis, she can't walk. I gotta look after her. I don't want to leave S'nives, but there you are, families come first, don't 'em?'

'Penzance! Such a long way. I'll miss you.' Jenny was shocked. She reached out and held Millie's hand. 'That's a bombshell. You've been like a mother to me, and the children.'

Millie nodded. She pulled the thread harder until it came out. 'It's only a train ride away. You can bring them down one day and we'll walk over to the Mount.' She spoke brightly but her eyes told a different story. A story of loneliness and poverty.

'That would be lovely,' Jen said, but they both knew it probably wouldn't happen. How could she ever afford the train fare for four of them?

181

'When are you going, Millie?'

Millie took a deep breath. 'Tomorrow.'

'Tomorrow.' Jenny was devastated.

A wounded silence trembled between them.

Millie's bust heaved with another deep breath. 'I want you to promise me something, Jen.'

'What's that?'

'You've gotta bury the hatchet with Nan, Jen. I know you don't like her – but you need her, and she needs you. Lottie's so happy up there – I went up to see Nan, to tell her I was leaving, and Lottie was there helping her pick the Victoria plums, and she looked so happy. She loves the animals and the garden, and did you know Nan is teaching her music?'

'No.' Jenny was tight-lipped.

'Nan wants to help you – if you let her – she grows all her own veg. Her garden's like a wonderland. Jen – you can't let yer silly pride ruin Lottie's life after what that child's been through.'

'I'll think about it.'

'Thinking about it's no good,' Millie said passionately. 'You gotta do it. Get over it. Put it behind you, Jen. You can't afford pride. I know I'm sticking me neck out, but I 'ope you'll take it from me, 'cause I love you like a daughter. A daughter I never had, Jen.'

Jenny's throat ached. Arnie's soulful eyes with their long lashes seemed to be close, looking into her heart, telling her Millie was right. So why, why was it so impossible?

'I will think about it, Millie,' she said, to keep the peace.

182

Alone in his spacious London apartment, John De Lumen took a last, appraising look at his painting, *Discovering Charlotte*. Since witnessing Arnie's funeral he had made subtle changes to the painting. The carefree child he'd seen on the sands at Porthmeor Beach must now be given a new depth and dimension. The sadness would be in her eyes, those dark blue, dreaming, knowing eyes. The innocent sparkle of them shone out from the ambience of the painting. The way the pale sands changed from white-gold to mirrors of silver reflecting the marbled clouds of a summer sky, and reflecting the bubbling fringe of each incoming wave. To John, the lines of surf were like a page of music, a blend of lullaby and power. Largo and fortissimo. As he painted, he found himself pausing to compose sea music on his Bechstein grand piano, his paint-stained fingers flying over the keys, his eyes searching Charlotte's eyes as she gazed out at him from the canvas.

The painting and the music were symbiotic, and never static, always flowing through John's solitary heart, and when the painting was finished it was like a bereavement. Not only was he letting go of his masterpiece, he was letting go of Charlotte. For now. What might happen as she blossomed into a young woman was a distant beacon of light on his horizon.

It was a large oil painting, three foot by two foot. Carefully, he laid it face down on the table, fitting it into the gold leaf Romanesque frame he had chosen. Each slender nail he hammered in brought a stab of nostalgia. His heart thumped with anticipation as he turned it over, propped it against the wall and stood back to see how it looked. The frame was perfect, complementing the blues of sea and sky and the rippling gold of the light on Charlotte's hair, the same ray of sunlight illuminating her small hand and the delicate seashells in her palm. He picked one up from the ceramic bowl on the windowsill, ran his thumb over it and pushed it into his leather wallet. For luck. His lucky shell. With him, always.

He gazed for a long time at his painting, walking past it, viewing it from every possible angle, imagining how it would feel to walk into a gallery and see it there. In beautiful italic script he wrote the label.

Discovering Charlotte
Oils
John De Lumen

In smaller print he added his London address, the date, and a note saying, *NOT FOR SALE*. Then he filled in the stout cardboard label for the Open Exhibition at the Mall Galleries, London. Taking a sheet from the airing cupboard, John wrapped the painting in it and tied it with bands of string. It was hidden. Gone from his sight.

Forgetting that he'd had no breakfast and no lunch, John set off carrying the painting under his arm to catch a bus and deliver it to the Submissions Room at the Mall Galleries. An awkward journey and an aching arm, but he was used to doing it. For years, he'd been submitting paintings to this major London gallery, but so far he hadn't had one accepted. With unquenchable optimism, he'd kept on doing it until disappointment hovered over his dreams. To be accepted would bring the coveted honour of being 'hung' for a month in this prestige gallery, with art critics, agents and wealthy art collectors viewing it. And this particular exhibition offered an unprecedented chance to have the painting exhibited in America.

Discovering Charlotte just had to get lucky.

Chapter 12

A Cornish Shovel

Nan's way of coping with the devastating grief was to rummage through the tool corner in the barn and find the Cornish shovel. Brushing the cobwebs from the handle, she reversed out with it, through a muddle of collapsing spades. A twinge of excitement ignited in her sad heart as she dug the blade of the shovel into the barn floor and held it at arm's length. *A monster,* she thought. *A monster of a shovel. It's taller than me.*

The day promised to be hot. Bees and flies were already buzzing around the pink marjoram flowers in Nan's garden and hundreds of butterflies flickered over the hedgerow flowers and the wild cliffs beyond. Nan's cats were in paradise, leaping and chasing the butterflies, bewildered by so many. Only Bartholomew abstained from the butterfly binge, trotting alongside Nan as she dragged the Cornish shovel across the paddock. Bartholomew was going to keep an eye on her. He settled on a dome of sea pinks which cushioned the top of the hedge, his attentive eyes sparkling in the morning sun.

Nan allowed herself one glance at the bay and the armada of Seine boats sailing out across the peacock-blue water. *ARNIE,* she thought, *always Arnie,* now a vivid memory flaring in her heart. It hurt too much to think about her handsome grandson who had died so tragically. Turning her back to the sea, Nan stood looking at a ten-foot high mountain of fresh soil and a pile of granite boulders. She'd had them delivered yesterday by two shire horses pulling a wagon. The driver, Tommy Tremain, had obediently unloaded it exactly where Nan wanted it but he had eyed Nan dubiously. 'And who is gonna build this Cornish hedge?' he asked. 'It's a skilled job – and a heavy one.'

'I'm doing it myself,' Nan said with a glint of defiance.

'Will you be wanting any help? If you can wait a week I'll come and show you how it's done.'

'No, thank you. I can't wait a week, and I know how to do it.' Nan gave him a piercing stare. 'You men don't have the monopoly on Cornish hedge building.'

She turned her back. Conversation closed. But Tommy Tremain frowned all the way down the lane. He sent the gossip bouncing through the town like a tennis ball. That mad old lady up at Hendravean thinks she can build a Cornish hedge. She could kill herself. At her age. Someone

186

ought to stop her. And anyway, women have got no business shovelling stone.

Nan had memorised the recipe for a Cornish hedge as if it was a cake. She'd watched her father build one many times, his pipe in his mouth, his keen eyes and calm voice giving a running commentary on what he was doing. 'Them lot up-country,' he would begin, 'they plant their hedges. Useless they are. Fresh air hedges. Wind goes straight through 'em. Now us Cornishmen, we build stone hedges. Last forever, they do. Wind don't go through 'em. The gorse and hawthorn grows on top, and the grass and wild flowers.'

Nan smiled to herself, remembering. Despite her confidence she found the two mounds of stone and earth daunting. But right now she needed an impossible project to bury her grief. *One stone at a time,* she thought, and found the courage to begin, picking up the first heavy lump of granite with her bare hands. It seemed permissible to groan with the effort since no one was there to listen except Bartholomew with his kind, bright face.

The section of hedge she was going to build was to fill a gap in the existing hedge around Mufty's paddock. It had once been a gateway and the two tall granite plinths still stood there with crystals twinkling in the sun. Nan was glad of the salty breeze from the sea cooling her hot face as she worked at laying the first two lines of stone. Before long, her hands were sore, her back ached and her heart chugged like an old engine, precariously, as if it might stop at any moment. Frankly Nan didn't care if it did. She drove herself on and with each intruding, bitter thought, she listened harder to the skylarks who sang high in the blue air, their wings beating ecstatically.

When the first two lines of stone were laid, Nan didn't pause but set about filling the gap with earth, staggering under the weight of the long handled shovel loaded with gritty soil. *Poor quality mining spoil,* Nan thought. Poor, but full of crystals. Smoky quartz and golden citrine. She picked them out and put them to one side, thinking Lottie would like them.

Too exhausted to walk back to the house for the drink she badly needed, Nan took a swig from her bottle of brandy. She leaned against the existing hedge, aware of its turfy scent and the scratchy grasses and seed pods prickling her skin through the worn cotton of her dress. A foxglove towered above her, its spotted bells burning pink against the sky. All was quiet and still. Yet her heart continued to race. She began to feel giddy and disoriented. She closed her eyes and there was a brief flash of Arnie's kind, eager face and a feeling of unresolved, unreachable, inevitable grief. She felt her body giving up, sliding to the ground, her mind cascading into sleep like water into a deep, dark pool.

It was Morwenna who found Nan. She'd gone up to Hendravean looking for Lottie. She crept through the house and found the chickens roosting contentedly on the stairs. Clapping her hands, Morwenna shooed them out into the amber sunlight of late afternoon. The house seemed empty but Morwenna was in awe of Nan and didn't

188

want to investigate further. It was Lottie she wanted. She had a slab of Nelson cake wrapped in greaseproof paper to share with her. She thought Lottie would like a picnic on the beach.

The yard and the barns were deserted, and Mufty was dozing in the cool of his stable. The paddock gate was open so Morwenna made her way over the cropped turf towards a heap of stones and earth, thinking Lottie might be up there working with Nan.

The grass was covered in loose soil with footprints in it. An enormous shovel was propped against the pile of stone. A flock of sparrows were all over the hedge and it was so quiet that the burr of their wings startled Morwenna as they flew up. She walked along the hedge towards the sea. Then she froze in horror. Slumped on the ground against the hedge was Nan's huge body in the mottled blue and white dress, her legs splayed, her eyes closed. She was covered in mud. It was over her legs, her arms and her face. Her mouth was open and flies were buzzing around her.

Convinced that Nan was dead, Morwenna ran screaming down the paddock. Bartholomew tore after her, his fluffy tail kinked, his ears flat. The chickens scattered in all directions as Morwenna fled through the yard and disappeared down Foxglove Lane screaming hysterically.

'What the heck is up with her?'

Jenny and Lottie were folding sheets in the street when Morwenna ran screaming towards them, her bushy hair flying, her mouth open.

'Don't drop the sheet,' Jenny said sharply to

189

Lottie. 'Finish folding it with me. She can wait.'

Lottie completed the last two folds of the heavy linen which was dry and cardboardy from the sun. She hung it over Jenny's arms and went to Morwenna who was bent double and gasping from the exertion. 'What a disgraceful fuss,' Jenny snorted.

Lottie was used to Morwenna's dramas. She put her arm round her friend's back. 'You're boiling hot. What's the matter?' she asked kindly, leaning close to look into Morwenna's wild, frightened eyes.

For a moment Morwenna couldn't speak. She was trembling and out of breath. 'I went ... up to...'

Jenny stood over the two girls frowning, her hands smoothing the folded sheet. 'Up to where?'

'To ... to Nan's place. I were looking for Lottie.' Morwenna sniffed noisily and Lottie unpegged a hanky from the line and gave it to her. 'I went up through the donkey paddock, and ... and...'

'You've no business up there, my girl,' said Jenny disapprovingly.

Morwenna glared right back at Jenny. 'And you got no business telling me where I can and can't go.'

Sensing a cat fight brewing, Lottie took Morwenna's hot, damp hands and held them firmly. 'Calm down, Morwenna, please, or you'll get a headache. Tell me what's wrong. What happened in the paddock?'

'I saw your nan, lying down on the ground. She looked 'orrible, all covered in mud. And ... and I think she's dead.'

'Dead!' Jenny and Lottie looked at each other, horrified. The shockwave hit Lottie hard. A huge piece of her world shattered onto the cobbles. Crashed and went tumbling down, out of control, towards the harbour, towards the place where Arnie had died.

'Oh, I'm sure that's not true, Morwenna,' Jenny said sensibly. 'You've made Lottie cry now.'

'I'm going up there,' Lottie said, shaking the tears away. 'I love Nan and she's kind to me, but she gets herself into trouble. She's reckless for an old lady.'

'Reckless she certainly is,' Jenny said. 'It seems to be a Lanroska trait, recklessness. Don't you cry, Lottie.'

'I'm not crying until I know the truth. I shall go up there, now. Morwenna will help you with the washing.'

'Oh no you don't.' Jenny caught hold of Lottie's arm. 'Not on your own, Lottie. We can leave the washing. I'll come with you and Morwenna had better come too. All right?'

Morwenna nodded. 'I got a slab of Nelson cake for Lottie.' She patted the pocket of her grubby apron. 'Me and Mum made it s'morning. It's yummy.'

'Thank you. Leave it in the kitchen. We'd better go and see what Nan has been up to.' Jenny put the folded sheet indoors on the table, her face set hard and her speech high-pitched and flustered. 'The boys are down the harbour getting coal. They know what to do when they get back. But if those little spriggans put that coal anywhere near the washing there'll be trouble.' She sighed.

'Trouble, trouble, trouble.'

Morwenna looked at her wisely. 'You need a pint of Guinness. That's what my mum has when she's upset.'

The three of them set off to walk to Nan's place. The worry was not whether they were fit enough to get there but whether the shoes on their feet would last the walk. Morwenna had a clumping pair of boots handed down from her brother and two sizes too big, the toes stuffed with newspaper. The leather sole was peeling off from the left boot and catching on the cobbled road. Lottie still had her slim Flora Day shoes, scuffed and worn, one with a broken buckle tied with string. Jenny's one and only pair of boots were nine years old, the soles now so thin she felt every pebble through them.

The sun was low over the Clodgy rocks, making a massive twinkling blaze on the water, and the sky was alive with the wide, sickle-shaped wings of gannets wheeling and diving for fish.

'Vic is out there somewhere,' Jenny said as they hurried along Porthmeor Road. 'I wish we could get a message to him, but we can't.' As they passed the gas works, she and Lottie glanced up at the hillside cemetery beyond, both thinking of Arnie. Lottie, who had been leading the way, waited and slipped her hand into Jenny's hand in silent empathy. They didn't go to Arnie's grave too often. 'He's not there,' Jenny often said with conviction. It sounded final but left an un-answered question flying in the wind.

Soon they were in the lane leading to Hen-dravean and the pinks of foxglove and campion burned down at them from the tops of hedges. The scent of meadowsweet and honeysuckle filled the air. To Lottie, Foxglove Lane was a magic tunnel to another world, the world of Nan's garden, away from the smell of fish and tar, a world of fruit and flowers and friendly animals. And Nan.

'Right, where was she, Morwenna?' Jen asked in a business-like tone.

'Up there.' Morwenna looked pale and frightened.

Jenny held Lottie back. 'You stay with me. I don't want you finding Nan on your own.'

The three of them trod cautiously over the silent turf towards the two piles of earth and stone. Morwenna's eyes rounded with fright. 'She's GONE,' she whispered.

'Well, she can't be dead then, can she?' Jenny snapped. 'You dragged us up here for nothing.'

As she spoke there was a crunching noise from behind the earth pile, followed by an unearthly groan, and an arc of soil flew through the air, the crystal clods glistening in the sunlight. Another crunch, another groan, and another arc of soil peppering down.

'I don't like it. Gives me the creeps.' Morwenna clutched Lottie who found her friend's fear infectious. The two girls held on to each other as Jenny marched round the earth pile. They heard the clang of a shovel being dropped. Then a moment of explosive silence.

'What the dickens are you doing here?' Nan's voice cleared the sparrows out of the hedge in a manically cheeping flock. Her eyes blazed out of the mud.

Jenny made herself six inches taller. 'For your information, we came up to see if you were all right. Is that a crime? Is it? Go on, tell me off for caring. I left me washing hanging in the street 'cause of you – and left the boys on their own when they're down the harbour scavenging coal.'

'And why shouldn't I be all right?'

'Morwenna thought you were dead. She saw you lying on the ground.'

Nan tossed Morwenna a look of scorn. 'Silly girl. And how dare you come up here and stare at me with those cow-eyes when I was asleep.'

Morwenna crumpled. She leaned against Lottie trembling and sniffing.

'Nan!' Lottie cried. 'Nan, stop it. Morwenna's my friend.' Lottie's clear little voice was lost in the almighty slanging match between Nan and Jenny.

'Look at the state of you, Nan,' Jenny yelled. 'Covered in mud. And you shouldn't be using a whopping great shovel like that, at your age. D'you want to have a heart attack?'

Nan picked up the shovel and rammed the blade into the ground. She leaned on it like a Viking warrior, the dried mud cracking on her cheeks as she bellowed at Jenny. 'Who cares if I have a heart attack?'

'I would. That's why I came up here when I should be home getting the boys' tea. What the heck are you doing anyway?'

'Building a Cornish hedge.'

'That's a man's job, Nan. You're crazy.'

'Why should it be a man's job? My old father taught me how to build a Cornish hedge. It's a precious skill – an old country skill – but you wouldn't know about that, would you? All you want to do is put on a silly dress and go dancing with some idiot in a top hat. And look where THAT got you.' The bitterness gathered like a cloud of stone dust between them, both of them inhaling its mind-crippling fog.

'Don't you accuse me like that.' Jenny moved closer to Nan, her cheeks burning. She had never felt so consumed by hatred. And yet, somewhere in the innermost pearl of her heart, a voice whispered reproach. Nan was an old lady. With a broken heart. Nan was Arnie's granny. But the words of pain and hatred ganged up in Jenny's throat. 'It's not my fault Arnie got drunk and fell in the harbour. I'm a good person and I work hard and I love my children – which is more than you do. You've been nasty to my boys, and to me – nasty. For years. Years and years I've put up with it. MY granny wasn't like you. She was kind and gentle. You're just a BULLY. That's what you are...'

'Get off my property, you conniving little hussy.' Nan lifted the shovel and brandished it at Jenny. Go on. GO. Leave me alone.'

'And you've been drinking. I can smell it.'

'Medicinal brandy.'

'Huh!' Jenny pointed to the empty brandy bottle lying in the mud. 'Look at the size of the bottle. I don't call that medicinal, you boozy old bag.'

'Will you GO AWAY. I don't want you here.'

Jenny stood her ground. 'No. I'm not going, Nan.'

'Yes, YOU ARE.' Nan raised the shovel and stuck it in the ground perilously close to Jenny's foot.

Lottie and Morwenna watched the confrontation in horror. Lottie felt her world collapsing. Arnie was dead, and the two people she loved were screaming at each other and Lottie was afraid for both of them. She didn't understand why Jenny was so angry with Nan for building a Cornish hedge. It was the kind of thing Nan enjoyed doing. Why did Nan hate Jenny so much? Lottie felt bewildered and powerless. And lonely.

'Your nan's crazy,' Morwenna whispered, her eyes rounded. 'She might kill your mum with that shovel.'

'She's not crazy.' The loneliness sharpened as Lottie now felt angry with Morwenna for her tactless choice of words.

'She is, Lottie. My mum says she ought to be locked up.'

Lottie clenched her hands. She swallowed the white-hot words jostling in her throat. She wanted to give Morwenna a mighty shove with both hands and send her spinning onto the stony turf. She closed her eyes for a moment and let the unbearable feeling thunder over her until it was gone, as if she was lying on a railway track waiting for a train to pass over her with its iron wheels.

'Kindly refrain from insulting my grandmother,' Lottie said, sensing her friend was about to say something even more hurtful. Bewildered by Lottie's vocabulary, Morwenna covered her mouth with her hand, her suntanned fingers with

196

their bitten-down nails digging into her cheek.

The row between Nan and Jenny was reaching new heights, each word a shard of broken glass from bottled-up rage. Even the seagulls seemed to be joining in, screeching at full throttle as they swooped and dived over Hendravean. Lottie was so upset that the words blurred. She was no longer hearing them. The air rang with pain as the two embattled women faced each other, their faces ugly with unsustainable fury.

Lottie was tempted to quietly step between them and appeal for calm but her natural sense of danger prevailed. She felt vulnerable, even with Morwenna beside her. *I don't belong here,* she thought. *Maybe I should run away?* Her eyes were drawn to the sparkling sea, the promise of peace far away in the bright blue of its afternoon horizon. Cormorants gathered on the rocks, their necks stretched out adoringly to the sun. Out in the bay, a cargo ship was steaming into Hayle while another one was steaming out into the diamond brightness.

Lottie hadn't thought about her mother so much recently but she did now, disturbed to find the image less vivid, the details of her face misty. Time was stealing the memory from her. What remained was the perfume her mother had used and the way it drifted through her clothes and hair. The flash of a magical smile, a smile that said everything would be all right in the morning. A smile that lied.

Morwenna pulled at her sleeve. 'We should go home,' she said kindly. 'Come on. Leave 'em to it. I got a slab of Nelson cake to share with you.'

Both girls were hungry and thirsty and the prospect of sinking their teeth into a slice of cool, moist, fruity cake was comforting. They grinned at each other, and ran away across the paddock and into Foxglove Lane, leaving Nan and Jenny's argument to echo over the cliffs without an audience.

They ran all the way to Downlong and burst into the cottage, starving hungry. They were greeted by Matt and Tom, grimy with coal dust but with toothy grins as they cleared the last crumbs of the Nelson cake from its greaseproof paper.

Morwenna picked Matt up by the scruff and hurled him against the china cabinet. 'You greedy pig, Matt Lanroska. That were for me and Lottie.'

The china cabinet jingled and the mantelpiece clock chimed when it wasn't supposed to. Shaken at being pushed over by a girl, Matt disguised his shock with an insolent grin. 'Shouldn't have left it on the table then, should you.'

Morwenna towered over him like a bird of prey, her feathers rumpled, her black eyes spangled with fury. Enjoying himself now, Matt reached out and lifted her skirt revealing her stout white legs. 'Let go,' she screeched, but Matt held on to the handful of skirt.

'I can see your knickers,' he taunted, singing the words like an insulting chant, 'Mad Morwenna Bartle.'

Chapter 13

Burning the Chairs

'I'm sorry, Lottie, but you can't go to school today.'

'But I need to go.' Lottie stood by the sofa, looking in despair at Jenny's ashen face and the uncanny brightness of her eyes. A year and nine long months had passed since Arnie's death, and the family were struggling to survive without him.

Jenny tried to speak, then gave in to the hollow, barking cough that shook her thin body lying on the sofa. She coughed, then cried with the pain. Lottie waited, smoothing her grammar school blazer and listening to the insistent tick of the mantelpiece clock. 'I'll be late,' she said, but Jenny looked at her with haunted eyes as another bout of coughing came from upstairs where Tom was lying in bed with a fever.

'Someone's gotta look after Tom,' Jenny croaked, 'and do the washing and keep the stove burning. I can't get up, Lottie, please understand that.'

In September, Lottie had started at the grammar school. She'd worked hard to pass the entrance exam, and Jenny was proud of her. Nan paid for her uniform and Lottie wore it with pride. The school was perfect for her and she

199

loved it, loved everything about it. The quiet, inspiring assemblies, the sense of hope and purpose, the chance to learn with other children who, like her, had dreams and ambitions that could lift them and their families out of the endemic poverty trap.

'I need to go,' she repeated, 'or I won't get my homework for the weekend. And today we've got Mr Jenkins for music and it's my favourite lesson.' Lottie tapped the recorder sticking out of her leather satchel. She glanced at the clock. It seemed impossible to explain to Jenny why she needed to go to school regularly. The education it offered was intensive and it moved on, every day, with or without Lottie. Missing even one day meant she would struggle to catch up. Missing two days meant she might never catch up.

'Grow up, Lottie,' Jenny growled. 'Look at me. I'm too ill to get up. You're nearly twelve now, and education is all very well but family comes first, my girl.' She reached up and tweaked the corner of Lottie's blazer. 'Go and take this off and put your work clothes on.'

'I want to go to school.'

'Stop being so selfish.' Jenny coughed again, holding her side. Then she cried out in distress. 'Tom could DIE, Lottie. Can't you see that? I can't take any more, not one more thing going wrong. Listen to me, will you? Tom could die, and … and so could…' she stopped abruptly. The clock struck eight o'clock.

It was obvious to Lottie what Jenny had been about to say. Reluctantly she headed upstairs and changed. She peeped at Tom and touched his brow in a gesture of concern. His skin felt clammy and his eyes were only half open. 'Am I ill, Lottie?' he mumbled.

'Yes, you are.'

'Am I gonna die?'

'No. Course you're not.' Lottie made her voice sound confident and cheerful. 'You'll soon be better.'

'My bed's wet. Matt will be angry with me. He'll fight me.'

Lottie pulled the covers back. 'It's all right, Tom. You haven't wet the bed. It's because you've been sweating. And I won't let Matt fight you when you're ill.'

Tom looked at her sleepily. 'Where's Mum?'

'Lying on the sofa. She's ill, like you, but you'll both get better.'

Tom's eyes rolled upwards, alarmingly, and he made a whimpering noise like a puppy. Lottie lifted his arm. It was limp. She didn't know what to do.

'I want Daddy,' Tom muttered.

'I know you do. So do I, Tom, but we can't bring him back.' Lottie peeled Tom's damp pyjamas off over his head and patted him dry with a towel. The boys only had one pair of pyjamas each, and it was raining. Washing clothes was out of the question. Lottie went into Jenny's bedroom and opened the rickety door to the dark oak wardrobe. She gulped, seeing Arnie's clothes still hanging there. A pair of his pyjamas, neatly folded, was on the top shelf. Miles too big for Tom, of course, but Lottie took the jacket down and pressed it to her face. The faded red and

201

white fabric had been nicely laundered and put away by Jenny. It was nearly two years since Arnie's death, but Lottie felt the sting of tears in her eyes. The fabric still felt as if Arnie was inside it. She thought maybe that idea would comfort Tom so she unfolded it, sat Tom up and put it on him, rolling the sleeves up. 'This is what your daddy used to wear, Tom, and it still feels like him.'

It worked. Tom snuggled into the clean, dry fabric, sliding down until even his head was engulfed. He went instantly to sleep with the edge of a smile curling his lips. Satisfied, Lottie kissed his damp cheek and went downstairs.

'What took you so long?' Jenny complained.

'I was looking after Tom. His pyjamas were soaking wet. I've put Arnie's jacket on him, the red and white striped one out of the wardrobe.'

'You shouldn't have done that,' Jenny groaned. 'I was keeping that nice. Now I'll have to wash it and iron it all over again.'

'But Tom needed it. I told him it was Arnie's and he settled down and went to sleep in it.'

'You've no business poking about in my wardrobe,' Jenny said crossly, and another bout of coughing shook her from head to toe.

'I was helping Tom.'

'Interfering, that's what you were doing.' Jenny's eyes looked agitated. 'And look at the stove! The fire's nearly out. You MUST keep it burning this time of year.'

Lottie went out in the rain and picked her way across the yard to the wood shed. It was February and the town was filled with the roar of the winter surf. Storms howled through the streets, driving hail and sand into corners and breathing out great banks of rolling sea fog. The wind chilled everything it touched, blasting through fabric, seeping through cracks in the stone walls, tearing at doors and windows. Lottie fought her way back into the cottage, empty-handed. 'There's no wood left,' she told Jenny, 'and no coal either – only what's left in the scuttle.'

'What d'you mean, there's NO WOOD?'

'There's no wood. We've used it all.'

'Oh no.' Jenny looked panic-stricken. 'Why haven't you children been out collecting it?'

'Tom is ill, and Matt and I have been in school. It's dark when we come home.'

'You are a MADAM.'

'That's not fair!' Lottie felt resentful. Every time she tried to speak calmly and reasonably, Jenny accused her of being a 'Madam'. It hurt. Her eyes welled with tears. 'Don't you love me any more, Jenny?'

'Aw, Lottie – course I do.' Jenny looked horrified. She held out her arms. 'Come here.'

The warmth and silence of sharing a hug was reassuring to both of them, like finding an island in a storm. An island with an inn where a log fire burned brightly, and soup bowls steamed, and there was laughter.

'I'm sorry, Lottie,' Jenny crooned. 'I'm an old cross-patch now – I feel proper poorly and weak. And ... and ... desperate.'

Lottie nodded. They looked into each other's eyes, trying to rediscover the bond of love. It was in there somewhere, a distant spark like a ship on a vast horizon out in the winter fog.

The stove sighed as the last cinder of burned coal collapsed into the ash bed. A handful of hail stones hit the window.

'You can't go out wooding in this,' Jenny said, 'and we need heat – we need to cook – and everything will get damp and mildewed if the fire goes out.' Her eyes searched the room and focused on a rickety chair. 'No one sits on that chair, Lottie. Break its legs off and we'll burn it.'

'What?' Lottie was shocked at the thought of burning a chair. What else would Jenny burn? 'I can't do that.'

'Yes, you can. Bring it over here and I'll do it.'

Lottie carried the chair, nervously, and put it by the sofa. 'It's not the first time I've burned a chair.' Jenny sat up on the sofa and turned the chair on its side. 'Chairs like this – you can pull 'em apart. Look! It's got no nails.'

Together they pulled the chair apart and suddenly they were giggling, despite the serious situation. 'If I had the breath I'd be singing *Trelawny*,' Jenny said. 'Let's burn the chairs and survive.'

For two miserable weeks, Lottie missed school to look after Jenny and Tom, and then Matt. She washed the heavy bed linen on her own, with Jenny barking instructions from the sofa. Then she carried a chair into the street and stood on it, precariously, to hang the sheets on the line in the pale winter sun. It took all the morning and her arms and back ached with the effort. Then she made pastry for the pasties and chopped up a very tough turnip and some onions, carrots and potatoes. There was no meat to put in, and no money to buy any, but Jenny had taught her how to spice up the vegetables with herbs and pepper. Stoking the fire to get the oven just right, getting her hands black and having to wash them under the street tap in the cold winter air, then go back to making the pasties seemed impossible to Lottie. She cried over it and learned to ignore the tears running down her face and just get on with it. She made eight pasties and carried the heavy metal tray to the oven, putting it on the floor while she struggled to open the door.

'You've got the oven too hot,' Jenny warned, as Lottie jumped back from the blast of dry heat hitting her face. It stung her eyes and the back of her throat. She heaved the tray of pasties inside and shut the door. 'We'll have burnt pastry and half-raw vegetables.'

Lottie looked at her miserably.

'You're a good girl,' Jenny said, and the kindness in her voice made Lottie crumple and give in to the looming deluge of tears. 'It's not easy, Lottie, I know.' Jenny stroked Lottie's blonde hair, and stroked her sore hands. 'You're shaking. It's all right, dear. We'll get through this. You're getting a taste of what my life is like – only I've had lots of practice.'

'I'm NEVER going to get married,' Lottie wept, 'if this is what women have to do.'

'Oh, you'll change your mind, Lottie – when you meet a handsome man like my Arnie.'

Lottie shook her head. 'My mind is made up. And there's not another man like Arnie in the whole wide world.'

'That's true.' Jenny closed her eyes. 'I need to sleep. I think I've got a fever, Lottie.'

'I should call the doctor.'

Jenny's eyes flew open.. 'No. We can't afford the doctor. You can look after me, Lottie.' She sat up. 'Take me to the toilet please.'

The toilet was outside, across the yard. 'My legs feel funny,' Jenny said. 'Help me get up.'

'Poor Jenny.' Lottie was filled with compassion and anxiety. Lovely, dancing Jenny. It was hard to see her so ill. She held out her hands, unprepared for the shock that was to come.

Jenny leaned forward, struggling to get up. Her legs buckled and she fell like a rag doll toppling from a shelf. 'My legs!' she cried. 'I can't feel them. Oh, no – no, I can't be paralysed, Lottie – not ME. What's wrong with me? What's wrong? And why has God got it in for me?'

Lottie knelt beside her, terrified, not knowing what to do.

'Touch my feet,' Jenny moaned.

Lottie did as she asked. Jenny's feet in her warm winter stockings had a strange new floppy feel to them.

'Go on – touch my feet.'

'I am.'

'I can't feel it.'

They stared at each other and shockwaves glided through the cottage. 'What am I gonna do?' Jenny whispered. 'Oh, Lottie...' She reached out and squeezed Lottie's arm. 'Don't look so frightened. I'm sorry – I panicked. I expect I'm just weak from the fever.'

'Try to get back on the sofa,' Lottie said, but

Jenny couldn't.

'The boys will be back from school – they need their mum – I can't let them find me like this, lying on the floor.'

Lottie looked at her in alarm. What if Jenny had polio? Lottie had heard of polio. A girl at school had died from it, and rumours had spread that the doctor had not been called in time. Lottie touched Jenny's brow. It was clammy. She observed the laboured breathing and made a decision. 'We can't afford the doctor,' Jenny had kept insisting, but Lottie was going to ask him anyway. She put on the warm winter coat Nan had given her, tucked her long blonde hair inside and turned the collar up. Leaving Jenny lying on the floor, she slipped out and ran through the winter air to the doctor's house in The Stennack, arriving out of breath and flushed.

'Hello, Lottie – what brings you here on such a cold day?' The doctor's wife looked down at Lottie from the grand porch. It had green and white tiles, highly polished, and gloomy plants with fleshy leaves hung from shelves. A black and tan dog with short legs and a gleaming coat growled and barked at Lottie. 'You stop that.' Mrs Tregullow picked up the dog and held it like a baby close to her ample bosom.

'Is that a sausage dog?' Lottie asked.

'Some call it a sausage dog. She's roly poly enough!' Mrs Tregullow patted the dog's plump belly. She looked at Lottie with caring, quizzical eyes. 'You look upset, dear. What's the matter?'

'Jenny's very ill. She's got a fever and she can't feel her legs,' Lottie said, standing very straight and willing herself not to cry, 'and we haven't got any money to pay the doctor – but, please, will he come because Jenny might die and then we'll be orphans.'

'Oh dear.' Mrs Tregullow seemed lost for words. 'Haven't you got anything you can sell? There's a good little pawn shop in S'nives.'

'No,' Lottie said firmly, but her mind flew to the black velvet bag, still hidden in Nan's cubby hole. Momentarily, she imagined herself selling its precious secret, walking home with the cash in her pocket. Then she saw the money vanishing like water down a drain, flashing silver as it sped past, spent on food and coal, and when it was gone, nothing changed. 'We've got nothing left,' she added, 'and we can't keep warm. We burned some of the chairs.'

The doctor's wife looked at Lottie with well-guarded compassion. 'You'd better come in, dear. Doctor is having his after-lunch coffee with a dash of whisky.'

Lottie followed her through the hall which was full of model ships in glass cases. Dr Tregullow was stretched out in a chair and she could smell his socks roasting by the hearth. His shoes were propped against a brass fender in front of an open fireplace piled high with glowing coals and spurting flames. The heat felt heavenly to Lottie.

'Come and have a warm.' The doctor looked at her kindly. 'Warm your hands, little one.'

'I'm nearly twelve now,' Lottie reminded him, and suddenly she couldn't speak. The warm, bright fire filled her with longing. She spread her sore, cold fingers and let the heat soak into her.

If only she could bring Jenny here. But she couldn't. It wasn't fair. It wasn't.

The Red Cross ambulance nosed its way through the cobbled alleyways of Downlong, its engine grinding and spitting out puffs of acrid smoke. Harassed women, their wrists red-raw from the wind and the washing soda, scurried to haul their lines of washing out of the way. Maudie Tripconey followed the ambulance without appearing to do so, her stout body engulfed in a trench coat, her eyes gleaming with curiosity as they peered from the folds of a thick maroon red scarf.

The ambulance came to a halt outside the Lanroskas' cottage. Maudie parked herself against a wall, out of the wind, a wisp of guilt drifting through her heart as she watched Jenny being carried out on a stretcher. They had covered her with a scarlet blanket and the colour was alarming, like a scream in the night. Maudie wondered why she should feel an unexpected rush of concern for a woman she had never liked. Jenny looked oddly dignified, asleep with her pretty face turned towards the sea.

Who's gonna look after those children? Maudie thought, and a little voice nagged in her heart. *It's time you did something to help, Maudie,* hotly followed by another, harder thought, *but not that older boy, Matt. He's evil. Those boys are always fighting, always filthy dirty. But Lottie – she's a lovely little girl.*

The slam of the ambulance doors, the ringing of its bell, and the way its protesting engine sent a shudder through the terrace of granite cottages was frightening to a quiet Cornish community. Maudie glanced at the serious faces of neighbours standing in their doorways or watching from windows. She made it her business to walk up to the Lanroskas' cottage and confront the doctor's wife who stood in the street, her arms around the three children. Maudie glanced disdainfully at grubby, snivelling Tom, swept over Matt's hostile stare, and smiled at Lottie who was trying to comfort Tom.

They all listened to the ambulance bell getting fainter and fainter as it headed along Wharf Road and up the long hill out of St Ives.

'Who's gonna take care of these children now?' Maudie asked.

The doctor's wife gave her an altruistic stare. 'They're coming home with me for now.'

'They've got no one,' Maudie reminded her. 'Their grandad, Vic – he's gone off – down Newlyn, he's gone. Couldn't bear staying here after he lost his son. And that old woman – Nan Lanroska – she's their great grandmother, and she's crazy.'

'As I said, Maudie, the children are coming with me for now.'

'Well, as far as I'm concerned, they're orphans – and something should be done about it.'

A plan hatched in Maudie's mind as she walked home. She'd heard the whispers. Jenny had lost the use of her legs. It had to be polio. Even if she did recover, it meant months, even years of being in hospital. Maudie knew the doctor's wife didn't want children, especially not a raggedy bunch like the Lanroskas.

Maudie walked faster and faster through the winter light. In her hall at home was a telephone. It had been installed six weeks ago, and Maudie was proud of it. She kept it dusted and polished, but she hadn't dared use it yet.

Inside she took off her trench coat and scarf, and hovered over the intimidating telephone, her heart thumping as she lifted the receiver.

'Nan would look after us,' Lottie said desperately.

The doctor's wife shook her head. 'Oh, I don't think so, dear. She's not fit enough to cope with three lively children.'

'I could live with Grandad,' Matt boasted.

'And where does he live?'

'Down Newlyn.'

'In a house?'

'No. He lives in a beach hut.'

'Then he can't look after you, can he?'

Matt shrugged. 'I don't see why not.'

The three children were huddled in the corner of the doctor's brown leather sofa. Mrs Tregullow had given them a meal of shepherd's pie and a mound of soft white cauliflower followed by apple dumplings and custard. They'd eaten every scrap, and the hot food had calmed them. Tom had eaten his too fast and he was burping and still crying as he leaned against Lottie. 'What's wrong with our mummy?' he kept asking.

'We think she's got polio,' Mrs Tregullow explained, again. 'She'll be well looked after in Truro City Hospital, but it will take a long time to make her better.'

211

'I want to see her,' Tom pleaded.

'You can't, dear. Not yet. When she's a bit better, you can go.'

'But I don't know where Truro is,' Tom said tearfully.

'I do.' Lottie held him close, finding the warmth of him comforting. 'I can take you when we're allowed to go.'

'There you are. You've got a lovely big sister, Tom,' Mrs Tregullow wagged a finger, 'and whatever happens, you three children must stick together. Look after each other. You remember that.' She got up to answer the doorbell.

Then everything happened so quickly. One minute they were huddled on the brown sofa, and the next they were being marched outside by two hefty policemen.

'But we haven't done anything wrong!' protested Lottie.

The policeman looked at her kindly, and he had long eyelashes, like Arnie. 'I know you haven't. We're just going to take you to a nice home where you can live until your mummy's better.'

'But we want to stay here,' Lottie said. 'I hope it's not an orphanage, because if it is, I won't go.'

Matt looked at Lottie with fire in his eyes. 'RUN,' he cried, and darted towards the door. The two policemen acted swiftly, one grabbing Matt and the other Tom. Matt howled and kicked. He struggled wildly but the policeman skilfully pinned his arms behind his back and handcuffed him. 'Sorry we've got to do this, lad, but if you won't come quietly, that's what happens.' He picked Matt up and carried him to the black police car parked outside. 'Don't you want a ride in our limo?'

Tom threw himself on the floor. 'Don't take my brother away!'

'We won't. We're taking all three of you. Now – do I have to handcuff you, young man? Or will you come quietly?'

Tom trembled from head to toe. He managed to stand up. 'I'll come quietly – but only if Lottie's coming.' He looked up at Lottie with tormented eyes.

'RUN, LOTTIE,' Matt yelled from inside the car.

'You remember what I said, Lottie.' Mrs Tregullow looked into Lottie's eyes. 'Stick together.'

Lottie felt torn. She watched Tom being bundled into the back seat of the police car, looking back at her appealingly. She thought of Nan. She thought of her long-ago mother. She felt responsible for the two boys, her brothers.

She stood on the doorstep, feeling desolate, feeling her life being wrenched and twisted with every scream of every seagull that dived over the streets of St Ives.

'I hope you're going to be sensible, young lady.' The policeman touched her gingerly, the brass button on his cuff catching in a tendril of her flowing honey-gold hair.

Lottie drew herself up taller. 'Don't you dare touch me,' she snapped, twisting out of reach. 'I shall walk to the car on my own.'

The two policemen jumped back and escorted her at a respectful distance, one leaning forward to open the passenger door. Lottie squeezed in, next to Tom. She sat up very straight and swung her legs in gracefully. 'You may shut the door,' she said to the policeman. She wondered why his eyes twinkled under those long lashes, since it was not an occasion for twinkles of amusement.

The car pulled away, lurching through Downlong, then purring along Wharf Road and heading out of St Ives. No one spoke. Lottie could feel Matt's fury and humiliation, she could feel Tom's anxiety, and she turned her head away from them, pressing her face to the window as the car climbed the hill, past the station and on towards Carbis Bay. The sea sparkled like never before, as if every single sparkle was waving goodbye. Would she ever see St Ives again? Would she see the sun and the moon shining across the bay, making a path of light? Would she ever see Nan again and hear her stories? As they drew near to Carrack Gladden, Lottie remembered the legend of the maiden's tears. She imagined the tears dripping through the rocks, for now they would be her own tears falling from a new and paralysing grief.

For the second time in her young life, Lottie had lost everything; everything and everyone she had grown to love.

Chapter 14

Separation

The police car bumped and rattled along the rough road out of St Ives, the sun setting behind them, a ball of fire in a wintery sky, its fading light dusting the estuary sands of Hayle. Vast flocks of birds flew in swerving patterns, their bellies lit like grains of wheat in the low sunlight. The policeman in the passenger seat turned and tried to smile kindly. 'My name is P.C. Roach,' he said, 'and you can talk to me if you want. I know it's a tough time for you.'

Nobody smiled back.

'Can I open the window please?' Lottie asked.

'Want some fresh air, do you? Turn the handle – go on, push it hard.'

Lottie struggled with the bright chrome handle and managed to wind the thick glass window down just enough for her to hear the haunting cry of the curlews and oyster catchers, and the majestic siren of a steamship out in the bay waiting for the tide. Thoughts of escape fluttered through her mind. She touched the door handle, waiting for the car to stop at a junction and she glanced at Matt who was curled up in a ball. His eyes gazed back at her and, oddly, it was the longest, most meaningful look that had ever passed between them. A sudden, overwhelming gift of friendship. Matt had never been her friend. But now he was, in this time of shared tragedy and powerlessness. A true friend, like Arnie reborn.

'The doors are locked,' said P.C. Roach, 'so don't even think about trying to get out.'

Lottie and Matt looked at each other, and at the ship out in the bay. Matt had never asked Lottie how she had managed to stow away on a cargo ship and now Lottie wished she had told him. Jenny had forbidden the boys to ask her about the shipwreck and about her old life, but there had been many times when Lottie could have explained it all to Matt. Words just didn't get through the dense layer of resentment he wore around him. Talking to him now, with the policemen listening, wasn't an option.

The views of Hayle Bay were soon gone, like the sunset, as if the light of the world was left behind in St Ives. Now they were winding between gorse-covered hills and Cornish hedges topped by bare winter hawthorns and sycamores bent over by westerly gales. A scattering of February celandines were closing their petals for the night, leaving a monochrome landscape of fields, farms and tin mines.

'I want to go home,' Tom said. 'I don't like this place.'

'Cuddle up to me.' Lottie put her arm around him and let him play with the wavy ends of her hair. It quietened him. She had no answers. Only questions.

The car travelled on, through the old mining towns of Camborne and Redruth. Once they stopped at a level crossing to let a train go steaming through.

'What's that hill?' Matt asked, his eyes suddenly alive. 'You can see it from St Ives. The one with the cross on top.'

'That's the Carn Brea,' P.C. Roach said. 'Lovely up there. You can see the whole of Cornwall – and at night you can see the lights of St Ives twinkling.'

Matt and Lottie looked at each other with a shared unspoken thought. *One day, when we are free, we'll go up there and sit on those high stacks of granite and see our home far away, twinkling in the night. When we are free.*

What had been an interesting journey became scary as they climbed out of Redruth.

'Wheal Buller Hill,' said P.C. Roach. 'Hold tight, you children. I've got to put my foot down.'

A thick blanket of mist hung over the hills and the driver headed up into it at breakneck speed. The smell of petrol filled the car and Tom was sick over the floor. 'I couldn't help it,' he cried, white-faced. 'Why are we going so fast?'

''Cause it's a hill, stupid,' Matt said, pretending he knew about cars when he didn't.

The driver didn't answer. The car lurched as he changed gear, roaring along the rough, stony road. Then down into first gear. 'If she won't go up, we'll have to get out and push,' he warned. 'Wouldn't be the first time I've pushed a car up Wheal Buller Hill.'

'What if it runs down backwards?' Tom asked.

'It won't, lad, it's got brakes.'

But the three children were terrified. Their only experience of being in a motor vehicle was the

Flora Day charabanc ride, out in the sunshine with everybody singing. In this dense fog and with darkness falling, and the harsh grind of the engine, even the two burly policemen seemed edgy. 'Can't see yer hand in front of yer face in this fog,' they complained, both leaning forward, straining to see the road, the headlights only making the mist look solid and yellowy like sheep's fleece.

'Where are we going?' Tom kept asking, and no one answered his question. 'And where's our mummy?'

Lottie held on to him tightly, trying to ignore the smell of sick and petrol. The mist came right inside the car, freezing cold and damp. She was glad of the warm coat Nan had bought her, but Matt and Tom had only the threadbare jackets they wore to school. Their warm fisherman's jerseys, knitted by Millie, were left in the cottage along with the things they loved. The boys' boxes of marbles. The storybooks imbued with happy memories of Arnie. Lottie's bed with the carved wooden animals. Her collection of shells and crystals. Her knitted doll. Her books. What would happen to it all? And her precious black velvet bag, still hidden at Hendravean. Would Nan guard its secret?

The car braked sharply as another car with glaring headlights came flaring out of the mist. The children were thrown forward and Lottie bruised her lip on the front seat. Tom banged his chin on the handbrake and started to howl the way he'd howled as a five-year-old. Loudly.

The exasperated driver shouted at Tom. 'Stop that noise. You're not a baby. We're nearly there

218

and you've got to behave. Be a big boy. If you don't behave, they won't take you, and I'll have to take you miles up-country to a home for bad boys.'

His aggressive tone silenced Tom. They drove on through the fog for what seemed like miles and miles of an invisible land, far away from the sea. An unfriendly, cold, landlocked place.

'Here we are. That's it.' The car turned into a gateway and came to a halt in front of a pair of towering iron gates. The car's headlights shone on rusting metal bars and glistening, mist-covered cobwebs strung between them. *Spiders,* thought Lottie, shuddering. *A house of spiders.*

She looked at Matt as the policeman got out to open the huge gates. Matt's eyes were frightened black bubbles in the darkness and he seemed to know exactly what Lottie was thinking. In a rare moment of empathy he reached out, found her hand and squeezed it. 'We stick together,' he whispered.

'Stick together,' Lottie whispered back. 'Together forever.'

'My children,' Jenny said desperately to one of the nurses standing around her bed. She felt in awe of them with their starched white caps and aprons as they bustled silently around the vast building. It was difficult to engage with them. They all seemed preoccupied with charts on clipboards, kidney-shaped bowls and trolleys stacked with medicines and bandages.

She kept drifting in and out of consciousness, waking to a bewildered sense of humiliation, strange young doctors in cardboardy white coats endlessly testing her useless legs and peering into her eyes with torches. It was like drowning. Coming up for air. Then sinking down into the deep dark. Each time she surfaced she asked a question and nobody answered except to tell her she was in hospital. She lost all sense of time, only aware that beyond the brightly lit windows was a blue-dark night muffled by a thick fog. Her children's faces danced in and out of her mind. Little Tom, still innocent, still needing a nap after school, still her baby. And Matt, heart-stoppingly like Arnie, his long legs and big feet and fathomless eyes. *I wish I'd been nicer to you, Matt,* Jenny thought. *Please God let me have a chance to make it right, be a mother to you, not an ogre.* And Lottie. Beautiful, mysterious Lottie. Jenny had wanted her happy and free. Wholesome and confident. But now Lottie was like Cinderella, downtrodden, overworked and desperate. Jenny could hardly bear it.

'It's all my fault,' she mumbled, and opened her eyes to see the tribe of white-coated doctors, students and nurses had moved on down the ward to stand like pillars of salt around someone else's bed. A nurse in a distinctive navy-blue uniform was drawing the curtains around her bed. She pulled up a chair and sat beside Jenny, offering her a hand to hold, and a pair of loving eyes. She reminded Jenny of Mrs Rabbit in the Beatrix Potter books.

'My children.'

'I know, dear. You're worried sick. Of course you are.' The nurse looked at her steadily. 'I'm Sister Jill, dear, and I'll be here with you every day. I know you're worried about your children. I'll send the almoner to see you tomorrow morning. She will find out what is happening to them and help you with any issues you have regarding your home and family.'

'But tonight? They'll be alone in the cottage.'

Sister Jill looked at her clipboard. 'It says on your admission notes that the doctor's wife in St Ives has taken your children in.'

'Oh – good. That's kind of her,' Jenny said, trying to imagine her two rough and ready boys conforming to Mrs Tregullow's orderly household. 'She doesn't like children. She'd cope with Lottie, but not the boys.'

'Where's their father?' Sister Jill asked.

'Dead and gone.' Jenny started to tremble. 'Almost two years ago now.' She tried to sit up. 'I'm a widow, you see and … and I can't possibly stay here in this hospital. I can't.'

'Why not?'

'I've no money. I can't possibly pay for treatment.'

'You'll have to stay – you can't walk, dear, can you?'

'It'll get better – won't it?'

Sister Jill shook her head. She held Jenny's hand tightly. 'It COULD get better, dear, but not for a long time. You are very seriously ill, Mrs Lanroska. I'm afraid you have polio.'

'Polio? But…' Jenny's eyes filled with desperate tears. 'Then … you must let me die. There's no money for treatment, I keep telling you. Just let me go home, please. Lottie's nearly twelve. She can look after me, and the neighbours will help.

But ... I don't want my children to watch me die.'

'We can't let you go home. You need special care and treatment.'

'But I can't pay for treatment,' Jenny repeated and added miserably. 'Just put me out in the street and let me die please, just let me die.' She turned her head away from Sister Jill's kind face. Again the terrible giddiness gyrated around her head, sucking her into a whirlpool of darkness. The starched white pillows seemed to reach up and engulf her. Jenny felt smaller and smaller, like an insect curled up and dying in the hot sun. The faces of her children whizzed past her as if going down a tunnel, but they were speeding towards the light while she was racing into a place of shadows.

Sister Jill let go of Jenny's limp hand and stood up. She called down the ward. 'Doctor – can you come quickly, please.' And the white-coated tribe hurried back to Jenny's bed.

A flight of cold, wet granite steps led up to the front door of Treskirby House. A few squares of light glowed from nearby windows but the rest of the house was hidden by the mist. P.C. Roach opened the car door and brandished the hand-cuffs at Matt. 'Don't you give me any trouble, young man.'

'He won't,' said Lottie firmly. 'We're going to stick together.' She took Tom's hand and offered the other one to Matt. Surprisingly, he grasped it and the three of them shivered as they climbed the steps between the two policemen.

The doorbell clanged far away and from

somewhere in the huge building came the creak of heavy, no-nonsense footsteps. P.C. Roach peered through the iron keyhole. 'Here she comes.'

In the light of P.C. Roach's torch, Lottie noticed another set of glistening cobwebs, one with a fat spider crouched in the centre. Nobody had opened that door for a while.

'Is this a prison?' Tom asked.

The door swung open, tearing the delicate cobwebs with utter disregard for the devastated spiders who had worked through the night making them.

'Come inside quickly. Before the fog gets in.'

They were bundled inside and the policemen let go of the children's hands. A weather-beaten woman with big feet turned her slow-blinking reptilian eyes on the three shivering children. 'What is that SMELL?' she asked, her lip curling in disgust.

'Sorry, ma'am,' said P.C. Roach. 'The youngest lad, Tom, was sick in the car.'

'Couldn't you have stopped?'

'Not on Wheal Buller Hill, ma'am.'

Tom hung his head and pressed closer to Lottie.

There was a brief, disgusted silence.

'So who have you brought me this time? Who are these children? Where are they from?'

'From S'nives,' P.C. Roach said. 'This is the Lanroska family. Matt, Lottie and Tom. They're not orphans. Their father was a fisherman and he was tragically drowned a couple of years ago. Now their mother's been taken to hospital.' He lowered his voice. 'It's going to be a long haul –

she has … polio.'

The reptilian eyes flickered. 'I hope they are not infectious.'

'No. The doctor's wife took them in. Fine healthy children, she said they were.'

'Hmmm.' The woman manufactured another silence, this time a sceptical one. Distant groans and thuds came in, as if the big house was clearing its throat around them.

'Can you take them?' P.C. Roach asked in his patient voice.

'I suppose we shall have to. Isn't there a relative they can go to?'

'No.'

'Our grandad lives in a beach hut down Newlyn,' Tom spoke up, bravely. 'He's got no room to swing a cat.'

'Be quiet.' The woman stamped one of her big feet at Tom. 'No one asked you to speak.' She opened a hard-backed navy-blue book. An ancient pencil hung from it on a frayed string. 'Right. Names. In full please, and ages.' She looked at Lottie. 'You first.'

Lottie straightened her spine. 'Lottie Lanroska. Eleven and three quarters.'

'What is Lottie short for?'

'Nothing.'

'Don't be insolent.'

'I wasn't. I'm called Lottie, at school and everywhere else,' Lottie said in her clear voice, 'and I go to the Grammar School. I passed the exam.'

'Well, you can't do that here. We have our own internal school. You will learn all you need to know.'

'I doubt that,' Lottie said, and P.C. Roach's eyes twinkled with amusement. He shook his head at her and put a finger to his lips. Lottie bit back what she wanted to say next. She turned her attention to Tom and gently wiped the smudges from his bewildered face with her hanky.

The boys mumbled their names and ages and the woman wrote them carefully in the book with the ancient pencil. She went to the wall in two beefy strides and pulled a cord which rang a bell deep inside the house.

'What should the children call you, ma'am?' P.C. Roach asked.

'Miss Poltair. At all times.'

'Right – thank you, Miss Poltair.' P.C. Roach nodded respectfully. He looked at the children with deep concern. 'We have to leave now. Try to be good Cornish children – eh? And try to be patient. It could be a long time, a very long time. You stick together and look after each other.'

Lottie looked into his eyes. She didn't want him to go. In this bleak, forbidding house, P.C. Roach and his long eyelashes seemed to be her last link with home, with loving, friendly Jenny and beautiful St Ives. And Morwenna. And Nan. Mufty and Bartholomew. The art of how to cry in silence was a skill Lottie had mastered long ago. She felt the pain and drew it in, a bitter tide soaking through the pores of her skin. It gave her headaches. She could feel one now, throbbing at her temples. Even the roots of her beautiful hair were hurting.

She watched the two St Ives policemen go out, letting in a grey wisp of weather, a skein of mist and a scent of bracken that fled into the waiting corridors. The three Lanroska children clung together, scared but proud, finding comfort in their closeness. *Stick together. Stick together,* Lottie thought.

But it was not to be.

A man with a bunch of keys came in through a side door and walked up to them. He was short with wide shoulders and a head shaped like a mushroom. He even smelled like a mushroom. His eyes darted everywhere and his fat fingers never stopped twiddling the keys or drumming the sleeve of his nicotine-encrusted jacket.

'Mr Gorda runs the boys' department,' Miss Poltair explained, and her expression softened just a little as she looked down at the children. 'Let go hands now and say goodbye. Matthew and Thomas, you will go with Mr Gorda. And Lottie will come with me.'

In the instant before all hell broke loose, it was Matt who Lottie turned to first. They looked into each other's eyes in horror, and beyond the horror there was love. Undiscovered and now forbidden.

'Excuse me but ... can't we stay together?' Lottie pleaded looking at Miss Poltair's forbidding slab of a face.

'Certainly not. Boys live in the boys' home. Girls in the girls' home.'

'Please?' Lottie begged even though she knew it was useless.

'No.'

She saw the word 'No' multiplying and growing, filling those grim, waiting corridors. The scars on her back tingled. She looked at Matt. She'd never told him about those scars. Perhaps she never would. But when she looked at Matt now, Lottie saw something new. Courage.

'Say goodbye to your sister,' Mr Gorda jingled the formidable keys, 'and you boys come with me.'

Matt gazed at Lottie as if he would never stop. Then he did something he'd never done before. In one swift, decisive, Arnie-like movement, he leaned forward and kissed Lottie on the cheek.

It was Tom who went berserk. He roared and howled and clung to Lottie, almost pulling her over. 'I want to stay with Lottie. She's my big sister. Why can't we be together? You've got to let us.'

Mr Gorda dragged him away and Tom lay on the floor yelling and kicking, making himself heavy and unmanageable. 'Get up!' Mr Gorda snarled, but Tom wouldn't. 'You little demon. And you – Matthew – don't just stand there, boy. Help me with your brother. What a baby!' Mr Gorda had a voice like rusty nails and Lottie could see the curve of his biceps straining the sleeves of his jacket. When Matt didn't move, he added, 'Or do I have to drag the pair of you? Because I will, and I don't care how much it hurts.'

Lottie winced as Tom was hauled roughly across the enormous hall, kicking and cursing. The last she saw of him was his tear-stained, screwed-up face and the soles of his shoes which were full of holes. The door slammed on both her brothers and Tom howled even louder. 'I don't want to go with my brother. He hates me. I want to stay with

Lottie.' The grey, granite walls soaked up his cries and the space rang with the sound of Mr Gorda's hard boots marching into the distance.

In deep shock, Lottie stood still, the feel of Matt's kiss lingering like a butterfly on her cheek.

'I hope you're going to be a good girl.' Miss Poltair's eyes had a sheen of satisfaction as if she'd actually relished the sight of Tom being dragged away.

Numbly Lottie walked beside Miss Poltair's flat black laced-up shoes in the opposite direction from where the boys had gone.

'Mr Gorda will soon knock some sense into those two,' Miss Poltair said. 'You will all be cleaned up, disinfected and de-loused. You will be given a clean set of clothes, a bed to sleep in, and a set of rules. See that you obey them at all times. Can you read?'

'Yes.'

'Yes, Miss Poltair.'

'Yes – Miss Poltair.'

'You will be kept in isolation until you have memorised the rules and repeated them to me. There they are on the wall.' She took Lottie into a gloomy room with a hard chair placed in front of the framed set of rules on the wall. 'You sit there and start learning them right now, and I shall send Matron to clean you up.'

'I'm perfectly capable of washing myself,' Lottie said.

'Read that first rule. Go on. Read it to me.'

Humiliated, Lottie began to read, theatrically. 'One – Respect your elders and don't answer back. Two – Girls are strictly forbidden to enter

228

the boys' side of this house.' She paused to ask a question. 'So how are we supposed to communicate? And when can I see my brothers? Matt and Tom are important to me.'

The reptilian eyes blinked. 'Read those two rules again and I shall be back to test you in one hour. If you haven't learned and understood all ten rules, you will go to bed with no supper.'

'That's unreasonable,' Lottie argued. 'What about my little brother, Tom? He can't read well enough yet to do that. Is this a children's home, or a children's prison?'

Miss Poltair looked shaken. She didn't seem to have an answer, so she leaned down with her hooky nose uncomfortably close to Lottie. 'If you don't conform,' she hissed, pointing a finger at the middle of Lottie's chest, 'you will have it beaten out of you.'

The scars burned on Lottie's back as if they were alive, warning her. Seeds of rebellion rooted in her soul. She kept her mouth shut and let Miss Poltair think she had won, when she hadn't.

Left alone in the grey little room, Lottie made up her mind that she would pretend to conform while her inner mind dreamed of escape, of going home to St Ives. She'd find a way of taking Tom and Matt, leading them on the long journey, walking and hiding and stealing food, surviving, believing they could do it. Inside the dream was another dream, curled up and far away, a dream of going to America and finding her mother.

Chapter 15

A Family – Gone

Nan had become increasingly reclusive in the time since Arnie's death. She spent February huddled indoors by the fire, reading her favourite books, making sachets from her jars of dried herbs, and knitting bobble hats to sell from Mufty's cart when the weather was warm enough to go out. She was plagued by a stubborn chest infection, and no matter how much honey and hot herb tea she took, it wouldn't get better. Every day she dragged herself out to care for Mufty and the chickens, and on bright days she wandered around the garden enjoying the mats of yellow celandine and the first violets along the base of the hedge. She put food out for the wild birds and retreated inside to watch them from the window, seeing flocks of yellowhammers and cirl buntings, and winter visitors like the beautiful redwings who sat around in the cold, fluffed out in their speckled plumage.

Nan had another reason to be standing at her window, always in the late afternoon when children were coming home from school. She was watching and hoping to see Lottie come running up Foxglove Lane. Nan had only seen her twice since Christmas. She missed the little girl's company, her bright chatter, her questions. The peaceful cosiness of reading a book with her by the fire were times Nan loved and treasured. She didn't want to lose touch with Lottie, especially now she was growing up fast. It must be the homework, and the dark evenings, Nan reasoned.

A sense of having been abandoned hovered over Nan, and she worked hard to keep herself busy and positive. She missed Vic, even though she understood why he needed to be away from St Ives and the memory of Arnie. He'd been to see her at Christmas. The sea in winter was too rough for him to bring the boat round to St Ives. So Vic had walked from Newlyn over the high, gorse-covered hills, and along the spectacular coast road that wound through Zennor. He'd spent Christmas Day chopping wood for Nan's fire and mending broken storm shutters on west-facing windows. On Boxing Day, he managed a brief early morning visit to Jenny and the children before tackling the strenuous hike back to Newlyn with the wind and the rain in his face, and the pressure of having to get home before the breath of winter darkness misted the hills. It was the last time Nan had seen Vic.

It was mid March before Nan felt well enough to harness Mufty, load the cart and go into St Ives. *Sod Jenny,* she thought, *I'm going to see the children and give them a hat each.* Driving Mufty along the lane between billows of pale yellow primroses, Nan felt optimistic. The sun was warm, the sea quiet, and the seagulls loud over the town as they nested on the rooftops. It was nearly Easter and a scattering of tourists and artists wandered around the town, many of them pausing to admire Mufty's bright cart and his harness decorated with tassels of coloured wool and some of Lottie's pompoms.

Nan found a place to park at the side of Wharf Road, thinking she would stay there until the church clock chimed four and the children would be home from school. Then she would go to the cottage in Downlong, give the children their hats and perhaps have a sing-song with them, if Jenny would let her. The piano accordion was in the cart and the tunes came floating into Nan's mind. She'd planned what she was going to say to Jenny. She'd look directly into those hurt, hostile eyes and tell her it was time to sing again, if only for the children's sake.

Selling her wares happened more by accident than effort. Shouting and bantering like a market trader wasn't Nan's style. She heaved herself onto the back of the cart and sat motionless like a huge Buddha. Only her eyes moved. Tourists were fascinated by her and would openly stare at her in disbelief. In previous years, Nan had enjoyed chatting with them but since Arnie's death, and the row with Jenny, she felt disinclined to talk to anyone, except Lottie. Everything hurt. The way the locals seemed to scurry past, avoiding her. The sight of a little fishing boat chugging home across the emerald water with seagulls wheeling and swooping, wanting their share of the shimmering basket of freshly caught fish. It could have been *The Jenny Wren*.

Nan felt marooned on an island of grief.

She managed the flurries of selling and the questions people asked her, mostly about Mufty who stood patiently in the sun enjoying the attention. When, at last, the church clock struck four, Nan packed up and headed for Downlong, leading Mufty and the cart slowly through the steep and narrow streets. She was unprepared for the shock that awaited her.

Her footsteps got slower and slower as she approached the silent cottage, sensing a change. In disbelief, she stood in front of it. The windows were boarded up, the door locked, the chimney smokeless, the washing line torn from the wall and coiled up against the doorstep. There were no children's voices, no clatter of tea cups, no smells of baking. Just an accusing emptiness.

My family, Nan thought, and the oncoming army of feelings hit hard in the centre of her being. Rage. *Why wasn't I told?* Terror. *Are they all dead?* Self-hate. *I should have helped.*

Shading her eyes from the sun, she struggled to read the small print on a white sheet of paper glued across the door. The key words jumped out at her. *BY ORDER OF ...* and *REPOSSESSED,* and *AUCTION.*

Bewildered fury took hold of Nan. It was Arnie's own cottage. He'd worked day and night to buy it for his family. How could anyone have a right to repossess it? What wickedness, in St Ives of all places. Beside herself, Nan began to rant in the street. 'WHO is responsible for this ... this outrage?'

Predictably, no one ventured out to face Nan. She lumbered to and fro, wringing her freckled hands, shouting at the sky, shouting at everyone who should have been there and wasn't. She

233

grazed her knuckles on the cottage door. Her knocking sounded hollow and precarious as if the floorboards upstairs were being shaken loose. Nan squatted down awkwardly with her painful knees and peered through the letterbox, smelling the cold, damp air inside. She could see the stairs still covered in sand and Lottie's school blazer hung from a peg, next to Arnie's old cork life-jacket and the boys' caps. Arnie's driftwood cart stood in the living room with two filthy sacks of coal on it. And Tom's treasured marble tin lay on the floor, the lid flung to one side, the glass marbles gleaming in the dim light.

A home abandoned.

A family – gone.

Nan straightened up gingerly and went to Mufty who was looking at her with empathy, his furry ears pricked, his velvet nose reaching out to her. In the harsh desolation of that moment, Nan felt Mufty was the only living creature on earth who cared about her. He was giving her his love in the way that horses and donkeys do, by press-ing the whole length of his warm face against her body. She held on to him, soaking up his silent kindness, allowing the simple, wordless comfort of a donkey to fill the jagged hole in her mind.

It was getting dark. Time to go home.

But tomorrow – tomorrow she would come back. She would ask everyone what had hap-pened. She'd knock on doors. Nan would leave no stone unturned until she knew the truth.

'Lottie Lanroska!' Miss Poltair had a whip in her hand. Malice glittered in her eyes as she rapped

234

the chair Lottie was standing on. 'Daydreaming again? You don't stop working for one minute. Do you understand me?'

'Yes – Miss Poltair.'

'And look at me when I'm speaking to you.'

Lottie turned her head carefully, afraid she would fall off the chair if she tried to look round.

'Say you're sorry!'

'Sorry – Miss Poltair.'

Every day the twelve girls of Lottie's age group were given a task – scrubbing, sweeping, polishing or washing up. The older girls in the home did the ironing or the mending or chopped vegetables in the kitchen. Today Lottie's age group were cleaning the tall windows along the corridors, a difficult job done with a rag dipped in vinegar, then scrubbed with damp newspaper. Lottie's arms ached from reaching up, standing on tiptoe on the chair to clean the highest of the small panes. Distracted by the views outside, she had paused to gaze and dared to dream.

Most of the windows in the building were too high for her to see much except sky. But standing on the chair, Lottie could see the green fields of inland Cornwall. Cornish hedges ablaze with gorse, sheep with baby lambs, a few horses and donkeys. She gazed with bitter longing. She wanted to be out there, free, playing and exploring with Morwenna.

She continued polishing the glass, but still her eyes were drawn to something in the distance. A hill with enormous stacks of granite and a stone cross on top. The Carn Brea. Lottie remembered what P.C. Roach had said about it. At night, up there, you could see the lights of St Ives twinkling far away. The Carn Brea was like a signpost. It was stage one of Lottie's incubating escape plan. To go up there, with Matt and Tom, study the landscape, and figure out how to find their way home to St Ives.

None of them had any knowledge of map-reading or navigating skills, and getting hold of a map seemed out of the question. Lottie thought Matt knew how to navigate by the stars. Vic had been teaching him that before he'd gone off to live in Newlyn. But it wouldn't be much use in the daytime. She thought sadly of the education she was missing. They'd just started doing Geography and Lottie found it fascinating. Seeing the vastness of America was both thrilling and alarming. Finding her real mother in thousands of miles of land wasn't going to be easy. *The only person who might help her was Nan,* Lottie thought. Nan had a magnificent set of Encyclopaedia Britannica, and one wet afternoon, she'd shown Lottie how to use them, and together they'd found the shipping routes to America. Lottie hadn't explained why this information was so important to her, but Nan had looked at her shrewdly as if she secretly knew the dream in Lottie's heart.

Hearing Miss Poltair's dreaded footsteps and cane-rapping at the far end of the corridor, Lottie pretended to be polishing vigorously. She was glad when they were allowed to get down from standing on the chairs and moved on around the corner to the dining room where the windows faced east. Lottie's arms ached, her fingers burned with sore skin, and she wanted a drink. All the girls looked tired but they were driven on relentlessly. There would be no break until lunchtime, and after lunch they went to school. Boring school for Lottie. Basic English and Maths well below her ability. Never any stories or poetry, no geography, no music.

'If those windows aren't spotlessly clean when I come back in half an hour, there'll be no lunch.' Miss Poltair rapped the cane on the palm of her leathery hand. 'Erica will supervise you while she's laying the table.' She handed the cane to Erica who was one of the older girls. 'Don't hesitate to use it, girl.'

Lottie quickly chose the window at the far end which overlooked the garden. She climbed onto a chair, and gave a gasp of delight. The window overlooked the kitchen garden, and a group of boys were out there working. She hadn't seen Matt and Tom since the foggy night when they'd arrived, so she stared out eagerly. Tom wasn't there but she could see Matt, his back hunched over a spade. When he straightened up for an instant she thought he'd grown taller. Her heart beat faster when she realised he looked so like Arnie, even from the back. Something about the way he stood, the shape of his legs and the way he moved. If only he would turn around and see her there in the window. She wanted to wave and shout. It was so good to know he was all right. Like her, he'd be hating it, but surviving. Lottie wanted to throw down her polishing rag, leap from the chair and hurtle out of the building and across the garden. She touched her hair which was tightly plaited and wound around her head.

Would Matt even recognise her? She'd tear the plaits out and run with her blonde hair flying, the way she had done in St Ives.

As if sensing her thoughts, Matt did turn round, very suddenly, and looked directly at the window. Lottie waved wildly, and he waved back.

'WHAT are you doing?' Erica looked up at her, power-drunk, the cane swishing in her plump pink hand.

'Waving to my brother.'

'GET DOWN. How dare you wave – to a ... to a BOY.' Erica's cheeks were a dark, unhealthy pink.

'But he's my brother.'

'I don't care if he's the king. Say you're sorry.'

'NO.'

'Why not?'

'Because I'm not sorry.' Lottie stamped her foot, furious with Erica for stealing her moment of joy. 'I haven't seen my brother since February. Why shouldn't I wave?'

Erica's hot hand crunched the top of Lottie's arm and shook her. She moved her face so close that Lottie could see the florid network of tiny veins on her cheek. Wielding Miss Poltair's whip-like cane, she whacked Lottie's bare legs and, having started, Erica couldn't seem to stop.

Lottie's fury at this violation of her simple human right to wave to her brother was stronger than fear. She knew how to fight now, from the times she'd watched Tom and Matt fighting. At first she'd been horrified, but gradually it became clear that despite the bullying and the crying, Tom was learning how to fight and how to survive emotionally, by himself, with no one to comfort him.

Lottie wasn't going to stand there meekly and let Erica beat her. She kicked and twisted and glared. She didn't cry. Crying would have been music to Erica's ears. Instead, she shouted and the words shot out like bullets, indiscriminate and deadly. Things her mother had said, like, 'Nice girls don't fight,' bobbed dimly in her mind, and were shot down. 'I AM going to survive,' she yelled at Erica's surprised face. 'You've got no right to beat me. I'm not having it. You stop it, right now, or you'll be sorry.' Lottie got hold of the cane in both hands and wrestled it. She gave Erica an almighty shove, one that Morwenna would have been proud of, and Erica fell backwards like a pillow, her eyes frightened, her mouth square.

Lottie stood over her with the cane in her hands, aware of the group of girls standing close clapping their hands, grinning and laughing with joy to see Erica on the floor. 'Beat her. Beat her. Go on, Lottie. Beat her fat bottom.'

Suddenly Lottie felt part of a tribe.

She felt like the leader of a tribe.

Erica didn't get up and fight back. She lay there, crying and trembling. *She's afraid of me,* Lottie thought, awed. She looked at the cane in her hands. Stupid thing. 'We don't need this,' she announced. With her head held high, she took the cane over to an open window and flung it, spinning, into the garden. It felt good.

Her moment of glory ended when the dreaded footsteps thundered through the vast building.

The girls fled and scrambled back to their window-polishing, except for Lottie who stood over Erica, her chin defiantly tilted, her dark blue eyes glowing, the backs of her legs stinging from the beating.

'WHAT is going on here?' Miss Poltair squeaked to a halt.

Erica sat up. 'It's her. She pushed me over. And kicked me. And she threw your cane out of the window.'

'Why?' The reptilian eyes glimmered a horrible green.

'She whipped me when I didn't deserve it,' Lottie said clearly. 'I did nothing wrong. I waved to my brother who is working in the garden. How can it be wrong? I explained that to Erica, but she obviously misunderstood.'

'She attacked me,' Erica said from the floor. 'Look at the bruises on my legs.'

'I was defending myself,' Lottie said. 'I don't see why I should stand there and let her beat me, do you?'

The reptilian eyes narrowed. Flecks of spittle appeared in the corners of Miss Poltair's miserable mouth. 'Lottie Lanroska – you...' She paused to bunch herself together. 'You are a demon. A demon child. Uncivilised.' Her arm shot out and grabbed Lottie. 'There's only one place for you. The cellar. Until you learn how to behave. And don't you dare struggle or kick, or I'll drag you.'

Lottie remembered Tom's resistance tactics and sat down, making herself heavy on the floor.

'Help me, Erica. Get hold of her other arm.'

Powerless between the two of them, Lottie felt

herself being dragged and bumped across the floor. She saw bricks of sunshine cast from the windows racing past as the two women pulled her along. *I won't give in. I won't,* she vowed. In a flash of memory, she saw Jenny tenderly carrying her home from the shipwreck. Such love. And now, here she was, being brutally hauled through this prison of a building.

As they dragged her through the entrance hall, Lottie's heart leapt when she saw the door to the outside world wide open, with two big girls brushing and polishing it. She'd never seen it open before. But next time, she'd be ready to seize her one chance and escape.

'I need a drink,' she pleaded, as Miss Poltair opened a thick wooden door and pushed her into the tomb-like darkness of the cellar.

'You'll get nothing until you learn to behave.'

Lottie turned around at the top of the stone steps and glared with burning eyes at Miss Poltair. 'Why are you so cruel to children?'

The reptilian eyes wavered just for an instant and then the oak door slammed shut in Lottie's face. She heard the scrape of bolts being shot. The door trembled. The footsteps walked away. And she was left alone in the ink-dark cellar.

John De Lumen stood in the art gallery in London, a glass of red wine in his hand. He was wearing his best suit, which smelled faintly of mothballs. It still fitted him, though he was thinner now that he lived more frugally as an artist. He'd polished his black shoes, found his favourite tie and his gold cufflinks. The wild edges of his beard had been trimmed, but not too much. He still wanted to look like an artist.

Thrilled that his painting, *Discovering Charlotte*, had finally been accepted for a major London exhibition, John went to the private view, not knowing what to expect. He didn't know any of the guests who filled the gallery so it was a lonely but exciting experience. Deliberately, he positioned himself close, but not too close, to *Discovering Charlotte*, watching people's reactions to it and listening to their comments.

One particular couple stood in front of the painting for a long time. They didn't look British. The lady wore a stylish dress in a heady mix of cobalt, soft orange and cinnamon, and the man had a blatantly brash checked jacket and a Stetson hat which he'd let slip onto the back of his neck. Both appeared to be conversing in an animated way, moving their lips a lot and gesticulating with their hands.

John eyed them discreetly, edging nearer to hear their comments on his painting. Evidently, his tactics didn't work for the lady looked at him directly, her eyes glowing with interest. Before he could escape, she swirled towards him in a drift of cobalt and orange. 'I guess you must be the lonesome artist,' she said in warm persuasive tones. 'Am I right?'

'Yes. Yes, I am an artist,' John said, edging away from her.

She pounced on his arm. 'Is this your painting? *Discovering Charlotte?*'

John nodded, putting down his glass. He didn't feel ready for this manifestation of a dream he'd been harbouring for years. He stood awkwardly, one hand in his pocket, the other stroking what was left of his beard.

'You're actually HIM,' the lady gushed. 'You're really, truly John De Lumen?'

He nodded, drawn to her wide smile and her flowing jet black hair. He imagined her as an Indian squaw with a feathered headband.

'I'm Coraline, and this is my husband, Rex.'

The two men nodded at each other and Rex took out a pack of Havana cigars and offered one to John.

'No, thank you very much.'

'Come and tell us about your wonderful painting, John– May I call you John? Don't be shy.'

He nodded. 'What would you like to know?'

'The history of it,' she beamed, 'especially ... who is Charlotte?'

John felt his eyes glistening. 'That shall remain a secret.'

'Oh – a mystery. I love mysteries – like the Mona Lisa. It makes the painting even more poignant – doesn't it, Rex?'

A friendly frown materialised through the blue wisps of cigar smoke. A frown of intensity. Rex looked searchingly at John. 'My wife and I own a gallery in New York. We travel the world looking for paintings – soul paintings which have a message and a mystery. Paintings you can gaze at, all your life, and still not figure out their meaning.'

John swallowed. *Kindred spirits,* he thought. A rarity. He felt deeply emotional.

'What does *Charlotte* mean to you?' Rex asked.

'Everything.'

The three of them gazed at the painting, and *Charlotte* gazed back, enigmatically, with her dark blue eyes.

'She is so innocent – but so knowing,' Coraline said, 'and there's sadness in those eyes. Can you tell us about that?'

John's mind went back to the day of the funeral. Little Charlotte, walking so bravely, with a black veil over her face. 'I could – and I might – but I don't feel ready to give that information.'

'No – and you shouldn't,' Rex said passionately. 'Let the painting speak for itself, because it does. It touches hearts.'

'Can you tell us where you painted it?' Coraline asked.

'In St Ives, Cornwall – on a lovely day,' John said. 'I sketched her. But I took the essence of her home in my heart and spent many, many months working on the painting.'

Rex seemed satisfied with his answer. He looked at his wife and raised his bushy eyebrows.

'Definitely.' Coraline gave John the warmest of smiles, glanced at Rex who nodded, his eyes bright with enthusiasm. Then she said, 'We would like to buy your painting, John. I know it says *Not for sale* in the catalogue but please consider our offer. *Discovering Charlotte* will have a good home in our gallery and it will be seen by art lovers, reviewers and collectors from all over America and beyond.'

John's heart began to beat very fast. Could he bear to part with his best painting?

Coraline seemed to read his mind. 'We know how artists feel. Parting with your best work is like a bereavement. It's a big emotional journey. The painting is like a beloved bird in a cage. You have to take a deep breath, open the cage and let it fly out, into the world.'

No one had ever talked to John in such an eloquent, openly emotive way. He was startled and moved by Coraline's words.

'But, John...' Rex leaned close, his big eyes beaming and business-like, 'what if this truly great work of art just stayed in your private studio? Who would see it? Surely when you painted it, you did it for the world to see ... didn't you?'

'I agree,' Coraline said, with passion. *'Discovering Charlotte* is a truly great work of art.'

John's heart beat even faster. He pressed his knees together to stop them shaking. The truth was that he'd painted *Discovering Charlotte* for one person only. And she would be in New York. Was his dream slowly coming true?

'When you did the painting – did you dream of where you wanted it hung?' Coraline asked.

John dared to meet her sweet, persuasive eyes. 'In America,' he said immediately.

'Oh, but – how wonderful!' Coraline gushed. 'Can you tell us why? Why America, when here in London you have so much art?'

John was finding it difficult to speak. Little Charlotte, with her honey-coloured hair and dark blue eyes, was vivid in his mind. Where was she now? At this moment? It was a golden evening in early spring and even London looked exuberant with swelling buds on the tall plane trees. He hoped Charlotte was outside, running free, playing and dancing on Porthmeor Beach. To him, her spirit would always belong there.

He touched his breast pocket, feeling the bump of the seashell in his wallet. His heart was speeding recklessly towards a YES.

'John? I'm sorry – have I asked you something painful?' Coraline asked. She touched his sleeve. 'You don't have to tell us why.'

'It – it's part of the mystery,' John said, 'but – well, we'll see what happens. My answer is YES – I will let go of the painting of Charlotte – but only to you...'

As he left the gallery, Coraline's words rang in his mind. 'It's like a bereavement.' And it was. But the money burned in his pocket as he headed for the bank. A new dream flared into life. Maybe – maybe now he could buy himself a little studio, in St Ives.

Chapter 16

The Cellar

There must be another way out of this cellar, Lottie thought, as she edged her way down the stone steps. She wasn't going to sit in the cellar and cry. She wasn't going to hammer on the door and beg to be released. She wasn't going to be afraid. And without fear there was hope.

At first the darkness looked solid and threatening but as her eyes got used to it, Lottie noticed light coming in from somewhere; the dim outline of walls, the odd twinkle of a crystal in the granite, the deep shadow of an alcove, the massive beams of the ceiling rim-lit by a secret infiltration of light.

Lottie paused to listen at the bottom of the steps. Number one sound was the *thud-thud* of her heartbeat and the huff of her breath. She heard mice, their tiny, scurrying paws creating a vibration, a sense of the life pulse. Lottie wasn't afraid of mice. Not since Nan had given her a dormouse to hold and she'd felt it quivering. She remembered its petal-like ears, the rapid beat of its heart under her thumb, and the ageless wisdom in the dark jewel of its eye.

Rats were a different matter. They had remarkably human feet which made a noise like bare feet on wet sand. Rats could fill an attic with the thump of their bodies, the squeaks of excitement as they went steeplechasing along water pipes and rafters. A rat was brazen and would look at you with unwavering knowing. A cornered rat would jump at you, at your throat. Lottie shuddered, listening for the heavyweight sound of them, and heard nothing. Nan had taught her a lot about wild creatures. 'Leave them alone and they'll leave you alone,' she'd said.

Standing in the musty twilight, she thought of ways to outsmart Miss Poltair and her cane and her 'big girls' who she'd trained to be clones of herself. What did Miss Poltair expect to find when she came to open the cellar door? A snivelling, terrified, apologetic wreck who had learned her lesson. Had Erica once been thrown into the cellar? Had she curled up in a ball and cried with

247

terror, her hot face pressed against the door? And did Miss Poltair stand gleefully listening on the other side? Had Erica given up and conformed?

A pioneer spirit gripped Lottie. She would be the first of Miss Poltair's victims to disappear, perhaps even escape. The thought fired her courage. She walked on, along a tunnel with an uneven stone floor, feeling disorientated in the dim light, and listening to the drip of water. At the end of the tunnel, a spring trickled from a hole into a carved stone basin, the clear water overflowing into a stone drain below. It felt good to cup her hands and drink the cold, sweet mineral water. She washed her hands and face.

Refreshed, she peered into the wider corridor at the end of the tunnel, going left and right. The light was brighter, more silvery on the granite walls. Muffled footsteps came from above and Lottie realised she had made a discovery. The cellar was vast, and its layout was the same as in the house – a corridor all the way round. Turning right would lead her to the boys' side of the building! She gave a little skip of joy.

Ahead of her were blinding stripes of sunlight blazing in through an iron grill. *A way out?* Lottie ran to it, excited. But it was high above her head. Filled with longing, she stared at palaces of cloud drifting over a blue sky, and breathed in the fresh air. It smelled of salt and ferns. How she had missed it, shut away in Treskirby House. She gulped. The cruel beating hadn't made her cry. But the yearning to be running barefoot along the shining sands was so powerful, like one of her intense headaches. The pain of being homesick rang through every fibre of her body.

The iron grill was impossible for her to reach, and far too heavy for her to lift.

She bobbed back, out of sight, as a crunch of many footsteps sounded above. Her hopes soared. The boys were packing up their gardening. Tools were being clanked and dragged along, and she could hear Mr Gorda's raucous voice telling them to hurry up, and not leave any tools behind. Lottie's heart pounded with excitement. Matt! Where was Matt? Would he walk right over the iron grill? How could she attract his attention without getting him into trouble? She jumped with fright when Mr Gorda's hard footsteps clattered right over the iron grill, sending clods of soil bouncing in to her hiding place. The hobnailed soles of his boots made the iron bars ring like a church bell.

Lottie listened, judging when the heavy footsteps got fainter. If only Matt would come close. She waited, then took a risk and called out. 'Matt. Matt, it's Lottie.' Her voice echoed eerily through the vast cellar.

There was a deathly silence. Then a boy's gruff voice. 'It came from down there ... under the grill.'

His face looked down and it wasn't Matt. It was a flushed face with frightened eyes. But then ... all the children in Treskirby House had frightened eyes.

'I am not a ghost,' Lottie said clearly, irritated by the shock on his face.

'A GIRL,' he shouted. 'There's a GIRL down there.'

There was no response. She imagined the boys frozen rigid with fear. Mr Gorda would punish anyone who dared to speak. 'Can you fetch Matt for me, please? I'm his sister.'

The boy grunted and disappeared. She heard whispers. Then, to her utter joy, Matt's face looked in at her with eyes so startlingly like Arnie that Lottie wanted to cry. It felt cruel to be so close and not able to touch him.

'What are you doing down there, Lottie?' Matt spoke in whispers, his eyes darting nervously to check if he was safe from Mr Gorda. 'I can't talk to you or I'll be beaten.'

'Is Tom all right?'

'Yes. He doesn't like it here, but he's all right.' Matt gave her a soulful stare. Lottie reached up to him and he reached down, lying on his tummy, but their hands were too far away to touch. The space between their reaching hands seemed alive, charged by an invisible, shimmering wire of energy. All they had was eye contact, intensified by the memory of home.

'We've got to escape,' Lottie whispered, 'and it has to be all three of us together. We must find the way home. To Nan. She'll take care of us.'

'I want to see Mum,' Matt said, sadly, and a big tear drop fell through the grill. 'Do you think she's dead, Lottie?'

Lottie stared up at him. Matt had never looked vulnerable and lost as he did now. Had Mr Gorda's cruel regime broken Matt's rebellious spirit?

'Of course she's not dead, Matt,' Lottie said confidently. 'She's got polio and people do get

250

better from it, but it takes a long, long time. She'll be missing us. When we escape we can go to the hospital and see her.'

Her bright words settled into Matt's consciousness. A flicker of light passed through his eyes.

'We've got to make a plan, Matt,' Lottie said, 'so we can escape at the first opportunity. We'll only get one chance. If they find out what we're doing they'll keep us prisoner. So don't tell anyone, and I won't. But every time you're in the garden, check this grill – I'll find a way to leave you a note.'

Matt nodded. He seemed edgy. 'I've got to go, Lottie. If the Gorgon sees me, I'll get a beating.' He started to get up, then lay down again, his face close to the bars. 'The Gorgon has a day off, on a Tuesday. We could do it then – you listen out – and Lottie – this is important. Make them trust you. Then they won't suspect us.'

Lottie nodded. She heard a shout in the distance. 'Matthew Lanroska! What do you think you're doing, boy? Inside – NOW.'

Matt rolled his eyes. 'I've gotta go.'

'Give my love to Tom.'

'I shan't tell him. He can't keep a secret.' Matt scrambled up and she saw his wiry shape against the blue and white sky. A clump of Alexanders hung over the grill, and Matt quickly snapped off one of the creamy umbels of blossom and threw it down to her.

'Thanks!' Lottie picked it up, moved to think Matt had remembered how she loved to breathe its sweet, exotic perfume. Then he was gone, his footsteps light and swift, fading into the distance,

251

leaving only the cheeping of sparrows and the pattering of sycamore leaves in the wind.

Matt's words lodged in her mind. 'Make them trust you.' He was right. It meant she had to find her way back to the cellar door and sit there, curled up in a ball of misery. Then apologise and pretend she had learned her lesson.

After staring up into the sunlight, Lottie's eyes took a while to adjust. Walking back into the darkness was difficult. What if Miss Poltair opened the cellar door and found she wasn't there? Would she just lock it and walk away? Would she leave her there all night without food or comfort?

Seeing Matt had been encouraging, but it had stirred up a whirlpool of emotions. Lottie felt drained. She didn't think she could take much more.

Nan turned herself round and clambered backwards down from the train which stood steaming at Truro Station. She reached in and slid her forked walking stick out from under the carriage seat. She stood for a moment, recovering from the effort, and fished in her canvas haversack for her cardboard rail ticket.

'Would you kindly direct me to Lemon Street?' she asked the ticket collector, her ringing voice and stature turning a few heads in the station foyer. She wore a different dress for once: her fruity dress in bottle-green cotton with a motif of peaches, pears and grapes. It had huge shoulder pads which made her look even more imperious. Instead of her usual battered old straw hat, Nan had a remarkably clean panama. Her ankles were

252

already swelling, bulging over the unfamiliar black court shoes.

She hadn't been to Truro for years, but on the walk to Lemon Street, she soon remembered it. She was shocked at the number of motorcars on the streets, and the appalling smell of them. Even so, she looked at each one with keen interest, especially after her long walk to St Ives Station, a difficult train journey, and now another long walk.

Sitting in the waiting room at the solicitor's office in Lemon Street, Nan took a swig from the glass bottle of elderflower cordial she had brought with her. Then, more discreetly, a swig of cherry brandy. She sailed into Bart Pascoe's office smelling like a Christmas cake.

'So what brings you to Truro, Mrs Lanroska?'

Nan paused to arrange herself on the hard leather chair, pulling the green dress over her wide-apart knees like a tent. She'd put on so much weight. And Bart Pascoe had aged; a ruff of grey hair circled his sunburnt bald scalp. His serious, attentive eyes were what Nan remembered, set in a long, narrow, Cornish face.

'I have lost my great-grandchildren,' she announced.

'Dear me. Lost – in what way?'

'The INFERNAL, INTERFERING authorities took them away, so I'm told – and I was the last to be told.'

'Dearie me.'

'Kindly don't interrupt.' Nan took a deep breath. 'I need to tell you everything, so pay attention, will you please, and make some notes. I have been wronged, grossly insulted and wickedly deceived. I love these three children, I'm perfectly capable and willing to take care of them in my lovely home.' Tears poured down Nan's wrinkled cheeks. 'And ... I will go to the ends of the earth to find them.'

The fragrance of the bluebell woods drifted over Cornwall, and the sky beyond the hospital window was the colour of bluebells. The air shimmered with heat and pollen and the wings of bees. Jenny's only comfort as she lay in bed was to imagine herself out there. But so often, her imaginings turned into an unbearable yearning, and when it did, she begged for sedatives and sleep.

Today she had burst into tears when the nurse told her it was the eighth of May. Flora Day. Lottie's birthday. And the second anniversary of Arnie's death. Nurse Jenkins, affectionately known as 'Good old Jenksie', had taken time to befriend Jenny through the long months of her illness. It was a blessed gift of friendship. 'I know your children so well now,' Jenksie often said. 'You've described them so vividly – so many times. I think I'd recognise them, Jen, and one day they're going to turn up here, you wait and see.'

No matter how busy she was, Jenksie spent time listening to Jenny's outpouring of grief and frustration. 'Why the tears?' she asked. 'Is the eighth of May a special day for you?'

'It's Flora Day. And I'll never dance again. Will I?'

'Never say never. You're a fighter, Jen. Look how far you've come! You've done miles better than the doctors expected.'

'And it's Lottie's birthday. Little Lottie. She's twelve, and I won't be there to wish her a happy birthday and give her a present. Why have my children been taken from me, Jenksie? Why, why, why?'

'You'll get them back. I'm sure you will.' Jenksie broke the rules and sat on the bed to give Jenny a cuddle. Matron walked past and deliberately looked the other way. Jenksie went on talking, soothingly, trying to bring glimmers of hope into Jenny's life. 'You've got something to look forward to this afternoon.'

'What's that?' Jenny looked up at her in surprise.

'Your leg iron. It's been made for you and they're bringing it in for a fitting. You might even take those first precious steps.' Jenksie's eyes shone as if she was giving a child an ice cream. She wagged a finger. 'And I shall be there, cheering you on.'

Jenny bit back a sarcastic reply. She pictured herself struggling around St Ives with her leg in an iron. 'Right.' She forced a smile. Her eyes turned again to the window. 'I need to sleep.' She felt her eyelids closing, and the sky beyond the window melted into a dream. Throughout her illness, sleep had become a refuge and a place of healing. It had an entrance gate of heavenly blue, and it had a password: 'My children'. Jenny pictured them on the sand, Lottie between the two boys, mothering them. She dreamed of waking up and finding them standing by her bed, their eyes solemn, their fingers clutching tiny posies.

In the three months Jenny had been in hospital,

255

she'd had few visitors. The difficulty of transport, lack of money, and pressure of work made it impossible for ordinary folk in St Ives to go on a trip to Truro. The hospital had a strict regime and 'Visiting Hour' was 3:00 to 4:00 and 7:00 to 8:00, beginning and ending with the ringing of a loud hand bell. Jenny learned not to expect anyone, and allowed herself to sleep through that hour of loneliness.

Having the leg iron fitted was stressful, despite the cheerful efforts of the physiotherapists and Jenksie. Feeling had returned to Jenny's left leg and she'd been rigorously doing exercises, building strength for the time when walking would actually be possible. Her arms had always been strong from the washing, bread-making and scrubbing she'd done in the Downlong cottage, but the early weeks of having polio left her weak all over, plus the effect of two years' malnutrition, the many times Jenny had gone without so that the children could eat. Her once thick glossy hair was scraggy and limp, her cheeks hollow, her skin pale. She felt very, very vulnerable when she sat in a chair looking at her withered right leg with its limp and twisted foot. The leg iron looked huge and ugly, like a piece of farm machinery. It was horribly shiny, cold and creaky, with stout leather straps and ferocious buckles.

'It's a good job I can't feel it,' she joked, trying to match the relentless cheerfulness of Jenksie and the team. When they stood her up, Jenny was terrified and giddy, and the leg iron felt cumbersome and heavy. She smiled bravely. 'I feel lopsided – as if I've been on the gin.' The giddiness passed and she was able to stand for a precarious few seconds, amid torrents of loud encouragement. She took her first steps between two parallel bars.

'Come on, Jen. Come on, Jen. You can do it.'

'Good girl. One more – well done. And another.'

'Well done! Six steps.'

'I'm shaking like a jelly,' Jen said.

'But you DID IT.'

She looked at the smiles and the glow of kindness in their faces, and felt a mixture of embarrassment and joy.

'You're on the way now, Jen,' said Jenksie as she helped her sit back in the wheelchair. 'On the way home, girl.'

A picture of her beloved Downlong cottage flashed into Jenny's mind. *But I don't have a home now,* she thought, while her face nodded and smiled. The almoner had gently explained to her, one dark afternoon, that the cottage had been seized and was up for auction to pay for her medical treatment. 'You must try hard to accept it, dear,' the almoner advised. 'A place will be found for you, probably in a nice home for...' she lowered her voice, '...for the disabled.'

'But – my children...' Jenny had cried and worried for days, and given up doing her exercises. Then the cry of a seagull passing over the hospital made her think of Lottie. How brave and composed she'd been after the shipwreck. How she'd settled down, bossed the boys about, and made a life for herself. Courage, like the rising sun, came blazing back into Jenny. She would fight to get better – for her children.

257

'It's Visiting Hour now, Jen,' Jenksie said as she wheeled Jenny back to the ward after her first go at walking. 'I expect you want to sleep, don't you? Shall I draw the curtains round?'

'No – I don't feel sleepy. I feel excited – as if something is going to happen. I think I'll just sit up for a while and watch people coming in,' Jenny said. 'Wouldn't it be wonderful if Lottie and Matt and Tom came through that door? Maybe I'll brush my hair, Jenksie. Can you find my brush?'

Jenny lay back against the stack of white pillows, the hairbrush in her hand. She found herself watching the door. Hoping.

The bell rang down in the corridor. The doors were flung open, and a bunch of flowers came in. A buzz of interest rippled around the ward. No one had ever, ever seen such an enormous bunch of freshly picked, bright flowers. There were scarlet and yellow tulips, Madonna lilies, blousy peonies, clouds of moon daisies and woodland ferns arranged in an extravagant spray like a peacock's tail.

A ringing voice came from behind the bunch of flowers.

'Where is she?'

'Bed three, on the left.'

The bunch of flowers swept towards Jenny in a wave of perfume. It stopped at the end of her bed, and a face under a panama hat looked round at Jenny with eyes that were fierce and brimming over with tears.

Jenny gasped. 'NAN! Oh ... Nan.'

Nan didn't speak. She lowered the flowers onto the bed and let their fragrance do the talking.

258

Then she lowered herself gingerly onto the visitor's chair. She took Jenny's pale hand and held it firmly between her rough, strong palms. The silence glistened over the flowers and around the bed, growing brighter with every heartbeat until it sparkled, and the work of the silence was done.

Jenny reached out and gave Nan a hug. The two women wept into each other's shoulders, sharing breath, sharing unspoken forgiveness. It was the first time they had ever hugged. Nan smelled of Madonna lilies and the earth they had grown in. She smelled of herb tea, and bluebell woods and Cornish pasties. And she smelled of home.

They moved apart, and looked into each other's eyes. The silence had one more healing moment to offer. A rare gift. The gift of looking into the eyes of your most deadly enemy, and finding a friend.

'This place pongs of Dettol,' Nan said.

'You haven't changed a bit,' Jenny said cheekily, and they both laughed. 'And – thank you for the flowers. They're gorgeous, and so extravagant – where DID you get them?'

'From my garden. I grow them.'

Jenny's mouth fell open.

'It's not difficult,' Nan said. 'They come up every year.'

'How did you get here, Nan? Surely you didn't carry this magnificent bouquet on the train ... did you?'

'I drove here.'

'You never did! Not in Mufty's cart?'

'No – I drove my motorcar.'

'You did what?'

'She's an Austin Seven, and she's a noisy old bird, but she goes like a scalded cat.'

'Nan! I didn't know you could drive.'

'Neither did I, Jenny. I just got in and found out. I've hit a few gate posts, and left some streaks of paint on those sharp corners in St Ives. It's been fun. I only just fit behind the steering wheel but, my goodness, people jump out of the way when they see me coming.'

Jenny looked at her in astonishment. 'But why, Nan? Why do you feel you need such a thing?'

Nan went quiet. She took Jenny's hand again, between hers, and looked at her intently. 'I'm going to find the children, Jenny. Nobody knows where they have been taken. The police wouldn't tell me, and nor would that stuck-up doctor's wife. So I've consulted my lawyer in Truro, and he's going to help me find them. He said it would be much quicker and easier if I had a car, and a telephone – so I've got both, and we're ready to go.'

'But I won't have a home for them, Nan,' Jenny said sadly, her pale fingers stroking the satin petals of a red tulip. 'Our cottage is up for auction to pay my medical fees.'

'I know. I know, dear.' Nan looked at her steadily. 'And that's why I'm here. I know we've had our differences – but it's water under the bridge – and I know I'm a wheezy old bat, but I intend to help you, no matter what. I intend to find those children and bring them home to St Ives, and I won't let the hospital send you to some nursing home. You can live with me – all of you.'

'But, Nan...' Jenny's eyes welled with tears again. 'I know you love Lottie – who wouldn't? But you've never liked the boys, have you? Are you sure it would work?'

'Of course it will work. We'll make it work,' Nan said reassuringly. 'It's never too late to start loving.'

Chapter 17

A Twist of Fate

Nan tripped over Bartholomew in her rush to answer the new phone. She'd christened it 'that hideous object'. It had such a loud, persistent bell and the other five cats had fled, wild-eyed, from the house. Shaking and cross with herself for falling, Nan heaved herself up, clutching the sideboard. It wobbled and the china horses toppled over and the gong swung to and fro. She was convinced the phone would stop ringing before she could answer it. This had happened several times, bringing her in from the garden in muddy boots, or struggling downstairs, only to find the bell had stopped ringing and all she heard was a buzz. She began to think there was something wrong with it.

This time she managed to get there. Breathlessly she lifted the heavy black receiver and looked at it, still not sure which end was which.

'Hello, Mrs Lanroska – are you there?'

'Wait a minute – let me turn this infernal thing

round.' Nan realised the voice was coming out of the end with the pepper pot holes. She turned it round and shouted into the cup-shaped mouth-piece. 'Hello. Can you hear me?'

'Yes, I certainly can, thank you. Are you all right, Mrs Lanroska? You sound a bit out of breath.'

'Of course I'm all right – I just tripped over the cat. Who are you?'

'It's Bart Pascoe, your solicitor. I've been trying to ring you. I have some good news. I've found out where the three children were taken. They are in an orphanage – Treskirby House. The name of the manager is Miss Poltair.'

'Oh, well done,' Nan said, excited. 'So where is this place?'

'It's in a remote location, at the top of Wheal Buller Hill – that's on the Helston road out of Redruth. Do you know it?'

'Not yet.'

'You turn left down a narrow lane and it's at the end – it's a big old place. I've drawn you a map and posted it to you with my letter.'

'That's wonderful news. I shall go and fetch them.'

'I wouldn't advise that course of action yet, Mrs Lanroska. The children are in the care of the welfare authorities and they won't let them go.'

'WHAT? That's preposterous,' Nan said firmly. 'They can't stop me, surely; can they?'

'I'm afraid they can. And if you go and try to take them, even if the children want to go, then it could make things worse. What I suggest, Mrs Lanroska, is a more subtle approach – a "softly-

softly catchee monkey" approach, if you see what I mean.'

'I am beside myself with anger.'

'Yes, naturally you are. But, believe me, the only way to get them back is to first go and visit them. Play the benevolent granny. Go and see their mother and get her permission. Then you must make a formal application to foster them – yes, I know you're their great-granny, but I'm afraid this is the only way. I will set the wheels in motion for you, and I hope you will take my advice.'

'That is appalling, wicked, abominable bureaucracy. No one is going to stop me from bringing MY great-grandchildren home to the place they love.'

'It's not as simple as that.' Bart Pascoe wearily explained it all again while Nan simmered at the end of the line. Then he said, 'You go and make yourself a nice cup of tea, Mrs Lanroska, and think seriously about what I've said. Calm yourself down. Don't go charging up there until you've had a chance to think it over.'

'I will not be spoken to in that patronising manner. Good morning.' Nan banged the phone down. Then, trembling, she picked it up again to see if she had broken it.

Seething, she took a basket and put six fresh brown eggs in there, carefully wrapping each one in a small square of newspaper. She packed three saffron buns from the batch she'd made yesterday, a roll of Cornish butter, and a small pot of her homemade blackcurrant jam. Orphanage food was pretty bland, she'd heard. She pictured the children's eyes shining when she gave them each a bun with the luxury of butter and jam.

The summer day was breezy and cool. It would be chilly up on those hills. Nan went to the window and scanned the distant blue hills across the bay through her telescope. She studied the Carn Brea with its stone cross and stacks of granite. Somewhere, beyond that hill, were the children!

Nan went out to the car and squeezed herself in behind the steering wheel, her mind too busy with what she was going to say. *A good omen,* she thought when the car started at the first go. Despite her anger, she deemed it wise to take Bart Pascoe's advice. This would be a 'benevolent granny' visit. Bittersweet, mandatory happiness. No ranting. No crying.

She was looking forward to seeing Lottie and she intended to make an effort with the boys. Then she'd go on to Truro, see Jenny and give her the good news. It had to be a lucky day. Lucky, lucky, lucky. Nan put her foot down and began to sing with unashamed abandon as the Austin Seven sailed along by the Hayle estuary. Mindful of the little car's needs, Nan stopped at a garage in Redruth and topped her up with petrol, oil and distilled water.

'Are you going Helston way?' the garage man asked her.

'Yes.'

'You'll be going up Wheal Buller Hill, madam,' he warned, 'and I'll give you a piece of advice. You need to go like hell at it, right from the start – you just have to hope there's no farm carts or herds of cows around.'

For the first time, Nan felt nervous and worried

about getting stuck or, even worse, rolling back. She could see Wheal Buller mine as she came to the hill, and the chimneys and slag heaps of other mines in the distance. She gripped the steering wheel tightly, put her foot down, and started to sing *Trelawny* at the top of her voice. She visualised Lottie's bright little face. 'I'm on the way, darling.' But on the last bit of the hill, the singing stopped, and she talked to the car, alarmed by the roar of the engine as she drove slower and slower, in first gear. 'Go on. Go on. Go on,' she prayed, sweating with anxiety.

At last, she was at the top. Seven hundred feet above sea level on the windswept moors of wiry grass, stunted trees and tiny fields. A place of ancient history where some of the fields had standing stones, and churches without towers crouched against the weather.

Nan felt jubilant as she swept down the narrow lane to the big, bleak house with its line of windows and tall chimneys. She'd made it. And the basket of goodies for the children was still intact. Play the benevolent grandmother. Go swanning in there with the basket over her arm, with a nice smile. Nice and calm. She imagined Lottie running towards her. It would be hard not to cry.

It was the right place. A weathered sign stood at the entrance gates. *Treskirby House.*

Then Nan went cold.

Something was wrong.

She parked and got out to open the high, wrought-iron gates and found them padlocked. A thick, brand new chain and a grey heavyweight padlock. Nan fiddled with it, not believing it would be locked, but it was. She let go of the chain and stood looking in, her hands on the rusting bars, expecting someone to come and let her in. She looked up at the house, hoping to see children's faces watching her arrive in her Austin Seven, all the way from St Ives. There was a large garden, even a well-tended vegetable patch, she observed. Surely there would be children out playing?

Nan went to the car, reached inside and blew a long blast on the horn. No one appeared, so she tried again and waited with the cold hilltop wind wrapping her mottled blue dress around her ankles. Lottie would be sure to see her from the window and cry, 'Nan! That's my Nan out there!' The imposing wooden doors would open and Lottie, Matt and Tom would come running down the drive, their eyes shining with joy.

Benevolent granny, she thought, optimistically ignoring the creeping shadow of disappointment. She felt shivery and extremely tired. Reluctantly she wedged herself back into the car and decided to rest and wait for a while. Maybe they'd taken the children on a trip out, judging by the two sets of wide tyre marks going under the gate.

She heard a dog barking and the clop-clop of heavy shire horses coming up the lane, and the sweet, heady scent of meadow hay. Nan got out and stood in the lane. 'Will you stop, please?' she asked the trilby-hatted farmer who was driving the wagon.

'Whoa there.' He pulled the reins and the two huge horses halted and immediately began to tear at the hedge, munching leaves and grass, their harnesses jingling.

'Do you know how I can get into this place?' Nan asked, hoping he would say there was another entrance. Yes, that would be it. She was at the wrong gate.

The farmer got down from the wagon, blue eyes glinting from a sunburnt face. He tapped his pipe on the roof of Nan's car and relit it. 'You 'ent gonna get in there, lady,' he said. ''Tis closed down. Gone broke or summat – lease run out – I dunno. I can't tell 'e why.'

Goosebumps prickled over Nan's skin. She looked at him in shock. 'But ... the children? Where are they?'

'Gone up-country. Saw 'em meself, yesterday, early in the morning. Saw 'em, poor little kiddies, all herded onto a great big blue bus – a private hire bus, it were. So big it nearly got stuck in the lane. Made such a mess it did. Worse than me 'aycart.'

'Is – that true?' Nan asked, looking at him through the curls of tobacco smoke.

'Course it's true. Saw 'em meself.'

'But how do you know they haven't just gone on a trip?'

'Believe me, I know, lady. 'Tis common knowledge. I 'eard it in the pub.'

'But where have they taken all those children?'

''Tis up-country. Plymouth.'

'Plymouth!' It sounded like the other end of the earth to Nan.

'They'm part of a big chain. They got orphanages all over the place – even in London, so I've 'eard. A girl who worked there was talking about it. She said they were taking 'em to Plymouth, and then splitting 'em up – a few in London and a few in Reading – some are going up to Leeds.'

'I hope they won't split up families,' Nan said, devastated.

'I wouldn't trust that lot as far as I could throw 'em. They don't care, do 'em? They'm just in it for the money. Wicked, I call it. Wicked.'

'When did the bus leave? Do you know?' Nan pictured herself tearing after the bus in her airborne Austin Seven. She'd overtake it and park in the road, blocking the way, then heave herself out with her forked stick and make them let the children go.

'Yesterday, about midday. Saw 'em meself, poor little urchins with their faces pressed to the window, some of 'em crying.'

The vision of driving to Plymouth faded.

'I'd best be on me way. I 'ope you find the kiddies.' The farmer doffed his hat to Nan, climbed onto the haycart, picked up the reins and set off in the creaking wagon, shedding wisps of hay over the hedges.

A throbbing mass of rage and despair barged its way into Nan's mind, body and soul. Arnie's children. Little Lottie, forever in her heart.

John De Lumen fidgeted and looked at his watch. For once the view of the sparkling sea failed to move him as the train pulled slowly into St Ives Station. It was ten minutes late, and that ten-minute delay could change his whole life. He was first out, opening the door before the train had even stopped. Dodging and apologising, he hurried down the platform, ticket in hand. Instead of his canvas haversack with its brushes and tubes of oil paint, he carried a brown leather briefcase with important documents inside, plus his lunch, a GWR cheese and tomato sandwich in white bread, with a mean little slice of Genoa cake without a cherry.

'Welcome to S'nives, sir. Nice to see you back again.'

'Please excuse me – I've got to dash.'

The ticket collector stared after him, puzzled as to why anyone should ever be in a hurry in beautiful S'nives.

John couldn't remember the last time he'd done any running. His legs weren't keen on the idea, but he forced them along, his leather-soled brogues pounding the slippery cobbles of The Warren, past the church, and onto Wharf Road. Today the sea was myriad colours, like an abalone shell, shimmering with opalescent gold and silver, turquoise and lavender. Normally that first glimpse of the harbour was a special meditative treat to John. He hardly noticed it, but ran hard along Wharf Road, scattering a flock of turnstones. People frowned at him as if he was an escaping thief. He didn't look like the sort of man who would have a reason to run.

Red-faced and out of breath, John arrived at the cottage in Downlong. It was the day of the auction. His heart sank when he saw the crowd gathered outside the cottage, and several expensive motorcars blocking the road, including a cream Bentley. John slid to a halt and leaned against a wall in the May sunshine, hoping his pulse was going to calm down and that he wouldn't drop dead before the bidding started.

He might be about to make the worse mistake of his life, he thought, looking at the small granite cottage. He was too late to view the inside and survey the yard at the back. All he had was the piece of paper with the description on it. *AN EXCELLENT INVESTMENT IDEAL AS A HOLIDAY COTTAGE OR AN ARTIST'S STUDIO.* It didn't say a pair of seagulls were nesting on the roof. All over St Ives the gulls were busy and stressed with the task of feeding and raising their speckled fledglings. There were two of them parked on the ridge of the roof, still fuzzy and awkward, screaming for food as the industrious parents swooped in with beaks full of fish.

'They mate for life, them gulls,' remarked the woman who was leaning on the wall next to John. Despite the sunshine, she was dressed in a long trench coat and a maroon scarf. Her eyes looked him up and down beadily. 'Where are you from then? You 'ent local.'

'London,' John said, still gasping for breath.

'So what d'you come all down 'ere for, eh?'

'We shall see.' John saw her eyeing his briefcase. He put it down, wedged it safely between his feet and focused on the auctioneer who was standing on the doorstep.

The church clock struck three, and the bidding started for the freehold of the Lanroskas' cottage.

'I will start at one hundred guineas.'

Even the seagulls fell silent as the auctioneer's keen eyes swept over the crowd. For a few seconds he locked eyes with John, but John kept

270

still, his hands in his pockets. He wasn't going to push up the price by bidding too early.

'Eighty then. Eighty guineas. Surely? What a low price for this sturdy little cottage in the heart of beautiful St Ives. Thank you, madam. Any advance on eighty guineas? Ninety – one hundred – one hundred and ten...'

It climbed rapidly to two hundred. John paid close attention, assessing each bidder with his dark blue eyes. Then it slowed down as bidders shook their heads and dropped out, leaving two, then one.

'Two hundred and fifty. Any advance on two hundred and fifty? I will sell...' The auctioneer looked directly at John as if he knew exactly what was going to happen. 'Two sixty?'

John raised his hand and nodded firmly.

'Ah – a new bidder. Two sixty – two seventy – two eighty.' There was a buzz of excitement. Heads turned to look at John.

'I will sell. Selling at two hundred and eighty guineas. Once. Twice. SOLD! To you, sir. Congratulations. Name, please?'

'John De Lumen.'

John's knees were shaking. But he signed with a steady hand. He'd done it! Thanks to *Discovering Charlotte*, which was now hanging in the gallery in New York, attracting lots of attention and favourable reviews.

'I hope you know what you've bought,' Maudie Tripconey warned, her beady eyes watching him open his mysterious briefcase.

'I'm sure I shall find out,' John said diplomatically.

'So what are you gonna do with it?' Maudie squared up to him, watched curiously by some of her neighbours.

'We shall see,' John said pleasantly, looking her in the eye.

Maudie walked away, muttering and tutting. 'A man on his own. 'Tisn't right, that's what I say.'

It was not until the crowd had gone and he was allowed to see the deeds of the cottage that John made a mind-rocking discovery. The name jumped out at him. *LANROSKA.*

What strange twist of fate had brought him to set up home in the very cottage where Charlotte had lived?

Where was she now?

As twilight fell over Cornwall on that balmy summer evening, the breeze dropped and the sea turned milky pale, with the mildest of waves lapping around the dark rocky headlands. On the great sweeping curves of beaches, the lighthouse flashed and the lights of ships shone like studs from lines of portholes.

A silver moon rose, reflected in the wet sand and the glistening dune grass. A clear, still summer night.

Beyond Godrevy, the distant coastline was an inky outline against the sky, and further inland were mosaics of light from the towns of Redruth and Camborne. Between them rose the granite tor of Carn Brea with its stone cross and massive stacks of rock, sculpted into extraordinary shapes by centuries of abrasive winds from the sea.

Twilight was wake-up time for the badgers who

had lived on the side of the hill for decades, their sett like a moon landscape of craters and heaps of excavated soil. Sometimes there were humans up there on the hill, picnicking or enjoying the view, and the oldest badger could smell them now, on the night air. Undeterred, he set out on his usual route, a path winding through the dense heather and gorse. It was like a sunken road, so deep and well-trodden by generations of paws that it even sheltered the old badger from storms. He trotted purposefully along it, his fur flouncing in the moonlight like a downy haze of light around his low-slung body. The white stripe on his head bobbed and his black nose glistened as he sniffed the air.

As he reached the top of the hill moving through the sharp moonlight shadows of the gigantic rock stack, the old badger hesitated. The smell of humans was close now. But there were no voices or movement. He listened, and heard them breathing. He crept nearer, cautious but intrigued, ready to flee at the first twitch of movement. It was his first time of being within touching distance of a human.

This one was very small. The badger sniffed her shoes, not liking the leather and the smell of different soil from some faraway place. He sniffed the night air. She had come from the east, this little human. Tentatively, the old badger dared to sniff her socks, and then her skin. He would have liked to touch a tendril of her long hair which was draped over her shoulders and get a better feel of who she was, what kind of energy she carried. But she was wedged in between two boys, an arm around each of them, their pale, unmoving faces close together as they slept deeply. The badger wanted to sniff the smallest boy's hand which was entwined in the girl's wavy hair. But it was too risky.

He stood still, his fur silvered by the moonlight, studying the sleeping children while the gentle moths of night fluttered around them. Then he turned and trotted on his way on soundless paws.

Chapter 18

The Stars of Home

A dream came true on that warm summer night.

Lottie awoke to find the heat haze of the day had cleared, and the night around her was indigo glass. The mighty, sun-soaked rocks of Carn Brea were still warm, their shapes black against a sky of brilliant stars. Mesmerised, she lay still, gazing, remembering Arnie teaching them how to find the constellation of Cygnus mapped out by the stars as a great swan flying across the heavens, with Deneb, the brightest star, in its tail. She was sure she could see it directly above her. It hadn't changed. It never would, Arnie had said.

Her time in the orphanage at Treskirby House had been the worst kind of imprisonment. Unreasonable discipline. Endless drudgery. A loveless, pointless existence. Lottie had ached with homesickness and she had held the dream in her heart, guarding it as fiercely as she had guarded the black velvet bag. The dream was beautifully simple, originating from the words of P.C. Roach: 'Up there, on the Carn Brea at night, you can see the lights of St Ives twinkling.' Lottie wanted to do that so much. She'd dreamed the dream, day and night, and had even given it a title, *The Stars of Home.*

She needed to stand up. Tom was deeply asleep and he didn't stir when she gently disentangled the ends of her hair from his fingers and put his hand on his chest. Matt lay curled up with his back against her, one hand clutching Lottie's coat which they'd used as a blanket. She stood up carefully, trying not to wake him. It was her dream and she wanted to do it on her own. Mindful of the steep and stony terrain, Lottie picked her way along the base of the rocks and stepped away from them. *I'm very small,* she thought, with the starry dome of the universe arched above her. Far below at the foot of Carn Brea were the lights of Camborne and Redruth. Excited, Lottie gazed beyond them, across the night landscape, and her heart leapt when she saw a light flashing. Godrevy! It had to be Godrevy Lighthouse. She counted between flashes, the way Arnie had taught her. Yes, it was Godrevy, and, with a sudden rush of joy, she tasted sea salt on her lips. With her whole being tingling, she followed the distant shimmer of the sea to the left and there, nestled into the cliffs, were the lights of St Ives. Home. But so far away.

For once, Lottie didn't try not to cry. She let the tears flow freely over her cheeks like a healing tide. Home. Home to St Ives where the sun and moon made paths of light across the water. She thought of Nan, asleep in her four-poster bed with Bartholomew purring under her chin. She thought of Mufty, safe in his stable, and the motherly chickens asleep in their shed.

Overwhelmed, Lottie hugged herself and gazed at the lights of home. It seemed miraculous and mysterious to have such a burden of anxiety and depression and yet be inside this intense diamond of pure happiness.

'What are you doing, Lottie?'

She heard a scuffle and Matt appeared beside her, shadowy but with the whites of his eyes shining in the dark. 'You're crying.' He hesitated, then put his arm around her shoulders.

Normally Lottie would have flicked him aside with a 'Don't touch me', but now she just leaned. Matt was taller than her now, and her head fitted nicely on his shoulder. His arm felt strong and brotherly. Lottie took some deep breaths.

'See those lights in the far distance, Matt? That's home – the lights of St Ives.'

Matt twitched with excitement. He stared and stared and Lottie watched the silhouette of his profile, a haze of light on his lower lip. Then he turned to her with a wide grin. She sensed the emotion quivering inside him. He balled his fists and did a thumbs-up at the sky. 'Let's wake Tom.'

'No,' Lottie said, 'let him sleep. We can tell him about it in the morning. The sleep will do him good.'

Matt shrugged. Already the old pecking order was emerging. Lottie was in charge, and he was content to let her be. 'I wonder what the time is?'

'Those are mostly lights from cottage windows,' Lottie said. 'People used to be in bed by eleven o'clock at home and the street lights were put out too. So it must be well before midnight.'

'Brain box,' Matt said, 'but a pretty one.' He tweaked her hair. 'What are we gonna do in the morning? I want to go and see our mum. Do you know where she is?'

'In hospital.'

'But where?'

'In Truro – probably.'

'How far away is Truro?'

'It's in the opposite direction, Matt – maybe it's about ten miles. And we don't KNOW she's there.'

'Tom's desperate to see her – really desperate.'

'Me too,' Lottie said, 'but we can talk it over in the morning, Matt. Let's just sit and gaze at the lights and enjoy the magic of the night.'

'Magic?'

Lottie couldn't read Matt's expression in the dark but she guessed it was one of scepticism. She sat down and pretended he wasn't there. To her surprise, Matt sat down with her in a brotherly silence which she appreciated. There were major decisions to make in the morning. How to get food. How to travel to St Ives without money or a map. How to trust that Nan would still be there and whether she could take all three of them. *Especially Matt,* Lottie thought.

'Listen!' Matt said suddenly. 'Someone's coming up the hill.'

It was too late to hide.

'Keep still,' Lottie whispered. 'They won't notice us in the dark. Pretend we're a rock.' She pressed close to Matt, so close that she could feel the beat of his heart inside the threadbare jacket.

The sound came steadily nearer. She pointed to where the bracken was moving, and a flash of white appeared low to the ground. She squeezed Matt's wrist to make him keep still and he did. Little pulses of amazement passed between them as a badger's white-striped face emerged, snuffling, from the bracken. With a flounce of thistle-down fur, the creature hesitated, looking at them, his black nose twitching. Tentatively, he came closer on quiet, complex paws. He padded right up to Lottie and sniffed her shoe. She felt gentleness and respect emanating from this wild badger. She dared to move, hoping to touch him, but in an instant he was gone, diving into the bracken at full gallop, his lush, furry tail dragging behind.

'Nan says animals are our teachers,' Lottie said, 'and maybe she's right. Maybe the badger was showing us how to be quiet and careful, run and hide at the first sign of danger.'

In the morning it was Matt who woke first. He had some thinking to do. His mind was a war-zone where the euphoria of freedom wrestled with the responsibility he felt towards Lottie and Tom. They should stick together. Despite letting Lottie be in charge, Matt felt he must protect them and see them safely home. But he had his own secret agenda. It was driven by guilt. Matt passionately wanted, and needed, to find his mother and say sorry to her for the cruel way he'd treated her. He wanted to know if she loved him. He didn't think she had ever loved him, not since Tom, and Lottie. If she didn't, then Matt intended to follow his burning need to be alone, to make his own way in the world, and grow into a man in peace.

The time in the orphanage had been hard, but in another way it had made him strong. The food had been boring but reliable and plentiful. Matt was now a mature thirteen-year-old, bigger and stronger than the leggy, resentful boy he had been. The work in the garden had built his muscles and given him a channel for his energy. When he saw himself in the mirror over the wash-basin he didn't see a lost, angry waif-like boy any more; he saw Arnie. His dad seemed to be right inside him, looking out, influencing him, trusting him. Matt longed to be reunited with *The Jenny Wren,* to find his dad's boat again, to own her like Arnie had promised. To Matt, *The Jenny Wren* was a person, a safe person, a sheltering friend. If only he could make enough money to buy her back from Terry. He could live on the boat, make himself a cosy den in the cabin.

Another puzzle was his changed attitude to-wards Lottie. He had hated her, and now, with frightening power, he loved her. It had begun during the car journey to the orphanage, and when they'd been torn apart. When he'd shouted, 'Run, Lottie,' he'd meant it with all his heart. He wanted Lottie to be forever free, running and dancing along the satin shore, her hair blowing in the wind, her dark blue eyes deep with secrets. He didn't want her to be turned into a miserable, servile orphan girl. He wanted Lottie to fly. But she would never love him. He'd treated her so badly. Matt felt he couldn't bear to live with that. He had to detach himself, give himself space to grow, give Arnie a chance to live within him and make him the sort of man he dreamed of being.

He definitely didn't want to live with Nan. *Nan hated him,* he thought. But then – Nan hated everyone except Lottie. Right now Matt was in a turmoil trying to sort out the mysterious, oscillating polarities of love and hate. When love turned to hate, he understood how and why. But when hate turned to love – that was unfathomable.

In the blue-white sunshine of early morning, he climbed the massive rocks of Carn Brea, and the climbing did him good. Climbing fired his confidence like nothing else. It lifted his spirits to another level, closer to the shining, uncomplicated sky. Up here on Carn Brea, the sky seemed extra enormous and the wind-sculpted shapes of the highest boulders were extraordinary. From the top he could see the land like a living map, peaceful with the early morning shadows of trees, winding lanes and farms with great granite barns, the chimneys of tin mines. He was so high up that the inland birds flew below him; flocks of rooks and jackdaws, their black plumage turned to beaten silver by the morning sun. Matt watched them, fascinated, and an idea seeded itself in his mind. *Maybe I could be an artist,* he thought, *and paint things nobody's ever seen before.*

Lottie didn't feel like climbing. Stiff and achy from a night on the damp ground, she sat beside

Tom, waiting for him to wake up, anxious about whether he was all right. Matt had made a bold escape plan, and the three of them had broken free from the orderly line of orphanage children queuing to board the train at Redruth. After yesterday's wild escape through steep, unfamiliar streets, could he face another day of running away? The hunger, the fear, the unknown, challenging journey ahead of them, and the constant worrying about being caught and sent back to Treskirby House was exhausting. She remembered how Tom had always been able to fall asleep if he was upset or stressed. A precious skill. She hoped it was helping him now.

'Come up here, Lottie!'

Matt was a triumphant silhouette against the dazzle of morning. She gazed up at him. Predictably, he was balanced on the very edge of a massive slab of granite, a sheer thirty-foot drop in front of him, his arms akimbo, his long legs confidently straight. Lottie waved to him. 'I'm staying here.' Studying the landscape, working out how to reach St Ives was important, and so was breakfast. She hadn't touched her packed lunch yesterday. She opened the haversack and unwrapped it, intending to split it between the three of them.

The sound of rustling paper woke Tom. He stretched and sat up, dreamy-eyed and disorientated, and when he saw Lottie a smile lit up his face. 'Lottie!' He gazed adoringly at her. 'Me and Matt missed you.'

'I missed you too.'

Tom sat up. 'Cor – look at them massive rocks.

Look where Matt is. How did them rocks get like that?'

'I expect there's a legend. Nan will know.'

'They look like a giant chucked them up there.'

'Look the other way and you can see St Ives,' Lottie said, pointing. 'See it? You can just see the island with the chapel on top, and last night Matt and I saw the lights twinkling, and Godrevy Lighthouse flashing.'

Tom's eyes didn't sparkle. He stared down at his scuffed brown boots. 'Have we got to walk all that way?'

'Don't you want to go home?' Lottie asked.

'I dunno.'

'Well – I'm going. You want to come with me, don't you?'

Tom nodded wordlessly.

Lottie was concerned. Something had changed. Tom never used to be stuck for words. He'd been a spontaneous chatterbox, full of life. Had it been beaten out of him? How could she bring it back? The time in Treskirby House must have been devastating for Tom, a deep shock to a happy, secure little boy.

'We have to go home, Tom. If we don't, the police will find us and send us back. Let's just get to Nan's place. She'll stick up for us, you know how fierce she is – and then she'll take us to see Mum. I promise.'

Tom looked at her, his eyes clouded with a muddle of confusion, pain and gratitude. 'I missed you, Lottie,' he managed to say.

Lottie opened the stale lunch pack and divided it into three, glad of the generous chunk of flapjack which was chewy and sustaining. They drank rainwater from a hollow basin in one of the rocks. Then Lottie organised the planning of the journey.

'We won't be up so high again,' she warned, 'so we've got to remember this landscape and plot the way to St Ives. Otherwise we could go round in circles and get nowhere.'

'We can't go across the fields,' Matt said. 'There's too many prickly hedges to climb. We've gotta go along the road and keep looking at sign-posts. Where's the main road? The one the police drove us up?'

'That's risky,' Lottie said. 'There are cars going along it – and carts and lorries. We'd have to keep hiding. We mustn't get caught. We'll never get another chance like this one.'

'But the little lanes are no good,' Matt said, pointing to one. 'They wind all over the place. It would take forever.'

'I know what to do,' Tom said. 'We could walk to the sea. It's only over there – and follow the edge of the cliffs 'til we get to St Ives.'

'No. There might not be a path, and we'd be struggling through gorse and bracken,' Lottie told him.

'And when we got to Hayle, we'd have to go all round the harbour, through the town and over the long road bridge,' Matt said. 'Someone would be sure to see us.'

Tom pouted. 'Can't we just tell people where we're going?'

'No,' said Matt and Lottie together, and Tom looked crushed.

'We're fugitives, Tom,' Lottie explained.

'What's a fugitive?'

'A person who is escaping.'

'But we escaped yesterday. You said we did.' Tom looked indignant.

'We've got to escape every day, Tom, until we find Nan's place in St Ives.'

'But I don't want to live with Nan. I want Mum. I want her a lot.' Tom's eyes burned with pain. 'And if ... if ... I can't have Mum ... I want to die. I do, Lottie, I really do.'

Lottie and Matt looked at each other in horror. Tom wasn't crying. He'd left the words smoking in the air. And he'd meant it. He seemed incapable of crying in the way he used to do. There was no safety valve now for Tom.

Lottie understood, but she still felt powerless. She gave Tom a hug, rocking him gently as he leaned on her. He felt tense and rigid, not like himself at all. Matt tried to offer some empathy, putting his hand on Tom's back. For a weird moment he and Lottie felt like parents.

They sat, silent, with Tom between them, searching the land spread out before them. *If only Nan had a telephone,* Lottie thought, *we could ring her up. Or I could write her a letter and tell her where we are. But I've got no paper and no money for a stamp.*

It seemed impossible.

Then, from far away came a familiar sound, a sound they heard in St Ives. The whistle of a train.

'There it is. LOOK!' Matt was fired with excitement.

Together they watched the Great Western Railway express steaming through the landscape, its plume of white steam flying like a scarf. Even as the train disappeared behind buildings and trees, the white plume still marked its path.

'The railway!' Matt shouted. He jumped to his feet. 'It goes in a straight line. THAT'S what we have to do. Get down there, get on the line and follow it – walk along it all the way to St Ives. It'll be easy. It's perfect.'

'But, Matt...' Lottie stared at him, unable to keep pace with his reckless plan.

'We could even follow it at night – under cover of darkness.' His bright eyes were like magnets drawing Lottie and Tom into his enthusiasm. 'And there's not many trains – we can easily hop out of the way. They make such a racket. We should start right now. Come on. It's our best plan. I know it is. We'll be in St Ives in no time.'

'But what about our dinner?' Tom asked. 'I'm still hungry.'

'Leave that to me,' Matt said. 'But get ready to run away fast if we get near a bakery or a market.'

Lottie frowned at him. 'You're not thinking of stealing, are you?'

'Course I am. How else are we gonna eat?'

'I could beg, like Oliver Twist,' Tom said.

'Or you could let me walk into the shop and persuade them to give us yesterday's bread rolls,' Lottie said.

'No.' Matt shook his head. 'It would draw attention to us and we don't want that. I can pinch food. It doesn't matter if I get caught 'cause I'm the bad boy anyway. Even the orphanage don't

285

want me. Now come on. Down the hill. Or am I going on me own?'

Lottie followed him, dragging Tom who was still eating flapjack. Along the badger's path through a bright tapestry of gorse flowers and pink heather, with the wild songs of skylarks, then down a rough track, the gritty mine-spoil crunching underfoot. It wound between two tin mines, one derelict and one busy with miners arriving for work, whistling and singing. They took no notice of the children.

Soon they were plodding past terraces of cottages on the outskirts of Camborne. The cottages fronted the street, as they did in Downlong, and there were bottles of fresh milk on the doorsteps. 'When I say RUN, you run,' Matt said, eyeing the gleaming glass bottles of creamy milk, 'and turn left at the end of this street.'

He winked at Lottie. She glared back. 'Matt, you can't steal from these people. They're like us – poor, like we were in Downlong.'

'I can.' Matt looked defiant.

Lottie drew herself up taller. 'If you do, Matt Lanroska, I shall stand in the street and shout it out to everyone. My brother, the milk thief.'

'That's why I shall survive and you won't,' Matt said ruthlessly. 'Tom wants a bottle of milk, don't you, Tom?'

'Nick it from the milkman's cart,' Tom said. 'He won't miss a few. He's down there – look.'

Ten minutes later, gasping for breath, the three of them sat in a field, their backs against a sweet-smelling haystack. Hearts thudding, they had fled through the streets of Camborne, each clutching

286

one of the thick glass bottles of milk Matt had pinched from the back of the milk cart which was standing, unattended, at the kerb, the pony dozing in the sun.

The milk tasted heavenly and, despite herself, Lottie drank gratefully.

'What shall we do with the bottles?'

'Stuff 'em down a rabbit hole.'

At the far end of the field, a colony of rabbits were sitting perfectly still, their ears erect, their fur silver in the morning sun. Beyond the hedge was a low embankment, pink with tall foxgloves and a fence of posts and wire. 'That's the railway! Come on.' Matt flung his empty milk bottle at the haystack and ran off, with Tom following, towards the railway.

Lottie collected the three empty bottles and stood them neatly in the lane, hoping the milk-man would find them. She felt exhausted, her tummy aching from too much milk, and the boys had run off without her. She didn't want to walk on the railway track.

'Come ON, Lottie,' Matt yelled, already on the other side of the wire.

Lottie trailed slowly across the field, carrying her shoes, her sore feet brushing through the lush clover and buttercups. She wanted to lie down and go to sleep. It was a power struggle now, between her and Matt, and she didn't feel up to it. She tried to ignore the GWR notice on the embankment saying *TRESPASSERS WILL BE PROSECUTED.*

Tom was standing in front of it. 'That's like the Lord's Prayer,' he said. 'Forgive us our trespasses. What's the other word, Lottie?'

'Prosecuted.'

'Does that mean you get your head chopped off?'

'No that's *executed.*'

'So what does *prosecuted* mean?'

'It means you go to 'ell,' Matt said. He held the wire down for Lottie to climb through. Then he bounded onto the railway track and stood victoriously. 'The way home! It's gonna be easy.'

'Lottie's tired,' Tom said. 'And me.'

'When we get to Hayle we'll have a rest,' Matt promised. 'We've got to keep going.'

The shining rails stretched ahead under a clear blue sky, the banks rich with cornflowers, ox-eye daisies and scarlet poppies. The children soon found it was easier to walk between the rails, stepping on the sleepers and avoiding the sharp ballast. Lottie found it fun to balance-walk along a single rail. They had plenty of warning when a train was approaching. At this end of Cornwall, the great GWR steam engines chuffed slowly between quiet little stations, and the rails carried the clatter of the metal wheels a long way down the track. The only dangerous places were in the cuttings where the flowery banks disappeared, replaced by walls of jagged rock covered in mosses and ferns. When they came to a cutting, they listened for trains, then ran through, following Matt. He led them on, relentlessly, never seeming to get tired.

But the proposed rest at Hayle Station didn't happen. Instead, they got a fright.

'Don't run. Act as if we're meant to be here,'

Matt said, leading them under a bridge and onto the platform. Lottie and Tom were so exhausted that they could hardly keep going. But the busy port of Hayle hummed around them and the air smelled of sea salt, tar and sawdust. Tantalising glimpses of the surf, the estuary and the piping cries of curlew and oyster catchers made Lottie feel emotional. So close to home now. She recognised the distant headland of Carrack Gladden. She decided not to speak in case she burst into tears. Her legs seemed to be walking up the station platform without her.

A few people were waiting on the opposite side with suitcases, but no one took any notice of three children trudging along in the hot sun.

At the other end of the platform, the rails curved inland going over a megalithic stone viaduct, its endless arches straddling the town. Matt didn't hesitate but attacked it in eager strides. Lottie yelled at him, 'Matt – NO! We can't walk over such a long bridge. It's too narrow.'

He kept walking.

'If a train comes, there's no room for us. There's no bank.'

He didn't look back.

'Matt!' Lottie was screaming at him now. She grabbed Tom. 'Don't go after him. Stay with me.'

Matt didn't even turn.

'If a train comes, it will CRUSH you against the wall.'

Lottie pushed Tom onto a bench and he sat obediently, too tired to do anything else. 'I've got to stop him. I'm going after him. You stay there.' She hurtled after Matt, running between the rails, over ballast and sleepers. How could Matt be so stupid? Or was he trying to kill himself? She had to stop him.

The rails started to clatter. She knew it meant there was a train about a mile away. 'MATT!' Lottie screamed until her throat was sore.

A new drama unravelled behind her. She heard Tom shout, 'Look OUT, Lottie!' Then the crunch, crunch of heavy boots running after her.

'GET OFF THEM RAILS.' A man's voice, louder than the town crier. 'What the 'ell do you think you'm doing? Get back on the platform – NOW. Right now or I'll skin you alive.'

Lottie turned, caught between two terrors. A station porter with a dark red furious face was tearing towards her. 'You stupid, crazy little girl.' Paralysed with fright, Lottie cowered in the middle of the railway, hearing the train.

The incensed porter thundered to a halt and grabbed her as if she was a doll, clamping his big meaty hands under her arms and lifting her up. 'Don't you move,' he warned and ran back to the platform, bouncing her up and down, her hair falling over her face. His shoulder smelled of nicotine and soot.

He flung her down with a bone-shaking thump onto the bench next to Tom, who was white-faced and indignant. 'Don't you hurt my sister,' Tom clenched his fists, 'or I'll fight you.' He wriggled close to Lottie and looked up at her. 'Are you all right?'

Lottie nodded, shaken. She studied the porter's furious face. He was breathing hard and sweat trickled from under his cap. 'My brother...' Lottie said desperately. 'He's on the bridge.'

And as she spoke, the train for Penzance came steaming into Hayle Station. Far below the great stone viaduct, people who were walking around the town looked up and gasped in horror as they saw a boy balance-walking along the parapet.

Chapter 19

Locked In

Lottie sat on the station bench, trembling from head to toe. A wild look of intent passed between her and Tom. Run, it said. But which way? Out of the station and into the town. Run until they found the end of the viaduct, and Matt. Stick together and never give up.

It was too late. The porter seemed to have read the intention in their eyes. Quick as a boxer's fists, his meaty hands grabbed both children, Tom by the ear and Lottie by a hank of her hair.

'Ow, you're hurting me. You're pulling me ear off,' Tom yelled, aiming a kick at the porter's substantial shins.

'Come quietly then or I will pull it off. And you, madam, if you wanna keep your flea-ridden hair.'

Lottie wanted to burst with rage. 'I have not got fleas. I've never had fleas. How dare you.'

'How dare you trespass on the railway line, you dirty little street urchins.' He dragged them

291

ruthlessly to a brown door marked *WAITING ROOM*, pushed them inside and locked the door from a bunch of keys hanging around his belt. 'You sit there and don't move. I'll be back when I've dealt with this damned train.'

They heard a slam of doors and the guard's whistle. Then the train's whistle as it chuffed out of the station and onto the viaduct.

'It'll kill Matt.' Tom curled up in a ball on the brown leather seat. 'I can't bear it, Lottie. First me dad – then me mum – now me brother.'

Lottie put her arm around him. 'No, it won't. Matt will be over the other side by now on a nice grassy bank.' She tried to sound reassuring, but she wasn't sure at all.

'Don't tell him about the orphanage,' she warned as the porter came back in.

'I'm Mr Roskenna,' he said, in a calmer voice. 'I'm not here to hurt you. It's my job to keep the railway line clear, and keep everyone safe – even the likes of you.' He sat down, took his hat off and pushed his hair away from his sweaty face. 'You could fry an egg on them rails in this heat.'

Lottie stood up and composed herself. She looked him in the eye. 'Mr Roskenna, you've no right to keep us here. Let us go, please, and we won't come here again.'

He peered at her. 'Are you Cornish children? Or tourists.'

'We're Cornish children.'

'Right – then why aren't you in school? Playing truant, I suppose. What are your names?'

'Lottie and Tom.'

'Lottie and Tom who?'

'Lanroska.'

'And where do you live?'

'In S'nives,' Tom said, pouting.

'So what are doing in Hayle?'

Tom looked up at Lottie. She gave his shoulder a warning squeeze. 'That's none of your business, Mr Roskenna.'

He looked her up and down. 'You are a little madam,' he said, 'and I don't believe you're Cornish. He might be, but you're not.'

'She came off a shipwreck,' Tom said, 'but she's our big sister now.'

'Is that so?' Mr Roskenna tapped his chin thoughtfully. 'And if I let you go, where are you gonna go to now?'

'S'nives.'

'And how are you gonna get there? Eh?'

'That's our affair,' Lottie said haughtily.

'Well, madam, I'm not letting you go until I know you're safe. I care about you – see? Where are your parents? Eh?' He looked at Tom.

'Dunno,' Tom said.

'That won't do. How do I know you're not on the run from somewhere? I heard some kids went missing yesterday from Redruth station. That's a job for the police, not me.'

Lottie's heart sank. She didn't know what it was safe to say. Mr Roskenna was putting his hat back on as if he'd already made up his mind. 'I'm locking you in, for now,' he said, standing up. 'I'll be back in about ten minutes. And if you're good, I'll bring you some orange squash and biscuits.'

He's going to ring the police, Lottie thought, and a cloud of depression engulfed her. The glory of being free, the Cam Brea and the lights of St Ives. Was the dream already over? Over and gone? So soon.

Up at Hendravean, Nan was getting ready to go to Truro for another meeting with Bart Pascoe. She wanted some action. Aware that she needed to look civilised, she chose a navy-blue dress she hadn't worn for years. It had voluminous sleeves and a full skirt which suited Nan's plan. She wanted to billow into the solicitor's office like a huge sailing ship. She chose a formidable navy hat with a wide brim to complete the effect. If she didn't get any sense out of Bart Pascoe, then she'd billow into the local press office. The *West Briton* would surely do a feature on how three Cornish children had been snatched from their home, imprisoned in Treskirby House, and now carted off to Plymouth, facing the prospect of being split up and relocated to up-country orphanages, while she, Nan, was a respectable grandmother with a home and heart big enough for all three children.

She'd talked it through with Jenny, especially the question of Matt's challenging behaviour. Between them, they'd manage him and, hopefully, Vic would get involved as well. Further down the line was another battle Nan intended to win. She had to prove to the hospital discharge team that she was fit to look after Jenny, who was now officially 'disabled'.

Nan had christened it 'Bureaucracy Mountain'.

Today's summit was to persuade Bart Pascoe to take immediate legal action to get the children back before they disappeared forever. Nan hadn't got the heart to tell Jenny about the children being taken to Plymouth. She'd try to resolve the problem first.

Instead of her beloved forked stick, Nan chose a respectable cane from her collection in the hall. She glanced at herself in the hall mirror, shooed the chickens off the stairs and sailed out, in warrior mode.

Bartholomew was sitting on the gatepost looking majestic and supervising Nan trying to start the Austin Seven in the hot sun. She was just squeezing herself behind the wheel when the cat gave a loud wail and ran to her.

'What's the matter with you?'

Bartholomew looked at the house and gave another echoing wail. Nan listened. The phone was ringing. Annoyed, she struggled back to the house, unlocked it and went in with Bartholomew galloping, kink-tailed, ahead of her.

Something's happened, Nan thought. She snatched the receiver off its pedestal. 'Hello?'

A man's voice answered. 'Are you Mrs Lanroska?'

'Yes, I am.'

'And are you the lady who lives at Hendravean in S'nives?'

'Yes.' Nan's heart began to beat wildly. 'Who are you?'

'I'm the porter at Hayle Railway Station. I have two children here who say their name is Lanroska. I caught them walking along the railway line. I was concerned for their safety and so I've locked them in the waiting room.'

Nan caught her breath. No, it couldn't be.

Could it? She began to shake with emotion. 'What are their names?'

'The little girl's name is Lottie.'

'Lottie,' whispered Nan and, without warning, tears trickled down her wrinkled cheeks. She couldn't breathe. Lottie was found. Beautiful, bright little Lottie.

'Mrs Lanroska? Are you still there?'

Nan tried to compose herself. Be responsible. And respectable. She swallowed. 'Yes – I'm sorry, I was just surprised.' She managed to speak calmly. 'How did they get to Hayle Station?'

'I don't know. They won't tell me anything. I guessed they were in trouble of some sort. But they did give me the name, Lanroska – and I found you in the telephone directory, a gurt thick thing it is.'

'There should be another boy with them; Matt, an older brother,' Nan said.

'Yes, they said they were worried about him. He went on walking – over the Hayle viaduct, little monkey. We checked the line and it was clear, no sign of him. He's hiding up somewhere.'

Breathe, Nan thought. *Stop acting like a jelly and pull yourself together, woman.*

'That sounds like young Matt,' she said calmly. She listened to Mr Roskenna ranting on about children and railway regulations and how he was responsible for Hayle Station. While he was talking, the chickens crept back in, nonchalantly, and re-established themselves on the stairs.

'These children keep asking me to let 'em go,' the porter said, 'but I've told 'em – no – not until I'm sure they've got a responsible adult there.'

296

'I'll come and fetch them in my car,' Nan said.

'Oh – you've got a CAR.' He sounded impressed.

'Keep them locked in until I get there. We don't want them running off again,' Nan said, 'and – promise me you won't let them go with anyone else.'

'Right. I'll give 'em some orange squash and biscuits. That'll keep 'em quiet.'

'Thank you,' Nan said, overwhelmed. 'Thank you so very much. I'll start the car and come now.'

She put the phone down and walked out into the sunshine, leaving the door wide open and the chickens on the stairs. In a burst of euphoria, she took off her formidable navy hat and sent it spinning over the chicken shed roof.

Lottie! She'd found Lottie.

Nan started the car, opened all its windows and went roaring out of St Ives, up Tregenna Hill, with the wind in her hair and a song in her heart.

Lottie and Tom inspected the waiting room window to see if it was possible to escape by climbing out. It had heavily frosted glass and it didn't look as if it had ever been opened. Tom kicked the door a few times to see if he could dislodge one of its panels, but it hardly creaked. Everything on Hayle Station was solid and unmoveable, especially Mr Roskenna. He'd brought the orange squash and biscuits, a big smile on his face. But seeing them both obviously waiting to dart out of the door and away, his mood had changed. He'd put the tray down on the floor and leaned his weight against

297

the door, the keys in his hand. 'Don't you try any-thing,' he warned, ''cause I'm ready for you – and I'm not letting you go. Look what I've brought you! Courtesy of Great Western Railway – squash and biscuits.'

'Thank you,' Lottie said politely. 'But we just want to be allowed to go home.'

'You will be going home, in about half an hour. I've arranged for a car to pick you up.'

'A car!' Nobody they knew had a car. Lottie and Tom looked at each other in horror, both sure it would be the police coming to take them back to the orphanage. Mr Roskenna's eyes twinkled with mischief. He'd been upset and angered by their behaviour, and now it seemed he was enjoying keeping them in suspense. He slid along the door, backed out, and slammed it shut. They heard him walk away whistling.

They drank the orange squash, and Tom stuffed biscuits in his jacket pockets. 'Don't you want one, Lottie?' he asked.

'I do – but I'm too upset to eat it.' Lottie slumped onto the brown leather seat. She lay down on her side, as if she was in bed, and held her head with both hands, shutting out the world.

'Aren't you well, Lottie?' Tom stroked her hair and she let him, knowing how much they both needed comfort. Worrying about Matt, and dreading the moment when the car arrived, Lottie drifted into an exhausted sleep. It was like a small oasis, too small for the huge desert under a burning sun. 'They can't keep us in an orphanage forever,' she muttered. 'We're going to grow up, Tom, and then we'll be free.' She opened her eyes and saw the deepening shadow of despair in Tom's sleepy brown eyes.

'When the car comes, Tom – listen to me!' Lottie sat up, a spark of hope in her mind. 'We could pretend to go with them nicely, as if we're not going to be any trouble. Then, just as we get to the car – we run, like we did at Redruth. It's our only, only chance now.'

'What if I can't do it?' Tom looked into her eyes, slowly, as if it was painful. 'You don't have to wait for me, or come back for me, Lottie. If you can escape, just go, and don't worry about me. Promise?'

Lottie saw a new shadow forming at the back of Tom's eyes. He'd had enough. Enough of running. But could she bear to abandon him? She didn't think so.

They pressed together on the brown leather seat as if it could be the last time they would see each other. From outside the quiet little station came the sound of a car backfiring as it came to a halt. There was a pause, then the car door slammed and there were footsteps, slow footsteps. Shoes, not boots. And the tap of a walking stick. A shadow billowed past the frosted glass of the waiting room window. A dear, remembered, bulky shape.

Lottie and Tom looked at each other, not daring to hope, yet hoping to catch the sudden flame of light in each other's eyes.

A ringing voice filled the station. 'Where are my great-grandchildren?'

The flame of light burst into a thousand sparks. They heard Mr Roskenna's boots scurrying, his voice being respectful, his keys jangling as if they were alive.

Lottie and Tom clung together, just in case. In case it was a dream.

The door swung open, and there was Nan. Nan with her toothy old smile, and her fierce eyes all misty.

'NAN,' Lottie breathed, and then they were hugging. Tom hung back, but Lottie dragged him into the hug, and Nan wrapped her huge freckled arms around both of them, their three heartbeats melting together into joy.

Nan sat down on the brown leather seat and pulled her dress over her wide apart knees. 'Let me look at you,' she said. 'You've grown – and put on weight – look at Tom! What on earth did they feed you on?'

'Porridge,' Tom said. He didn't smile at Nan. 'I want to see our mum.' His bottom lip trembled. 'Where is she? Is – is she dead? No one told us nothing. I wrote her a letter and Mr Gorda chucked it in the bin.'

Nan shut her eyes for a few seconds, waiting for the right words to settle like birds into her mind. She knew she had to try very hard not to be fierce with Tom. Mentally she classified Mr Gorda in her 'black book'. 'That was appallingly cruel,' she said, 'and your mum is in hospital in Truro. I've been to see her, and she's getting better every day. She's had polio, and one of her legs doesn't work any more. They've made her a calliper, which is an iron leg, and she's learning to walk on it.'

'Poor Jenny,' Lottie said, remembering how

Jenny had loved to dance.

'Right now, I'm going to take you home,' Nan said, 'and home is my place. I've told Jenny you can all live with me. She's longing to see you – and I'll take you to see her in a few days' time.'

A smile passed through Tom's eyes but didn't reach his mouth. 'But – I thought you and Mum hated each other,' he said, 'and what about my box of marbles?'

'I've got your box of marbles safe,' Nan said, 'and Lottie's bed. Jenny and I are good friends now.'

Lottie beamed and clasped her hands together joyfully. But Tom looked sceptical. 'How come? I thought you and Mum hated each other forever.'

'Well, I know a magic spell for getting rid of hatred,' Nan said, lowering her voice to hypnotic mode. 'I put it in a bubble of purple light and let it blow away across the sea, and St Ia came out of the waves. She seized the bubble of hatred and took it far away west into the deep Atlantic, to the place where storms are made. And there it will stay, 'til the end of time.'

Lottie and Tom gazed at her in awe, and suddenly it was like the old happy times by the wishing well at Carrack Gladden.

'I know I've been a grumpy old granny,' Nan said, 'but I'm going to try to change.'

Lottie slipped her arms round Nan and kissed her wrinkled cheek. 'We missed you, Nan. You're lovely, and I don't want you to change.'

Crossing the viaduct at Hayle had been a turning point for Matt. He'd seen Lottie and Tom being captured, and so he wasn't going to risk returning to Hayle Station. Like the great rocks of the Carn Brea, the viaduct appealed to his eternal quest for danger. He enjoyed challenging himself, celebrating his perfect balance and confidence. Frightening people who were walking below was part of the fun. It came to an end when he saw the train pulling into Hayle Station. Realising he had only minutes to save his life, Matt had covered the length of the viaduct in spectacular leaps and strides, arriving gasping for breath at the far end. There still wasn't much room for him on the narrow strip of blackened earth so he flung himself face down and clung to the tough roots of ragwort and couch grass. He feared the massive, hissing power of the steam engine would suck the flesh from his bones and blast the life out of him. When it had passed, discovering he was still intact was like being reborn.

His hands and clothes were black with soot and he guessed his face was too. He yearned to find the beach and plunge into cool, invigorating surf. But Hayle was a busy, complicated port. He'd have to find his way to the other side of the Red River, a treacherous fast current colliding with the surf, polluting the water with waste from the inland tin mines. Everyone knew it was a dangerous place to swim.

So Matt walked on, following the railway as it curved inland and the banks widened into flowery expanses of rosebay willowherb and evening primrose. It ran past some close-cropped paddocks where there were goats and skewbald horses. Matt climbed through the wire and went to the stone water trough, cupped his hands and drank the clear, peaty water, then took off his jacket and shook the soot out of it, watched by a small audience of horses. He felt so hot and grimy that he plunged his whole head in, letting the water flood deliciously into the roots of his hair. Emerging refreshed and sparkling clean, he walked on along the railway, the heat shimmering on the rails in the distance. Ahead of him was a signal box and sets of signals where the rails diverged at St Erth Station.

Mindful of being seen and caught, Matt approached the little country station cautiously and, once his feet were on the platform, he sauntered along as if he'd every right to be there. Mercifully no one challenged him. It seemed a sleepy place, with a few tourists slumped on benches. St Erth Station was a good place to hide. The St Ives branch line platform was a few steps below the main London line, and it had little recesses with seats where he could be invisible and think.

Matt didn't want to live with Nan. He didn't want to go back to school either. He felt too old. Beyond school. Matt wanted a life of his own. He wanted to have a go at being free, living on his wits, maybe even finding a job. He'd lie about his age, and he was confident that he could steal food for himself and sleep rough. Deep down, Matt believed no one loved him, so nothing mattered. He'd be a bad boy and enjoy it.

St Erth Station with its diverging rail tracks was the perfect place to make a decision. The tourists were standing up and hanging on to their luggage as a magnificent, highly polished steam train pulled in. Matt bounded up onto the platform to watch. He listened to the announcement. 'This is the train for London, Paddington, calling at Hayle, Camborne, Redruth, Truro...'

Matt sauntered up the platform and boarded the train, walked down the corridor and locked himself into the toilet. The guard blew his whistle, waved his green flag, and the train pulled away, gathering speed as it headed for London through the hot afternoon.

Chapter 20

'Don't You Make Trouble'

Jenny was snoozing in the armchair next to her bed. The heat made her drowsy and she was tired from the effort of learning to walk again. She was still hobbling, on crutches, afraid to trust the gleaming calliper strapped onto her useless leg. It looked awful and it made an annoying, unfeminine clonk on the floor. Getting used to it was emotionally draining and humiliating but the alternative was a wheelchair, and that would be impossible in St Ives.

She wasn't enjoying her snooze. Always there were nightmares about losing her children, and the battle against poverty. In her dreams, Jenny often saw Arnie but he was out of reach, on the other side of a river, or on a boat with miles of sparkling water between them. But today, in her dream, Arnie was close, at last. She sensed his presence. She woke up with a jump, and stared at him. Those long lashes. That slow, caring smile.

But he looked so young.

'Arnie!' she whispered, and the image flickered like a reflection in water. She looked down and saw his legs, boyish legs in scruffy shorts and badly darned grey socks.

'It's not Arnie, Mum. It's me, Matt.'

'Matt?' A shimmer of disappointment fled through Jenny's eyes, swiftly followed by a flare of incredulous joy. 'MATT!' she screamed. 'Matt – DARLING!'

Matt gulped. Never, in his whole life had she called him 'darling'. It felt like the most healing word, melting in the air, pouring over him.

'But you've grown so 'andsome,' Jenny said, her face bright. 'You look SO like your dad now. I can't believe you're actually here. Come on, give us a hug.' She held out her arms.

'I'm a bit grubby, Mum.'

'I don't care. I wouldn't care if you were covered in tar. You're my boy.'

Matt tried, but he found the hug overwhelming. Being held close, like a baby, on his mother's breast, his chin on her shoulder, tore his self-control to pieces. But he still couldn't let go of his burning need to cry. He gave her what he hoped was a friendly squeeze, and pulled away.

'How did you get here, Matt?'

'We escaped – Tom and Lottie and me – from the orphanage. They lied to us, Mum – told us we were going on a trip when really they were taking us – all of us – up to Plymouth to be relocated in another orphanage. They took us to Redruth Station on a bus, to catch a train, and just as it was about to leave we opened the door, jumped out and ran like hell. We ran all the way through Redruth and up onto the Carn Brea and we slept there under Lottie's coat. Tom slept all night but Lottie and me were awake and we saw the lights of St Ives twinkling in the distance.'

Jenny listened, enthralled. She gazed at Matt in awe. 'You're very, VERY brave. I'm so proud of you, Matt.'

Matt nodded. He waited, for the awkward questions. He looked at Jenksie who was standing behind Jenny's chair. Jenksie had rescued him from the hospital entrance after a fierce, navy-uniformed dragon had evicted him: 'We don't admit dirty unaccompanied boys to this hospital.' Jenksie had been about to go home, her nurse's cape swinging around her shoulders. She'd dealt briskly with the navy-uniformed dragon: 'I am Mrs Lanroska's nurse. I will take Matt in to see his mother, and he will be the BEST medicine she could have. Come along, Matt.' Matt had loped gratefully beside the swinging, confident Jenksie, and on the way she'd given him some wise advice. 'DON'T tell your mother anything that will worry her.'

So when Jenny asked, 'Where are Lottie and Tom now?' Matt found that question difficult. He thought for a moment, then offered an explanation. 'They're safe, Mum. But the porter at Hayle station yelled at us. He ran after us, mad as hell he was, and he grabbed Lottie and Tom. I saw him pushing them into the waiting room. I

306

didn't go back 'cause I reckoned he'd catch me as well. I wanted to go home to St Ives, but I wanted to see you first, Mum. I – I didn't even know if you were alive. No one would tell me. So when the London train pulled in at St Erth, I got on it, hid in the toilet, and got off at Truro – and ... here I am.'

'So what's happened to Lottie and Tom?'

'Dunno.' Matt gave a guilty shrug. 'The police might take them back to the orphanage – but Lottie will find a way of escaping, Mum, she's really smart. She'll get to Nan's place if she can.'

'Oh dear – I hope they're both safe.' Jenny looked at him with troubled eyes. Immediately, Matt felt her love drifting away from him, the wondrous moment of being called 'darling' disappearing into the great complicated world like a sugar crystal stirred into hot tea.

Jenny looked at him shrewdly. 'We've got to find them, Matt.'

Jenksie leaned over Jenny. 'I'll go and see what I can find out,' she said. 'I'm sure Matt wants to know about your leg and how well you're doing.'

Matt looked at the gleaming metal calliper on his mother's leg. He remembered how she'd loved to dance. He wanted to say something kind, but the words that came out of his mouth were, 'You smell of Dettol, Mum.' And the words he'd intended to say remained stubbornly locked in his heart.

Jenksie was soon back, a smile forming two deep dimples on her cheeks. 'I've got some VERY good news.'

'What?'

'Nan has telephoned to say that Lottie and Tom have been found, alive and well, and she has taken them home in her car. She'll bring them in to see you as soon as she can.'

Jenny clasped her hands together and her face shone. 'My children! I've got my children back. Oh, I'm so happy – I think I could WALK!' She pushed herself up, out of the chair. 'Give me your arm, Matt, just for balance. See – I can do it. I can.'

She was radiant, but Matt was secretly shocked and upset to see the painful, awkward steps. His mother had been a free spirit, dancing, running across the beach, marching along the streets of St Ives, proud and agile. He didn't think he could bear to see her like this. Would it be forever? *What a death sentence,* he thought privately. He wanted her back, the way she was. Then he hated himself for being so selfish. Matt's mind was in a terrible muddle. He wanted, more than ever, to get away by himself and think.

'Well done – oh, you're flying now, Jen!' Jenksie beamed encouragement as Jenny reached the window, turned laboriously and walked back, dragging the heavy calliper, trying not to mind its ugly weight. She fell back into the chair, shaking a little, drained by the effort.

'Mum...' Matt took her hand. There was so much he wanted to say and to ask. He picked the thought which bubbled to the top of his cauldron of worries. 'I don't want to live with Nan.'

Jenny shut her eyes, then opened them into an expression Matt knew only too well. Exasperation. Rejection would come next. 'Same old

Matt,' she ranted, and the old fire came into her eyes. 'You should be grateful we've got Nan and she's offered to put up with us, Matt. You know what she's like. It's a big thing for her to do at her age – and God only knows how we're gonna manage. But for Nan, we'd be homeless.'

Matt frowned. 'Why? We've got our cottage.'

'No, Matt, we haven't. It's had to be sold to pay my medical fees. We've got nothing – nothing except Nan's goodwill – so don't you go making trouble.'

Matt felt himself go dark. Dark and bad, all over again. The shock crawled over him. First the boat, now the cottage. And how could his mother so casually tell him their home was gone? They were homeless. Did she think he hadn't got feelings? Was she still trying to shock him into 'behaving'? He'd done his best to bring Lottie and Tom home, and all of his effort and courage counted for nothing, swept ruthlessly away under the shadow of those old words, those cruel words, 'Don't you make trouble'.

'I won't make trouble,' he said, lifting his head and narrowing his eyes. 'I'm leaving. On the train. I'll make a life for myself. And I'm not coming back.'

He turned and swaggered out of the ward. Once out of sight, he ran, wild and angry, out into the unfamiliar streets of Truro, a long grey thread trailing from one of his socks.

'He's painting it white.'

'White!'

'Yes – white – he's got it in a big bucket and a

brush wide enough to paint an elephant.'

'He's not painting the granite, is he? He'd better not be!'

Maudie Tripconey and a group of neighbours from Downlong stood at the end of the cobbled street, collectively complaining about what John De Lumen was doing to the cottage. Their voices were shrill with indignation and John could clearly hear every word. Unperturbed, he calmly continued sloshing white paint over the rough stone walls. He'd done the inside, painting everything white, even the stairwell and the quaint little wrought-iron banister. The result was exactly what he wanted; clean and fresh and full of light. Satisfied, he'd sat on an upturned bucket sipping Cornish scrumpy cider from a ceramic tankard, and he'd enjoyed watching the sunlight changing on the white walls. Slabs of lemon yellow, and shadows of deep blue, like a snowfield. At sunset, it turned rosy pink and gold.

John's furniture hadn't yet arrived from London, so he was managing with a few oddments. Most of his stuff wouldn't fit into the cottage and he'd spent hours with a tape measure working out a plan. Bookshelves. A table and chairs. A small armchair. An art cupboard. He'd have a simple life with no china cabinets or family silver. What he'd miss was his piano.

On that first night, he'd slept in Lottie's old bedroom on two rolled up dustsheets, the window wide open to the tang of salty air and the lamentations of seagulls. He awoke with a feeling of deep, deep peace in body and soul, so different from how he felt in London. He wasn't going back. From now on, he'd be part of St Ives and its loving, vibrant community.

Upsetting the neighbours hadn't been a great start but John wasn't going to rise to the bait.

'We've gotta confront him,' Maudie said. 'Come on, girls.'

She led the way up the cobbled street, her hips rolling, her cheeks shining with righteous glee. John was up a ladder, his bucket of white paint dangling precariously. 'Please don't shake the ladder,' he said calmly when Maudie banged her fist on one of the rungs. He went on painting, engrossed in the difficult task of filling every crack and crevice with the whitest of white paint.

'Well, excuse me, sir, but you can't paint your walls WHITE. That's good Cornish granite. 'Tis a sin to paint over it.'

John went on painting in silence.

'That Cornish granite's been here for centuries. St Ives Town Council won't like this. They'll make you scrub it all off – and that'll be some job.'

'What about 'ow it looks – one white cottage in a terrace of granite? It'll look awful.'

'Where's you from anyway?'

'He's from London,' Maudie said, proud of her knowledge. Then she added, 'People come down 'ere from up-country and think they can do whatever they like.'

John dipped the wide paintbrush into the bucket.

'And look what you'm doing – dropping drips all over the street. We don't want our granite cobbles covered in white spots. You're standing in

311

it, Maudie. We'll 'ave white footprints next.'

'What do you want it white for? I wouldn't have my place all white like that – show the dirt, wouldn't it? You wait 'til winter and the storms come in. Your white walls will go green, you wait and see.'

John continued doggedly painting until the women went quiet. They had run out of things to say. He climbed down the ladder, carrying the bucket which he put down on the doorstep. His dark blue eyes sparkled as he surveyed the group of women. 'Good morning, ladies.'

No one answered. John plunged the enormous paintbrush into a bucket of water and wiped his hands on a remarkably clean rag, his every move scrutinised by the hostile stares. Quietly, he turned to face them. 'I'm John De Lumen,' he said, 'and I'm so sorry if my white paint has upset you.' He paused for a response but there wasn't one. Humility wasn't something they were used to. 'I think it looks rather nice actually,' he said pleasantly. 'I do hope you'll try to get used to it. It's going to be an art gallery and I hope it will bring some new prosperity to the town.'

Nobody spoke. John smiled, showing a set of perfect white teeth inside the pointed grey beard. He directed the smile to Maudie. She sniffed, tutted and walked away. 'Nice to meet you, ladies,' John said, and quietly gathered his tools and disappeared into his snowy white cottage.

'What's the thing you most want to do?' Nan asked Lottie and Tom on their first morning back in St Ives.

'Go in the sea,' said Tom.

'Brush Mufty,' said Lottie, 'and go in the sea.'

'Right. Today we shall play, and tomorrow we'll go and see your mother,' Nan said, and she'd driven them down to Porthmeor Beach in the car. She even took off her shoes and paddled, with two towels over one arm, keeping a close eye on the two precious children.

Lottie felt ridiculously happy as she ran down the shining sands with Tom. Happy at seeing the summer sky reflected in the wet sand. Happy at the feel of the velvety foam rushing between her sore toes. Happy to see the glittering dark blue waves curling over into clean white surf. Happy that the ocean was an eternal presence in her life.

After days of being hot, grubby and desperate, it was a fabulous treat to dive into the crystal water and let it stream through her hair. She never wanted to get out. Seeing Tom, pink-faced and radiant, with his hair plastered down by the water, seeing him rolling and diving, swimming like a seal, was part of the homecoming joy. Lottie only wished for Matt to be there. Where was he? They knew he'd been to see Jenny, and it had gone badly wrong. What would Matt do? Where was he now? Roaming the streets, hungry and alone? Or was he hurt? Or caught?

Nan met them at the edge of the sea, giving them each a clean towel. What luxury. Then she headed for an ice-cream booth at the top of the beach and bought them a pink cornet each. Tom's eyes rounded and Nan had to explain why he must eat all his ice cream now, not try to stuff half of it into his pocket for later. 'It melts,' she

313

said. 'Look – it's running down your arm.'

'Can't I stop it melting?'

'No.'

'Why?'

'Because it's cream that's been frozen, Tom,' Lottie said. 'Like snow in the winter.'

'But how does the man make it freeze?'

'Ask him,' Nan said. 'But finish eating it first or it'll run away.'

'He's got a box of eternal winter – like in a fairy tale – and he keeps the ice creams inside,' Lottie said, but Tom still needed a conversation with the ice-cream salesman.

'It's liquid nitrogen,' he told Lottie. 'In an insulated box. And if you sat inside the box, you could eat ice cream forever and it would never melt.'

Nan laughed her wheezy laugh, her rolls of fat wobbling under the old mottled blue dress.

'I wanted to save an ice cream for Matt,' Tom said dolefully.

'You can't save ice cream,' Nan said. 'Ice cream is like time. Enjoy it before it's gone, never to return.'

'Can I take one into hospital for Mum tomorrow?'

'Not unless you want to leave a trail of pink ice cream all along the corridors and up the stairs.'

Lottie and Tom were looking forward to seeing Jenny. But in the morning, at breakfast time, Nan said, 'I've got some bad news.'

They both stopped eating and looked at her anxiously.

'Is Matt dead?' Tom asked.

'Not as far as I know.' Nan tried to look kindly

into Tom's tormented eyes. The bright, bubbly little boy she remembered had been replaced by an oversensitive, deeply hurt child who couldn't take much more.

'No, Tom, Matt is missing at the moment. He's well able to take care of himself, and he'll turn up one day soon, like a bad penny.' Nan cut Tom a generous slice of bread and put it on his plate. 'There's Cornish butter and honey from my bees. Help yourself.'

'Your eyes are twinkling, Nan,' Lottie said. 'It's not really bad news, is it?'

'You don't miss a trick, do you, Lottie?' Nan chuckled. 'The bad news is that we won't be going to visit your mum today. But – the good news is that she's coming home – tomorrow! I was going to send you both back to school but, under the circumstances, I need you here to help me get Jenny's room ready.'

Tom brightened. 'Can we pick her some flowers?'

'I can do the bed linen,' Lottie said. 'I know how Jenny likes it.'

'Good girl,' Nan said. She drummed her fingers on the lid of the honey jar, her eyes moving from Lottie to Tom and back again. 'You're all right here, aren't you?'

Tom and Lottie nodded. 'We will be when Mum is back,' Tom said, 'and Matt.'

So far, their new life with Nan was going well. They had a bedroom each and there was a room ready and waiting for Matt. Nan had plenty of furniture, most of it unused, and with help from Vic she'd set the bedrooms up weeks ago when she'd first started searching for the children. Vic had cleared out the cottage in Downlong and everything was crammed into the downstairs room Jenny was to have. Now she needed Vic again to sort it out.

'I can trust you two, can't I?' Nan said. 'Because I need you to do Mufty and the chickens while I drive down to Newlyn and fetch Vic, if he can come. Lottie knows what to do. Will you show Tom, Lottie? Can you remember what needs to be done?'

'Of course I will.' Lottie got up and started to clear the table. 'You go, Nan. I know exactly what to do.'

'Matt might be at Grandad's place,' Tom said.

'He might be – but don't count on it,' warned Nan. She watched, perplexed, as Tom tried to pick up Bessie, lifting her by her front paws, leaving the rest of the cat dangling awkwardly. 'Show him how to pick up a cat, Lottie, will you?'

Lottie picked up Bartholomew who leaned against her, purring and giving her his golden-eyed gaze. 'You have to make your arm into a chair, Tom,' she said. 'Tuck it under Bessie's back legs.'

Bessie was patient while Tom sorted out her legs. She seemed to know how much Tom needed a loving, purring friend.

'She likes you,' Nan said, and Tom beamed.

'I never held a cat before,' he said.

'They're good company, if you're kind,' Nan told him. 'If you're lonely at night, leave your bedroom door ajar and Bessie might come and sleep with you.'

This clearly appealed to Tom. He'd never had a pet and didn't know much about animals. Every day, at Nan's place, was going to be an adventure for him.

Nan put on her battered panama hat, ready to go out and start the Austin Seven. 'If anyone comes here while I'm gone, Lottie – don't go with them – and don't let them take Tom either. You stay together, and if anyone comes – you run like hell and hide.'

'But not if it's Matt,' Tom said.

'Not if it's Matt,' agreed Nan. 'When your mum is here, we'll sit round the table and decide what we're going to do about finding him. We don't want the police carting him off to the orphanage again, do we?'

Chapter 21

Matt

The Carn Brea seemed to have a strange power over Matt. He didn't need to make a decision about going up there. He just knew it was where he had to be. When he'd climbed those magnificent rocks in the early morning, he'd had a life-changing moment, and it had gone, swept away in the turbulence of escaping with Lottie and Tom. But was the moment still up there, waiting like a stranded, rainbow-cheeked bubble? Could he drop back into it and read the secret message encoded in its fragile membrane? He wanted to try.

This time, he wouldn't go there with nothing. He had to set himself up for survival.

After leaving the hospital in Truro, he ran down to Boscawen Park in the twilight and crawled under a clump of laurel and rhododendron bushes where he cried himself to sleep. The crying was cathartic, washing away the negatives in his life, starting with Jenny. Then Nan. His dad dying. The shock of learning his home had been sold. Matt thought his heart must be broken. But was it true? Did hearts really break? His was still faithfully thudding, after everything it had been through.

In the middle of the negatives, Lottie was on a golden pedestal. Matt had tried to hate her, and ended up feeling he loved her, even if she didn't love him back. During the time at the orphanage, Matt had missed Lottie and realised how much she meant to him, and regretted the way he'd kept his feelings a secret. He admired and respected her. Her beauty both haunted and sustained him. He fantasised about growing up and marrying Lottie. Since she wasn't his real sister, it would be possible. But each time the dream floated into his mind, he dismissed it, rejected it, stamped on it. Lottie was out of reach. After the way he had treated her, Lottie would never love him.

He was an outcast.

In the morning, Matt crawled out of the bushes, his eyes red, his face swollen from crying. He found his way back to Truro Station and boarded the first train to Redruth, again hiding in the toilet. In the morning sun, he strolled down the steep street of shops as if he lived there. He noted where the bakeries were, and the greengrocer, and right at the bottom of the hill was an art shop. Exactly what he needed.

Matt returned to the top of the street, his heart racing with excitement and nerves. He mustn't get caught. First he followed the baker's pony and cart under the railway bridge and past the church into the residential streets. He waited until the baker took his basket and walked off down the path of a big house, leaving the cart un-attended. Matt helped himself to a loaf of saffron bread and a few rolls, stuffing them into his haversack. Unobserved, he sauntered back along the street, adding a bottle of milk from a door-step to his hoard. Next he discreetly pinched two apples from the box outside the greengrocer's. It was hard not to run and panic, but nobody challenged him. At a steady walk, he reached the art shop and went in, an apple in each pocket. It had to be done quickly because now he was trembling and his face felt red. The door activated a bell and a voice shouted from the room beyond, 'Won't keep you a minute.' How lucky. All he needed was a minute to grab a sketchbook, two pencils and a sharpener. Then he fled, out of the door, running hard through the streets and into the lanes, over the fields and up to the Carn Brea, happy enough to sing.

A hollow place in his mind echoed with one of the Ten Commandments which had been drummed into him at school. THOU SHALT NOT STEAL. *Sorry God,* he thought, *but I can't*

319

help it. I'll make up for it d'reckly. The guilt soon vanished as he climbed towards the sky and sat on the spacious top of the rock stack. *Anyway, I deserve it,* he added, tearing a honey-scented chunk from the loaf and sinking his teeth into its warm sultanas, currants and deep-yellow bread.

Nestled into one of the sculpted hollows of granite, he fell asleep, his hands clutching the strap of his laden haversack, and no one disturbed him except for two magpies who strutted nearby. He awoke in the clear air with St Ives shimmering in the far distance, and the tapestry of gorse flowers and purple heather sloping away from the rocks.

Matt felt like the King of the World.

He took out the sketchbook, smoothed its pristine, creamy cartridge paper, and began to draw. The weekly art lesson at school had been very basic. How to shade with a pencil, how to make an apple appear round, an eye look bright, a cat look fluffy. How to draw a horse's hind legs. How to understand perspective. It was never creative. Only now, in charge of his own life, did Matt feel he could explore the tantalising world of his imagination. As soon as his pencil touched the paper, he was back inside the mysterious bubble, using a gift he had never used before.

Many times in St Ives, Matt had hung around the artists who worked along the harbour or out on the cliffs, fascinated by the quirky way some of them interpreted the scenery. Some had paints. Others, like him, just had a sketch pad and pencils. Tourists would come along and ask to buy a picture and the artist would peel it off

320

the pad and get paid three, four or even five pounds for it. An absolute fortune. Paper money! Matt had never even touched a pound note.

His first sketches were inspired by the way the huge rocks framed bits of the distant landscape. There was something bold and rebellious about the massive, wind-sculpted granite, the way it dominated, making the cottages and the tin mines, the trees and squares of field look so tiny, like toys. He longed for a paint box. Then he could paint the delicate misty blues of the landscape captured in glimpses between the dark powerful rock shapes.

There must be a beach nearby, where tourists went. Portreath, he remembered. In a few days he'd go there, where nobody knew him, and try to sell his drawings. He turned the sketch pad over and began to practise signing his name with a flourish: Matt Lanroska.

His first paper money would buy him a paint box and a hat to shade his eyes while he was working, and a sizzling hot Cornish pasty. *All he needed now was a beard,* he thought, stroking the down that was beginning to grow on his chin.

Seeing the Red Cross Ambulance turning in to the gates of Hendravean, bringing Jenny home, was an intensely emotional moment. Lottie stood back, waiting on the doorstep with Nan, letting Tom go out there first. He'd picked a bunch of marigolds, lavender and montbretia and Nan helped him arrange it into a beautiful posy, tied with an orange satin ribbon. 'I just know he's going to drop it,' Nan said, but she let Tom take it out. 'Don't rush at your mum,' she warned. 'You might knock her over. She's very precarious.'

The ambulance came to a halt and Tom hopped from one foot to the other while two confident Red Cross ladies opened the doors, put a ramp there, and wheeled Jenny out in a chair. 'A wise move,' Nan said. Lottie held her hand tightly, a lump in her throat as she caught the first glimpse of Jenny. Tom's heartfelt cry of 'Mum!' was something she'd never forget. Jenny held out her arms to catch Tom as he hurtled towards her and the flowers went flying. The Red Cross lady picked them up and shook them back into shape, then stood, misty-eyed, watching the reunion. Tom clung to Jenny and she leaned her cheek against his hair, patting his back and whispering to him. The seagulls marked the occasion by circling over Hendravean, their orange beaks filling the sky with wild spirals of music.

Lottie fidgeted. She looked up at Nan standing so solid and reliable. 'Go on – you go!' Nan said, but Lottie felt suddenly desolate and lost. *Jenny's not my real mum,* she thought. *I wish my real mum would stop living in America and come to find me. I'd hug her the way Tom is hugging Jenny. I wish I knew who my real father was. I'd love him too, and we'd read stories together and go to the beach.*

But Jenny was Jenny, and Lottie felt a bond with her, so she skipped over to her, glad to be part of the welcoming hug. Tom looked at her with sleepy eyes, dreamy and content, the way he used to be.

'Lottie!' Jenny gazed at her. 'You've grown – quite a young lady now, aren't you? How I've missed you.'

The three of them hugged, Tom on one side, Lottie on the other, all silently aware of the empty space where Matt should have been.

'Can't you walk, Mum?' Tom asked.

'I can, a bit. I've got to practise every day.'

'We'll lend you the chair,' the Red Cross lady said, pushing Jenny towards the house, 'until you don't need it any more.'

Nan looked pale, her jaw set tight as if she found this moment difficult. She and Jenny smiled at each other, and the smiles were like book covers, hiding the pages of love and hate, laughter and regret.

When the ambulance had gone, they sat around Nan's kitchen table, sharing mugs of tea and gingerbread. Jenny fished into the big carpetbag she'd brought with her. Balls of bright wool and knitting needles tumbled out. 'I've been busy,' she said. 'I couldn't do much but I made a little present for each of you. Here's yours, Tom.' She handed him a brown paper bag.

Tom's eyes shone. He pulled out a hand-knitted beanie hat with the Cornish flag of St Piran embroidered on the front. He put it on immediately. 'It's warm.'

'When you wear it, remember I knitted it, and every strand of wool passed through my fingers and picked up the love I've got for you,' Jenny said. 'I even said some prayers for you and knitted them in. You can't see them, but they're in there – for always.'

Tom looked impressed, and so did Nan. Jenny took out another paper bag, bigger, with something knobbly inside. 'This is for you, Lottie. It took me ages to make – but it's got love and prayers knitted into it too. I'll bet you can't guess what it is!'

Lottie felt the shape inside the paper bag. 'I don't know what it can possibly be,' she said, intrigued. She opened the bag, peeped in and gasped in surprise. Out came a beautifully knitted donkey in soft greys and browns, like Mufty. It had two shiny black beads for eyes, with clever white stitching around them. It had a dark dorsal stripe down its back and a tassel for a tail. Jenny had made a bridle from scarlet wool and had even managed to stitch the name, *MUFTY*, on the browband. It had a tiny bell, and brightly coloured flowers along the reins.

'Oh, Jenny!' Lottie was overwhelmed. 'I can't believe you made this. It's wonderful.'

Nan's eyes sparkled with interest. 'It's exquisite. Well done.' Praise indeed from Nan.

Jenny looked pleased. 'He's got pipecleaners inside his legs so you can bend them. You can stand him up or sit him down.'

'I LOVE him,' Lottie said. 'I'll keep him forever; even when I'm an old lady, I'll still have him.'

'Now yours, Nan.' Jenny handed a bigger, fatter paper bag to Nan.

Nan looked moved. 'I'm too old for presents ... but it's very kind of you.' The paper crackled and she drew out a plump knitted tea cosy with an embroidered cat on each side, with their names neatly stitched. *BESSIE* and *BARTHOLOMEW.* 'How lovely!' Nan said, and she fitted it over the brown teapot.

'I didn't know you were so clever, Mum,' Tom said, wide-eyed.

'That's 'cause I was always washing and cooking,' Jenny said. 'When you're ill, like I was, you can do all sorts of wonderful things.' Her happy face went sad again, and she took one more present out of the bag and put it on the table. It had a name on it. *MATT.*

Everyone looked at it in silence.

'Is it a hat like mine?' Tom said at last.

Jenny nodded.

'And did you knit prayers and love into it?'

She nodded.

'Don't cry, Jenny.' Lottie noticed the tears brimming and she walked round the table, the model donkey in her hand, to give Jenny a cuddle.

'What are we gonna do?' Jenny whispered, looking round at the concerned eyes. 'Matt said ... he said...' She paused and took a deep, shuddering breath.

'Said what? You can tell us, Jenny.' Lottie held on to her tightly.

'He said he was gonna make a life of his own. He said he was never coming back,' Jenny wept, and suddenly her lovely gifts looked too bright, almost mockingly bright. 'I mean – he's only thirteen, coming up fourteen. How can he live on his own? Where's he gonna sleep?'

'Matt's clever,' Lottie said. 'He's a good survivor.'

'Living rough is all very well in this weather,' Jenny wailed, 'but what'll he do when the storms come in? Where can he shelter? What's he gonna eat?'

Tom and Lottie looked at each other in a silent pact. But Jenny knew.

'He'll go thieving,' she said, 'and then he'll get in trouble. If the police catch him stealing – they'll send him to a Borstal.'

Nan opened her mouth and shut it again, biting back her version of how Matt would get his come-uppance.

'What's a Borstal?' Lottie asked.

'It's a terrible, terrible place. It's for bad boys, and it's worse than an orphanage,' Jenny said.

Tom looked at her. 'Matt thinks you don't love him.'

Jenny looked horrified. 'Oh – but I do. I DO. I just always seem to get it wrong with Matt. Oh, what are we gonna do? How can we get him back?'

Nan broke her silence. 'We can't. The only strong thing to do is to let go. Let him go – and one day he'll come home, Jenny. Believe me – to possess is to set free.'

Matt was on his way to Portreath a few days later. He travelled early in the morning, on foot, his precious sketch pad half full of his drawings of the Carn Brea. He'd run out of food but he didn't intend to steal in Portreath but use the money he hoped to make by selling his drawings. In Portreath he'd be a respectable Cornish artist. So as he walked past South Crofty tin mine, he again followed a baker's delivery cart and pinched saffron bread and doorstep milk. No one challenged him. His luck held, and he felt jubilant as he walked towards the sea along the bright green banks of a stream, seeing tiny blue butterflies and turquoise dragonflies.

What he wanted, more than anything, was to go in the sea and come out refreshed and clean. The beach was quiet in the early morning and a group of seals were sunning themselves on the shoreline. Away to the right was a harbour, hidden behind a substantial granite pier. Matt walked along the beach, picking up unusual pebbles of banded agate, and gazing up at the high, dark cliffs. A steep rocky island loomed beyond the shore, white with seagulls, gannets and guillemots. At the far end of the sandy beach was a spectacular sea cave, open at both ends, with cool green rock pools and fragmented views of the surf. Obviously at high tide the waves would come surging through it. Portreath was full of pictures just waiting to be drawn.

Matt had endured the humdrum, frugal regime of the orphanage by letting his mind detach and dream. He'd dreamed of the moment when he would dive into the sparkles between waves and let the incoming surf pound his body with thousands of salty bubbles and sinuous curls of emerald water.

Leaving his clothes and haversack high up on a rocky ledge, Matt splashed through the sea cave and plunged into the surf. He swam out, beyond the waves, and floated blissfully on the swell, his face to the sun. A seal came close and looked at him with limpid, dark eyes. It gave him an idea. He swam with it, underwater, rolling and twisting, looping over and under each other, the seal's face coming close to look at him, playing and responding like a dog, its huge, appealing eyes seeming to communicate with him. They sent each other peaceful thoughts. Matt knew seals sometimes attacked and bit people, but he felt totally at ease with this wild creature. They didn't try to touch each other but there was a closeness and a tingle between them.

He emerged from the sea feeling reborn, aware of the seal's mysterious, motherly face watching him from the shimmering water.

A glaze of salt covered his skin as it dried in the sunshine, and the hot sand filled the spaces between his toes. Matt felt confident as he pulled his clothes on, knowing he was clean, and his hair would dry tousled and shiny. Tourists were strolling up the beach now. It was time to start drawing. *A friend doesn't have to be human*, Matt thought, and using the thick, dark 2B pencil, he began to draw swirly pictures of seals on the wet sand.

A man and a woman stood behind him, edging closer, watching the picture appearing on the creamy white paper. Matt had learned to draw fast, in swift, bold strokes. His first few pictures had been tight and fussy. Girlish. While he was drawing now, he felt strong and bold. Totally absorbed, he jumped when the man spoke to him.

'That's a beautiful drawing. Would you sell it?'

'D'reckly.'

The woman laughed pleasantly. 'Ah – you're a Cornish artist.'

'Yes.' Matt went on shading the seal's underbelly.

'How much would you want for it?' she asked.

'I'd like it so much.'

Matt was going to say two pounds, but the seal looked back at him from the paper. Like a wise woman. Be careful what you say. Matt signed his name with a flourish. 'Make me an offer,' he said, feeling very daring. His heart began to race. What if she suspected he was a schoolboy on the run?

There was a pause, and a rustle of paper money.

'Would you take five pounds for it?' The man held out five crisp new pound notes.

Matt pretended to be unimpressed. 'Yes – yes, I will.' He peeled the sketch away from the pad and handed it to him, without smiling.

'Oh, how wonderful – thank you,' the woman said, warmly. 'And good luck with your work, young man. You're going to be a top artist one of these days.'

They walked away with his picture of the seal, leaving Matt sitting on the sand, round-eyed as he stared at the five pounds. FIVE WHOLE POUNDS. In his hand.

The euphoria froze in his mind like ice. The years of learning not to trust happiness gathered around him on the sand. He'd sold his best picture. He wanted it back. He could have given it to Lottie. Eventually. When he went home, if he ever did.

Another feeling taunted him. He had no one to share his success. No one he could run to and say, 'I sold my first picture for FIVE POUNDS.'

Freedom was glorious, and cold as ice.

'I could have a baby now if I wanted,' boasted

329

Morwenna as the two girls strolled along Porth-meor Beach.

Lottie gave her a candid stare. 'How come?'

Morwenna's eyes gleamed. She lowered her voice. ''Cause I started my periods. I'm a woman now.'

Lottie went quiet. She'd noticed her friend's breasts and the way she flaunted them. It was confusing. In the orphanage, the girls had been collectively told about periods in a passionless, military style by Miss Poltair who looked as if her breasts were made of concrete. The big girls whispered horror stories to the younger ones about the 2Bs – bleeding and bellyache – and how terrible it was.

'Haven't you started yet?' Morwenna asked.

'No, and I don't want to either.'

'Don't be daft – course you do.'

But Lottie shook her head, suddenly feeling vulnerable in Morwenna's assured presence.

'Why not? You're so quaint, Lottie. Don't you want to grow up?'

'Not yet.'

'But why?'

Lottie sighed. She knew Morwenna would peck and peck at her like a bird until she got an answer. 'Growing up has got nothing to do with periods,' she said.

'Yes, it has.'

'No, it hasn't.'

'It has.'

'It HAS NOT.'

The two friends came close to falling out and Lottie didn't want that to happen. She towed

Morwenna up the beach past the row of little tents used by the tourists. She sat down in the warm, dry sand. 'I'll explain it to you, but only because you're my best friend. But you've got to promise to keep it a secret.'

'Promise. Cross my heart.'

Lottie scooped a handful of sand, letting it trickle through her fingers. 'I never thought I would grow up without my mother, my real mother, not Jenny. I want to find my mother while I've still got some childhood left.'

'I get that, Lottie. But how can you find her? The world is so big.'

'My mother went to America. So that's where I shall go to look for her.'

'You can't go to America!'

'I can.'

'How?'

'I shall stow away on a ship. That's how I came to St Ives. But this time, I shall be very organised. I shall take a map, and a picnic, and some money, and some envelopes and stamps so that I can write and tell Jenny where I am, and tell her I still love her. Jenny's had enough upsets in her life.'

'What about your father?'

Lottie shrugged. 'I don't remember him. He was never there. My gran told me he was working far away in another country. I wish I knew where he was and if he ever thinks about me.' Lottie stared into Morwenna's concerned eyes, finding it comforting to share her secret pain with her friend.

'But you CAN'T go to America,' insisted Morwenna. 'You're my best friend and I only just got you back.'

'It's a dream,' Lottie said, staring at the flare path of the sunset over the water. Somewhere out there was America. 'But dreams can come true – if you make them come true.'

Chapter 22

A Telegram

On the other side of the Atlantic Ocean in New York, Coraline was busy preparing the Rex and Coraline Gallery for its morning opening time. She swirled around, dusting frames and polishing glass, arranging the table and chair where she would spend her morning, making sure she had a tall glass of water, pen and paper, and a few art reference books. She took the Visitors' Book from its drawer and laid it out at the other end of the table, next to an ornate glass inkwell and a carved onyx box with a Waterman fountain pen and a freshly sharpened royal blue pencil.

Coraline did a final check, her black court shoes tapping briskly over the polished wood floor. She took her job very seriously, honouring each painting as she passed. Every one of the 108 pictures had a message and a story, all from artists she had met, encouraged, and listened to. She felt their presence with her in the gallery, gazing through canvas and paper and glass. *Discovering Charlotte* was in Room 3, and Coraline often paused in front of it, thinking of John and praying he would one day reconnect with the little girl who had stolen his heart.

She unlocked the door, releasing the fragrance of sandalwood polish and oil paint into the busy street where the morning air smelled of horses, motorcars and coffee houses. She put the OPEN sign up and sat down at her table, a book on Monet open in front of her.

The usual kind of people came in. Wealthy old ladies staring eagerly into the distance. Charismatic art dealers and reviewers who frowned, scribbled on notepads and gave nothing away. Couples looking for an unusual picture to hang in their home. Students brimming over with questions. And mysterious loners, like the tight-lipped young woman coming in now.

She wore dark glasses and gave Coraline the briefest of nods as she glided in. Her powder-blue suit hung limp around her as if she had lost weight. It had once been smart, but Coraline noticed the slightly frayed cuffs and the way its buttons had lost their lustre. Like the eyes, she suspected, only those were well hidden. Coiled hair, drawn back from a sweet, doll-like face which was spoiled by the tense jaw and pursed lips. *She radiated suffering,* Coraline thought, keeping a discreet eye on her as she wandered around the gallery in silent shoes, her toes pointed outwards like those of a dancer.

Something about her made Coraline uneasy. The young woman didn't seem to be engaging with the paintings in the responsive, contemplative way that most people did. The gallery was uncannily quiet with only a few elderly visitors sitting, deep in thought, in front of individual paintings. Watching from her chair by the entrance, Coraline lost sight of the enigmatic young woman when she moved on into the second and third rooms of the gallery.

She heard a sudden low-pitched gasp, followed by a pulsating silence, and then a crash that made the polished floorboards tremble.

Coraline ran through the gallery, into the second room. Nothing. Into the third, and there she found the young woman, face down on the floor in her powder-blue suit, the badly worn soles of her shoes upturned, one arm stretched out, her delicate white fingers splayed as if reaching towards the painting she'd been looking at.

It was *Discovering Charlotte*.

September brought a golden peacefulness to St Ives. The children went back to school, the swallows and the sand martins left for South Africa, and the tourists headed home to their up-country lives. Most of the September visitors were artists, seeking to paint the mellowing light, the sunsets and the harvest moon shining on the water. Despite the quiet weather, the surf was building, the swell coming from the hurricane season far away across the Atlantic. The waves were huge, indigo and a long way apart, roaring into Porthmeor Beach and Porthgwidden like steam trains with their plumes of white. At full moon, the highest tide of the year swept over Wharf Road, driving foam and seaweed into the fish cellars, the shops and cottages. Behind the lifeboat house, the spray flew right over the rooftops and poured down into the street.

In the morning, after the night tide, wedges of soft sand and blue mussel shells, orange crab claws and ribbons of seaweed filled the streets.

Jenny wanted to go to the cottage in Downlong which had been their home. She'd heard rumours about an artist buying it and having the audacity to paint it white, and she wanted to see it for herself. Her walking was improving every day and she felt better for being in St Ives again. It was still like summer in the harbour, the tide far out, exposing the pale sands stretching to the distant shore of Porthminster Beach.

'You'll be fine. Just take it steady,' Nan said, taking her enormous willow basket out of the car. 'I've got plenty of shopping to do.'

Jenny hobbled off towards Downlong, self-conscious about her iron leg. Women were still out sweeping the sand from doorsteps and corners, and most of them were pleased to see Jenny back in St Ives. She felt her smile getting wider and wider, her eyes brighter with every conversation. By the time she reached the cottage, she was radiant.

The white walls shone in the morning sun. The windows sparkled and pots of red geraniums stood outside the door. A man with a silver beard was watering them gently with a brand new watering can. Jenny chuckled to herself, imagining what Arnie might have said about that. She couldn't believe how lovely the cottage looked, painted snowy white, and with a board across the top of the door, saying:

ARTIST'S STUDIO
OPEN

It looked so different that Jenny didn't experience the sadness she'd been expecting. A sense of light and optimism hovered over the white cottage. For some absurd reason, Jenny felt glad she had chosen to wear a pretty dress and forget about her iron leg. She decided to go in and see what kind of paintings this man did, and she wouldn't tell him she used to live there.

She waited until he'd shaken the last few drops from the watering can, and then followed him inside. *I could pretend I'm a wealthy Emmet,* she thought mischievously.

He took the can into what had been her kitchen and put it on the draining board. Jenny gasped with surprise. 'TAPS!' Two shiny metal taps. He'd had water put in!

John turned slowly to look at her.

Jenny's hand flew to her mouth. 'Oops – sorry, I didn't mean to be rude. I was just surprised to see the taps. Not many people have them in Downlong.'

John looked at her quietly, an unassuming warmth in his gaze. She saw him glance at her iron leg, then up at her face. She felt drawn to him.

'Good morning, young lady.' He held out his hand. 'I'm John De Lumen. Welcome to my studio.'

Jenny swapped her walking stick to her left hand, and shook hands with John De Lumen. His fingers held on to hers just a fraction longer than normal, and in those few seconds Jenny saw something deep and shadowy in his eyes. A closely guarded wound of the spirit.

'I hope you enjoy looking at the paintings,' he said in a kind voice, as if he was cutting her a slice of cake. 'Most of them are mine, but there are a few that friends have done.'

'Thank you. I'll have a look round,' Jenny said, noticing he wore a heavy cotton fisherman's smock, covered in smears of paint. An easel was set up in a corner, with boxes of rolled up tubes of colour, bottles of turps, lots of rags, and an earthenware jar crammed with brushes, their handles encrusted with paint.

Jenny walked out into the back yard. *A broken heart,* she thought. *John De Lumen has got a broken heart. I'll bet it's a woman.* She stared in amazement at what had been a scruffy back yard. *He's covering his broken heart with white paint.* The dilapidated sheds were gone, replaced by an elegant colonial style veranda which ran all the way round, sheltering the paintings hung on the white walls. In the centre of the yard, a small square of granite cobbles remained, well scrubbed and twinkling with tiny flecks of mica and crystal. Even the devoted pair of seagulls stood on the roof in shock, looking down at Jenny. 'Hello, my birds!' she called, remembering the years of nest building, and mess, and fun, and joy she'd had from watching them.

Her legs were aching now but she walked round, looking at the paintings of St Ives. They were colourful and interesting, mostly seascapes, cliff top flowers and sunlit, cobbled streets. One of them stopped Jenny in her tracks. A painting

337

with an odd title. *The Queen of St Ives.* 'That's Nan!' she cried, and laughed out loud at the way he'd captured her charismatic figure, sitting like a Buddha on Mufty's cart surrounded by the colourful posies, hats and pots of chutney, punnets of fruit and lavender bags.

Hearing her laughter, John hurried to her side. 'You like that one?' he asked.

'I LOVE it,' Jenny said, and hesitated. She didn't want to tell him who she was. 'I know that old lady. Everyone calls her Nan. You've got her – absolutely. She'd love it.' She grinned at John's slightly anxious face. 'It's a bit cheeky – but who cares?'

'Look at the next two,' John said, and they moved on to the next painting which was a comical back view of Nan going home through the narrow street on Mufty's cart. The third one, entitled *Still Going Home* was a perfect tiny silhouette of Nan and Mufty against the sunset.

'They're wonderful,' Jenny breathed. 'If I had money I'd buy them – all three.'

John looked pleased. His eyes hung on to her as if he badly needed the warmth and friendliness.

'How long have you been an artist?' Jenny asked.

'Not long – about ten years.'

'And what were you before?'

'I was an engineer,' John said. 'Mostly abroad. Canada, and South Africa. Building tunnels through mountains for the railway – and I worked on the diamond mines.'

'You must be very clever,' Jenny said, impressed.

'Perhaps.' He looked pensive. 'But being clever isn't a recipe for happiness.' He looked down at her iron leg. 'You seem happy, my dear – despite...' He paused awkwardly.

'Despite me poor old leg,' Jenny smiled, rescuing him. 'I had polio, but I'm well now.'

A new spark of interest lit his eyes. 'Ah – you must be Jenny. Jenny Lanroska?'

Jenny felt cornered. She couldn't say no, and she didn't want to say yes. So she kept quiet.

John noticed her discomfort immediately. He took her hand and held it warmly between his, and shut his eyes in a moment of silent reverence. It moved Jenny profoundly.

'Forgive me, my dear.' John looked at her intently. 'I don't wish to intrude – but – hmm ... let me think about this.' He held on to her hand and she noticed the flecks of oil paint embedded in his cuticles. He seemed to be deep in thought. Untold secrets flew between them like owls in the twilight on silent wings.

Whatever might have been said remained unspoken, as they were interrupted by a shout from the door. 'Mr De Lumen – are you there?'

John let go of her hand and became businesslike again. 'I'll come back.' He went to answer the door and Jenny walked after him thinking she should go now.

'A telegram for you, sir.' The postman handed him a yellow envelope. 'From New York.'

Lottie didn't feel like herself. The conversation with Morwenna had disturbed her. Over the summer she noticed her own breasts growing but she didn't feel proud of them like Morwenna. She wanted to push them flat. She felt robbed of her

339

childhood. At first, going to live with Nan had seemed like Utopia. But nothing was the same. Secretly, Lottie wanted Nan to herself. She craved the times of magic when she and Nan would read together, or Nan would tell her stories from Cornish folklore, or teach her music. Nan herself was different, changed by the effort of living with Jenny and Tom. Lottie didn't think driving the car was good for Nan. She held on to the steering wheel grimly and nobody dared to speak when she was driving. Cooking for four was another worry, and Nan had more or less given up her kitchen to Jenny who was used to feeding a family. But it meant Nan no longer had fun, spreading her herbs on the kitchen table, making pot pourri, flipping pancakes and laughing her wheezy laugh if things went wrong. Lottie helped as much as she could, but often felt torn between Nan's way of doing things and Jenny's way. Even the chickens were upset, their feathers ruffled when Jenny chased them out of the house with a broom. Only Mufty and the two cats were peaceful.

Nan never mentioned Matt, and Lottie sensed she was glad he wasn't there. Jenny, Lottie and Tom worried about him and talked it over together, and shared their sadness and the ache of missing him. Jenny was convinced Matt would be caught and sent to Borstal. Tom kept asking if his brother was dead. But Lottie's feelings were so different that she kept them to herself. She didn't long for the old Matt who teased her. She longed for the new Matt who masterminded their escape. The new Matt who looked like Arnie. The new Matt who was kind and courageous.

Increasingly, Lottie wanted time on her own and she often ended up sitting in the straw with Mufty, in his cosy stable, telling the listening donkey her troubles. Or she spent time curled up in a chair, poring over one of Nan's encyclopaedias, always the same one, the one with the map of shipping routes from Great Britain.

'It's time for bed, Lottie.' Nan looked over her shoulder one evening. 'Are you reading that AGAIN? You must know it by heart by now.'

Lottie gave Nan a look that said everything about how she was feeling. Nan heaved herself down onto the window sill seat, facing Lottie's chair. 'Tell me – why on earth are you so obsessed with shipping routes? Is it something you're doing at school?'

Lottie shook her head miserably.

'Lottie?' Nan sat there in her Buddha pose, her storm-coloured eyes kind. 'You can tell Nan, surely?'

'If I do, you mustn't tell Jenny.'

'I won't. Promise.'

'Jenny would be upset,' Lottie said, not sure whether she would dare to tell Nan.

'You tell Nan. I'm not moving until you do.'

Lottie sighed. She'd water it down. Pretend it didn't really matter. Nan was looking at her expectantly.

'I want to ... to find out where my real mother is.'

'Oh, my dear girl,' Nan said, radiating compassion. She held out her arms. 'You'd better let me give you a cuddle. Come on. Or does Mufty get them all now? I'm sorry I haven't got big furry ears.'

Lottie shut the navy-blue encyclopaedia. She leaned against Nan's comforting bulk. A ring of pain circled her throat, and her temples throbbed. The sharp light from the window hurt her eyes. 'I'm getting one of those headaches, Nan. Do I have to go to school tomorrow?'

'Not if you've got a headache, dear. What's brought it on?'

'Worrying,' Lottie said, and Nan squeezed her tighter.

'What about?'

'Matt.' Lottie felt sheltered as if Nan was a sun-warmed rock in a storm. She listened to the old, steady heartbeat under the mottled blue dress. Her hand crept up and curled a finger around Nan's deep purple amethyst beads. They felt like familiar friends. 'And – I don't want to grow up, Nan. Not without knowing where my mother is and why she didn't want me.' Suddenly her head seemed to burst with pain and she sobbed and sobbed. 'And why didn't my father come and find me? Why?'

'You have a good cry,' Nan crooned, rocking her. 'It's the best medicine in the world.'

As always, Nan was right. The sobs went on, relentlessly, like footsteps carrying the headache and the worries away to a distant mountain.

'We don't really grow up,' Nan said. 'I haven't. I'm still a little girl inside. That's how I keep the magic alive. And little girls are strong for ever. Indestructible and invincible.'

'I miss the magic,' Lottie sniffed. 'Everything is so serious now.'

Nan went on rocking her. 'Maybe you're right,

Lottie. We need some nostalgia. Some fun time.'

Lottie sat up. 'Why don't we go to the nut grove? It's September. Tom would love it – and we could take a picnic.'

Nan smiled her toothy old smile. 'I don't see why not. On Saturday, while the weather is good.' She smoothed Lottie's hair away from her hot face. 'You'll always be my little girl, even when you're grown up, Lottie – and – I don't want to lose you. Have you got that?'

Lottie nodded, suddenly feeling more stable. 'I love you, Nan,' she whispered.

John stood at the top of the stairs, hands on hips, looking up at the loft hatch. In the early morning, before the gallery opened, he reckoned there was time to inspect the loft. One of the neighbours had given him a finger-wagging warning. 'You take a look in the loft, before the winter storms come in. That roof was leaking badly when the Lanroskas were there.'

It wasn't the only reason, and the other one gave him goosebumps. John had slept with Coraline's telegram under his pillow. And in the pre-dawn twilight, with the sound of hundreds of seagulls circling over St Ives, there had been a presence by his bed. Dimly, as if in a dream, John saw a shining face and heard a whisper – 'In the loft – in the corner – a forgotten box. You must open it – open it – open...' The image faded with the dawn, and John wasn't sure whether he'd been dreaming, or not. Could it have been the young fisherman who had died so tragically? Why was he telling John to go into the loft?

He lit an oil lantern, and carried a ladder upstairs. Annoyed with himself for feeling nervous, he climbed up, lifted the hatch and pulled himself through. The rafters looked ancient and riddled with woodworm. John stood up gingerly, balanced on one of the beams. He held the lantern high. The cramped space smelled musty and fishy and he could hear the two seagulls paddling over the roof tiles on their webbed yellow feet.

Slowly he swung the lantern round, spilling brassy light into every cobwebby corner. And there it was – a box, thick with dust, lurking under the eaves. John nearly stopped breathing. After all his years of engineering tunnels and diamond mines, this was the most spooky thing he'd ever experienced. A box, in a loft, in a Cornish cottage.

John's ability to keep calm, no matter what, clicked into place in his mind. Yet he felt vulnerable, having nobody there to witness his hair-raising discovery. *It's only an old box,* he told himself. Not trusting the strength of the beams, he crawled towards the box and touched it, leaving a handprint in the dust. It was cardboard; a wide, shallow box with a fitted lid, such as a tailor might use to put a new suit in. It wasn't heavy, but there was obviously something inside.

Putting the lantern down, John eased the lid up, holding the two front corners, intending to briefly assess whether it was worth the effort of dragging it across the loft and down the ladder. He made a slot big enough to put his fingers in and what he touched spooked him even more. Velvet. John withdrew his hand smartly and pushed the cardboard lid shut again.

Had it been china, or metal, he could have coped. But velvet? Velvet was mysteriously feminine. Some secret seductive power that women used. Something he wasn't supposed to investigate. John made a swift, business-like decision. He slid the box towards the hatch and manhandled it awkwardly down the ladder. He carried it outside into the yard and brushed a cloud of dust from it, then took it inside, put it on the kitchen table and lifted the cardboard lid right off.

Sunlight streamed through the window onto rich, red velvet. A dress. A child's dress with a full skirt and layers of quality lace petticoats.

John's eyes burned. He felt his defences crumbling. He recognised that dress. He'd bought it in Canada and sent it over for Christmas. It had to be the same one. Slowly, he gathered its muffled softness and pressed it close to his face, feeling the shock bending him in half, allowing himself to stroke the scarlet velvet, lovingly, as if the little girl was still inside it. 'Charlotte,' he whispered, 'I've found you. It was you, in the painting. It really was you – and I was so close.'

Afraid to breathe, he stared at the sky outside the window, seeking to calm himself. John didn't know how not to cry. He straightened his spine and carefully put the red dress on the table, diverting his mind into searching for an answer to the great mystery of how on earth Charlotte had ended up in St Ives. Was there something else in the box?

There was! Under the layers of tissue paper, he found a light green school exercise book, and on the front was a name, *Lottie Lanroska*. Someone, perhaps the young fisherman, had thought it important enough to be hidden in the box with the dress.

John's hands shook with excitement as he opened the book and began to read the words Lottie had written on her first day at St Ives School in her clear, childlike but flawless script.

AN INTERESTING JOURNEY

Until I was four I had a happy life with my mother. We lived in Swansea. My father was working abroad and I hardly ever saw him. My mother said she loved me, but she didn't because she abandoned me. She went to live in America with a soldier and he didn't want me so I was left behind to live with my Granny. When I was six she gave me a secret treasure and told me to look after it forever, and then she died and I was taken to an orphanage, where I lived until I was eight.

I was very unhappy and they made me do horrible work like scrubbing the floor. At night in the dormitory we were freezing cold. All of us were crying and afraid of the manager, Mr Burlet. One day I told him we needed an extra blanket each. His face went purple and he shook me hard. I told him to stop it but he dragged me into his office and left me there for hours. He had two birds in a cage and I let them out. I was glad to set them free but when I told him that, Mr Burlet went crazy. He took off his belt and beat me. I tried not to cry but in the end I was screaming.

The next day was an adoption day and we had to wear our best clothes. I decided to run away and I took my secret treasure out of the hole I made in my mattress. I ran all the way to the docks and hid on a ship. I thought it was going to America and that I would find my mother.

A storm blew up and the ship was wrecked at St Ives. I was thrown into the sea and I clung to a piece of wood. The waves were like hills and valleys. I was scared and icy cold but Arnie rescued me and took me home to live with his family and I like it. I like Jenny and my two brothers, but I love Nan best.

My name is Lottie now and I like it. My real name used to be Charlotte De Lumen, but I'm not going to tell anyone because I'm very happy here in St Ives. I'm looking forward to my birthday on 8th May. I will be nine, and Jenny is going to take me to Flora Day at Helston.

John held Lottie Lanroska's exercise book tightly over his chest. For a few moments he could feel the fast, powerful thump of his heartbeat through the pages. Again he waited for calm to return. He visualised the sea on a winter night, perfect silk stretched out under a silver moon. His mind sang a line from a favourite hymn. *That still small voice of calm.* Another line from the same hymn poured its music through his heart. *Forgive our foolish ways.* And look what his foolish ways had done to his beautiful daughter. How she had suffered while he was far across the world, totally, selfishly obsessed with his work as an engineer. He'd sent money home, and gifts. He'd sent prayers. But he hadn't been there for Charlotte. Would she ever forgive him? Could he ever tell her he was here, in St Ives?

John got up, the book still clutched to his heart.

He paced to and fro, trying to think sensibly against the crazy mix of guilt and joy. His impulse was to find Charlotte, immediately, and tell her the good news. Or was it good news? He realised he must handle this very carefully. If he got it wrong, he could lose Charlotte as quickly as he'd found her.

It must remain a secret. For now.

Cool, calm decision-making had been part of John's life. He needed a plan. He put Lottie's book into his brown leather briefcase. Then he took it out again, kissed it and put it back in. He added Coraline's telegram and a notepad. It was ten o'clock, time to open the gallery. Instead, John put a notice in the window:

GALLERY CLOSED TODAY.

Carrying the briefcase, he headed for the station.

Chapter 23

Perfect Timing

John's carefully constructed plan collapsed like a card house on a Saturday morning in October. He'd done everything the solicitor suggested. Shaved his beard off because Bart Pascoe said little girls found beards alarming. Sent for a copy of Charlotte's birth certificate from Somerset

House. Written out a 'Statement of Intent'. Drafted a formal letter to Jenny Lanroska. Planned and rehearsed his first meeting with Charlotte. He was waiting for the letter from America. He planned to proceed in a calm, un-hurried, non-threatening way to make the reunion with his daughter go smoothly. He didn't want her to feel frightened, or angry with him. Their first meeting must lay the foundations of a new, life-long bond. John was quietly excited and opti-mistic, but he felt he was walking a tightrope, and he was glad he hadn't encountered anyone from the Lanroska family during those tense weeks of planning.

On that Saturday morning, there was a storm brewing. People were tapping their barometers and watching the pressure drop. The sea was blue-black and clouds of spray flew high against Godrevy Lighthouse. It was still quiet in the har-bour, but no fishermen ventured out, and the smaller boats were being winched out of the water and lined up neatly along Wharf Road. The town was busy with locals stocking up on essentials ahead of the storm.

John was packing up a painting for a customer, taking the money and exchanging pleasantries. He was unaware of who had walked into the gal-lery while he was busy. When the customer had gone, he heard laughter coming from the yard area. A wheezy, ringing laugh, some girly giggling and banter. Intrigued, he headed down there, and came face to face with Nan and the entire Lanroska family – including Charlotte – no, he must call her Lottie.

John felt emotionally shipwrecked. He longed to talk to Lottie, to be close to her, to see her eyes. But Nan filled the doorway. She had stopped laughing and was assessing him with storm-coloured eyes, her chin lifted high. John's knees trembled. He felt terrified of her.

'Ah – so you're the culprit!' Nan's voice rang through the gallery and out into the street. There was a wheezy silence during which she looked him up and down. 'Well, my man, you're a MOST accomplished artist. I haven't laughed so much for years and years.' She wiped her eyes with the sleeve of a voluminous, multi-coloured hand-knitted cardigan, and she smelled of chrysanthemums and pickling vinegar. 'I must say these paintings of me with Mufty's cart are superb caricatures. The Queen of St Ives indeed! The audacity of it! – but I like it. Well done, my man.' Nan offered him her hand.

John grasped it warmly, reassured by her humour. He found himself saying something totally inappropriate, given the gravity of the situation. 'I can see you've been making chutney.'

Nan kept hold of his hand. 'Well then – it's a case of paint meets chutney,' she said and a gale of laughter followed.

John hadn't yet looked at Lottie, but it was good to hear her giggling. He wasn't used to laughing now, but he managed a chuckle, conscious of his face without the beard. Jenny was there, with her iron leg, and she threw him a cheeky grin. 'You look SO NICE without that beard. I can see your smile – and you look years younger, John.'

'Thank you,' John said, still mesmerised by Nan. He knew what was going to happen. No one else was in the gallery. He thought he ought to go and shut the door, lock it and put the CLOSED sign up. But it happened so fast, as if a master chess player was up there making great sweeping game-changing, life-changing moves. John hadn't time or the power to intervene.

There was even a gust of wind from the heavens, whirling leaves in the middle of the yard.

Jenny brought the children forward. 'Lottie and Tom, you must meet the artist – John ... oops, I've forgotten your surname. Remind me.'

'De Lumen. John De Lumen,' he said, and finally he and Lottie were staring at each other with their dark blue eyes.

There was no more laughter.

Only shock.

No one spoke. A spell had fallen and ripples of magic pulsed out from the mysterious moment of truth.

Again, John was captivated by Lottie's beauty. It wasn't just physical. It was an aura of light around her as she came to shake his hand. John was very afraid. But Lottie wasn't. In the moment of contact, she gazed up into his eyes with perfect clarity.

'John De Lumen,' she said, and a smile made her eyes luminous with incredulous joy. She noticed he was afraid, and she gave him both her hands. 'I'm Charlotte De Lumen, but you can call me Lottie. You're my daddy, aren't you? I know you are.'

He nodded helplessly. It was over. Lottie was in charge. She reached up and slipped her arms

351

around his neck, and became part of him, as if she'd always been there. It felt natural to rest his cheek on the silky top of her head, and rest his hands lightly on the plume of bright hair around her shoulders.

She'd made it easy. So easy.

It was over.

'Don't cry, Jenny.' Lottie put Jenny's mug of cocoa down on the windowsill. 'What's wrong?'

Jenny could hardly speak. She sat in the window, watching the storm through salt encrusted glass. The tide was out, but the beach was covered in foam, and the sea was a mass of white. Huge clods of foam detached and flew inland, across the sand, over the rocks and onto the grassy cliffs. It blew into the town, piling against walls and into corners. It was even in Foxglove Lane, clinging to the hedges in great shivering drifts of creamy white.

'Is the storm upsetting you?' Lottie asked.

'It's Matt,' Jenny said in a low-pitched, desperate voice. 'Where is he? Where will he go in this storm? Why hasn't he come home? I'm breaking my heart worrying, Lottie, and trying to understand – why?'

Lottie hardly knew what to say. She worried about Matt too, and so did Tom. She stood close to Jenny and leaned on her shoulder. 'You're shivering. Come and sit by the fire.'

Jenny shook her head. 'I can't. I keep thinking – what if he's out there trying to get home? No one is out. No one can even stand up in this wind. In the town it's dangerous with the roof slates flying everywhere. I feel so helpless. And it's his birthday soon. He'll be fourteen – and I want him home.' She cried even harder.

'Matt is strong now, Jenny,' Lottie said, 'and he knows how to survive. He really does. He brought Tom and me home and he was brave. I didn't used to like Matt but now I do. I love him and I want him home, and Tom does, even though they used to fight.'

Jenny sipped her cocoa, wrapping both hands around the mug. 'You're such a comfort to me, Lottie. I hope – I hope I don't lose you as well.'

'You won't,' Lottie said firmly. 'Even if I go to America and find my real mum, I'll never love her like you and Nan. I want to live in St Ives for all of my life – and now I've got my father here too.'

Jenny nodded. 'I'm happy for you, darling girl, and John is proper 'andsome. I like him. He's a gentleman and there's not many of them around. He says he'll come up here later, at teatime, and he's bringing all the documents, even your birth certificate, and he'll tell you about your real mother.' Jenny paused to dry her eyes. She tried to smile. 'I wish it was me.'

The wish hovered in the silence. Lottie didn't know what to say, how to comfort Jenny, so she just listened, her hand on Jenny's knee, her eyes attentive.

'Are you happy about it, Lottie? Will you be pleased to see him later?'

Lottie didn't answer. She felt happy about her father, but her feelings about her mother were confused, swinging between anger and an ache of

353

yearning. She stared out of the window at the darkening sky. 'I hope he doesn't try to go out in the storm. He's not used to Cornish storms.'

'There you are – now you're worrying about him. We are a pair of worriers,' Jenny said in a brighter voice. 'Come on, we've gotta make pasties, and a cake for when he does come up here. A celebration cake – with ICING.' Her eyes lit up and she looked kindly at Lottie. 'It's a big thing for you, isn't it? Finding your real dad like that – so unexpectedly.'

Lottie gave her a hug. 'But I still love you, Jenny. I'm getting to know my father, and I expect I shall love him in time, but he'll never be as good as Arnie.' She lowered her voice to a whisper. 'And Matt looks like Arnie now, and he's clever and brave, like Arnie was.'

'Don't start me off crying again.' Jenny swallowed the rest of her cocoa. 'Now. Kitchen. Pasties.'

A stormy day was cosy at Hendravean. Lottie trusted the strong old house. Its walls were thick, and the fire burned steadily. All the cats were inside. Mufty had been bedded down the night before in an extra deep layer of straw, a net bulging with sweet meadow hay, and plenty of water. The chickens were shut safely in their shed. Nan was upstairs trying to teach Tom how to play the piano accordion, so fragments of tunes and long breathy chords echoed down the stairs.

Lottie felt lucky and contented. A good feeling on a stormy day. Meeting John, and talking about her mother had changed her longing to go to

America. Yes, she still wanted to go and see her mother, but Hendravean was home.

Dear John,

Every day, every hour of my life, I have grieved for my lost child, little Charlotte. She was so beautiful and wise beyond her years. I should never have left her. Please forgive me for what I did.

When I saw your painting in the gallery I'm afraid I collapsed with the shock, but the lady, Coraline, was so kind to me and I am all right now. I have been ill for years, and I live alone in a tiny apartment. I would love to come back home to England and see Charlotte but sadly I have no money for the fare.

I hope Charlotte is happy. Please, if you get the chance to talk to her, tell her I love her and I pray we will meet again some day and that I will be forgiven.

My love, always,
Olivia

Lottie folded the letter and handed it back to John. 'Poor Mummy,' she said. 'I wanted so much to find her. I was even going to stow away on a ship again.'

John looked thoughtful. 'You won't have to do that, Lottie. I shall take you to New York, one day, I hope. We shall go on the luxury cruise ship, which sails from Southampton. It's enormous – like a floating palace, with lovely cabins and a posh restaurant. You'd love it.'

'That would cost a fortune,' Jenny said. 'I hope you're rich.'

'I'm not.' John looked round at the Lanroska family and Lottie sensed he was finding it difficult to be honest, especially with Nan who was still eyeing him sceptically. 'I was moderately wealthy once, but I gave it all up to follow my dream of being an artist and running my own gallery in St Ives.'

Nan tutted and picked up Bartholomew who set about kneading her lap with his soft paws. 'More fool you,' she said bluntly. 'But who am I to criticise when I did something similar myself. Gave it all up to mess about with a few chickens.' She laughed but nobody else did.

'What were you, Nan?' Jenny asked.

'A musician. LRAM. A music teacher.'

'I never knew that.' Jenny looked impressed. 'You're a dark horse, Nan.'

'So you won't be taking Lottie off to America just yet,' Nan said, looking at John in a challenging way.

'I can't make any promises,' John said. 'Even if I had the money, we couldn't go until Easter. The Atlantic is no fun in winter. To be honest, I don't expect to make more than enough to live on from the gallery – but we can dream – can't we, Lottie?'

Lottie smiled at her father. 'We'd need enough money to go there on the ship, and bring my mother back.'

'I'd like to bring the painting home as well,' John said, 'because that's what started it all – it's how I found you. It belongs here in St Ives – but I'd have to buy it back from Rex and Coraline. Yes, we shall need a lot of money. A lot of money.'

'Well, come on, let's finish this cake. Get your strength up!' Jenny said, slicing up the remaining wedge of the iced cake.

Lottie thought her father's first visit to Hendravean had been a success. She watched him walking away in the sunset, the light glinting on his silver hair. A flame of happiness burned in her heart. But there was something else. An idea. She wanted to shout it out, but, no, it must be a secret. It had always been a secret, hiding in the dark, waiting for its moment in the sun, the right moment.

She couldn't wait for it to be midnight.

The air was calm now, full of a briny, peaty tang after the storm. The waves were still enormous and spaced out, but the surface of the water moved like folds of satin. A pale marble moon broke through the clouds and etched a silver blaze over the sea. Lottie sat in her bedroom window, unable to sleep. She thought of Nan telling her about the shimmering pathways of the sun and moon in St Ives Bay and how it inspired artists like her father to give up everything for the joy of painting that special light.

Tired out, she got into bed and managed to fall asleep, only to wake at the perfect time. Nan's grandfather clock breathed in and started its Westminster chimes down in the hall. Lottie sat up and counted. Twelve. It was midnight.

The moon looked tiny now, high up in the sky, making silver slabs of the slate rooftops and silver threads from the masts of boats in the silent harbour. Down in Nan's garden, it cast shadows over the silver grass and flickered in the tiny windmill on the chicken shed roof.

Lottie lit her candle with a match and watched

her own shadow leap onto the wall like a wild-haired giant. She pulled her fisherman's jersey over her nightie, took the candle and tiptoed along the landing, past Tom's room, and Nan's room, and Matt's empty room. She crept down the stairs, trying to breathe quietly, her eyes big and bright in the darkness.

John was standing in the open doorway of his white-painted gallery, sipping strong tea from a blue and white enamel mug. It was early morning and the cobbled road glistened with the sunrise. He heard the throb of boats in the harbour and the clamour of circling seagulls. Then running feet, and Lottie appeared, pink-cheeked and out of breath, her eyes full of light. Her beauty startled him, throwing his orderly thoughts into chaos.

'Charlotte – no – I mean Lottie! Whatever are you doing here so early? You're welcome, of course.'

'It's a secret.' Her eyes shone with excitement. 'Can we please go inside, as it's private.' She led the way in and sat down at the kitchen table. 'You sit there – Daddy – and don't interrupt. Listen until I've finished.'

'Right.' Astonished, he sat down and tried to look Daddyish. His skin chilled, and his spine turned to ice when Lottie calmly put a small black velvet bag on the table. 'Is – is this...?'

Lottie put a finger to her lips. 'Please just listen.' Her eyes were compelling, holding his like magnets.

He listened.

'When Granny died, I was only little – six, I

358

think. The day before she died, she gave me this. I knew what it was because I'd seen it in her jewel box. She told me it was a family heirloom and it was given to her by my grandad. She said he had brought it all the way from the diamond mines in South Africa where he worked. She asked me to keep it hidden until I was grown up, and then think very carefully about what to do with it. She told me it would be difficult for me to do, and she was right.' Lottie paused, stared out at the sky and sighed. 'It's been hard for me. I wanted to give it to Jenny when we were very poor, and Jenny was ill and we had to burn the chairs to keep warm, here in this cottage.'

John waited, concerned at the obvious stress the memory brought to Lottie's young face.

'But I thought about it, and saw that it would be wasted, and we'd still be poor, so I kept quiet. Nan hid it for me in a secret cubby hole, and there it stayed, until – until you came into my life. Granny said the timing would be perfect, and I would know with all my heart what to do with it.' Lottie put the black velvet bag into her father's hand. She sighed and suddenly looked bright again as if a great burden had been lifted from her young shoulders. 'You must have it now, Daddy. It was meant for you, not me, and I've done it in secret because I didn't want to hurt Jenny or Nan.'

John nodded, overwhelmed by his daughter's philosophy.

'The timing is perfect,' she concluded, 'because if it's worth a lot of money, you can use it to bring my mother home from America, and the painting.'

'Can I speak?' he asked.

Lottie grinned, looking happier. 'Yes.'

'I'm proud of you,' John said. He took a pair of scissors from a drawer. 'Shall we look at it together?'

'Yes – please – I've never looked at it, but I wanted to.'

The moment when he cut the tightly knotted cord seemed sacred, like a ship being launched. With his steady artist's fingers, John slid the diamond brooch out from its dark bag into the lattice of sunlight on the kitchen table. Its sparkle was deep. Blue, and gold, and crystal white.

They gazed and gazed.

'If you squint your eyes, you get rainbows,' Lottie said, awed by the perfect geometry and wonder of the diamond. 'It's too beautiful to touch.'

'I think it somehow belongs to St Ives,' John said, 'as if St Ives is, itself, a diamond.'

It was nearly Easter, and in Cornwall the bulb fields were ablaze with daffodils. On the cliffs, the green domes of sea pinks had plump little buds, and the wiry grass was studded with purple violets. Abundant primroses cushioned the winding lanes. Even the abandoned tin mines were a paradise of wild flowers, mats of bright blue heath speedwell, and the polished petals of celandines opened to the sun. This was Cornwall at its best, ironically a time when few tourists ventured down.

It was the day before the long awaited trip to America, and Lottie was sitting on the warm timber at the side of the harbour slipway with Jenny, their faces to the west where the late afternoon sky was pink and gold, reflected in a calm sea, the tide lapping higher and higher at the granite walls, lifting the boats as it flooded across the sand.

'I can't believe you'll be away for three whole weeks,' Jenny said. 'I'm going to miss you. It'll just be me, and Tom and Nan.'

'I'll miss you too, Jenny.' Lottie was trying to keep a conversation going with Jenny but her mind wanted to be dreaming. Her dreams followed the sun over the shining sea. She dreamed of arriving and seeing her mother waiting on the quay. Would they recognise each other? Would they hug? Would there be tears of joy? She couldn't imagine beyond the point of arrival, but only take a leap forward to the time of coming home, seeing Jenny and Tom there to welcome her as the luxury cruise ship sailed in to Southampton. Imagining Nan at home, caring for Mufty and the chickens, keeping the fire burning. Lottie wanted to go but she didn't want to miss a single day of the spring in Cornwall. By the time she got home, the bluebells would be out.

She felt nervous about going on the ship. Memories of the shipwreck kept looming in her mind. Her father would be with her. He'd look after her, he assured Jenny. Lottie wasn't sure how she felt about that, or whether she actually wanted to be looked after. She thought the roles might be reversed, and she would be looking after him.

'You will come back, Lottie, won't you?' Jenny was working herself up into a state of anxiety.

'Of course I will,' Lottie assured her. 'This is my home, Jenny. I just want to be Lottie and live in St Ives.'

'You're growing up so quickly now,' Jenny said, 'and you look wonderful, Lottie. I hope some American lad doesn't take a fancy to you.'

Lottie grinned. 'I doubt that.' She stared out to sea, one hand twiddling the ends of her hair. Freshly washed, and dried in the sun, it was thick and shiny. She had a new light blue dress with a slim skirt, a dark blue softly draped jacket, and a string of blue lapis lazuli beads which Nan had given her. The colour suited her and she felt good in it. Tom had gazed adoringly at her. He didn't want her to go. She glanced across at Smeaton's Pier where Tom was playing with some friends in a sunny wedge of soft sand against the wall.

The church clock chimed six, each chime travelling far across the water and through the ancient stones of the harbour. Jenny stood up. 'I can see Nan's car there now. Shall we go?'

Lottie hesitated. She had a funny feeling that something was going to happen. Something that came from the sea, out of the golden evening. 'You go home with Nan, Jenny. I want to stay a bit longer and say goodbye to St Ives – and Tom can come with me.'

Jenny looked at her dubiously. 'Don't be long then, Lottie. Early start tomorrow.' She stood close to her for a moment, both of them watching a boat coming in from the west, chugging steadily over the shining water. Lottie saw Jenny's eyes change, a sudden dark welling up of grief. 'Don't that sound like Arnie's boat?'

'I don't know,' Lottie said, lost for words to comfort Jenny.

A young man was standing, balanced with careless grace on the boat, bringing it in from the open sea.

'He even looks like Arnie,' Jenny said. 'But perhaps it's just me, imagining it – wishful thinking – I'm not going to stand here and watch. See you later, Lottie.' Jenny hobbled off, determinedly, without looking back.

Lottie stayed there, a slim figure alone on the slipway, her honey-coloured hair lifting gently in the breeze. Some mysterious force compelled her to watch the boat coming in to the harbour, going too fast, a bow wave fanning out from it making the moored boats rock a little. Intrigued, she studied the young man from a distance, noting his blue fisherman's cap, his blue-as-the-sea shirt, his long straight legs, his confidence. Obviously he intended to land on the slipway where she was standing. Maybe she ought to move.

She turned to walk away.

'Lottie! Lottie, wait.'

She froze.

'Lottie!'

She knew that voice – didn't she?

She turned back to see him climbing out of the boat onto the slipway. They stared at each other.

The last brim of the sun flared pink on the horizon. The boat rocked gently. Neither of them moved.

'Matt!' she cried, in disbelief.

Matt had grown tall and strong. Lottie gazed up at him, feeling suddenly small and feminine.

She wanted to ask where he had been, but she didn't want to yell at him like Jenny would have done. She tried to smile, but the smile wouldn't come. He moved closer, his eyes full of the light on the sea.

'Lottie,' he said, in a new voice, low and deep, and she sensed he wanted to say more. But the way he said her name said everything. It glowed in the air. Just 'Lottie'. Matt looked down at her and his eyes sparkled under the long lashes. The old hostile, rebellious glint had gone. Matt had come home. Not just home to St Ives, but home to his true self.

Lottie searched her soul for something beautiful to say, and the moment had points of light, a brilliance, like the diamond brooch emerging out of the black velvet bag. 'You're precious, Matt,' she said, 'like a secret diamond.'

'Lottie,' he said, again, as if he couldn't say anything more meaningful. His eyes moved over her. He reached out a suntanned hand and gently brushed a tendril of her hair away from her face.

She gave his rough brown hand a squeeze. 'You've come home – have you?'

Matt shook his head. He waved at the boat. 'That's my home now. Recognise her?'

The boat was freshly painted in a new shade of blue, with the cabin window frames glossy white and yellow. A new St Piran's flag flew proudly on the cabin roof. Lottie gave a squeal of joy. '*The Jenny Wren!* Is it really her? Really Arnie's boat?' The smile came then, on both their faces. 'How did you get her, Matt?'

'I found her.' Matt had tears in his eyes. Happy

tears. 'She was doing nothing, moored in Hayle. Terry wasn't using her and he said I could have her cheap. So I worked for him all winter, mending lobster pots and nets. And selling my pictures at weekends – 'til I'd got enough to buy her. Terry didn't care – he didn't even ask how old I was – he just helped me 'cause Dad was his friend.'

'Your pictures?' Lottie asked, still smiling, still holding his rough hand between her own. 'What pictures?'

'I'll show you them – we'll go on board d'reckly,' Matt said. He started to explain how he'd come to do the drawings and sell them, when they were interrupted by the sound of running feet.

Tom came belting along Wharf Road and onto the slipway, his cheeks red, his eyes bright with excitement. 'Matt! Matt!' he yelled, and flung himself at his brother, wrapping his arms around him. 'I missed you, Matt. Are you home now?'

'I'll be around,' Matt promised, 'but I've got me own home now – *The Jenny Wren.*'

'Dad's boat!' Tom jumped up and down with enthusiasm. 'You got Dad's boat back.' He took a wild leap from the slipway into the rocking boat.

Matt looked at Lottie. 'Where's Mum?' A shadow crossed his face.

'Up at Nan's place. She's all right, Matt – but she misses you.'

Matt looked sceptical. Then he nodded. 'I'll take you out in the bay. Just a little way and back,' he said, 'but you'll have to sit still, Tom.'

Tom sat down on one of the blue painted seats. 'I won't move. Promise.'

Matt helped Lottie into the boat, and she sat

365

down next to Tom. With a wide grin on his face, Matt started the engine, turned the boat around and *The Jenny Wren* went purring across the harbour and out into the vast expanse of shining water. *Today* The Jenny Wren, Lottie thought, *and tomorrow the luxury cruise ship sailing out to America.* But she wouldn't tell Matt now. She didn't want to spoil his obvious joy. It was so healing to be out in St Ives Bay with the sunset still pink and gold in the west, the rippling swell gentle but heavy enough to remind them that this was the mighty Atlantic Ocean.

Matt cut the engine and they floated blissfully, looking back at St Ives where the cottage walls glowed in the golden evening. The window of Hendravean winked in the light, and Lottie wondered if Nan was up there gazing out at the eastern sky. Waiting, as she often did, for the moonrise.

'Lottie.'

She felt Matt's hands on her shoulders, turning her round. He sat down, between her and Tom, his arms round both of them. She gasped. 'The MOON – it's enormous.'

'And look where it's rising, Lottie,' Matt said.

Far away, silhouetted against the radiance of the moon was a hill with a stone cross. 'The Carn Brea.' Lottie smiled at Matt, then at Tom. 'That's where we were – so far away – so lost – so long ago. And look at us now – so lucky and free.'

'I made my own luck,' Matt said, and he gave *The Jenny Wren* a pat, started the engine, and took them safely home to the harbour.

Author's Note

I lived in Cornwall for many years, so it is close to my heart. It's a beautiful and charismatic land with its own language, its own St Piran's Flag, its unique customs and folklore, and a thriving culture of music, dance and theatre. The town of St Ives, where my novel is set, has always been a magnet for artists who enjoy the particular quality of light, the narrow, cobbled streets and breathtaking seascapes. It began in the 1920s when artists from London came down on the train to set up their easels and paint. As well as numerous small galleries, St Ives now has the Barbara Hepworth Museum and Sculpture Garden, and Tate St Ives, a great honour for the town.

In writing and researching *A Cornish Orphan*, I have tried to weave some of the lesser-known culture and legend into the story. The male voice choirs which are awesome and an experience not to be missed. The bakeries, not just pasties but saffron bread and Nelson cake, clotted cream and honey. The folklore, rich with stories of wicked giants, sea spirits and spriggans, many of them brought alive by street theatre such as the Hal-an-Tow which is part of the Helston Flora Day, featured in the book. Last, but not least, the warm-hearted, resilient, creative people of Cornwall.

Included in *A Cornish Orphan* are the legends of St Ia, and The Maiden's Tears from the fern cave at Carrack Gladden, the legend of The Stone from Outer Space and the Unwinding Spiral Dance from the Helston Flora Day. Thank you to the St Ives Archives and the St Ives Museum who helped me with my research, and the St Ives Bookshop who stock so many interesting books on Cornwall, and who support West Country authors, including me, by selling and displaying our books.

Acknowledgements

My grateful thanks to Rita at the St Ives Archives for her time and meticulous research, to Beth Emanuel for her perfect typing and friendly help, to Jo and Emma at Simon & Schuster UK, and to my agent, Judith Murdoch, for her wise guidance.

I thank St Ives Bookseller for their warm welcome (they have sold all my books since *Solomon's Tale*) and for helping me choose books for research, particularly the work of Cyril Noall and *Helston Flora Day* by Jill Newton.

The publishers hope that this book has given you enjoyable reading. Large Print Books are especially designed to be as easy to see and hold as possible. If you wish a catalogue please ask at your local library or write directly to:

Magna Large Print Books
Cawood House,
Asquith Industrial Estate,
Gargrave,
Nr Skipton, North Yorkshire.
BD23 3SE